Rigged

A
Shagball and Tangles
DICK Files Adventure
By

A. C. Brooks

Other Shagball and Tangles Adventures Include:

Foul Hooked-2011
Dead on the Dock-2012
Weed Line-2013
Deep Drop-2014

For more information go to **www.acbrooks.net**

This book is a work of fiction, like a fictional book should be. Names, characters, places and events are products of the author's increasingly disturbing imagination and/or are used fictitiously. Any similarities to real events, locations, or persons, whether living, dead, or in a zombie state, are coincidental. Some famous names may appear to be misspelled but they are not. They are fictional non-celebrities who have no interest in suing the author.

ISBN: 1519148798
ISBN 13: 9781519148797

Acknowledgements

Once again I must thank my fantastic wife, Penny, for keeping me in check. I know that may be hard to believe, but not if you had a chance to read my growing collection of deleted chapters. Maybe some day. Anyways, without her love, support, and encouragement, I never would have written book one, let alone five. So there you go.

I would also like to thank the *Coastal Star* for being kind enough to have included an article about each of my books in their superb magazine. Hopefully that continues with *Rigged.* I greatly appreciate the exposure.

I would also be remiss if I did not thank my good friends at the Old Key Lime House in Lantana for promoting me and offering my books for sale in their gift shop. Thank you from the bottom of my liver (knock on wood).

Last, but certainly not least, I must thank my loyal readers. Without you, you wouldn't be reading this, as I would have called it quits after *Foul Hooked.* It is solely because of your growing attachment to my characters, stories, and humor, which keep me writing. Hope you enjoy Shagball and Tangles first DICK Files adventure.

What they are saying about *Rigged* :

"There's funny and then there's funny. I should know, but I don't. I can dance though. Watch me dance."

- Ellen Degeneress

"This book isn't silver, it's gold. Solid fucking gold. Get some. What's in your IRA?"

- Actor William DeVayne

"When I read *Rigged* I laughed, and laughed, and laughed, and laughed, and then I cried, and then I laughed one more time, and it was over. Kind of like when I lost my virginity."

- Jimmy Kimmell

"A. C. Brooks is fabulous. He's going to be HUGE! Just like the big beautiful wall I'm going to build. Of course after this book he's going to need one around his house. Mexico will pay for that one too."

- Donald K. Trump

"I thought I was bad but A.C. makes me look like a choir boy. A ninety year old Jewish choir boy, but a choir boy nonetheless."

- Don Rickels

"Where in the hell did this A.C. Brooks guy come from and what makes him tick? Now there's two questions I don't want the answer to. He's sick I tell ya. Sick!"

- Jerry Sienfeld

"If you've ever looked at a goat with lust in your eyes, this book is not for you. If you can't say the words, "Radical Islam," this book is not for you. If you serve tacos at Thanksgiving, or drive a Subaru, this book may not be for you. If, however, you have a sense of humor, and get that I write purely for entertainment value, this book is definitely for you. That being said, does anyone know Salman Rushdie's number?"

- A.C. Brooks

Prologue

There's a saying that goes something like this: "The two happiest days in a boater's life are the day he buys it and the day he sells it."

If you know the feeling, then you know how painfully true it can be. But there's no saying for the two worst days in a boater's life. Now there is: "The two worst days in a boater's life are the day his boat gets hijacked and the day it blows up with all his shit on it."

Sometimes it's the same day. It was for me. And the only thing worse than having the two worst days of a boater's life in one single day is when somebody tries to kill him in the middle of it. I know, I know, it would be worse to be killed, but then there would be no new saying. So let it go. A story has to start somewhere.

Chapter 1

Me, Holly, and Tangles were met at our arrival gate at Norfolk International Airport by a familiar face. It was the guy who had saved our butts in Saint- Martin. He told us at the time his name was Rafe (pronounced like "safe" but with an R). He appeared to be of Mexican or Latin American descent, was a good shot, and worked for the secret government agency that had recruited us. That much had been established during our previous encounter in the Caribbean.

After exchanging pleasantries, Rafe said, "Please, no talking until we're in the vehicle. Follow me." We did as we were told, and after picking up our luggage, he led us curbside to a big black Suburban with government plates, parked next to a NO PARKING sign. *Nice.* Holly rode shotgun, and me and Tangles sat in the back. As he pulled away from the curb, I said, "I can't believe the new boat's finally ready. It's been two years since that fucking McGirt blew up the *Lucky Dog.*"

"Will you watch the language, please?" Holly said.

"Sorry. I think I have posttraumatic some-asshole-stole-my-boat-and-blew-it-up syndrome."

"I can't believe he showed up in the Bahamas and tried to do it again. That guy's like an evil shadow," Tangles said.

"He should be thankful he's in jail because if I ever see him again, I swear I'm gonna strangle that squirrelly snake."

"Kit, will you *please* forget about him?" Holly said. "You know darn well you're never going to see him again. Think about positive things...like the new boat."

"Hey, I'm totally fired up about the boat."

"You should be," Rafe said.

"Shit," Tangles said. "Nobody's happier than me. For two years you've been Minnie-the-Moochin my Robalo. I'm tired of getting on it to find it low on gas."

I looked at the little ingrate with heightened disdain. "That happened once. The fuel dock closed early."

"Sure it did. Once too many times."

"Once too many? Nice English. Learn that on the shrimp boat?"

"C'mon guys," Holly warned.

"Now hold on a second," I protested. "He called me a mooch after I *gave* him the Robalo. That's *gave* with a capital G. You know what that means, Tangles, right? Like when you *gave* that waitress from Benny's—"

"Stop it, please." Holly turned in her seat to face me. "Nobody wants to hear it...seriously."

"I'd kinda like to hear it," Rafe said.

Holly looked at him and shook her head. "You guys are all the same, I swear."

Tangles tried to act innocent and held his little hands out with the palms facing up. "The only thing I gave her was a big tip, I swear."

"That's not what I heard," I mumbled, just loud enough for everybody to hear.

"That's bullshit! I didn't even—"

"All right, all right, I was just kidding." I gave him a light punch in the shoulder, and he looked at me suspiciously.

"You better be. It's hard enough for a man of my stature to get dates without someone saying I gave a waitress…uh, whatever."

"Crabs? I did not hear that."

"Kit!" Holly was not pleased.

"You are such a *dick,*" said Tangles. "A big moochie dick."

"Well, you got part of it right."

"Yeah, the moochie dick part. Big is the wrong adjective—right, Holly?"

"Oh no he *didn't.*" Rafe chuckled. The way he said it, like a *Jerry Springer Show* participant, elicited a laugh from Holly. Nevertheless, it was an unsupportive and uncalled-for laugh.

"What are *you* laughing at?" I asked her.

"I'm laughing because it's true."

"WHAT?!" I couldn't believe my ears.

"Oh, boy," Rafe murmured.

"Holly, what the hell?" I glanced at Tangles, who scooched closer to the door and averted his eyes out the window.

"Kit, c'mon." Holly smiled. "You know damn well it's true. You've been using the Robalo a lot the last couple of years. Maybe even more than Tangles."

"Are you serious?!"

"Gotcha!" She winked, and Rafe started laughing.

"I'm standing pat," said Tangles. "You gave me the boat, and then you mooched it back…minus the gas."

"Sorry. I can't imagine what I was thinking."

"Me neither."

"No, I mean I can't imagine what I was thinking when I saved your worthless little life."

Rafe was grinning, but Holly not so much. "Kit! Please."

"Sorry."

"I saved yours, too, asshole," Tangles replied.

"No more," Holly said. "Seriously."

After a few minutes of semiawkward silence, we passed over a bridge. Tangles asked, "What river is that? Where are we going?"

"That's part of the Chesapeake Bay. We're going to the US Naval Shipyard."

"The naval shipyard?" I wondered out loud. "What does the navy know about building a fishing boat?"

"Very little, but their expertise in other areas is second to none. Plus, this is one of the few places in the world where we could build such a unique vessel without attracting attention. Security and secrecy are of paramount importance, and they're two things the navy's good at."

"Cool," Tangles said. "A secret navy fishing boat."

"Like I said, it's not really a navy boat per se; it was just built here and uses some of their tried-and-true technologies. A slew of private contractors with specialized talents was brought in to put it all together."

"Like with the computer and security systems?" Holly asked.

"Among other things, yes, exactly."

"So what's so secret about it?" I asked.

"You'll find out shortly. I'll tell you one thing, though—the boss pulled out all the stops on this one. It's unbelievable. This will be a shakedown cruise like none other."

"You're coming too?"

"You bet your ass. On top of being the project coordinator, I spent the last two years working on the propulsion system, and I'm anxious to see how it performs. I also need to make sure you're capable of captaining it."

"Shit. You kidding me? If it floats and it's got a motor, I can run it. End of story."

"It's got a motor, all right. Here we are. Let me do the talking."

Holly looked back at me with a puzzled look on her face. I just shrugged. I didn't know *what* to expect.

Rafe powered the window down and handed one guard an ID. Another used a long pole with a mirror on it to check the underside. Rafe popped open the trunk, and a third guard quickly rifled through our luggage. After checking with the other two guards, the first guard handed three passes to Rafe and said, "Have a good day, Commander."

As we drove past the gate, Holly said, "Commander? You're a commander in the navy?"

"I'm whoever I need to be, whenever I need to be." He smiled.

"Now just hold on a second. Don't you think it's time somebody leveled with us? What exactly *is* your job? Who do you—"

"Work for? You'll find out once we're on the boat."

Frustrated, Holly blew some air into her bangs and pushed them to the side.

As we wound through the shipyard, Tangles commented on its size. "Man, this place is big."

"Yes it is—twelve hundred and seventy-five acres. This is where every ship ever built by the navy comes for servicing, repairs, or upgrades. And when I say 'every ship,' that means guided-missile cruisers, subs, amphibious vessels, and supercarriers, including nuclear-powered ones."

"Wow," I said. "Must be a busy place."

"Very. And it's a place where needing top-secret clearance to enter certain areas is the norm, which has worked out well for us. As far as the base personnel are concerned, this is just another secret government project, which it is…for the most part." He smiled.

"What's with all the smiling?" Tangles asked. "You look like you're auditioning to be a model on *The Price is Right.*"

"You're damn right I'm smiling. We took her out the other night to test some systems, and she performed flawlessly. If she does as well on the shakedown cruise as she did in the bay, which I expect she will, you'll be smiling too…all three of you."

I caught Rafe's eye in the rearview mirror. "You know when I'll be smiling?"

"When?"

"When I'm trolling along a big fat weed line. Does she have outriggers? She better have a nice set of outriggers."

"Oh, she's got outriggers, all right. Outriggers like you've never seen."

"Man, you're killing me. How much farther?"

"Not much. In fact, here we are."

We pulled up to what looked like a small aircraft hangar perched perpendicular to the waterway behind it. The hangar was surrounded by barbed-wire fence that had HIGH VOLTAGE signs attached to it. An armed guard stepped out of a small guard shack by the gate. Rafe powered the window down, and the guard acknowledged him as he handed over our ID badges. After jotting something on a clipboard, he handed back our IDs and waved us through. Rafe pressed a button on the visor, and an overhead door on the end of the hangar trundled open. We drove inside to an enclosed area and piled out of the Suburban. After unloading our gear, Rafe led us to an interior door and stuck his hand into a contraption on the wall.

"Fingerprint scanner?" I asked.

"Yes, followed by a retina scanner." The light on top of the fingerprint scanner went from red to green, and he pulled his hand out. When an electronic eye popped out from the wall, Rafe positioned his left eye directly in front of it, and a second or two later a series of locks on the steel door snapped open.

"That's pretty cool," Tangles said.

"You ain't seen nothing yet. C'mon."

We followed him into the dark hangar, and I was immediately hit by one of my favorite smells in the world—saltwater, the smell of the ocean. He flicked the lights on, and the space looked about a hundred to a hundred and twenty feet long, maybe seventy to eighty feet wide, and fifty feet high. It wasn't a hangar, of course; it was a boathouse. There was a channel cut right down the middle, and an overhead pulley system held up a black curtain. It was draped over what I assumed was our new boat. It looked to be in the fifty-foot class. I was more than ready to check her out, and the anticipation was killing me as we followed Rafe to the gangway that led to the boat. He stopped at the foot of the gangway and pulled a small gadget out of his pocket that looked like a keyless device for a new car. He pressed it, and a faint humming sound emanated from under the curtain.

"What's that *sound?*" Tangles asked.

"I'm firing up the boat."

"*Firing up?* Firing *what* up? It sounds like a...I don't know. Like a Vulcan force field or something."

"Maybe 'firing up' was the wrong way to put it."

"A remote starter," Holly commented. "Very handy. I'm guessing there was some female input involved."

"You guessed right."

I couldn't take it anymore. "Enough with the dramatics already. Raise the curtain, and let's check her out!"

"You asked for it. Prepare to have your mind blown."

"It's a little late for that," Tangles quipped.

"For once I agree with you," Holly added.

"Very funny," I deadpanned. "Please, Rafe, the curtain?"

He pressed a button on a piling next to the gangway, and the curtain slowly lifted up. It went up until it collapsed in on itself, revealing...nothing. There was no boat.

"What the hell? Is this some kind of sick joke?" I looked at Tangles, who looked as confused as I was.

"It's no joke, believe me," Rafe replied.

Holly's expression slowly shifted from perplexed to a rueful grin. "No way," she muttered. "No way, no way...no *frickin'* way!"

"No way *what?* Where the hell's the boat?"

"It's right in front of you."

"What?"

"I present to you the world's first invisible fishing slash spy boat."

"Oh my God," Holly muttered. "The cloak of invisibility? For real?"

"The cloak of *what?*" Tangles's head was twitching like a hungry mutt waiting for a treat.

"Good Lord, haven't you guys ever seen *Harry Potter*? Cloaking technology—it's the latest thing."

Rafe held out the device and pressed it again. Like a wavy mirage taking shape in the desert, a sleek, gleaming, blue-hulled, fifty-footish, sport-fishing-style yacht appeared in a matter of seconds. I felt my knees go weak, and Tangles's jaw, which was naturally close to the ground, may have actually hit it. I stood stunned and hung on to a piling for support. Rafe lowered the gangway, and Holly followed him aboard.

"This is incredible." She beamed. "I love *Harry Potter*!"

Chapter 2

I blinked a few times, shook my head, and even pinched myself, but the boat was still there. *Un-friggin'-believable.* With great apprehension I eyed the gangway that led to the boat. Like Indiana Jones in *The Last Crusade*, I fully expected it to vanish once I stepped on it, and I'd end up in the drink. *An invisible boat?* I thought. *Impossible. Right?*

"C'mon, Kit." Holly waved at me to come aboard. "I thought you were anxious to check it out." Tangles brushed past me and climbed aboard. I held tight to the gangway rail and followed him.

"Are you all right?" she asked me. "You look a little pale."

"*No*, I'm not all right. I just saw an invisible boat, for Christ's sake!"

"That doesn't make any sense," Tangles said. "How could you see—"

"Oh, shut up, will you? You know what I mean. This is crazy." I pointed at the center of the cockpit and added, "Nice fighting chair." Tangles beat me to it and hopped on the chair.

"There's a toggle switch on the bottom of the rod gimbal," Rafe said.

"Yeah? What's it for?" Tangles turned his head to look at him.

"I haven't deactivated the security system yet, so if you don't flick the toggle switch in the next fifteen seconds, you'll be ejected from the boat."

"Say *what?* Who's gonna eject me?"

Holly and I shared questioning looks as Rafe started counting down from ten. "I'd listen to him if I were you," Holly said.

"Rafe's full of it. Nobody's gonna eject me." As Tangles squirmed in the seat, I found myself wanting to fuck with his head—a common occurrence.

"I'm with you," I said, thinking the opposite. "He's probably just bluffing."

Rafe started speaking louder when he got to five and signaled for me and Holly to step back.

Tangles looked nervous. "Why are you stepping back? You know something I don't?"

"Stupid question."

"Asshole."

"THREE."

"Better get off," Holly urged. Like me, she sensed Rafe wasn't kidding.

"TWO."

"Okay, okay," Tangles conceded. "Where's that switch again?" He reached down between his legs.

"ONE."

Tangles was too late. With a loud *whumpf!* Tangles flew out of the chair like he was shot from a cannon. He somersaulted high through the air. His feet clipped a light hanging above the canal. It shook and made a loud *clang*. He was still screaming when he splashed down about thirty feet from the stern.

It was flat-out *hilarious.* I instantly regretted not having recorded it on my phone. I looked at Rafe. "Dude, I'd pay big money to see that again. That was *awesome!*"

"Don't worry. The HD cameras started rolling as soon as the pressure sensors indicated activity in the cockpit."

"You mean we're being recorded right now?"

"Yep."

"Sweet. I wanna freeze-frame the part where he hit the light and make it my screen saver."

Tangles popped to the surface, muttering and sputtering.

"Tangles! Are you all right?" Holly yelled.

He swam toward us, and we crossed the cockpit to greet him. Rafe reached under the gunwale by the tuna door, and a low drone could be heard as a swim platform magically extended out from the stern.

"This boat has a retracting swim platform?" Holly asked. "Wow, I've never seen *that* before."

"Wait a second," I cut in. "This boat just appeared out of thin air, and you're impressed with the swim platform? *Really?*"

"Hey, unlike you, I'm familiar with the cloak of invisibility. You know what a big *Harry Potter* fan I am."

"But that's fiction! It's make-believe! This is for real!"

"Look," Rafe said. "There are a lot of things on this boat that nobody's seen before. But you're right, Kit. To the few who are privy to what this vessel can do, everything else pales in comparison to the cloaking technology."

"Not for me," replied a smiling Holly, with her hands on her hips.

"Bullshit!" Tangles slapped a hand onto the swim platform. "There's nothing that pales beside sitting on a pile of dynamite. Thanks for the warning."

Rafe helped him up but wasn't the least bit apologetic. "I *did* warn you. Maybe next time you'll listen when I tell you to do something."

"I doubt it. He's a slow learner," I commented as I inspected the booby-trapped fighting chair. "I think his brain stopped growing when the rest of him did."

"What do you know? You thought he was bluffing, jerk."

"Or did I?"

"Kit! C'mon," Holly said.

Tangles pointed at the stern. "Hey, check out the name of the boat: *LD3*."

I stepped onto the swim platform and looked for myself. Below *LD3*, it read LANTANA, FL.

"Not bad," I commented. "Not bad at all. But why the *LD3*? My last boat was the *Lucky Dog*. Shouldn't this be the *LD2*?" I looked at Rafe for the answer.

"Since your last boat was blown to smithereens, the boss wanted to put a little distance between the names. Plus, it sounds better."

"Works for me. The important thing is the *Lucky Dog* is back!"

"Back and on track. In with the game fish and out with the jack," Tangles said.

"*That's* what I'm talking about!" I low-fived him and shouted, "They're gonna be *thick*!"

Holly shook her head and rolled her eyes at Rafe, who said, "You have a lot to learn about captaining this vessel before any fishing takes place." He pointed to the seat cushion for the fighting chair, which was floating nearby, and asked me to retrieve it. I was directed to an extendable boat pole under the gunwale and fished out the cushion. Unwilling to let a soaking wet Tangles traipse through the new boat, Rafe sent him off to the showers. He pointed out where they were and explained they were put in for the contractors that worked on the boat. Tangles grabbed his overnight bag and disembarked after Rafe assured him he wouldn't start the tour without him. Just as Tangles reached the locker-room door, Rafe called out, "Be quick about it, and stay out of the sauna!"

"There's a sauna in there?" I asked.

"You're damn right. It gets cold in the winter."

Chapter 3

As soon as Tangles disappeared into the shower, Holly started peppering Rafe with questions about the cloaking technology. Rafe didn't claim to know exactly how it worked as it wasn't his field of expertise, but he mentioned 3-D holographic imagery, nanotechnology, electromagnetism, and the need for a superior power source to make it all work. He went on to add that it worked best when the boat was stationary, but it could also be used while the boat was moving at slow speed—up to seven and a half knots per hour.

"That'll work," I said. "Not fast enough to invisibly troll for wahoo, but perfect for mahimahi."

"It's not a gimmick, Mr. Jansen. The cloaking system is to be used only when necessary." Rafe was not amused. I could tell because he called me Mr. Jansen like when I got scolded in school.

"What, uh…what would make it necessary for us to go invisible?" Holly asked.

"There is a possibility that an assignment will take us into dangerous waters—waters known for piracy, among other things. That's when the cloaking technology might be used."

"But I thought we'd just be doing some information gathering, right? I mean, that's what we were told."

"That's what we do. But like I said, sometimes we have to go to dangerous places to do it. Better safe than sorry, and this boat is the safest thing on the water…by far."

"Good. I like safe. Safe is good." Holly was exhibiting her nervous Nellie side.

"I got a question," I said. "You said it doesn't work as well when the boat is moving. Why?"

"Well, the obvious problem is the wake the boat leaves behind. There's no way to cloak that. The other problem is the effect increased wind speed has on the hologram imagery. The faster the boat moves, the more difficult it is to project the surrounding scenery. At eight knots the boat starts looking like a blur. Someone with a sharp eye could detect something moving in the water, even if they don't know what it is."

"What about radar?"

"Look, I know you've got a lot of questions, but I'm not going over this again with Tangles. When he gets back we'll cover everything. For now, let's get you two entered into the onboard security system. C'mon over here."

We trailed him to the door that led from the cockpit to the interior salon. He reached inside his jacket and pulled out a phone and a UBS cable. He plugged one end of the cable into the phone and the other into a port on the side of a chest-high panel that was adjacent to the door. He pressed a button on top of the panel, and the cover slid open to reveal the image of an oversize hand. After entering some commands into the phone, he nodded at Holly and said, "Ladies first. Press your right hand firmly against the image until the backlight shows green."

Holly did as instructed, and the backlight went from red to a flashing orange and then green. "That's it?"

"Yes, now it's your turn, Kit. Just give me a second." Holly pulled her hand away, and Rafe entered some more instructions on his phone. "Okay, you know the drill. Go ahead and press your hand firmly on the screen."

"I always liked patty-cakes." After I got the green light, I stepped back while he entered more commands on his phone.

"Now for the retina scan," he announced. "Holly, place your hand back on the screen." Holly stepped up and placed her hand on the screen. This time when the light turned green, a small circular port above the screen slid open to reveal a tiny camera lens. "Just stand still, look directly at it, and don't close your eyes."

"It scans both?"

"Just this time, so it has both in its memory."

The lens appeared to change angle as it shifted from one eye to the other, and then just like that, the small port slid shut.

"That was fast," Holly said.

"Just like the boat."

"Really?" I asked. "What kind of power does it have?"

Rafe chuckled. "Don't worry about the power. Put your hand back on the screen, please."

Being six foot two, I actually had to look down at the camera eye, which was only about neck high. "Why is the retina scanner set so low?"

"That's as high as we could mount it and still have the necessary angle for the camera to work on Tangles."

"Of course."

"Talking about me again?" Tangles was toweling his thick mop of hair as he approached the gangway.

"Yeah, Rafe was just telling me why the—"

"Kit. C'mon. Give it a rest." Holly gave me a nudge.

"What."

"You know what."

"All right, all right."

"All right what?" Tangles stepped onto the boat.

"All right, it's about time you got back. We need to get you programmed into the security system. Over here, please." Rafe waved him over, and Holly and I stepped into the cockpit. As Tangles got his hand and eyes scanned, I walked over to the fighting chair.

"Is it okay to sit in this thing?"

"Go ahead," Rafe said. "The charge has to be reset before it's live."

"Good to know." I plopped down in the chair and swiveled around to face the bow. As I looked up at the enclosed flybridge, I noticed something unusual. The outriggers were white and so was the railing holding a row of rod holders (otherwise known as a rocket launcher), which were white, too. Normally, all of it would be chrome. I got up and looked around the side of the boat, and the bow rail was also white. I had never seen a white bow rail before. *Strange.* In fact, as I looked around, there wasn't a single piece of exposed chrome or metal hardware anywhere—including the pop-up cleats and the hinges on the hatch covers. It was all white. *Were they painted?* When I sat back down in the chair, I noticed what appeared to be a fresh scratch on the rod holder attached to one of the arms, perhaps the result of Tangles being ejected. I scratched at it with my fingernail. It was black underneath. It *was* painted. I flicked it with my finger, and it felt like plastic. *Plastic?*

"What are you doing?" Holly asked.

"This thing's plastic."

"So?"

I heard Rafe tell Tangles he was good to go.

"Look at the bow rail, look at the riggers. Hell, look at the cleats." I pointed. "You see any chrome or metal anywhere? I think it's all plastic. Chintzy, friggin' plastic."

"I was wondering how long it would take you to notice," Rafe said as he and Tangles walked over. "But chintzy? Nothing could be further from the truth."

"Notice what?" Tangles asked.

"You're right," said Holly as she lifted a hatch on top of the transom. "This finger latch is too light to be metal. In fact, the hatch seems lighter than normal, too." She popped up a cleat in the corner and shook her head. "But this cleat's not plastic, that's for sure. It's way too heavy."

"You're right on both counts," Rafe replied. "Kit, you asked me earlier about radar?"

"Yeah."

"Not only can the boat be made invisible to the eye, it can be made invisible to radar. The hull is made of Kevlar-reinforced carbon fiber, the same carbon fiber used in the stealth bomber. That's what the rod holders and the riggers and everything else that's normally metal is made of—except the cleats and the propellers. Those are made of a proprietary alloy and then dipped in a carbon composite paint with a special antiadherence compound. Nothing sticks to it."

"No way."

"Way."

"Whoa," Tangles said. "That's seriously cool."

"You've seen that car commercial where they dump mud and gunk on the hood of the car, and it rolls right off?"

"Yeah, I think it's a Nissan commercial."

"It's the same stuff. Everything that's painted, including the cockpit deck, has that type of paint on it. Of course, we put a nonskid texture on the deck."

"Sweet. Should make cleaning up a cinch."

"Wait a second," I said. "Either the boat's invisible to radar, or it isn't. You said that it can be made invisible to radar. What's that mean?"

"Actually, I should have said it the other way around. As it sits now at the dock, it's invisible to radar. But whenever the boat is moving, a signal is put out from the radar arch that makes us visible to radar. We figured more often than not it's prudent to be seen, especially if you're crossing shipping lanes at night, or if you're approached by the coast guard or some other steward of the sea. If someone has a visual on you and you're not showing up on radar, that'll invite the kind of scrutiny we want to avoid."

"So you can disable the signal if necessary?"

"Yes. The navigational screen at the helm has a stealth mode, which I'll show you when we get there. First, let me show you the rest of the cockpit."

Rafe showed us the eighty-gallon live well in the transom and the large fish box sunk in the deck on the starboard side. When he lifted the hatch in the deck on the port side, I assumed it would be another empty fish box, but it was filled with ice.

"That's a lot of ice," Tangles said. "I don't suppose you have any margarita mix in the cabin."

"Very funny. Both fish boxes are refrigerated; this one is actually closer to a freezer. The desalinated ice is pumped in from a reverse-osmosis unit below deck. We can make our own water. That makes the boat pretty much self-sustaining, assuming you guys really *do* know how to fish."

"Hey now. Don't be dissin' our fishin'."

"Damn straight," I added. "We buy tartar sauce by the gallon."

"Look at this," Holly said. To the left of the cabin door was a short cushioned bench, and next to that was a fairly long counter with a sink. Below the counter, Holly held open the door of a refrigerator that appeared stocked. "Anybody want a bottle of water?" Everybody took a bottle while Rafe pointed out the cleaning station to the right of the cabin door. It also had a sink and a number of drawers to the side and below—pretty standard stuff on a sport-fishing yacht.

"Looks like a decent setup," I commented. "But I'd like to see what we have under the hood. I noticed we're not plugged into shore power. Is there a generator running? Why don't I smell any fumes?"

"There's no generator running, at least not in the traditional sense, and you won't smell any fumes unless you want to."

"What?"

Rafe walked over to Holly and slid open another panel on the bulkhead. He pressed a button and in moments the familiar sound of a diesel engine could be heard as it rumbled to life. It got louder as what I presumed to be the second engine started running. It was soon followed by the smell of the diesel as some smoke wafted out from the stern.

"There's your generator," said Rafe.

"Hold on now. The fish box full of ice has power to it and so does the fridge that Holly pulled the water out of *before* you fired it up. Besides, that doesn't sound like a generator. That sounds like the ship engines."

"That's the idea. There's actually a digital recording being played through the speakers in the engine room to make you think it's an engine. It's on a continuous loop. When I pressed the button to start the recording, it also started a small diesel generator with a rich fuel mix that produces enough of an emission to sell the ruse."

"*Ruse?* What ruse?"

"Yeah," Tangles said. "What are you hiding under the hood?"

"I'm confused, too," Holly added. "Where's the power coming from?"

"Open the engine compartment," I urged. "Quit toying with us."

"As you wish. Please step to the side."

Tangles and I retreated to opposite corners of the stern, and Holly stood next to Rafe as he pressed the button to kill the generator and the recording of the engine sounds. Then he pressed another button, and the large center hatch on the deck began slowly tilting up toward the bow. Rafe led Holly around the side. When the opening was big enough, Tangles scrambled down the ladder.

"Don't touch anything!" Rafe warned. The hatch finished opening, and I squatted down to take a look. It looked like a normal engine compartment on a brand-new boat. It was clean, and there were a pair of big diesels in the center. Tangles was scratching his head as he looked around the compartment.

"Are those CATs?" I asked him.

"Yeah, but they're not even turbos. What's up with that?" He slowly waved his hand over the top of the nearest engine. "The engine's not even warm." He waved a hand over the second engine and shook his head. "Like Rafe said, they weren't running." He pointed to the starboard side. "There's a small generator mounted on the side there, it's only 2500 watts. Shit, that could barely run my margarita blender. What the hell."

"Don't worry about having enough power for a blender—or anything else, for that matter," Rafe said. "Those engines are just for show. They've never run, and they never will. They can't. Take a closer look."

Tangles knelt down by the closest engine and rapped his hairy little knuckles on the manifold. "What? It's…it's *plastic*!" He rapped on a few other spots and cried, "It's all plastic!"

"That's right." Rafe looked at me and added, "*Chintzy* plastic, if you will. They're just lightweight replicas with hidden speakers built in."

Tangles scrambled up the ladder, and I stood up, more confused than ever.

"This doesn't make sense," Holly said.

I looked Rafe square in the eye. I was tired of being jerked around and let him know it. "The jig's up, Rafe. Time to come clean."

"Easy there."

"I'm serious, man. How the hell are we supposed to leave the dock without engines?"

Tangles stepped in front of me and pointed at him. "You heard the man. Where's the power coming from?"

Rafe raised his hands up defensively and smiled. "All right, all right. Sorry about drawing it out like this, but I couldn't resist. You're the first people I've had the opportunity to spring this on, and I wanted it to be a surprise."

"Dude," I said. "A little while ago you made this boat appear out of thin air. You got your surprise in—cloaking technology. I still can't believe it, and I saw it...or didn't see it. Or both. Whatever. What could possibly top that?"

He pointed down at the engine compartment and looked at Tangles. "You saw where the engine compartment ends?"

"Yeah, it stops at a bulkhead that looks to be about midship."

"That's right. On the other side of that bulkhead is an inaccessible lead-sealed chamber that contains the power source. The power source drives a turboelectric transmission that provides electricity to the motors connected directly to the propeller-drive shafts. It also powers the electrical systems for everything on the boat. Hell, it could power this whole shipyard."

"So what the hell's in there?" Tangles asked.

I was focused on "lead-sealed" and looked at Holly with concern. Apparently she was focused on "lead-sealed" as well, because she started shaking her head and said, "No, no it can't be."

"Oh yes it can." Rafe smiled.

"What are you talking about? What the hell is it?" Tangles cried.

"Why, it's a 44-megawatt, fast-neutron nuclear reactor. What else?"

Chapter 4

"WHAT?!" Tangles looked freaked. "We're not wearing radiation suits! We're gonna fry! We're gonna—"

"Relax, okay?" Rafe looked at me and Holly. "Everybody calm down. It's perfectly safe. The reactor has a neutron shield over the cone, and like I said, the midship bulkhead is lead-lined and sealed. Plus the reactor housing itself is solid lead. We had to go nuclear to make the cloaking technology work, and it offers numerous advantages over—"

"Whoa, whoa, whoa," I cut in. "Lead this? Lead that? Sounds heavy. Sounds *real* heavy. And you said there's a pair of turbines, too. Where are they? How does this boat even float?"

"The turbines are beneath the engine-room floor where the gas tanks would normally be. The weight savings by not having to carry fuel or real engines helps offset the weight of the turbines and the lead. So does the carbon-composite hull."

"You telling me there's only a carbon-composite hull between the water and the reactor?"

"Of course not. The entire forward hull, starting from the reactor chamber, is reinforced with ribbing and plating made from the same proprietary alloy used in the props and cleats."

"So how is the boat invisible to radar?"

"All the reinforcement is below the waterline."

"This is insane," Holly commented.

Tangles was unconvinced. "You sure we're not gonna fry? I saw this movie called *Chernobyl Diaries.* When the tourists wandered too close to the reactor, they started—"

"Knock it off already. That was Chernobyl…and it was a movie. Nobody's gonna burn up. We had the best nuclear physicists and engineers in the world design the power plant."

"So what kind of range does it have?"

Rafe laughed. "Range? There is no range. You wanna go trans-Atlantic and fish for great whites off South Africa? Have at it. The fuel rods shouldn't need to be replaced for seven or eight years. It all depends on how hard and how often the boat is run. You're only limited by the weather and how much food you can carry. Since water's not an issue with the reverse-osmosis system, you could be at sea for years.

"If we don't burn up," Tangles said, "this could be awesome."

"You're not gonna burn up, and it *is* awesome. Nothing like this has ever been built."

"No gas needed," I marveled. "That's incredible. Diesel runs almost five bucks a gallon on the water—more in the islands."

"That's right. No fuel and no emissions—unless you're trying to fool somebody. Then you run the little diesel generator with the piped-in engine sounds."

"This is crazy," Holly said. "Amazing, but completely nuts."

"It's amazingly quiet, too, thanks to the turboelectric transmission."

"Yeah, about that," I wondered out loud. "It's all below the engine room floor? How far below? What's the draft on this thing? How big is the boat, fifty feet?"

"Fifty-five. Unfortunately, since we had to hide the reactor and turbines, it increased the draft to five feet eleven inches, about a foot more than normal."

"That could be problematic in the islands."

"Not really. There are plenty of marinas that accommodate much larger boats with a six-foot draft. But remember, you're never gonna need fuel. You can stay offshore, depending on the weather."

"What about going ashore for provisions? I didn't notice a tender."

"We got it covered." He grinned. "Follow me."

After Rafe closed the hatch to the fake engine room, we followed him around the port side to the bow. There was an unusual rise in the center of the bow that was about six feet wide by twelve feet long and rose from the deck maybe two and a half feet. It was tapered to the sides and toward the bow to make it look like a design feature of the boat. A seam ran down the middle, and the periphery of the protrusion was encircled with a rubber seal. I pointed at it.

"You got it covered…cute. Why?"

"The cloaking technology works better. Plus it helps protect the advanced electrical systems from the elements." He pulled out his phone and tapped it a couple of times. The seam in the middle separated, and the two halves began retracting under the rubber seal. He pointed at the expansive window across the front of salon, which was divided by a semicircular tube running from the deck to the top of the glass. "The davit is concealed in the tube. I'll show you later how to employ it. The glass on the boat is bulletproof Plexiglas, almost an inch and a half thick."

"Let me guess," Holly said. "Better safe than sorry."

"Always."

With the tender exposed, Tangles commented, "Looks pretty sweet."

Rafe broke down the specifications. "That it is. It's just less than eleven feet long in the stowed position. The pop-up swim platform puts it at twelve. It's five and a half feet wide, and as you can see, it's designed to carry up to five people. From the bottom of the hull to the top of the miniwindshield it's only three feet, but when you raise up the removable T-top that's folded over the bow, the clearance is six foot four from the deck."

"Glad I won't be bumping my head," I commented. I crouched down and pointed at the stern, noticing the lack of an engine. "This is powered like a wave runner? Like a jet boat?"

"Sort of. See that round shroud on the bottom of the hull?"

I leaned forward for a better look. "Yeah, what is that? It looks like a jet turbine."

"That's pretty much what it is. At only twenty pounds it delivers almost 500 percent more thrust than a typical water jet pump you'd find on a personal watercraft—the equivalent to a 200-horsepower gas motor. This little baby can go from zero to sixty in three seconds."

"*What?* That's crazy."

"Don't tell me this thing is nuclear powered, too," Holly said.

"Anybody else feeling hot?" Tangles waved a hand in front of his face. "Is my face starting to blister? I think I'm starting to blister."

"You're not starting to blister," Rafe said. "Of course it's not nuclear; it's electric. Sandwiched between the deck and the bottom of the hull is a bank of lithium-hybrid batteries. They account for over half of the tender's thousand-pound weight."

"So what kind of range does it have?" I inquired.

"Approximately thirty miles, going thirty miles an hour. Naturally there's a power gauge on the dash."

"Naturally. So let me see if I got this straight. We got ourselves an invisible, nuclear-powered spy/fishing boat with unlimited range and a fast-as-hell tender that runs on electric?"

"The boat's not exactly slow either. It should do eighty knots."

"Eighty knots? In a boat *this* size? No friggin' way."

"Maybe even ninety, but there's concern over the structural integrity at that kind of speed. Hopefully, at some point on the shakedown cruise the conditions will allow us to open it up."

"Holy crap. I think I'm gonna like this setup. I think I'm gonna like it a lot."

"I got wood," Tangles quipped.

Holly rolled her eyes. "You guys are so predictable. We haven't even seen the inside yet."

Rafe looked at his watch. "Let's get moving, then. Daylight's burning."

Chapter 5

In an elementary school basement in the heart of Raqqa, Syria, the leaders of ISIS (the Islamic State of Iraq and Syria) gathered for a group meeting. Such meetings were rare as they posed a security risk, and the atmosphere was tense. The senior official who called the meeting, Abdullah al-Mullah, tried to alleviate the pervasive mood.

"Everybody relax, please. The Americans will never bomb a school, certainly not while it is in session."

"Don't be so sure, they bombed a hospital not so long ago," said one of the leaders.

"I should have said 'intentionally.' Their incompetence is certainly a factor."

"So what are we waiting for?" another leader asked. "School will be out soon."

"Yes, why have you called us here?"

"As you all know, ever since the great leader al-Baghdadi was killed, we have operated on many different fronts, sometimes coordinated, sometimes not. While we have had some success, like in Paris and with the Russian airliner, and our territory has grown, this strategy is unsustainable. We are like an octopus without eyes whose arms lash out randomly, never certain what the other arms are doing. We need a leader with extraordinary vision. Someone who can guide and unite us in a strike at the heart of America."

"Someone like bin Laden," one of the leaders commented. Several of the other leaders murmured their consent, and al-Mullah agreed.

"Yes, someone like bin Laden."

"But who?" The leaders looked at each other, wondering if somebody present might be asked to fill such a giant turban. Al-Mullah glanced at his watch, and as if on cue, there was a knock on the basement door. The guards flanking the door cocked their AK-47s as the leaders pulled out automatic weapons from beneath their robes.

Al-Mullah raised a hand. "Please! Don't shoot! I'm expecting someone." He quickly crossed the room and waved the guards away from the door. After receiving the password from the person on the other side, he opened it. As al-Mullah hugged the mystery guest, another man stepped into the room and pulled down the *ghutra* (head scarf) concealing his face. He held his arms wide open and announced, "My brothers, we have returned to join the fight!"

Cries of astonishment filled the room as the former head of intelligence for the Taliban, Abdul Hasiq, stepped forward to greet them. The leaders were stunned because he was supposed to be incarcerated in Qatar with the other four senior Taliban officials who were released from Guantanamo Bay in exchange for the American deserter Bowe Bergdahl. Like the proud father of the bride in a wedding reception line, Hasiq shook hands and hugged each leader in turn.

After a long hug and welcome greeting from al-Mullah, the second man acknowledged the guards and watched from behind his ghutra as Hasiq finished the warm reception. When Hasiq turned to face him, the man turned his jet-black eyes toward al-Mullah and nodded. Al-Mullah looked at the eight men in white robes and pointed at the mystery man next to him. "This is the reason I called this meeting. The octopus is no longer blind."

The man standing next to him pulled his ghutra down, and all but one of the leaders cheered, "Fazi! Fazi!" They instantly recognized him as Mohammed Fazi, the ruthless Taliban defense minister who was responsible for the massacre of thousands of Muslim Shi'ites in Afghanistan. Also known as the Beast, like Hasiq, he too was part of the trade for Bowe Bergdahl.

Fazi was imposing at six foot three and a solid 260 pounds, large for an Arab. Like all those in attendance, he had a bushy black beard that was also streaked with white. What made him stand out from the others, besides his size, was the thick unibrow over his shark-like eyes. While a unibrow wasn't necessarily a unique feature for a radical Muslim terrorist, what *was* unique was the singular hair that stuck out from the unibrow over his left eye. It was almost four inches long and occasionally moved from side to side like the feeler on an ant or some other creepy-crawly critter. He had a habit of twisting it between his thumb and forefinger while in deep thought or conversation. He had been doing it for so long it had earned its own nickname…Hair of the Beast.

The Beast broke out a rare smile and laughed, exposing a broken tooth. "I have been called many things, but never the eye of the octopus." Most of the leaders chuckled along with him. He put his hand on al-Mullah's shoulder and added, "Let us get down to business." He gave al-Mullah a nudge and followed him down the stairs. There was a ring of chairs surrounding a large map of the Middle East on the floor. After the Beast was greeted, everyone took a seat.

Hasiq, the intelligence expert, was the first to speak. "While being held in Qatar, we were able to closely monitor the progress of the caliphate state. All of you are to be commended for your role in it. The use of social media to attract Westerners to our cause has been more effective than anyone could imagine. Yet despite the beheadings of journalists and American aid workers, President Obama refuses to declare war on us. Do any of you know why?"

"Of course," one of the leaders said. "Because he is a Muslim who hates Christians and Jews as much as we do." The other leaders nodded and murmured their assent.

"That is exactly right. He is by far our greatest ally. But time is not on our side. He has less than a year left in his term, and the American people have finally grown wise to his deception. The Senate is controlled by the warmongering Republicans, and it is possible they will retake the White House this year. And if Trump wins, we may face the full wrath and fury of the US military, which should not be underestimated."

"The US military is not what it once was," another leader commented. "Obama has removed all his best commanders from the field—more than a thousand of them. He even issued their dismissal papers while they were on active duty—a demoralizing move and further proof that Obama has our back. *Fox News* has correctly reported that he has decimated his own military more than he has ISIS."

A round of laughter ensued but quickly stopped when the Beast raised his hand. "This is no time to be overconfident. Like Hasiq said, time is not on our side. We must conquer as much territory and cause as much death and destruction as possible while Obama is still in office. This is why we have enacted a plan that is so audacious it will shock the world and leave America in a death spiral of social, economic, and racial discord. Obama has set the table for us. Now it is time to feast."

"Wait a second!" The young leader of the Khorasan group dared to protest. "You have already enacted a plan? Ever since al-Baghdadi was killed we have operated as a council of equals. No major strikes or missions have been carried out without the consent of the council. Was anybody else aware of this plan?" He looked around at the other leaders who all shook their heads no. When al-Mullah failed to shake his head, the young leader pointed at him. "Of course you knew. You brought them here. Who made you Allah? Did I miss out on—"

Al-Mullah raised his hand to cut him off. "First of all, never disrespect Allah. Second, everybody here knows that the only one with a less coherent strategy than ours is Obama. If he wasn't on our side, we'd be in serious trouble. Fazi has devised a brilliant plan that will be more devastating to America than the World Trade Center attacks and will free our greatest warriors from detention. I am telling you, Osama bin

Laden will be but a footnote to history if the plan succeeds, which I have no doubt it will."

The young Khorasan leader looked around the room but could tell nothing from the stoic expressions he was met with. He glanced over his shoulder at Fazi, who had sidled closer while he questioned al-Mullah. Fazi's eyes were closed as he slowly rubbed the Hair of the Beast between his thumb and index finger. The young leader found it disgusting, which was saying something in itself. Looking back around the room, he shook his head and continued to vent his frustration.

"This is goat shit. With all due respect to Fazi and Hasiq, they've spent the last ten years behind bars. The world has changed. The social media campaign that I have championed is what is turning the tide on the war on the West. Europeans are joining our ranks every day—even Americans. Even American women! The next time you are procreating in the name of Allah and your partner doesn't go *baaa*, you can thank me."

There was some nervous chuckling, and Fazi inched closer to him as one of the leaders agreed. "He has a point."

'You're damn right I do. On whose authority—"

Like Michael Douglas pulling out a shotgun from an over-the-shoulder holster in the opening scene of *Romancing the Stone,* Mohammed Fazi, a.k.a. the Beast, unsheathed a gleaming sword. Seizing the hilt with a second gnarled hand, he slashed down and across the young leader's neck in one fluid and devastatingly powerful stroke.

"That would be on *my* authority!" the Beast proclaimed as the severed head rolled onto the map on the floor. As blood spewed from the savaged carotid artery, the headless body slumped and fell out of the chair.

One of the guards pulled out an iPhone and began recording the scene as the shrinking circle of leaders instinctively scooched their chairs away from the carnage. Never one to let an opportunity to establish control pass, the Beast put his foot on the empty chair and casually rested an elbow across his knee. "The great thing about an octopus is that if it loses an arm, another grows in its place. His replacement will be named shortly." He raised his sword in triumph and added, "Now, who would like to hear my plan?"

It was like a kindergarten teacher asking if anybody wanted to go to recess. A chorus of "I dos" echoed off the basement walls, and all hands shot in the air.

Chapter 6

The Beast stepped forward and skewered the severed head like it was a cocktail-party meatball. Holding it up for all to see, he commented, "Getting too wrapped up in technology and social media can lead a man to forget his roots. The Khorasan is just another name for the Taliban. Insulting the defense minister of the Taliban is a mistake that is only made once."

"But Fazi, your sudden appearance was a surprise to us all. Perhaps you acted a bit impulsively. You should have let him speak his mind. He was a smart and capable warrior. Besides, you are no longer the defense minister." The nervous leader glanced around at the others and didn't need to be a mind reader to know what they were thinking. He could see it in their eyes: *Are you fucking crazy?*

Fazi flung the head across the basement, and it came to rest against an old boiler. He pulled a rag out from his robe and wiped the bloody blade clean.

The outspoken leader feared he was about to be Fazi's next victim and moved to save himself. "What I, uh, meant was, you are no longer the defense minister of the Taliban because you are the new leader of ISIS.

All praise Fazi!" He raised a fist and was joined by the others as they shouted, "Fazi! Fazi!"

Fazi stepped across the bloody map on the floor and stuck the point of his sword only inches from the trembling leader's throat. The room fell into silence. "As your new leader I must be convinced of your unquestioned loyalty." He looked at the others. "Of *everyone's* loyalty!"

"You have it, Fazi," one leader said.

"We are yours to lead," another said. One by one they consented—except for the outspoken leader, who seemed frozen at the point of Fazi's sword. Fazi turned back to face him. "Are you sure my treatment of your brash Khorasan friend will not cloud your loyalty to me?"

"Of…of course not," he stammered. "You are the leader of ISIS. You may administer justice anyway you see fit. Besides, technology is overrated."

Fazi considered his words and lowered his sword. "You believe this in your heart?"

Relieved to no longer have the sword at his throat, he tried to break the tension. "Absolutely, my iPhone 6 is so big it won't fit under my turban."

Everyone laughed, including Fazi, with his broken tooth. Concerned with the time, Hasiq used the moment to redirect the meeting.

"School's out in twenty minutes. Why don't you tell them your plan, Fazi? Once they hear it, they will know why you were destined to be our leader."

Fazi nodded. "Very well." He slipped the sword back into its concealed sheath and asked one of the guards to remove the headless body of the Khorasan leader. Once the guard dragged the body out of the way, Fazi addressed his fellow terrorists.

"It is true that much has changed since I was captured, but it has been welcome change. The warmonger Bush has been replaced with one of our own, Obama. His policies could not be more effective if they had been crafted by those in this room. He has divided America both economically and racially to the point where it is on the verge of another civil war. The community organizer has become the national disorganizer. Like a true follower of Allah, he has supported the Muslims while disparaging the Christians and Jews. His actions are clear: he favors Sharia law more than the US Constitution. He even preempted us by bringing ebola into the United States, and now he is pushing to allow us into his country by simply posing as Syrian refugees. Truly incredible. Yes, much has changed since the dark days of the patriot Bush. So while I was imprisoned, I thought to myself, what can we possibly do to America that Obama has not already done? What will shock and awe them, so to speak?"

The leaders chuckled at the use of the words used to describe Bush's invasion of Iraq.

"Well, thanks to a breach of security at the White House, I found my answer. It started a few years ago when the Secret Service showed their lack of professionalism in Cartagena. Two dozen agents along with some White House staff were entertaining prostitutes in the same hotel Obama would soon be staying in. When it came to light, in true Obama fashion, the agents were punished while the White House staff was promoted. I assumed the ensuing shakeup would change the way they protected the president, but I was wrong. Last year there were no fewer than five fence jumpers at the White House. The last one made it through the front doors and deep inside the building before being subdued by an off-duty agent. Can you imagine that? One man, armed with nothing but a knife, made it into the White House. The president's security is a joke. We protect our goats better!" Another round of laughter erupted before he continued. "I believe Obama has let his security down on purpose."

"But why?" one of the leaders asked.

"The answer is obvious. He is looking to become a martyr. It is the only way to help mitigate his failed presidency in the eyes of American historians. Even though he will be hailed triumphantly in the Muslim world, and as someone who makes Narcissus look like Forrest Gump, this is important to him."

"Who is Forrest Gump?" another leader asked.

"We saw many American movies in Guantanamo Bay," Hasiq said. "Forrest Gump was a humble retard, like Biz Markie."

"Who is Biz Markie?" Looks of bewilderment and questioning murmurs filled the room.

Fazi took charge. "Silence! We will fill you in on what we learned of American pop culture some other time. The important thing to take away from this is that the Secret Service is lax on security, and that is where we shall strike."

"But I am confused," said the outspoken leader who'd had Fazi's sword at his throat only minutes earlier. "Like you said, Obama is our biggest ally. Why would we want to kill him?"

"We wouldn't. That is not the plan. But it got me thinking. If Obama's security is so lax, think of how bad it must be for former presidents."

"*Former* presidents?"

"Yes, *former* presidents. Did you not see the news reports that it took the Secret Service thirteen months to fix the home-alarm system of the elder Bush? Or how a postman was able to fly a lawnmower through thirty miles of restricted airspace and land on the Capitol steps? It's unbelievable. The Secret Service is a worse mess than a steaming pile of camel shit. How serious do you think they are about protecting Carter? Or Clinton?"

"You want to kill Bill Clinton?"

"I wouldn't mind it, but no, he is not our target. Our target is the great infidel George W. Bush, the forty-third president of the United States and a proven enemy of Allah. We are going to kidnap him." At the mention of kidnapping Bush, nearly all of the leaders snapped to attention, straightening up in their seats.

"This is a bold plan to say the least. What is the ransom?"

"If the Americans do not want to see his head on a stick, they will release the rest of the Guantanamo Bay detainees."

"That is not much of a ransom. Obama is already releasing them. It was one of his many unfulfilled campaign pledges—to close Guantanamo Bay. As much as he despises Bush and uses him as a scapegoat for his policy failures, he will gladly agree. After all, he traded a deserter for five senior Taliban commanders, including you and Hasiq."

"That is exactly right. He will look at it as a blessing. But that is not the only demand."

"What is the other?"

"That the Jews release all of their prisoners of war."

"The *Jews?* Do you think they will go for that? Netanyahu had a good relationship with Bush, but that's a lot of prisoners. If his name was Bushowitz, I'd say yes, but I'm not so sure."

"Unfortunately for Bush, I'm sure the answer will be no. There is no love lost between Obama and Netanyahu, to say the least. Obama will try to persuade him through diplomatic channels, as always, with that buffoon Kerry leading the way. Netanyahu is still understandably upset over the Iran deal and will say no. Obama will then resort to threats and bullying, as he always does. He will threaten to cut off all aid to Israel and to defend Iran against any attacks directed toward their nuclear military complex. This will cause Netanyahu to appeal to the UN to prevent such action, which will take time. By then, our brothers in Guantanamo Bay will be free and fighting alongside us.

"At that point we will chop off the infidel's head and broadcast it for the world to see. The American people will demand the United States declare war against ISIS, but Obama the Nobel Peace Prize winner will never do it. This will divide the United States even more. Netanyahu's refusal to release prisoners to save Bush will ironically give Obama the excuse to do what he has wanted to do for years. He will oppose his military advisers and announce a US alliance with Iran. When that happens the Jews will go nuts, and it will destroy what little is left of American-Israeli relations. It won't be long before the Jews believe Iran has nuclear weapons within reach, and they will bomb their nuclear facilities into oblivion. The Russians have established a foothold in the region—thanks to Obama's blunders in Syria, not to mention his withdrawal of troops from Iraq and Afghanistan—and Putin will be quick to step in. The Chinese will have little choice but to protect their oil interests and will also enter the conflict. And that, my brothers, is how we will start World War Three—the ultimate goal of the plan. While the superpowers are busy battling each other, we will push into the other Arab states, then Turkey, Greece, Italy, and Eastern Europe. Soon, the entire European continent will be under our control."

The room was eerily silent as the terrorist leaders and guards sat slack-jawed. Finally, the outspoken one who had dared to question him earlier spoke.

"And how do you plan on capturing Bush? He lives on a ranch in central Texas. It's fairly remote and reasonably well guarded. We have looked at satellite photographs. To pull off a successful kidnapping would be nearly impossible."

Fazi nodded at Hasiq and signaled for him to speak.

"We came to the same conclusion, which is why we will seize him when he is away from the ranch. Bush has a longtime trusted Mexican American ranch foreman, who is from a small town outside of Matamoros. Matamoros is on the Mexican side of the Rio Grande, south of Brownsville, Texas. He is going there tomorrow with his wife and daughter to attend a family reunion. After the reunion they will be kidnapped. The wife and daughter will be held hostage while we send the foreman back to Bush's ranch. Assuming the foreman doesn't want his wife and daughter raped, tortured, and killed, he will tell us of Bush's travel schedule.

"We have learned that he regularly travels to Houston and other coastal cities to visit friends. His travel plans are generally not known to the public, but when he travels in Texas, he seldom has more than two Secret Service agents guarding him. The next time he travels to the coast, we will strike like a cobra and take him to an abandoned oil rig in the Gulf of Mexico. We have already prepared the rig for our guest. Four of our brothers, including two of the Taliban Five, are in Matamoros to help the esteemed Mohammed Zahvi carry out the plan. They are being assisted by fringe members of the Sinaloa cartel, who have been enlisted to smuggle our fellow jihadists across the border, and found us the abandoned oil rig. They have proved to be unwaveringly loyal to the dollar, which soon will not be so mighty."

The questioning leader put his hands together in prayer, looked at the ceiling, and said, "Praise Allah." Suddenly, a bell rang, signaling the end of school, and they heard the sound of children running into the street. "This plan is both brilliant and devious in nature," he continued. "I shall never question you again, Fazi. Praise Fazi!" He pulled a semiautomatic handgun out from under his robe and fired several rounds into the ceiling. In an instant everybody fired their weapons into the ceiling, the earsplitting sound drowning out the chants of "Fazi! Fazi!"

Chapter 7

Oskar Medina stood on the deck of the *Taladro Grande* and watched the helicopter disappear from sight. After thirty years working for Mexico's state-owned oil company (Pemex), he had been promoted to OIM (offshore installation manager) of the newest fixed platform rig in the fleet. The executives being flown back to the mainland had presented him with an eighteen karat gold necklace during a short but touching ceremony. It had a charm dangling from it in the design of an oil barrel and he fingered it proudly. He had started as a roughneck in the Mexican lowlands and was now the man in charge of a state-of-the-art drilling rig nearly a hundred miles off the coast of the Texas Mexico border.

He had spent the last twenty years on a smaller jack-up rig named the *Dinero Majado* that been decommissioned only six months earlier. At twenty-eight years old, it had been pushed to the brink of its useful life. It was now nothing more than a rusting hulk and refuge for marine life that sat ten miles to the southwest of the *Taladro Grande.* The rig had been a good producer for Pemex. It was where he learned the ins and outs of offshore drilling and worked his way up the ranks. Unlike the *Taladro Grande*, it sat in only 250 feet of water on the edge of an undersea step of the continental shelf. The reminiscing came to an abrupt end when somebody yelled for him.

"Boss Hombre!" He turned to see his lead technical analyst approach with a knowing grin.

"Will you quit calling me that? We've been working together for fifteen years, Fernando. My name's Oskar, like it's always been. Que pasa?"

"A sensor on the number-two support leg indicates the presence of a possible stress fracture forming on a cross strut."

"How far down is it?"

"Two hundred and eighty feet."

"Send Pago down to check it out."

"As soon as he gets back, I will. I just wanted to let you know."

"What do you mean, 'as soon as he gets back'? He's not on shore leave."

"He's fishing on the skiff. The OTL (operations team leader) gave him the day off because he was working deep yesterday. I guess he needed some uptime."

"Uptime, my ass. If he's clear to go down again, that's where I want him. This rig shouldn't have any stress fractures—it's brand-new. Get me the OTL."

Ten miles away, the deep-dive specialist named Pago relaxed in the shade of the *Dinero Majado.* It was only the second time he had returned to the old rig. Without a calm sea like the one that currently presented itself, it was too risky in the small work skiff. He had it tied off to a support structure and watched his fishing line with sinker and baited hook quickly disappear into the depths. Although he was a diver by trade, he was a born fisherman like his father and his father's father before him. And like any good fisherman worth his salt, he knew how to take what the sea gave him and turn it to his advantage. After catching a few snappers, he managed to pull up a small barracuda before it cut through his mono leader. In quick order he cut the belly into several strips and threw the remains overboard.

After rerigging for bigger game with his last few feet of eighty-pound mono leader, he sent the new rig down with heightened anticipation. He knew that barracuda belly was a favorite of big groupers and mutton snappers. A few minutes later he was rewarded with a powerful thump on his line and struggled to reel up whatever was pulling on it. Worried the line might get severed on the support structure, he untied the skiff with one hand and drifted away from the rusty rig. Five minutes later a large grouper broke the surface only six feet from the tiny skiff. Excitement coursed through his veins as he grabbed a small gaff and began maneuvering the grouper alongside the skiff. Without warning a large hammerhead appeared from the depths and savagely chomped down on the helpless grouper with a row of razor-sharp teeth. Pago recoiled as the hammerhead thrashed its tail, and the boat nearly capsized when he grabbed the side. It was over in an instant. The hammerhead quickly disappeared with the grouper and Pago's severed leader, leaving nothing but some blood and guts on the surface.

"Shit! Are you kidding me!?" Pago waved a clenched fist, but he knew it could have been worse. *Much worse.* Still, he was angry. He had two more barracuda strips but was out of leader. Or was he? He had spent some time on the old rig before the new rig was finished. He was pretty sure he didn't leave any fishing gear behind, but he wasn't the only one who fished. Several of the maintenance guys were known to fish, too. Maybe one of them left behind some heavy mono or wire leader. It was worth a look, provided nobody had changed the lock and he could still get on the rig. He fired up the small outboard and quickly motored over to the rusty metal ladder that extended down from underneath the rig. After retying the skiff, he grabbed a small penlight out of his tackle box and clambered up to the trapdoor in the deck. *Yes! The old combination lock was still there.* With one hand holding the top rung, he used the other to manipulate the combination to O-I-L, and snapped it open. He set the lock on a makeshift plywood platform off to the side and pushed open the creaky door.

The trapdoor led to an electrical room connected to an office. He was glad for the penlight as he made his way through the darkened interior. He exited the office onto the grated walkway and followed it up a set of stairs that led to the upper levels. He glanced at his watch. It was five o'clock. He had a couple of hours of daylight left. There was plenty of time to try a few more drops and still make it back to the *Taladro Grande* by dark—*if* he could find some leader. He crossed through the mess hall and stopped by a window to look down at the water some seventy feet below. It was one of those rare days when the gulf was nearly flat, and the sunlight gave it a mirror effect. Off the kitchen and down a short flight of steps was the maintenance room. When he got there he was puzzled to find all the tool bins and miscellaneous cabinets in the hallway. He swung open the door to the windowless room and shone the penlight around.

"What the hell?" he mumbled. The room was about sixteen feet square, and there was a circle of spotlights ringing a chair positioned in the center. He walked around the room and found a brand-new generator and small refrigerator where the tool bins used to be. On the floor next to the refrigerator were ten cases of bottled water and four cases of Spam. Perplexed, he scratched his head. On another wall was some recently installed shelving that held a monitor and some electronic equipment he didn't immediately recognize. He traced the cables with his penlight. The thickest one ran up through a hole in the ceiling. Beyond curious, he exited the room and made his way to the dorm level above. He found the bunk room where the cable passed through and saw that it too went through the ceiling. Shaking his head, he made his way topside and found what he suspected—a satellite dish. *What in the hell was going on?*

The walkie-talkie clipped to his belt beeped twice, and he heard the voice of his direct supervisor (the OTL). "Pago, pick up."

He unclipped it from his belt. "I'm here."

"How's the fishing?"

"Not bad until a big hammerhead almost capsized me."

"Good for you. Engineering spotted a possible stress fracture on one of the cross struts. Boss Hombre wants you to check it out el pronto."

"How deep?"

"Two-eighty."

"Can't it wait till morning? It's getting late."

"No. Boss Hombre just had his big promotion ceremony, and he doesn't want any screw-ups. Get back here now. Over and out."

Pago clipped the radio on his belt and had an idea. He found a pair of old wire cutters in one of the tool bins and went back into the maintenance room. With penlight in hand he reached behind the electronic equipment and snipped off a four-foot section of cable. He walked into the mess hall, where there was better light, and quickly stripped the rubber covering off. The stranded copper wire wasn't much, but it would do.

Back in the skiff, he secured a hook to the makeshift wire leader, attached it to the fishing line with a swivel, and then stuck one of the barracuda bellies on the hook. Then he fired up the engine and put the rod in a holder angled out to the side. When he was fifty yards from the old rig he started letting line out. He throttled up to a comfortable seven knots and settled in for a leisurely troll back to the *Taladro Grande.* No sense letting a good 'cuda belly go to waste. He looked past the bait as it skipped on the surface and wondered what the hell was going on in the maintenance room of the decommissioned *Dinero Majado.*

Chapter 8

After Rafe showed us the electric tender, he led us into the cabin for a tour of the interior. The layout of the main salon was somewhat similar to a Hatteras, with a big wraparound sofa to the port side and a table in front of it like a dinette. Inside the doorway to the starboard side was a set of stairs leading up to the bridge. Past the stairs was another sofa along the starboard side with a raised counter top running perpendicular to it at the end. On the opposite side was the step-down galley with another counter and three stools perched in front of it. And like on the newer Hatteras models, the entire forward bulkhead was glass from beam to beam, matching the bridge above. As Holly checked out the galley, the ringtone on Rafe's cell started chiming.

"Yes? Yes, she's expected. Escort her in and have her come aboard." *Click.*

We followed Rafe down two steps to the galley level and then down two more to the forward berths. On the port side there was a mate's berth with two sets of bunks and a small head with a shower that was also accessible from the hallway. Opposite the mate's berth was a stateroom with a queen-size bed and a more generous bathroom. In the bow was the master stateroom spanning the width of the boat, which Rafe reported to be nineteen feet. A king-size bed faced the stern, and directly above it the ceiling dipped down about eighteen inches. I pointed at it. "What's with the ceiling?"

"That's where the tender sits," Rafe said.

"Oh, right." I ducked under it and rolled onto the bed.

"Kit, c'mon. That's rude." Holly shook her head as Tangles dove onto the bed next to me. He put his hands behind his head and exhaled.

"Ohhhh, this is nice. I got dibs."

"You wish," I chided him. "You got dibs on the bunk beds. You should take a top one so you could pay homage to your simian ancestry by swinging from bunk to bunk like a marmoset."

"A marma-*what*?"

"Kit, c'mon." Much to Holly's dismay, Rafe laughed. Holly gave him a look and added, "You're not helping."

"Sorry."

"So where's all the high-tech surveillance and security monitoring equipment? Where are the computers?"

"I thought you'd never ask. Check it out." There was a vanity next to the door leading to what I presumed was the master bath. In between the vanity and the door was a small strip of paneling. Rafe pressed the light switch, and several cabin lights turned on, including a wall sconce above the switch. "The light switch has to be on to activate the one-eighty on the vanity," he explained. "Just press your index finger on the top of the sconce and...voila." He did just that, and the vanity began to slowly rotate.

"No way," Holly said.

Tangles scrambled off the bed, and I swung my feet over the side to get a better view. Within fifteen seconds the vanity rotated out of sight, and in its place was a computerized dashboard and a display console that would make Captain Kirk proud. The center-mirror section of the vanity was now a computer screen. It was laid out in Brady Bunch fashion, with multiple shots of the cockpit, the bow, the bridge, and the port and starboard sides of the boat on separate surrounding screens.

"Wow, is that cool," Holly said. "Those are live shots of the exterior?"

"Yes."

"It's sorta like the Batcave," Tangles agreed with a nod.

"Pretty slick," I added. "I didn't even notice the cameras."

"That's a first."

"Ha-ha-ha. Can it."

Rafe pointed behind me. "Press your finger on top of either of the sconces on the headboard."

When I did, a compartment attached to the ceiling at the foot of the bed silently slid open, and a flat-screen TV swung down. It showed the same split-screen shots of the boat's exterior minus the center computer screen.

"Huh," was all I said.

"What's the matter? Is the live-video feed not coming through?"

"No, no, it's fine. It's just—"

"Just *what?*"

"It's kinda small. What is it, a twenty-seven-inch screen? I didn't even know they made those anymore."

"Are you kidding me?"

"You are unbe*liev*able sometimes." Holly shook her head, and I held my hands open defensively.

"I'm just saying."

"Please don't start saying that again. You know how much I hate that."

"It *is* kinda small," Tangles confirmed.

"Thank you very much."

"I'll be sure to tell the boss how you feel about it," Rafe replied.

"No, no, it's fine, really. So is the bed."

"What's wrong with the bed?"

I pushed my hand down in the center of it a couple of times. "Nothing, considering it's not a Tempur-Pedic."

"Oh my God," Holly said. "When did you turn into such a prima donna?"

"Hey, with all the heavy reeling I do, I need a good mattress for my back. If I sleep on a cheap mattress I might wake up with spina bifida one day."

Rafe shook his head, and Holly's mouth hung open for a couple of seconds.

I smiled. "Gotcha."

"That's not even funny…joking about that."

Tangles laughed, and I pointed at him. "*He* thinks it's funny."

"He doesn't count. He *never* counts."

Rafe and I laughed as Tangles complained. "Hey, what the hell does that mean?"

As Holly apologized, I noticed movement on the TV monitor and pointed at it. "Looks like we got company."

Rafe looked at the vanity display, which showed somebody stepping into the cockpit. "Good," he said. "Now we can get the show on the road. You guys wait here." As he went to escort our unknown visitor in, I leaned back on the bed and closed my eyes. It was actually pretty comfortable, considering.

"Will you get off the bed already?" Holly pleaded. "You too, Tangles. Let's show some manners for once."

I tried out my Matthew McConaughey impression as I got off the bed and drawled, "All right, all right, all right."

Holly looked at me funny. "What was *that?*"

"What was what?"

"The way you said that, you sounded drunk. Don't do that again."

Undeterred, I gave it another go. "All right, all right, all right."

"Dude, that's pretty good," Tangles said. "Foster Brooks, right? Nice impression."

"It's not Foster Brooks." I shook my head in disbelief. "It's Matthew McConaughey. *Foster Brooks?* How old are you again?"

"My dad was an alkie, and Foster Brooks was his favorite. Just say you're doing Foster Brooks. That was pretty good."

"It's not *Foster Brooks*! It's Matthew McConaughey. I think it's a pretty good one, too."

"Well, you thought wrong," Holly said. "I, sir, know Matthew McConaughey, and you are no Matthew McConaughey. So please...don't ever do that again. It's *horrible.*"

"Wow, tough crowd."

"Not really, just one with ears."

"Ouch, that's gotta hurt," Tangles said. "Maybe you could pass it off as Matthew McConaughey impersonating Foster Brooks. That might work."

"You know what else might work? Me stuffing you in the fish box. Oh, wait, what am I thinking? There's *plenty* of room for your scrawny little ass in the fish box. Maybe you should bunk there."

Tangles puffed his little chest out. "Why do you always—"

"Hey everybody," Rafe interrupted. "I'd like you to meet Judy Larson; she's the former head of IT for Homeland Security." An attractive librarian type with semigeeky glasses stepped forward and shook everybody's hand. After we introduced ourselves, Rafe gave us a little more background on her. "Miss Larson is a computer and mathematical genius who has done extensive work on supercollider magnocellular receptivity and quantum statistical analysis. Did I get that right?"

"Yes, thank you."

"She's also won the Cole prize in algebra and number theory, as well as the prestigious Fields Medal."

"Wow," Tangles gushed. "All that and you can cook, too. Impressive. You single?"

"Tangles!" Holly appeared mortified as Rafe and I chuckled.

Miss Larson looked taken aback and somewhat confused as she responded to Tangles. "Yes, I am single. Very *happily* single, as a matter of fact. But what gave you the idea that I can cook?"

"The Fields Medal. The Mrs. Fields Medal. You gotta have some serious baking skills to take top honors in that. My mom entered it one year but her chocolate-chip po' boy with shrimp-and-oyster mousse didn't make the cut."

"You're kidding, right?"

"No, I'm not kidding. It was *awesome.* She got screwed. What did you win with?"

Miss Larson looked at Rafe with disbelief written all over her face. "*He's* one of the new agents?"

"Don't worry. You'll have limited interaction with him."

I started laughing, and Holly elbowed me in the side.

"What?" Tangles said. "What did I say? I was just complimenting—"

"It's not a compliment!" Miss Larson scowled at Tangles. "The Fields Medal is awarded for outstanding discoveries in the field of mathematics. *Not* for baking cookies."

"How was I supposed to know there's two Fields Medals?"

"There's not. There's only one. And I won it. Again, not for baking...okay?"

"Okay, okay, sure...sorry. Geez, you try to pay somebody a—"

"Look," Rafe said. "We're behind schedule already. Miss Larson—"

"Please, just Judy, okay?" She glanced at me and Holly.

"Right, sorry. Judy is here to train Holly on all the computer systems, so why don't we let them get to work. Kit, you and Tangles come with me. You need to learn how to run this vessel, among other things."

Holly told Miss Larson she'd be right back and excused herself to use the bathroom. Rafe headed down the hall, and as I slipped past her, I nodded and said, "Nice to meet you, Judy."

She reciprocated, and Tangles said, "Look, Judy, I—"

"It's Miss Larson to you."

"*What?*"

As I was prone to do, I came to his defense. "I know we just met, Judy, but believe me when I tell you he meant no disrespect. He's just an idiot sometimes, like me…more often than me, but still. He's trustworthy, and he's a helluva mate. You know we have a fishing show, right? We're using it as cover to help you guys do what you need to do."

"So I heard."

"You just *heard?*" Tangles asked. "You mean you haven't seen our show?"

"Uh, let me think about that. No."

"Don't you have cable?"

"Yes, I have cable…satellite, too."

"Well, maybe your provider doesn't carry ESPN." He looked at me. "What number are we on again?"

"Ten, I think. ESPN 10…or maybe it's eleven. They keep bumping us down the damn line."

"You heard him. Maybe your provider doesn't get—"

"Between cable and satellite I get over three thousand channels, and I've never seen you on any of them."

"Whatever. The show's very popular in southeast central Palm Beach County. If you play your cards right, maybe we'll work you into an episode, if you know what I mean." He winked at her and smiled just as Holly came out of the bathroom. *Oh shit.*

"Did you just wink at me? Who does that?"

"Tangles, get out of here!" Holly pointed down the hall. "You too, Kit. *Now.* We have work to do." She turned to Judy. "Don't pay any attention to them. I never do."

Rafe yelled for us, and I grabbed Tangles by the shirt. It was time to go nuclear.

Chapter 9

Rafe spent a good hour on the bridge explaining how the boat ran. I was no stranger to boats, and my mind wandered until he started using words like "fast neutron" and "turboelectric." It reminded me we were going to be fishing and snooping the oceans in what amounted to a high-speed, invisible-on-demand, floating nuke plant. *Sweet.*

"You paying attention, Shagball?"

"Huh? What? Yeah, of course I am. I used to have a turboelectric razor. It worked great unless you didn't have a full charge. Without a full charge the blade had a tendency to tug. It's not a big deal unless you're manscaping the short hairs—that could be painful."

Tangles chuckled, but Rafe wasn't pleased.

"What the hell does *that* have to do with anything?"

"Well, I would think you need to keep the turboelectric part of things fully charged, or things could start going haywire."

"The transmission? The turboelectric transmission?"

"Yeah, what else?"

"Sounds about right to me," Tangles agreed.

Rafe rubbed his temple like he was getting a migraine and dropped an F-bomb, followed by something that sounded suspiciously like "Chernobyl." He mumbled it, and I couldn't be certain, but then again, I couldn't think of anything that rhymed with Chernobyl.

"What was that?" I asked.

"Nothing."

"So it *does* need to be kept on full charge?" Tangles said.

"Who said anything about charging?"

"Sorry, I was just—"

"Look, I obviously shouldn't have mentioned the transmission or the reactor or anything regarding the propulsion system, but I thought you might like to know. Clearly, the technical stuff is way over your head."

"*Everything*'s over his head," I pointed out. "But don't worry, I think I have a pretty good grasp of things. Where's the ignition switch again?"

I knew there was no ignition switch. The first thing Rafe showed us was the push-button start, which only worked if the pusher's fingerprint was encoded into the start system.

Rafe looked at me in disbelief. "I'm starting to think the boss made a huge mistake by—"

"Oh c'mon, man. I was just kidding. I know how to fire this baby up."

I went to push the button, and Rafe grabbed my wrist. He was quite strong and let me know it.

"Not now. Now we finish going over the instrumentation."

He let go of my wrist, and as I discreetly massaged it, Tangles said, "I was hoping Judy would handle that."

"Forget about her. She's not interested in you."

Rafe started to talk about the Raytheon depth sounder, but Tangles wasn't having it.

"Whoa, whoa, whoa. Hold the phone. What do you mean she's not interested in me? We just met."

"It's not just you; I'm pretty sure she likes women."

"*What?* Oh, man, you're kidding me, right?"

"'Fraid not."

"What makes you think she likes women?" I asked.

"She drives a Subaru."

I looked at Tangles and shook my head. "You heard the man. She drives a Subaru. Forget about her."

"What the...what the hell does that mean? Who cares what she drives?"

"You should, so you don't waste your time fawning all over her. Don't you know *anything?*"

"You're saying that because she drives a Subaru, she's gay? That's ridiculous. I never heard that before."

"Really?" Rafe said.

"Yep." I nodded. "That's what I heard, too. You can take it to the bank, just not the sperm bank." Rafe laughed, but not Tangles.

"That is *the* most absurd, sexist, gay-stereotyping thing I ever heard in my life. I like Subarus, and I'm not gay."

"Well, you're not a lesbo. I'll give you that...at least not yet."

"Please!" Rafe cut in. "I'm sorry I mentioned it." He glanced at his watch and shook his head. "C'mon, follow me." We followed him into the salon, and he called for Judy and Holly. Rafe had us take a seat at the dinette, and Judy and Holly joined us.

"What's going on?" Judy asked.

Rafe's phone chimed, and he held it up. "Conference call—it's the boss."

Rafe walked over to the bar area on the starboard side and slid open a cabinet. There was a flat-screen TV inside, and below was what looked like stereo equipment. Rafe pushed a couple of buttons and then sat down with us and placed his phone in a cradle in the center of the table. "Hello? You there, boss?" On the TV screen was a live picture of the inside of the salon.

"Yes, I'm here," said a familiar voice over the recessed speakers in the ceiling and walls of the salon. "I can see everybody is present. Good."

Holly whispered in my ear, "Whose voice is that?"

I had previously told Tangles and Holly about the voice-mimicking device the mysterious man in charge used, but before I could figure it out, the answer came over the speaker system.

"It's the friendly voice of the late Tom Bosley, who played Mr. C on *Happy Days.*"

"Oh. Right. How did you hear what I said?"

"Rafe, please explain to our agents in training how the system works."

Rafe pointed at the speaker in the wall directly behind where Holly and I were sitting. "Each of the speakers has a built-in microphone. Once you put your phone in the cradle and turn on the TV and sound system, it activates the group-speak feature. There's also a camera on the TV that allows him to see everybody in the room."

"Oh, okay."

"Pretty slick," Tangles said.

"This whole boat's pretty slick," I added.

"I told you it was worth the wait," said the voice of Mr. C. "Did I not?"

"You certainly did. And it was. At least I *think* it was. I can't be sure until I see how well she raises fish."

"Mr. Jansen, do I need to remind you—"

"I thought we were past the Mr. Jansen thing. Please, can we stick with Kit or Shagball? Just pretend I'm one of Richie's friends."

"Okay then, Kit, do I need to remind you what the primary purpose of this boat is? It's for intelligence gathering, not fishing. I didn't spend a billion dollars just so you could go fishing."

"Did you just say a *billion*?"

"Yes, that's a billion dollars with a B. Not a million, a *billion*. It's nearly a quarter of my annual budget, and I expect everybody to take good care of it."

"A billion dollars?! Holy gold-plated sea cow," Tangles said.

"I bet it was the cloaking technology that drove up the cost," Holly commented nonchalantly. Amazingly, she didn't seem too fazed by the sticker price.

"Well, truth be told, building a one-off nuclear propulsion system isn't exactly cheap, but yes, developing the cloaking technology proved to be extremely challenging and costly. It's the first of its kind."

"You mean the first after *Harry Potter*."

"No, I mean the first in reality. Not the movies. So what did you think of the demonstration?"

"It was amazing, but—"

"But what?"

"Who exactly *are you*? I mean…you're speaking in a dead actor's voice. Why all the secrecy?"

"She's right," I added. "Isn't it about time you leveled with us? You did just call us 'agents in training.' Agents in training for who?"

"You mean *whom*."

"Sorry, Mom."

"Yes, it's time. I was getting to it. You're agents in training for the Department of International Criminal Knowledge."

"Never heard of it," Tangles said.

"The Department of International Criminal Knowledge?" Holly repeated. "I never heard of it either."

"Same here," I said.

"That's because it's a secret organization. So secret that it was long ago decided my identity should remain hidden, even from my own agents."

I pointed at Judy and Rafe.

"You guys don't know who Mr. C is? You never met him?"

They both shook their heads no. I couldn't believe it. "For real?"

"We've all speculated," Rafe said. "But it's true. Nobody really knows."

I looked at Holly and Tangles, who both looked skeptical.

"Believe it," said Mr. C. "Nobody knows but those who know and there's not too many of those." Then he chuckled. *Cute.*

"This is crazy," Holly said.

"Maybe, but it's worked for nearly fifteen years now. Like they say, if it ain't broke, don't fix it. And this DICK isn't broke."

"Excuse me?" Holly's eyes about popped out of her head, and she looked at Judy, who looked nonplussed and sighed. I looked at Rafe, and he smiled. *Huh?*

"C'mon, guys, don't you get it? I'm talking about DICK. D-I-C-K, DICK—the Department of International Criminal Knowledge."

Holly's mouth hung open for a second before she said, "Oh my God. You cannot be serious."

"I can, and I am. DICK is the most top-secret terrorist- and international-criminal-hunting organization in the world…as far as we know."

"I always knew I'd end up working for dick," I lamented.

"So, Jude, do *you* like working for DICK?" Tangles said. He might have gotten away with it, but then he winked.

"Stop winking, and don't call me Jude."

"Does that mean no, or is the Subaru a loaner?"

"*What?* How did you know I—"

"Enough fraternizing for now," Mr. C said. "It's time to get this show on the road."

Judy protested that she wasn't fraternizing, but he shut her down. She apologized, but not before giving Tangles the evil eye.

Mr. C continued, "Kit, when you agreed to use your fishing show as cover to aid our intelligence-gathering efforts, you only had one stipulation."

"That's right. It was to help find Holly's long-lost cousin, Lucky."

"His name was Patrick," Holly corrected me. "Patrick VanderGrift. Millie nicknamed him Lucky when she saw his birthmark. Did you find something about him?" Holly bit her lower lip. She was clearly hoping for some good news.

"Yes, I believe so. As part of our mission to hunt terrorists and international criminals, we process vast volumes of data for the major security and law enforcement branches of the United States, including the Department of Defense. I ran the name Patrick VanderGrift through our system but struck out. Holly, you mentioned that Patrick was running away from his abusive father, so I ran his adoptive mother's maiden name instead—thinking he might have used it."

"LeRoux?"

"Yes. When we ran the name LeRoux, we had a hit. In 1966, a Rick LeRoux enlisted in the navy. He signed up at a military base in the South Pacific, in American Samoa."

"*Rick*? American Samoa? I don't know, that's halfway around the world. That doesn't sound too promising."

"The date of birth listed was February 22, 1948."

"What?! That's gotta be him! Where is he now?"

"I'm sorry, Holly, but he was killed in action in Vietnam. He was on a navy patrol boat in the Mekong Delta…July 17, 1970." Holly's temporary euphoria was just that—temporary. She covered her mouth with her hand and Judy put a hand on her shoulder.

I was about to console her, too, when Mr. C added, "But it's not *all* bad news."

Holly had tears in her eyes, and I put an arm around her.

"What do you…what do you mean?" she managed to choke out.

"A second LeRoux from Samoa enlisted in the navy in 1985. He was also eighteen years old, and his full name was Alexander Hamilton LeRoux."

"Alexander Hamilton?" I asked. "Wasn't he a founding father or something?"

"That's right. He fought in the Revolutionary War, was secretary of the Treasury to George Washington, and started the first political party in the United States—the Federalist Party. He was also a relentless interpreter and promoter of the Constitution. But there's one fact regarding his formative years that I think you will find most interesting. Do you know where he was born and raised?"

"No. I suck at *Jeopardy*."

"I'm sure. He was born out of wedlock in the West Indies, on the island of Nevis. Soon after, his mother moved with him to…drum roll, please… Saint Croix."

"*Saint Croix?* You're kidding," said Holly.

"While the jovial Mr. C was known to occasionally kid Potsy and company, I assure you I am not kidding. Young Mr. Hamilton's mother died of a fever when he was just eleven years old, leaving him orphaned. He was adopted by a cousin and wrote an essay about a hurricane that devastated the town of Christiansted, Saint Croix, on August 30, 1772. Community leaders were so impressed they pooled their funds and sent him to the American colonies for a formal education. The rest, as they say, is history. He is easily the most important historical person to ever come from Saint Croix, where he is deservedly revered for his accomplishments to this day."

"That can't be a coincidence. Maybe Patrick shortened his name to Rick. Alexander must be related to him, right? Maybe he's his son. Please don't tell me he's dead, too."

"I doubt it. At least he wasn't dead as of a couple of weeks ago. Navy SEALs are known to be rather tough."

"He's a SEAL?"

"*Was* a SEAL. He retired in 2005 after twenty years of decorated service. He was regarded as one of the navy's top divers. After he retired he dropped off the grid. And I mean dropped off as in disappeared. We couldn't find anything on him...zilch. Then, a few months ago, he resurfaced."

"Where?"

"Thanks to the Patriot Act, which was passed simultaneously with the secret formation of DICK, domestic oil companies are required to file personnel reports for all their employees. So are all their subcontractors. One of my assistants did a follow-up search for Alexander Hamilton LeRoux, and bingo, we found him. He's doing contract work as a deep-dive specialist on an oil rig named the *Taladro Grande,* about a hundred miles southeast of Brownsville, Texas, in the Gulf of Mexico."

"Brownsville's on the Texas border, isn't it?" I asked.

"Yes. The rig is actually owned by Pemex, the Mexican national oil company. One of Pemex's partners is Navajo Oil, out of Houston. LeRoux works for a subcontractor of Navajo."

"I've got to see him," said Holly. "I'd like to skip the shakedown cruise and fly to Houston as soon as—"

"Hold on a second, young lady. You haven't even *begun* to learn how to operate the computer systems that run the *LD3*. We've invested tens of thousands of man-hours and an incredible amount of money to put this one-of-a-kind vessel together. Needless to say, there are a couple of high-ranking insiders who have been critical of this project and especially of the crew I've put together. That means you and Shagball and Tangles. I'm hoping to prove them wrong."

"But—"

"But nothing. We made a deal, and I held up my end of it. I expect you to do the same. Fortunately, there's a way we can both get what we want."

"I'm listening."

"Both the NSA and Homeland Security have reason to believe a Mexican drug cartel may have struck a deal with ISIS to help smuggle terrorists over the southern border. There may already be a planned attack of some sort in the works. FBI agents in Brownsville have been hearing the same rumor on the street, giving it more credibility. I think it would be a good test of our surveillance capabilities to head over there and see what our parabolic mics, and eavesdropping drones, can pick up. While you're in the area, you can stop by the *Taladro Grande* and see if Alexander Hamilton LeRoux is your cousin."

"Yes!" Holly cried. "Thank you, thank you, thank you!"

"Hold on, boss," Rafe said. "This was just supposed to be a shakedown cruise. We're a long way from Texas."

"Which is why you'd better get moving. Obviously, if you find any problems that need immediate attention, turn around and come back. A trip like this should be perfect for getting everybody up to speed with how everything works."

"Excuse me, sir," Judy said. "I hadn't planned on an extended trip. I'll need to make some arrangements to take care of my dogs, my mail, my—"

"Subaru?" Tangles said with a raised eyebrow.

Judy shot him a look. "And my car, too."

"You'd better get on the horn, then. I'll be monitoring the boat's operating systems and progress from headquarters. Good luck and God speed." *Click.*

Chapter 10

Franklin Post leaned back in his command center recliner and gazed up at the starry-domed ceiling of his Puget Sound estate. It had been fourteen years since he accepted the task of creating and running the world's most secret data-collecting/spy agency. As a self-made IT billionaire, he wasn't in it for the money. He was in it because he loved his country, and he loved his sister. She had been on Flight 19, which crashed into the Pennsylvania countryside when terrorists took control of the cockpit on September 11, 2001.

The forty-third president of the United States knew this when he pitched him the job. The president also knew his wife had left him, and he was going through a difficult time in his otherwise extraordinary life, correctly anticipating he would be unable to resist the chance to build and run DICK. Despite the president's persona as a word-stumbling, not-too-bright overachiever, Franklin Post (a.k.a. Stargazer) knew it was all an act. Well, at least most of it was. He regarded him as the Columbo of presidents, someone who was nearly always underestimated. He remembered the words of Saddam Hussein emerging from a rat-hole in the Iraqi desert after being bombed into near oblivion during operation Desert Storm's shock-and-awe campaign. He told his American captors, "I never thought Bush would do it. I thought he was bluffing."

He smiled as he scrawled through the voice-mimicking device, called the Oralator, he had invented. It was time to call the former president. He would be using the voice of Peter Falk, of Columbo fame, in his honor. After double-checking that he had his laugh rag handy (something to gag himself with in the likelihood that the president would say something hilarious, whether intentional or not), he hit the hyperdial on his phone.

A couple of thousand miles away in Crawford, Texas, George W. Bush stood by a fence overlooking part of his vast ranch. He was watching his ranch foreman, Manny Gonzalez, herd up some steer. Manny had just arrived back from a trip to Mexico for a family reunion, and he seemed out of sorts. Maybe it was because his wife and daughter didn't come back with him. Manny told him they stayed behind to visit with family a little longer. Maybe he missed them, and that was why he didn't seem to be himself. Or maybe it was something else. He was about to flag him down and see if he wanted to toss some horseshoes over a frosty glass of iced tea when his phone vibrated in a pocket of his blue jeans. When he pulled it out and saw the name "Stargazer" appear on the display, his heart skipped a beat. He only got one or two calls a year from Stargazer, and he relished being kept in the DICK loop. He also loved not knowing what voice Stargazer would use when he called, even though he knew his true identity.

He answered in typical Dubya fashion. "Stargazer! How the hell are you?"

"I'm doing well, sir. How are you?"

The president held the phone away from his ear and stared at it for a second before resuming the conversation.

"I'm doing good. Real good. That's a new voice you're using there. Who is it? Wait a second. I think I know. Say something again."

"Something again."

"Heh, that's a good one, Stargazer, but I got you figured. You're using the voice of that actor, Vic what's-his-name. You know the one I'm talking about. The one that got killed filming *The Twilight Zone* movie in the early eighties. A helicopter crashed on him."

"Vic Morrow?"

"Yeah, that's right. Vic Morrow—helluvan actor. Can't believe he got demancipated. What a way to go."

"This isn't Vic Morrow's voice."

"*What?*"

"It's Peter Falk."

"Hey, watch your language. I'm a Christian."

"I said Falk, F-A-L-K, Falk. You know, Columbo."

"Oh, right...Columbo. The guy with the cigar and the raincoat. He sounds just like Vic Morrow. You know, before his head got helicoptered."

"I hadn't thought about it until now, but you might be right. I'll have to watch some of his old movies and check it out. Maybe add him to the Oralator."

"Check out *The Bad News Bears.* I loved him in that. What a great movie. He shoulda stuck to making *Bad News Bears* sequels—no helicopters required. So, detective, to what do I owe this call? You bag another terrorist? Go on, gimme all the juicy details."

"I'm afraid it's not one of those calls, sir."

"Don't be scared, Stargazer, just spit it out. If you can dish it, I can take it. If you ever tasted my wife's cooking, you'd know what I'm talking about. Heh."

"Okay, then. The leader of ISIS, al-Baghdadi, was critically injured in a drone attack, and we captured one of his wives and a daughter."

"Sounds good to me. I mean, except for having more than one wife. That's just plain nuts."

"We also finally got Jihadi John, the one in the videos seen cutting off heads."

"That's great. So what's the bad news? Don't tell me *Duck Dynasty* is goin' off the air."

"No, sir. It has to do with al-Baghdadi. When one leader goes down, another one steps in to fill the void."

"Hey, I've filled a few voids in my day. That's what happens when the cat's away—the mice play. You smell the cheese, you eat the cheese. Nothing you can do about it. It's called human nature. He'll get over it... assuming he lives."

"Sir, what, uh, what are you talking about?"

"What do you mean? You brought it up. I'm talking about the void. The wife's void. So what if she's been bumpin' burkas with some goatherder."

"No. No, that's not what I meant. I'm talking about the *leadership* void. ISIS has a new leader, and you're not gonna like who it is."

"Oh, right. That makes more sense. Who is it? Ben Affleck? I saw he grew a beard."

"No. It's Mohammed Fazi. Ring a bell?"

"What'd you say?"

"Ring a bell?"

“Before that.”

“Fazi. Mohammed Fazi, otherwise known as the Beast.”

“That’s one of the sons of bitches I locked up in Geronimo Bay!”

“You mean Guantanamo Bay.”

“Guantanamo, Geronimo, Obamano. That’s what they oughta call it—Obamano, ’cause Obama no wanna keep it open. When did Fazi get out?”

“Last year. Obama released him along with four other Taliban commanders in exchange for the suspected deserter, Sergeant Bowe Bergdahl.”

“*Fazi* was in that group? I didn’t realize that. Gallupin’ goatburgers!”

“It gets better.”

“No it doesn’t. It doesn’t *ever* get better when someone says it gets better. It always gets worse. Ever notice that?”

“You’re right. It gets worse.”

“See what I mean?”

“At least one other of the so-called Taliban Five has joined Fazi’s command team. We’re not sure where the others are at this point, but it’s safe to say they haven’t joined the Red Cross.”

“Of course not! What the hell’s the matter with Obama? Did he think they were gonna go home and work for the Baghdad Geek Squad? Those guys are hardened terrorists. I know, I waterboarded the shit out of ’em. Closest thing to a shower they ever had, the smelly bastards. Didn’t get much information, but I guarantee you one thing—every time they hear a leaky faucet they’ll be praying to Allah. Heh.”

Franklin Post reached for his laugh rag but was somehow able to control himself without deploying the gag.

"As always, sir, you certainly know how to speak your mind."

"A mind's a beautiful thing to waste—especially if it belongs to a terrorist on the receiving end of an M-16. But don't tell me you called just to say that the vermin I corralled got let out by Obama and now they're tryin' to kill us again."

"No, sir. I just wanted to give you a heads-up and get the bad news out of the way first."

"So what's the good news? They bringin' back *Bonanza?*"

"No. Remember the fishing-show guys who had their boat blown up in the Caribbean? You suggested we consider making them DICK agents."

"Sure I do. They got the greatest show on earth. Well, the wet part, at least. *Fishing on the Edge with Shagball and*...what's his psychic's name?"

"You mean his sidekick?"

"That's what I said, his psychic."

"Right. Of course. It's Tangles."

"Tangles. That's it. How could I forget? That little feller's a riot. So, what about 'em?"

"The new boat that we built them is finally finished. They just left Norfolk on their maiden voyage."

"They got maidens on board? Damn, you're really rollin' out the red carpet for a couple of newbie agents."

"That's not what I meant. It's a shakedown cruise. They're taking it to the Gulf of Mexico if it doesn't have any problems—and it better not, given the time and money we poured into it."

"Why the gulf?"

"Well, one reason is the FBI and Homeland Security have been hearing rumors that one of the Mexican cartels is helping ISIS smuggle terrorists across the border and they have something planned. We're gonna test our new surveillance equipment to see if we can pick up any information to corroborate it."

"It'd be nice to verify it, too. If talk is cheap, then rumors are worthless. Unless they're true. Then they're, uh, worthful. Or something like that."

"What?"

"You know what I mean. What's the other reason?"

"The only stipulation to getting the fishing guys to join us was that we help locate Shagball's girlfriend Holly's long-lost cousin, and I think we might have. He may be working on an oil rig a hundred miles east of Brownsville. I agreed to let them go there after Holly threatened to jump on a plane when I told her. She's part of the new team, too, and needs to learn the computer systems. I brought in Judy Larson to train her and couldn't afford to have her go running off."

"Judy Larson?"

"Yes, she's been with DICK from the start. You know, the mathematical and computer genius."

"Oh, right. The one that drives a Subaru."

"*What?* What does that—"

"Hey, to each his own. Or *her* own, if you know what I mean. That's what I say. Some girls like the carpet, some like the hardwood, and some like both. Those can be a real handful. But who cares? The only thing I care about is they're coming to my neck of the woods."

"Why?"

"Last time we talked, you said this boat was special—that it was a superduper spy boat disguised as a fishing boat."

"I did say something like that. Your point is?"

"Do I have to spell it out for you, Stargazer? I like to fish. F-I-S-ish…fish. "

"You do?"

"Damn straight. I also like to paint, ride horses, and chase illegals, but that gets old after a while. Every now and then, I like to fish…deep-sea fish. You know, over-your-head kinda deep. It sure would be great to take a spin on the new DICK boat and meet the guys. Maybe they could teach me a few tricks."

"Sir, I don't know if—"

"I do. I'm buddies with some Halliburton execs, and we founded a program to help hire more veterans. Halliburton's a contractor on a rig called the *Bluewater,* somewhere off Corpus Christi, and they got a bunch of vets working on it. I'm making a surprise visit on Memorial Day to thank the vets for their service. Maybe the DICK boys can swing by and take me fishing for a couple hours. I sure would appreciate it, Stargazer…Stargazer? You there?"

"Huh? Yeah. I was just looking to see where the *Bluewater* is in relation to the *Taladro Grande.*"

"*Taladro Grande*? Sounds tasty. Is it anything like chile rellenos? Heh. Just kidding. Not about the chile rellenos, though, I love those things."

"Found it. The *Bluewater* is about ninety miles north of the *Taladro Grande.*"

"Yeah, but in nautical miles that's practically next door, right?"

"Not exactly. I just don't know if it's such a good idea, sir. You'll draw attention to the boat, which is a nuclear-powered, next-generation—"

"Hold your horses pardner. Did you say *nucular*? This baby's *nucular?* Oh, man, is this great! Does it have cruise missiles? I *love* cruise missiles."

"No, sir. It's not a battleship. It's mainly for surveillance, although it does have defensive weaponry and more than a few nifty gadgets, if I do say so myself."

"So what are you worried about, then? There's not gonna be any press with me, and we'll be in the middle of the gulf. Nobody but the workers on the rig will see me get on the boat, and even then they won't see much. You ever been on an offshore rig, Stargazer? I have. It's a long way from the deck to the water. They won't be able to see spit."

"What about the Secret Service guys that travel with you?"

"What about them? They're the Secret Service. They know how to keep a secret."

"You know the problems the service has been having. I don't know."

"I'll tell you what. I'll only bring my most trusted agent with me when I go on the boat—Blinky. What do you say, Stargazer? What's the big worry?"

"It's Shagball and Tangles."

"Heh. Good one. But I'm willing to take my chances."

"Well…all right then. I'll try to arrange it."

"For real?"

"Yes. As long as the boat doesn't have any major issues, they should be able to make it to the *Bluewater* by Memorial Day."

"Great! So, that's it?"

"That's it, unless you have something else."

"Aren't you supposed to say, 'Well, there is *one* more thing.'"

"What?"

"That's what Columbo always says. You know, the suspect ushers him out the door, and he turns and says, 'Well, there is *one* more thing,' and then he *nails* 'em."

"Oh, right. Well, sir, there is *one* more thing."

"What's that, detective?"

"Don't forget the sunscreen." *Click.*

The president slipped the small phone into his shirt pocket and laughed as he tugged the brim of his cowboy hat a little lower. "Heh. Sunscreen. Who needs it when you got one of these on your noggin?" He waved at his ranch foreman and hollered, "Hey, Manny! Manny, commere!"

Manny held up a finger, and after securing the last steer in the pen, he jogged over.

"How about a glass of iced tea and a game of horse-shoes?" the president asked.

"No thank you, señor. I have much work to do."

"A lemonade then? I had the missus whip up a batch. It's hand squeezed just the way you like it—from a frozen tube."

"Thanks, but not today, sir. I am fine."

"The hell you are. Since when did you ever turn down a lemonade? What's going on, Manny? You miss-ing the wife and kids already?"

"Sí."

"Sí. What a word. To you, it means yes. To others, a vitamin. To me, it's the ocean—the great blue sky in the water. When I'm on the sea, I forget about the daily grind of retirement. You know, painting, horseback riding, chasing, uh...armadillos. All my worries just seem to melt away like a warm iceberg. Like if that blowhard Al Gore was breathing on it. Heh. Yup, the sea is the answer to your troubles, mi amigo. I wish I could take you with me."

"You are going to the sea?"

"Sí, I'm going to the sea. Heh. Didn't know I could speak Spanish, did you?"

"No sir, you speak it very well. What are you going to the sea for?"

"Sea for. Heh. You say that in an airport, and they'll arrest you. That's what we call an *explosivo.* I'm going to an oil rig in the gulf on Memorial Day to surprise some veterans and maybe slip in a little deep-sea fishing, too."

"Where in the gulf?"

"It's a rig off Corpus Christi called the *Bluewater.*"

"I thought you had plans to spend Memorial Day weekend with your family on Padre Island."

"I did. I mean, I do. I still am. It's just that on Memorial Day my buddies at Halliburton are gonna have their helicopter service fly me out to the rig for the day. I'll be back on Padre Island for dinner. As much as my family means to me, service to my country means even more. The thing I miss most about being president is the opportunity to meet and salute the fine men and women who serve to defend our great nation. It gives me chills just thinking about it. Like when I found out I passed English at Yale. That was a close one. Heh."

Manny glanced at his watch and said, "Sir, I just realized I need to get to the feedstore before it closes."

"Well, you better get moving, then. A hungry cow is a mad cow, and a mad cow gets a disease. I guess it makes your brain go to mush, like if you watch too much MSNBC. Get as much feed as you want. Keep those cows fat and happy."

The president tipped his hat and walked toward the house. Five minutes later, Manny was bouncing down the road in his old pickup. He didn't really need any feed, he just didn't dare make the call he was about to make from the ranch. He had been given specific instructions by the kidnappers, and he stuck to them. With conflicting emotions he reached in the glove box and pulled out the prepaid cell phone the kidnappers had given him. The last person on earth he wanted to betray was the man he worked for, the forty-third president of the United States. He had given him a good job and benefits and always treated him and his family fairly and with kindness. Manny genuinely liked the man, but he loved his dear wife and precious daughter even more. He pulled into a dusty strip-mall parking lot, put the truck in park, and dialed the number he was given. Three rings later one of the kidnappers answered.

"Who is it?" The kidnappers had assigned a code name to both him and the president, and he answered accordingly.

"It's the Indian."

"You have new information to report?"

"Yes. The Cowboy is traveling to an oil rig in the Gulf of Mexico called the *Bluewater.* It is somewhere off Corpus Christi. He will be using the Halliburton helicopter service."

"Halliburton?"

"They are an oil company. The president is flying out to meet some veterans who work for them."

"When?"

"On Memorial Day."

"You said he would be on Padre Island with his family."

"That's why I called. He will still be spending the weekend with his family there but will spend part of Memorial Day going to the Bluewater to meet some veterans."

"The helicopter service will be picking him up on Padre Island?"

"Yes. I did what you asked. Now please, I beg you, let my family go."

"Not until we have the Cowboy."

"But you said—"

"Never mind what I said. What I am saying now is they will be released unharmed *after* we have the Cowboy. Call if you hear of any other changes in his plans."

"Wait! I need to speak with my wife. I need to know she is okay. Please!"

Manny held his breath as he heard voices conversing in Arabic. A few seconds later his wife was on the line.

"Manuel? Is that you?"

"Maria, are you all right? Have they hurt you?"

"No, not yet. But I'm scared, so scared. So is Isabella. Please do what they say, Manuel. Please do it for the sake of our family."

One of the kidnappers snatched the phone out of her hand and said, "That's enough!"

"Don't hurt her! Don't hurt my baby!" Manny cried. "I'll find out everything I can."

"If you ever want to see your family again, you will." *Click.*

Chapter 11

In the backyard of a not-so-safe-house on the outskirts of Matamoros, the wiry terrorist ringleader Mohammed Zahvi terminated the call and smiled. *It was all coming together.* The petrified ranch foreman had just confirmed what their intelligence had anticipated: that Bush would be traveling to the Gulf Coast of Texas. He did a quick Google search on his phone and discovered the *Bluewater* was only one hundred miles north of the *Dinero Majado*. Was it mere luck or coincidence that they had chosen to hold the president captive there? No, he truly believed it was the will of Allah. It was a kidnapping that would send shock waves throughout the world and possibly light the fuse leading to World War III. *Praise Allah!* Before he gave the news to ISIS headquarters, he wanted to discuss it with his colleagues. The ranch foreman had mentioned that Bush would be using an oil company helicopter service. *A helicopter service.* A germ of an idea was slowly replicating in his demented mind as he closed his eyes and prayed to Allah to help him see the light. For a full minute he stood in silence. A lone tumbleweed bounced over the rickety courtyard fence and brushed his robe as it continued its random journey to nowhere.

Suddenly, the idea stood in front of him like a young virgin ready to be taken.

He turned and walked across the dusty courtyard in the fading sunlight, pushing aside some garments on a clothesline as he made his way to the back door. The two members of the Sinaloa cartel who held the hostages at gunpoint nodded at him as he entered.

Chaco, the one who first suggested the abandoned oil rig as a possible place to hold a hostage, said, "It is time for us to eat. Have your friends stand guard for a while."

"Where are they?"

"In the back room."

"I need to speak with them for a few minutes. When we are done you can eat." Without waiting for a reply, he walked down the short hall and opened the door to the room that served as their data and security center. His fellow terrorists were playing chess.

"Don't you ever get sick of that game?" he asked.

Khalullah shrugged, but Noorbi, the security expert, replied, "What else are we supposed to do? It's a waiting game."

"Not anymore. The wait is over. We have work to do." He went on to explain his conversation with the ranch foreman and added, "I think I see a way we can snatch the Cowboy without it appearing he has been kidnapped. At least long enough for us to make a clean getaway and secure the prize before the authorities figure out what happened."

"And how is that?" Khalullah asked.

"The oil company, Halliburton, has a helicopter service that will be flying the Cowboy out to a rig called the *Bluewater.* We find out which service it is and where they are located, and we hack their computer system. This will allow us to know exactly when and where he is supposed to be picked up."

"But how does that help us abduct him without immediately alerting the authorities? How do we neutralize his security detail without—"

"Let me finish. You're right. We obviously can't kidnap him at an airfield, or anywhere else in public for that matter. We need to employ a ruse, a trick, a sleight of hand. I prayed to Allah and he has given me the solution."

"Which is?" asked Noorbi.

"The Cowboy is flying out and back on the same day from Padre Island. He's just going for a few hours to shake some hands, take some pictures, have lunch, and return. It is on the return that we shall strike."

"How so?"

"First, we trick the helicopter service into believing the Cowboy has delayed his scheduled return flight by a couple of hours. Nothing unusual, I'm sure. We hack the scheduling system and put in a call if necessary. Then we arrive in our own helicopter to pick him up at the scheduled time. Once we are airborne, we can neutralize the Secret Service agents. By the time the real helicopter service shows up and everyone realizes the Cowboy is missing, it will be too late. The cowardly infidel will be in our avenging hands on board the *Dinero Majado,* and the world will soon hear our demands."

The two rapt terrorists agreed that the plan was indeed brilliant.

"Fazi will love this idea," Khalullah said.

"Only if it works. Like I said, we have much work to do."

"Like getting a helicopter and a pilot," Noorbi said.

"Yes, and we need to make it look like it belongs to the helicopter service we are duping. Why don't you go on the computer and see if you can find out who they are? Khalullah, go relieve Chaco and tell him to come here. He needs to find us a helicopter and pilot."

"Okay." As he left, Noorbi crossed the room and sat at a table with a laptop hooked to a large monitor. When he tapped the keyboard the full screen came up, and he noticed something wrong. He clicked on one of the split screens, the one that had a live feed of the maintenance room on the *Dinero Majado,* and it was blank. "Goat shit," he muttered.

"What's the problem?" Zahvi asked.

"The live feed to the *Dinero Majado* is dead. There's nothing—look." He clicked the computer mouse on the image a few times, and it was blank.

"It's recorded, right?"

"Of course."

"Play it back."

Noorbi changed screens, and his fingers fluttered over the keyboard.

Chaco came walking in and asked, "What do you want? I'm hungry."

Zahvi looked away from the computer screen and eyeballed him.

"We need a helicopter and a pilot."

"What do you mean? We have one."

"No, not the one we've been using to ferry the gear out to the *Dinero Majado.* We may need to keep using them. This is for a one-way trip. The helicopter will be ditched at sea when we are through."

"What about the pilot?"

"What about him? Somebody has to ditch it. There can be no witnesses."

"That's going to cost you."

"So you can do it then?"

"This is Mexico, amigo. I can do anything for a price."

"We need one within a week. It needs a paint job, too."

"The helicopter is no problem. We buy them from the army all the time. My brother-in-law is a mechanic who has a chop shop not too far from here. He can do the paint job."

"And the pilot?"

"That is trickier. Nobody wants to lose a good pilot."

"He doesn't have to be good. He just needs to be able to land and take off from an oil rig."

"Still."

Zahvi reached under his robe and pulled out a wad of hundred-dollar bills. He peeled off three and handed them to the grinning Chaco. "Why don't you think about it over dinner? Go somewhere nice, if there is such a thing around here. Take your friend and put your heads together. Make some calls. Whatever it takes. Find us a pilot. You will be well compensated as always. We'll watch the hostages."

"Gracias, señor."

Chaco turned to leave, and Noorbi cried, "What in the name of Allah?" Chaco and Zahvi turned to look at the computer screen. The concealed night-vision camera showed a man walking around the converted maintenance room of the supposedly abandoned *Dinero Majado.*

Zahvi pointed at the screen. "Who is that? What is going on?" Then he turned to Chaco and pointed a finger at his face. "You said the rig was abandoned!"

"It is! My cousin said so."

"That's no ghost! What is he doing?"

Noorbi held up a hand. "The video feed cuts out at the end. Let's see what happens from the beginning. I'll replay it." Seconds later the three watched in silence as the man entered the maintenance room and looked around. He walked over to the generator and shone a penlight on the bottled water and provisions stacked against the wall. He scratched his head and then shone the light on the electronic equipment. Using the small beam from the penlight he traced the cables that ran up to the ceiling. Then he turned and walked out of the room. "What's he doing?" Zahvi wondered out loud.

"How should I know?"

"When did this happen?"

Noorbi checked the time on the video. "In the last forty-five minutes."

"Damn it! All our work is going down the meerkat hole! How could this happen?" He looked at Chaco again.

"Don't look at me, amigo."

"Of course I'm looking at you. You're the one who told us about this supposedly abandoned rig!"

"My cousin assured me the oil company was through with it. They pulled out over six months ago. There is no reason for them to go back there."

"Well, *somebody* has! Our plan is blown!"

Noorbi pointed at the screen. "Look! He's back." The three watched as the man reentered the room, holding something in his hand. He walked over to the communications equipment and reached behind it. A second later the screen went blank.

"I think he cut the video feed! Let me zoom in." Noorbi rewound the feed and zoomed in on the object in his hand as he entered the room. He froze the frame, and the three men leaned forward to get a better look at it.

"Those are wire cutters," Zahvi said. "He sabotaged our equipment! Who is this man? Where did he come from?"

"Hold on," Chaco said. "Can you zoom in on the front of his shirt when he walks in the room? It looks familiar." Noorbi zoomed in on the shirt and froze the frame again.

Chaco shook his head. "That's a Pemex T-shirt. He probably works for them. He must have come from the *Taladro Grande*, even though my cousin told me it is off limits to everyone."

"The *Taladro Grande?*"

"The oil rig my cousin works on. It's only ten miles away."

"So what is this man doing on the *Dinero Majado?* How did he get there?"

"They have a couple of skiffs they use for maintenance work. He must have taken one. For what purpose, I don't know."

"I do. To sabotage our equipment. Who *else* is he working for? That's the question. We must find out. He has to be stopped."

"Sabotage?" Noorbi questioned.

"What else would you call using a pair of wire cutters on the cable?"

"I'm not so sure. If you noticed, when he first entered the room, he looked around and scratched his head. It looked to me like he was surprised to see the equipment and supplies. If he came to sabotage, he would not have been surprised."

Zahvi shook his head, confused. "I don't know. I don't know what to think except—wait a second. You said this just happened?"

"Yes, within the hour."

"He appears to be working alone. Even if he immediately returned to the other rig, it takes time to go ten miles in a skiff. With a little help from Allah, perhaps we're not too late. Chaco, call your cousin."

"What do I tell him?"

"Tell him he has an opportunity to earn a bonus. This man is a saboteur, or he inadvertently stumbled onto our operation. It is preferable that your cousin determine which he is, but either way, he needs to be silenced. I am sure oil rig accidents are not uncommon."

"This, too, will cost you, amigo."

"What doesn't? Whoever said Mexico was cheap has goat shit for brains. Make the call—now."

Chapter 12

It was just before dark when Pago arrived back at the *Taladro Grande*. He guided the small skiff onto the lift that would hoist the craft some thirty feet up to level three. As he passed the second level, he heard the hum of the elevator over the small lift motor. Figuring it was likely the OTL, he had to decide whether to tell him about what he saw in the maintenance room of the *Dinero Majado*. Why? Because the oil company made it very clear that due to liability issues, nobody was permitted on it for any reason. He could be fired if he admitted to scrounging around the old rig looking for fishing leader. Of course *could* was the operative word. As a deep-dive specialist, he wasn't a cinch to quickly replace and might not get the ax—*might* being the operative word.

The elevator door opened, and sure enough, the OTL, Luis, strode out.

"I called you over an hour ago!" he shouted. "What took you so long? It's almost dark!"

Pago held up the fifteen-pound dolphin he caught while trolling a barracuda belly and smiled. "I got delayed when I hooked this on the way back." He tossed it onto the deck, and it slid into the side of Luis's work boot.

Luis nudged it away, unimpressed. "That's it? One stinking dolphin?"

"Plus these." Pago opened a small cooler and tossed a couple of snappers onto the dock.

"You were gone all afternoon. Where were you?"

Pago set the cooler and the fishing rods on the deck and climbed out of the skiff. Luis seemed more agitated than usual, even if he *was* a little late.

"Since when do you care where I fish? The water's flat, so I took advantage."

"Took advantage? Hmmm. You came from the direction of the *Dinero Majado.* Is that where you were?"

The accusatory tone surprised him a little. *Should he tell him about what he saw there?* It wouldn't be the end of the world if he got fired—not by a long shot. But as usual, he planned to finance his next treasure-hunting expedition with the money he earned on the rig. If he did get fired, it would take some time to get work on another rig. That would set the expedition back. Having the expedition set back was as unacceptable as touching his nest egg—his navy pension. That was one egg he wouldn't crack until he was ready to eat omelets and spend his golden years snail snorkeling off the beaches of Pago Pago. He looked at Luis. He was a likable enough guy for a supervisor, but the trust factor was zilch. The answer was no.

"Uh…yeah, like I said, Luis, I took advantage. There's thirty years of barnacles on the support structures. I usually can't get there because the conditions have to be just right, like they were today. It's a great place to fish."

"Doesn't look like it was so great today."

"That's because a big hammerhead snatched a grouper off my line, and I ran out of leader. I was lucky the skiff didn't capsize."

"Yeah? Well, looks like your luck ran out. Engineering thinks there might be a stress fracture on one of the supports. Boss Hombre wants you to suit up and check it out."

"And I will." He smiled.

"*Now.* He wants it checked out *now.* Pronto."

"Pronto, that means tomorrow, right?"

"No, that means get your stinky ass back in the water."

Pago looked at Luis in disbelief. He had been out in the hot sun most of the afternoon. He was tired, hungry, and in no condition to dive. Especially a night dive to 280 feet.

"I don't care *what* Boss Hombre says. You don't go down two hundred and eighty feet unless you're ready—e*specially* at night. It's a safety issue. I need to rehydrate and get some food in my system first. It's that simple. This is a new rig, so I seriously doubt there's a stress fracture, but even if there is, it's not like it's going to suddenly collapse. I'll check it out in the morning after a good night's rest." If he got fired, he got fired.

Luis eyed him as he put the snapper in the cooler and pulled out a bottle of water. As he chugged it, Luis's radio crackled to life. Luis turned his back to Pago.

"Luis, here." As Luis walked away, Pago put the fish on the cleaning table set on the edge of the grated walkway and began cleaning them. He had the dolphin filleted out and was scaling the first snapper when Luis returned.

"Okay," said Luis. "I explained to Boss Hombre what you said. You'll go first thing in the morning, right?"

"Sure, no problemo. I'll go down at first light, check everything out. Thanks for making him understand. You want some mahimahi?"

"Sí." As Pago reached in the cooler and placed some fillets into a zip lock bag, Luis picked up the bigger of the two rods propped against the cleaning table. "You catch the mahi with this?"

Pago glanced at him and nodded. "Yeah."

Luis fingered the unusual leader that was attached to the hook. It looked like two thin copper wires stranded together—like speaker wire or something.

"I thought you ran out of leader."

Pago looked up from the cleaning table and saw Luis fingering the leader. "I, uh…did. That's a makeshift leader."

"Makeshift? Makeshift out of what?"

"Out of, you know…some old wiring I found on the skiff."

"Is that right. It doesn't look very old…how resourceful."

"That's my motto: be resourceful and recycle."

"Is that right. You know what my motto is?"

"No, what?"

"Do what the boss says. And starting tomorrow, it better be your motto, too." Luis grabbed the bag of dolphin fillets off the cleaning table and walked away without another word. As he got on the elevator, Pago yelled, "You're welcome!" When the door closed, he added, "asshole."

Pago finished cleaning up, and ten minutes later he opened the door to the small dormlike room he shared with a member of the engineering staff. He set his fishing gear in the corner and stripped down to his skivvies, preparing to take a shower. When he opened his dresser drawer to get some fresh clothes, he did a double take. Being an ex–Navy SEAL, he was a neat freak. There was a place for everything, and everything was in its place. At least that's the way *he* operated. His clothes were always folded properly and placed in the drawer just so. He could immediately tell by looking at his T-shirts that somebody had been in the drawer. They weren't just so. He opened up a second drawer where his shorts were, and it was the same thing. They were just slightly askew. Concerned now, he opened the small drawer on top of the dresser and was relieved to find his wallet and navy ring undisturbed.

He shook his head, wondering if his roommate had been rifling through his shit for some reason. He got along well with Arturo and considered it unlikely. *Huh.* He would think about it while taking a nice hot shower down the hall. He grabbed some clothes and a towel and opened up the cabinet above his bunk where he kept his toilet kit. He grabbed it, and as the cabinet began to swing shut, he stuck his hand back in and reopened it. His Microsoft Surface tablet was gone! *What the hell?* He quickly opened the second cabinet where he kept some other personal belongings, but it wasn't there either. It was gone. He quickly checked the cabinet where Arturo kept his own laptop, and it was there. Why would Arturo borrow his tablet when he had his own? He wouldn't. *What the fuck.* He would check with Arturo, but he was pretty sure he knew what the answer would be: somebody swiped his tablet.

Chapter 13

Chaco led the way into the seedy Matamoros saloon and took an empty booth in the back of the bar. His compadre, Jorge, slid into the booth first. Chaco sat next to him, so they both faced the entrance. There were marginally nicer and safer restaurants he could have chosen, but he preferred the familiarity of Juanita's. He also preferred keeping as much as possible of the dinero that the terrorista had given him for a "nice" dinner. He knew that when it came to Mexican food, nice was a relative term. It was Mexican food: tacos and burritos. Nice, but certainly not as nice as the hundred-dollar bills in his pocket. And as far as safety went, it was he and Jorge who were the ones to be feared as known members of the Sinaloa cartel. Few patrons dared make direct eye contact with them. Even the waitress who took their drink order did so while staring at her order pad. As the bartender poured two shots of tequila and set a couple of cervezas on the bar, Chaco surveyed the scene. No strange looks, nothing unusual. Good. They sat in stony silence until the waitress returned with their drinks and took their dinner order.

After they downed the tequila and chased it with a beer, Jorge said, "I don't trust the terroristas."

"So what? The money is good."

"Why do you think they plan to dispose of a perfectly good helicopter and pilot?"

"I don't know, and I don't care. What I *do* know is they are going to pay out their stinking asses, and what I *care* about is finding a pilot."

"Finding a pilot who is expendable."

"Yes, this could be difficult."

"Maybe not."

Chaco raised a thick black eyebrow.

"What do you mean?"

"A couple of weeks ago I noticed a gringo sitting at the bar when I came in for lunch."

"Here?"

"Yes."

"A *gringo?*"

"Yes, I know. That's what I thought too. He looked nervous, as he should be, playing with a matchbook at the bar. I thought maybe he was a fugitive from the States. He was scrawny—an easy mark. When the bartender brought the food, I asked if he knew anything about him. He said he's been around for a few weeks. He used to smuggle for the Colombians and speaks really bad Spanish."

"Used to?"

"That's what he told the bartender. Now he's working for the Zetas."

"The *Zetas?* The stinking *Zetas?* So then what? You killed him?"

"No, he slipped away while I was talking to the bartender."

"That's not like you to miss such an opportunity. I assume there is a reason I should care."

"There is. The bartender said he was a pilot."

"A helicopter pilot?"

"I guess. How many kinds are there?"

"Why would he tell this to the bartender?"

"Because he's looking to do some work on the side. He gave the bartender two hundred dollars to steer him some under-the-table work. He doesn't want the Zetas to know."

"That's a good idea, assuming he wants to keep his dick attached to his cojones and his head to his neck."

"He has a neck like a toothpick. I could cut his head off with this." He picked the cheap butter knife off his napkin, and they both laughed. Chaco signaled the waitress, and she brought them another round. As she walked away, Chaco looked at Jorge.

"If this gringo can fly a helicopter, he could be just what we need. The terroristas will be pleased so long as he can fly, and we can eliminate a Zeta pilot. So how do we find this gringo?"

"I'll talk to the bartender. He must have a way to reach him." Chaco slid out of the booth to let him out, and as he slid back in, Jorge just stood there. Confused, Chaco asked, "What are you waiting for? Go talk to him."

"He'll be more helpful if I slip him some dinero." He held his hand out.

"I only have hundreds."

"One should do it."

"*A hundred dollars?* Fuck that, amigo. Tell him you will kill him if he doesn't cooperate. Or I'll kill him… either way."

"Are you sure? This could be a good break for us. If we return and tell the terroristas we found a pilot, they will happily pay more. You could say we paid the bartender five hundred, and we could split the difference."

Chaco nodded and grinned before handing over a hundred-dollar bill. "I like the way you think, amigo." Jorge tucked the bill in his shirt pocket and made his way to the bar. Chaco watched him exchange words with the bartender and then reach in his shirt pocket and slide a bill across the bar. After a quick glance, the bartender deftly palmed the bill and was soon talking into his cell phone. Jorge winked at Chaco and flashed a broken-tooth grin because he still had the hundred-dollar bill in his pocket, having given the bartender a twenty. Less than thirty seconds later, the bartender flipped his phone shut and said, "He'll be here in fifteen minutes." He pointed at the waitress who was setting a tray of food down at their booth. "Go enjoy your food before the gringo gets here. He's greasier than the burritos."

Chapter 14

The career criminal they called "the Gringo," kept his head down as he traversed the dark and dangerous side streets of Matamoros. His beady eyes danced around like Beyonce on crystal meth as he scanned the alleyways and shadows for lurking threats. He silently cursed his misfortune at having ended up in such a hellhole. His plans for living the good life sipping umbrella drinks on a tropical beach had been squashed flatter than Michael Moore's wallet, thanks to a chance encounter with an unlikely foe from his past. He spit in the road and tried to convince himself it was better than being in jail, but it didn't seem so at the moment. He'd certainly be safer in a federal penitentiary than on the streets of Matamoros. *Shit.* He bumped into a trash can, and the noise startled him. He looked to see if the noise attracted anyone's attention, and when he saw the profile of a head peek out from behind a doorway, he broke into a jog.

Jorge was just finishing his cow cod burrito when he saw the Gringo come through the door and approach the bartender.

"The Gringo's here."

Chaco looked up from his tripe soup. "The one talking to the bartender?"

"Yes, he's walking this way."

"Search him before he sits down."

"Of course."

Chaco let Jorge out of the booth, and the Gringo said, "Where are you going? I thought you wanted to talk."

"I need to check you out. Don't move." Jorge dropped to a knee and started patting his way up the Gringo's legs.

"Oh, shit. Better be careful what you touch. I haven't been laid in—"

"Shut up."

As Jorge stood up, he pulled a .45 semiautomatic out from the Gringo's waistband. It had been tucked into the small of his back, hidden under a sweaty T-shirt. "What do we have here?"

"It's a gun. You shoot people with it. I think in Matamoros you get frequent flier points every time you fire one. It would explain a lot."

Jorge slid the gun on the table, and Chaco examined it.

"This looks like military issue. Were you in the military?"

"What is this? A job interview for Taco Bell?" The Gringo snorted out a laugh, but Jorge and Chaco were not amused. Chaco nodded at Jorge, who punched him in the gut, and he keeled over. As he massaged his bruised rib cage and fought to regain his breath, Chaco spoke.

"You told the bartender you were a pilot. Were you a pilot in the military?"

"Yeah, sort of. Man, that hurt. You don't have to punch it out of me, guys. I mean, c'mon, you asked to meet. You don't wanna hire me, then don't hire me, but this is ridiculous."

"What do you mean, *sort of*?"

"You know, like uh, I'm *sort of* thirsty. How about I sit down, and we can talk over a cold one? Besides, everybody's looking, and I wanna keep this on the QT." Chaco nodded at Jorge, who ushered him in the booth, and then sat next to him, pinning him in.

"So," Chaco said. "What kind of pilot are you?"

"How many kinds are there?"

"That's what I said," Jorge commented.

Chaco scowled at him. "Shut up."

"I'm just kidding. It's a good question. But fortunately for you, I can pilot anything. Planes, trains, automobiles, boats, submarines, hot-air balloons... I've smuggled shit in all of them. When I was six years old, I smuggled a Slinky out of a K-Mart and made my getaway on a skateboard. That's where it all began."

"That's not smuggling. That's shoplifting."

"Diversification—that's the name of the game. Diversification and adaptability. That's what makes me so valuable. I've done it all, and I can do it all and—"

"You didn't say helicopter."

"Helicopter? Is that what this is all about? *Shit.* What's the big deal? So it's a plane without wings, so what. I once smuggled a ton of northern California sinsemilla from Canada to Alaska by dog sled. That's like a snowmobile with an engine that eats and shits. Did I mention snowmobiles? I've used those too. I'm like the postal service. I always deliver. Like I said, you gotta be—"

Chaco slammed his fist on the table. "I don't care about fucking snowmobiles! I only care about helicopters. Can you fly one or not?"

"Sure I can. I mean, it's been a couple of years, but no sweat. It's like riding a bike. You never forget. Only difference is, if you stop pedaling, you crash and burn. How about that beer now?"

Chaco stared in his eyes for an uncomfortable moment. "You said you forget."

"No. No, I said, 'You *never* forget.' Never...that's like nada in Mexican."

"*Nunca.*"

"Nunca what?"

"Nunca means never. I hope you fly helicopters better than you know Spanish."

"So maybe I'm a little rusty. Rust needs lubrication. Get me a beer for chrissakes."

Chaco held up three fingers, and the bartender nodded. As he waited for the waitress to bring the beers, the Gringo looked at Chaco's soup and wondered what godforsaken animal parts were floating around in it—assuming they *were* animal parts. Once the waitress delivered the beers and left, Chaco pointed at him.

"If you lie to me, I will cut you to pieces."

The Gringo wiped the foam from his lips and set his beer down with a belch. "I don't doubt it. Looks like that's how they make the soup here. But speaking of getting cut to pieces, let me ask you something. You notice I got all my limbs attached? All my fingers? All my toes?" He held out his hands and wiggled his fingers. Then he stamped the floor with his feet. "You notice how I'm not missing nothing? I got my ears, I got my arms, I got my legs...bad helicopter pilots can't say the same thing. When a chopper goes down, it's like being trapped in an elevator with a Cusinart on top. Chop, chop, chop." He made a chopping motion with his hand to accentuate the point. "You either fly that baby or you're getting the Edward Scissorhands treatment. As you can see, I'm neither chopped up nor dead. Hence, I can fly a whirlybird. So why don't you tell me what it is you need transported and where you need it transported to, and I'll tell you what it's gonna cost. That's kinda the way it works."

"Is that how it works for the Zetas?"

"Shhh. Don't even *say* that word." The Gringo's head swiveled as he nervously checked out the other patrons. "Everybody's related to somebody around here—no offensivo. Like I told the bartender, mums the word."

"How did you come to work for them?"

The Gringo took another swig of beer and smiled. "They wanted the best, they hired the best. I think the word is primo." He pointed a finger at his chest and added, "that's me. El Primo."

Chaco and Jorge both laughed knowing that *el primo* means "the cousin" and that "the best" is *el major.*

Jorge said, "El Primo?" and laughed again.

"Sí. That means yes. El Primo. I once zip-lined two hundred kilos of coke across an Amazonian tributary onto a makeshift trailer hooked to a herd of donkeys. El Primo always delivers."

"Is that when you were working for the Colombians?" Chaco raised an eyebrow.

"Yeah, that's right. You wanna be the best? You gotta work for the worst. I did, and I'm done. At least I am with *those* crazy bastards. Now I work freelance."

"I am surprised they would let el Primo go so easily," Jorge said.

"It was amicable. You know, amicabueno. At least it was on my end. Everything was good until they blamed me for a shipment that went missing that I had nothing to do with. That's when I vamoosed. Their loss, your gain. Now, are we ever gonna talk turkey? I can only take so much aroma. That soup smells like dirty ass."

"You want soup?"

"No. Lord, no. No soupo. Just tell me what you need my vast arsenal of skills for."

Chaco looked at Jorge, who shrugged. Still wary of the scrawny gringo who called himself el Primo, Chaco shook his head.

"What are you shaking your head for? You guys should be high-fivin' over the chance to work with me. I'm warning you, though. I don't come cheap."

"How much?" asked Chaco.

"Depends on the cargo and where I have to take it."

"You will need to pick somebody up and drop them off, and it must be done with a helicopter. That's all we know," he lied.

"Are you kidding me? You don't know the where, when, or who?"

"Not yet, but you will be leaving from Matamoros."

"Well *that* narrows it down. All right, I'll give you the basic rates. Ten grand up front, ten grand every time I refuel, and ten grand every time I land. The rate's at least double for drug lords or anyone on the FBI's Ten Most Wanted list. That's doble."

"Congratulations. You finally got one right."

"All fuel costs and helicopter-related expenses are on top of my fee, of course."

"Por supuesto."

"What about the soup? I said I don't want any. In fact, thanks to that heaping bowl of stench, I may never eat soup again."

Jorge laughed. "Not soup. 'Por supuesto' means 'of course.' How long have you been in Matamoros?"

"Three weeks, tres weeks." He lied. "But it feels like three years."

"I can't believe you lasted three days," Chaco commented as he finished his bowl of tripe.

"Yeah? Well, you can't keep a good hombre down. So when can I see the whirlybird? I need to give her the once-over and take her for a little spin. Make sure she's up to el Primo's standards."

"We'll call you in a few days. Give Jorge your number."

"What kind of chopper is it?"

"Military."

"I notice you're not big on details."

"What difference does it make? I thought El Primo could fly anything."

Jorge laughed so hard beer started coming out his nose, and Chaco flashed his "summer-teeth" smile. Some were here, some were there, and what few teeth he had were broken and discolored.

"Funny man. I see why you eat soup. You could bleed to death gumming a taco." He took a card out of his pocket and handed it to Jorge. "My number's on the back. I guess we're done, for now. Can I have my gun back?"

"Where are you staying?" Chaco asked.

"Some shithole called the Matador. I'm not saying it's dirty, but their roaches have fleas. Great place. There was a knife fight in the laundry room last night."

Chaco laughed.

"My nephew owns the Matador," Jorge said. He wasn't laughing.

"Your nephew? Oh well, you know, on the plus side, I appreciate the security. I think there's six dead-bolts on the door to my room. Good, uh, mattress, too. Bueno mattress. Firm. Very firm. Muy firmo."

Chaco pushed his gun across the table. "Jorge will tell his nephew that you are working with us. You won't have any trouble at the hotel. We'll talk to the bar-tender, too. That should help you get out of here in one piece."

"How comforting. Gracias, I guess." Chaco nodded at Jorge who slid out of the booth. El Primo followed and tucked his gun under his T-shirt as he stood up.

As el Primo headed out the door, Jorge sat down and looked at Chaco. "So, what do you think?"

"I think he talks too much. I don't trust him."

"You don't trust anybody. That's good. If you trusted him, I would be worried."

"He sure thinks a lot of himself. El Primo. If he's as good as he says he is, why would he be staying at the Matador? Something doesn't add up. Tell your nephew to search his room."

"I'm sure he already has."

"Then see if he found anything. Tell him to keep an eye out. We have a big payday coming, and I don't want some cocky gringo screwing it up. El Primo. What a joke. He is lucky we need him, or I would have killed him for being such a wiseass. You told me he had a chicken neck, but I say he has a cuello lagarto."

"Lizard neck. Yes, that is perfect." Jorge laughed.

"No, es primo."

They were still laughing when the waitress brought their next round.

Chapter 15

We left the secret boathouse cloaked and in stealth mode. Tangles and I were on the bridge with Rafe, and Holly was below deck with the certified computer genius and Subaru driver, Judy. Driving the boat while it was cloaked was going to take some getting used to. Looking aft from the bridge toward the cockpit and stern, the view was rippling water reflecting the setting sun. That's it. There was no stern, no cockpit, no nothing. We were in an invisible boat, but on the inside, everything was visible. Try getting your head around that one.

"This is really weird," I said.

"I feel like I'm in a fishbowl with invisible walls," said Tangles.

"Yeah, I know," Rafe agreed. "It can be a little disorienting."

"Fishbowls are made of glass," I pointed out. "Clear glass. They *are* invisible. But they don't have walls. You know why? 'Cause they're bowls. Otherwise, it'd be called a fishwall, which makes no sense, like most of the stuff that comes out of your pint-size pie hole."

Tangles surrendered and raised his little arms. "Okay, okay, I'm sorry about the joke about the size of your penis. I shouldn't have dropped that one in front of Holly."

"Not that, you idiot. Don't be calling me a mooch. I hate mooches."

"Everybody hates mooches," Rafe said.

"Exactly."

"You know I was just kidding, Shag. Mooch is the wrong word. You can use the Robalo anytime you want. Truce?"

"Seriously?"

"About the truce or the Robalo?"

"I *gave* you the Robalo. You do remember that, right? Just like I *gave* you life when I plucked your sorry ass out of the gulfstream."

"Of course I remember. *Everyone* remembers. You bring it up all the time. Thanks for that. It's not like I haven't tried to make it up to you. I saved your life too, you know."

Somehow, I felt guilty. Why? I have no idea. But I did. *Shit.* "Okay, okay, I'll try not to do that anymore," I conceded. I held a fist out. "Truce."

"For real?"

"Sure, why not." We fist-bumped. "Sorry about what I said earlier about the waitress from Benny's and for wondering why I ever saved your worthless little life."

"No prob, bro. You really mean it?"

"About the waitress or your life?"

"You never stop, do you?" Tangles shook his head.

I pointed at him. "That's what she said." We both laughed and fist-bumped again. The truce was on.

"Madre de dios!" complained Rafe. "Are you guys done making up, or do you need to go below and share a cabin? It's time to focus. There's a lot to learn."

A lot to learn was a slight understatement. It was like saying Hillary has a lot to hide. I thought I knew my way around a boat pretty good after thirty years working my way up the boaters' food chain, from a fifteen-foot Whaler to a twenty-foot Robalo to a thirty-eight-foot Viking that now resided in pieces at the bottom of the Caribbean. Hell, I didn't *think* I did, I did. But when you step up to the fifty-five-foot class and throw a fast-neutron nuclear reactor into the mix, well, there's a bit of a learning curve. There was also next-generation radar, sonar, and GPS chart plotters to consider, not to mention the elaborate and highly lethal weapons-defense system. That was gonna take some time.

The weather was clear for the run down to Florida, and for three days Rafe drilled us on the operating systems and let us run the boat in shifts. The first time I was left alone at the helm, I put the pedal down, so to speak. I wanted to see how fast the *LD3* could go. The answer was at least sixty knots. That's how fast we were going when Rafe came scrambling up the steps and shut me down. He reiterated in no uncertain terms that we were to run at excessive speed only when required. It was mainly because running so fast could draw unwanted attention, but it also had to do with not wanting to unnecessarily jostle the highly sensitive and extremely expensive equipment on board. *Boo-hoo.* The problem was, I now knew how awesome it was to run a fifty-five-foot dream machine at sixty knots and wondered what it would feel like at seventy. Or eighty. Call it a hunch, but I was confident it wouldn't be long before excessive speed was required.

At times (usually in the wee hours) the boat ran by autopilot synched to a collision-avoidance and weather-alert systems to sound an alarm if needed. That was how we made it to Palm Beach in three days. That and the fact that we hadn't fished once, despite passing some sweet-looking weed lines and diving birds. Why, you ask? Because there wasn't a single fishing rod on the boat. Not one. It was a completely unacceptable situation that would normally drive me nuts. *Normally*. But after Rafe explained that I was in charge of outfitting the boat with the necessary fishing gear and presented me with a credit card from the boss, well, all was forgiven.

The plan was to dock at Holly's house on Sabal Island and spend a day provisioning the boat for the trip to the western Gulf of Mexico. That's what we did. Rafe stayed on the boat to tinker with the propulsion system while Holly and Judy went to get the provisions. Even though I knew it would take us all day just to get the boat ready to fish, I put us in charge of the alcohol, too. As Rafe was prone to say, "Better safe than sorry." Since we weren't sure how long it would be before we could reprovision, I planned on being safer than Rosie O'Donnell's panties in a game of strip poker. We were *not* going to run dry, especially with a no-limit AmEx Black card in my possession—thankyouverymuch.

After dropping nearly three grand for libations from Total Wine and Liquor at the boat, we hit Tuppen's in Lake Worth for some gear: rods, reels, line, leader, hooks, swivels, gaffs. You name it, we got it. I found it to be so much more fun shopping when you know you'll never see the bill—particularly when it's for $5,475.86. After we unloaded the gear on the boat, I asked Tangles to get things organized while I ran over to Florida Native to stock up on bait and anything else that looked good.

Mission accomplished, I returned to the boat to find Tangles making live rigs and stocked the bait freezer full of prerigged ballyhoo, squid, sardines, and split-tailed mullets. While I prefer to rig my own baits the way my old buddy Tooda taught me, prerigged is always better than not rigged if you don't have the time. Tooda also taught me that prerigged is better when somebody else is paying for it. Tooda was right. Not that the squid and ballyhoo were cheap, but the split-tailed mullets were eight bucks a pop. Feeling the gifted AmEx effect, I took all they had: four dozen.

With the girls still shopping and Rafe still tinkering, it was time for the piece de resistance; a trip to Black Bart's in West Palm. No proper fitting of a world-class fishing boat could be said to have been done without a trip there. I had the guys in back rig up some lures I picked out while Tangles and I went through the store loading up on high-end tackle and gear. There was a pair of fighting chairs on the display floor that each had a heavy-duty rod and gleaming oversize reel sticking out of the gimbal. I checked out the price tag hanging off one of the reels; it was twenty-five hundred marked down from three grand. Knowing a good deal on a rod/reel combo when I see one, I bought both. We got some Gore-Tex rainsuits, new boat shoes, shorts, shirts, and a little this and that. Of course at Black Bart's, a little this and that adds up fast. When the dust settled, the total damages were nearly ten grand. The manager was so happy he gave me and

Tangles a Black Bart visor, and Tangles talked him out of a couple of T-shirts on the way out the door.

When we pulled into Holly's driveway with our Black Bart's booty, Holly was standing next to the Jeep, and Judy was placing something in the backseat. I parked on the side, and Holly pointed at the rods sticking out of the backseat of the Beemer as Tangles and I exited the car.

"You got *more* fishing rods?"

"*More?* Hell yeah, I got more. I'm just getting started, babe. It's a big job outfitting a boat like the *LD3*. I even got Gore-Tex rainsuits for everybody. Not that I plan on fishing in the rain, but like Rafe says, better safe than sorry."

Judy shut the rear door of the Jeep. "Okay, I'm ready when you are."

"Ready for what?" Tangles asked. "Where you going? It's happy hour at the Old Key Lime House."

"I'm taking Judy to the airport," answered Holly.

"What? Why? I thought—"

"There's a systems emergency. I have to catch a plane. Nice meeting you two and good luck." She shook my hand.

As she was shaking Tangles's hand, I asked, "What about training Holly on the computers and—"

"*Me* train *her?*" She snorted. "Except for the security interface operating system, there was very little I could teach her. In fact, she taught me a few things, which is something I haven't said in a long time. Once I take care of this emergency, I may rejoin you in the gulf, although I have little doubt Holly can handle things from here." Judy tried pulling her hand away from Tangles, but he kept shaking it.

"Thank you," said Holly. "I really enjoyed working with you. Please keep your phone handy. I'm sure I'll have some questions about that security interface."

"You can call me anytime. Anytime at all." The smile she gave Holly made me wonder just how bad she wanted her to call. *Hmmm.*

Judy tried pulling her hand away from Tangles for the second time, but he kept holding on. Judy scowled at him. Tangles must have got the message because Judy's hand finally jerked free.

"Oh, sorry. It's just that, I thought, you know—"

"Thought what?"

"I thought we had a little, you know, chemistry going on here."

"*Chemistry?*"

"Yeah, chemistry. You know, sparks?"

"Oh, you mean like when you mix nitric acid and hydrazine? A fiery explosion?"

"You feel it too, huh? I knew it."

"Actually I would describe our compatibility as more like ammonia and bleach."

"How's that?"

"It creates an extremely toxic chloramine vapor when mixed. There's your chemistry for you. Thanks, but no thanks." She nodded at Holly and walked around the Jeep to the passenger door. Tangles stood stunned for a second before muttering, "Shit," and then hurried over to the Beemer. Holly got in the Jeep, and I leaned in to give her a kiss after she started it up.

"You going to Palm Beach International?" I asked.

"Yeah, I thought we'd take A1A. Go for the scenic ride."

"Call me after you drop her off. We'll meet you at the Old Key Lime House for the rest of happy hour and dinner."

"Sounds good."

I looked at Judy, who had just buckled up. "Have a safe trip."

"Thanks. I wish I could join you for dinner. Holly's amazing...amazingly, uh, talented—seriously. You're very lucky. Good-bye."

Holly pulled away, and Tangles ran in front of the Jeep with a bag in his hand. "Wait! Stop!"

Holly jammed on the brakes, and Tangles went around to the passenger door. Judy powered down the window, and Tangles handed her the bag.

"I almost forgot. I got something for you."

Judy looked in the bag, puzzled. "Why would you get me something? What is it?"

"It's just a T-shirt. I thought you would look good in it. Not that you don't look good in what you have on now." As much as I could tell Judy wanted to lay in to him, she was clearly caught off guard and appeared a little flustered.

"Oh, I, well...well, thank you. It's completely uncalled for, but thanks." She quickly stuffed the bag in her carry on and then stuck her hand out the window to shake Tangles's hand again. Rather than shake it, though, Tangles held it up to his lips and gently kissed the back of her hand.

"Until we meet again, m'lady," he murmured, and she pulled her hand away before he could plant a second kiss.

"*M'lady?* In your dreams, Tangles. In your hot and twisted dreams. Good-bye."

As they pulled away, Tangles grinned. “She wants me. She totally wants me. I can feel it.”

I wasn’t so sure, and as they headed down the road, I yelled, “Holly drives a Jeep! Notice the Jeep!”

Chapter 16

Chaco and Jorge had just finished telling the terroristas about their meeting with the smuggler known as el Primo. As expected, the terrorists were very pleased that they'd found a helicopter pilot and had no qualms reimbursing them for the money they claimed to have paid the bartender. Chaco licked his cracked lips as he watched the one called Zahvi pull a stack of bills out of a duffel bag and count out five one-hundred-dollar bills.

"You sure this el Primo is what he claims to be?" Zahvi asked as he handed the money to Chaco.

"No, but we'll know soon enough. The helicopter is being delivered to my brother-in-law's tomorrow. El Primo is going to take Jorge for a test ride. Then we'll know."

"What?" said Jorge. "Why me?"

"Why not?"

"Because I...I've never even been on a plane."

"So? You're not *going* on a plane."

"I'm not going on a helicopter, either. I prefer to stay on the ground."

"And I prefer not to slice open that fat belly of yours, but I will if you don't go. *You're* the one who found this *lagarto cuello*, so *you're* the one going on the test flight."

"What is a lagarto cuello?" asked Zahvi.

El Primo has a lizard neck," Jorge explained. "That's what lagarto cuello means."

"I see. Well, I don't care what his name is. I only care that he can fly a helicopter."

"Jorge cares, too, because if he can't, it's chop-chop-chop for Jorge." Chaco chuckled and made a slicing motion with his hand just as his cell phone rang. He pulled it out of his pocket and looked at the screen before announcing, "It's my cousin on the *Taladro Grande*."

"Put him on speakerphone," Zahvi said.

Chaco did as he was told. "Cousin, I have you on speakerphone so our friends can hear. What did you find out?"

"A diver took the skiff. He said he was fishing by the *Dinero Majado* but nothing about going on the rig or seeing anything unusual."

"I told you he's a spy!" Zahvi said. "Why else would he keep quiet about what he saw?"

"That's what I thought, too, but I searched his room, and it was clean as a whistle. I took his computer. It's one of those small devices like an iPad. He's only sent a handful of e-mails since he's been on the rig, and they were all to what appears to be friends or family. There was nothing suspicious. I searched his Facebook page, too, but he hasn't posted anything in six months—no messaging either."

"Wait a second, how did you access this information? How did you find his passwords?"

"I didn't have to. It wasn't protected."

"*What?* How could that be?"

"I don't know. I'm just telling you what I found."

"There must be something there. We watched him cut the video feed on the *Dinero Majado.* He must be working for somebody."

"I'm not so sure. If he was, I think I would have found something. What do you want me to do?"

"I want to see his computer for myself. Can you arrange to have it sent on the next flight back?"

"Are you crazy? He's already reported it stolen. If I'm caught with it, I will be fired. I'm tossing it overboard as soon as I get off the phone."

Zahvi shook his head in disbelief. "Who *is* this man? Where is he from? What is his background?"

"He is from somewhere in the South Pacific. That's all I know."

"You said he was a diver?"

"Yes. In fact, he's supposed to go on a dive first thing in the morning—a deep dive. Engineering thinks there's a stress fracture on a support strut. He's going to check it out."

"Sounds like dangerous work."

"It is."

"Make it *more* dangerous then. An accident will be fine. Make it so he never returns to the surface."

"And how would I do that? I don't know anything about diving, and I don't usually work on the lower levels."

"Then do what you need to do. I don't care if it is an accident or not. He must be silenced as soon as possible."

There was an awkward silence on the line until Chaco said, "Cousin? Are you still there?"

"Yes, I'm here. This is more than I signed up for, Chaco."

Chaco looked at Zahvi, who said, "I will double your pay."

Chaco nodded and kept the dialogue going. "He has the money, cousin. Make it happen, and we will celebrate when this is over."

"The sooner the better."

"You'll do it then?"

"Yes, of course."

"I knew I could count on you."

"You always do. One of these days the tables will be turned."

"When they are, I will sit you at the head and treat you to a feast like you have never imagined."

"So long as it's not at that place called Juanita's. Their burritos are greasier than Ricky Martin's *culo.*" *Click.*

Jorge started laughing.

"Culo?" Zahvi asked. "Ricky Martin? What does this mean?"

"You don't wanna know, amigo," answered Chaco with a frown. "But he's wrong about the burritos. I eat the beef ones all the time."

Jorge laughed even harder. "So does Ricky Martin."

"ENOUGH!" The ex-Taliban commander slammed the butt of his AK-47 into the floor, breaking a Mexican tile. The room went silent as Jorge and Chaco suddenly remembered who they were working for. "I don't care about burritos! The only thing I care about is whether your cousin is reliable!" He pointed at

Chaco. “Our whole operation is in jeopardy if your cousin doesn’t take care of the problem.”

Chaco waggled his index finger and gave him his best semitoothless smile.

“Trust me, amigo, this diver is a dead man…D-E-D, dead.”

Chapter 17

After a quick shower, Pago tracked down his roommate, Arturo, who confirmed what he suspected; Arturo had no idea where his computer tablet was. Pago went to report the theft to Luis (the OTL), but found Luis's assistant, Roberto, sitting in the small office instead. Roberto informed him that Luis had retired for the night. When told of the missing tablet, Roberto didn't seem too concerned, suggesting he had misplaced it.

"Misplaced it? Are you kidding me? There *is* nowhere to misplace it. Our room is smaller than this office. I know where it was when I left this morning, and it's not there anymore. Arturo says he didn't take it. Why would he? He has his own. Somebody else had to take it."

"You sure you didn't leave it in the lounge or the cafeteria?"

"I wasn't *in* the lounge or the cafeteria today. I was fishing."

"Oh, that's right. You were fishing by the *Dinero Majado*. You do know that it's off-limits, yes?"

The statement caught him a little off guard. He was simply trying to report a missing tablet, and for the second time since returning, the focus was back on the *Dinero Majado.* "Of course I know. But there are no rules against fishing near it, right?"

Roberto's eyes narrowed a little. "Not yet, but is that *all* you were doing?"

"*What?* What do you mean by that? What else would I be doing?"

"I don't know. Did you have your tablet with you?"

Now Pago was getting pissed. "My *tablet?* Why in the *fuck* would I take my tablet fishing?"

"Oh, I don't know. Maybe you wanted to use it away from prying eyes. Maybe when that hammerhead took your grouper and almost capsized the skiff, the tablet went overboard. Maybe you're looking for the company to buy you a new one. Maybe—"

"And maybe I'm going to grab you by the fucking throat and squeeze it until—"

"Relax, amigo. Okay? Just relax. I was only speculating, just like you're speculating someone stole your tablet."

"I'm not speculating, asshole! My tablet *is* gone. Just like your common sense. Even if I had it on the skiff, which I didn't, what could I do with it a hundred miles from shore?" He pointed to a small window that framed the imposing darkness of the vast gulf beyond. "There's no wireless network out there, and even if there was, it was so bright today you couldn't read the display screen anyways. *Shit.* You been drug tested lately?"

"Watch it, Pago."

"Yeah? Well, watch this. I'm outta here." He spun and headed for the door.

"Where are you going? I have a few more questions."

Pago stopped at the door and turned to face him. "Too bad, I've heard enough. I'm diving at first light and need to go gas up some tanks."

"Okay, then. I'll tell Luis about your missing tablet in the morning."

"Super." Pago turned and slammed the office door shut.

Pago was still steaming as he headed to the elevator. On the way down to the dive locker, he reexamined his conversation with the idiot Roberto. Luis had obviously told him about his fishing trip to the *Dinero Majado* and his run-in with the hammerhead. That much was clear. What wasn't clear was Roberto's bizarre line of questioning. *Taking his tablet on a fishing trip?* That was crazy talk. Unless...suddenly he remembered the satellite dish hidden on the top deck of the supposedly abandoned *Dinero Majado.* Maybe there *was* a wireless network out there. *Did Roberto know that?* What the hell was going on?

Pago let himself into the dive locker and began filling a tank with a mixture of helium and nitrogen. Why helium and nitrogen? Because that's what divers use on dives down to three hundred feet.

While diving can be dangerous at any depth, below the recreational level of 110 feet, the risk increases exponentially. Once a diver descends past that level, the immediate threat is the onset of nitrogen narcosis, which is the anesthetic effect that certain pressurized gases have on the human consciousness. A diver suffering this condition will feel drunk and sluggish and have difficulty maintaining a coherent train of thought. That's why it's also called "the martini effect." The deeper the diver goes past 110 feet, the worse the condition gets. The condition is reversible, but only if the diver realizes what's happening and ascends before becoming incapacitated or running out of air. The diver must also stop his or her ascent at predetermined levels for a calculated amount of time to prevent decompression sickness. Decompression sickness, also known as "the bends," results when certain gases dissolve into the bloodstream on depressurization. The condition can be extremely painful and usually results in joint pain and rashes, and sometimes paralysis and death. Through painful and sometimes fatal experimentation, divers discovered that they could go well below the 110-foot level by breathing a mixture of gases other than oxygen. Not only could they dive deeper, but they didn't have to stop on the ascent to decompress. This in no way minimizes the risks of deep diving, because having any type of problem or equipment malfunction at 280 feet is likely to be your last.

As Pago filled a second tank, he continued to ponder what was going on in the maintenance room of the *Dinero Majado* and what, if anything, he should do about it. Both Luis and his assistant seemed unusually interested in his fishing trip, to say the least. It was almost as if they knew he had boarded the decommissioned rig. *Did they? How was that possible?* And what about his missing tablet? What was going on there? He finished gassing up the second tank and then checked his regulator, buoyancy compensator, and the rest of his gear. Everything was set to go. He glanced at his dive watch. It was almost ten o'clock. It was time to get some much-needed rest.

All was quiet and dark on the lower levels of the *Taladro Grande* as Pago pulled out the keys and began locking the door behind him. Quiet, that is, except for the drone of machinery and drilling gear that was so constant it was almost inaudible to those who worked and lived on the rig. It was similar to how people who live near active train tracks eventually tune out the blowing horns and rumbling engines of passing locomotives. So despite the noise emanating from the huge structure, Pago heard something above the din and turned to look. That was all the warning he had before something smashed into the side of his head and his world went black.

Pago crumpled to the deck, and the perpetrator quickly dragged him back into the dive locker. He flicked on the light after he shut the door and quickly scanned the room. He didn't have much of a plan other than to slit his throat and throw him overboard, but as he looked around he had an idea. Pago had laid out all his dive gear and that included a weight belt. The perpetrator saw a second weight belt on a shelf along with some loose weights. He quickly added the loose weights to the two belts and tied them together around Pago's waist. After checking to make sure the coast was clear, he dragged him out onto the walkway. Then he maneuvered Pago's body so his head and torso were hanging over the middle rail of the four foot high railing. He pulled out a knife and was about to slit Pago's throat when red lights started flashing along with the wail of a siren. It startled him so much that he flinched and dropped the knife. *It was a fire drill.* He'd forgotten about the fire drill that was scheduled that evening. He heard the knife clatter on a walkway below and cursed. Panicking at the thought of being caught in the act, he grabbed Pago by the legs and shoved him over the railing head first. He peered over the rail in time to see Pago's midsection hit the top rail of the walkway below. There was a loud clang as he somersaulted into the void. Like a tree falling in the woods with no one to hear it, Pago was swallowed up unnoticed by the dark and deadly sea.

Chapter 18

We left early the next morning out the Boynton Inlet and took advantage of the good weather by hammering the *LD3* down the coast at a nice forty-knot clip. Tangles proposed that we stop in Key West to have lunch with our old friends at the Big Iguana, but Holly and Rafe both nixed the idea. Rafe was all business and Holly wanted to get to the western Gulf of Mexico as fast as possible to see if the boss had indeed located her long-lost cousin. It was weird not having to worry about when and where to refuel. Despite knowing the *LD3* was nuclear powered, I couldn't shake my range anxiety and kept looking at the phony fuel gauge. When we were in the Dry Tortugas, I powered down the boat.

Tangles looked up at me. "What are you doing?"

"What am I doing? What do you think? We're in the Dry Tortugas, let's do a little bottom fishing. Get the gear ready."

"Alright! I never fished here before." Tangles scampered down the stairs, and I was right behind him. Rafe, who had been going over some security-system issues with Holly, came walking into the salon.

"Why are we stopped?" He asked.

Tangles brushed by him and disappeared down the hall to gather a few rods. Clearly, Rafe needed to be enlightened, and I was more than happy to be the one to do it.

"Because we're in the Dry Tortugas. That's why."

"So?"

"So, it's a beautiful day, and this is bottom-fishing nirvana, my friend. It's time to test out the HD cameras and catch us some dinner, captain's call."

"Captain's call? *Puhleeze,*" Holly said, as she appeared behind Rafe. "Now you're calling yourself 'Captain'?"

"Well, I'm sure as hell no Tennille. Who do you think's been at the helm while you two do whatever it is you've been doing?"

"We've been working on a security-system glitch. Believe me, I'd much rather be in the cockpit, getting some fresh air."

"Well, now's your chance. You too, Rafe. Right after Tangles and I catch a few for the cameras. Have to make sure this fancy cockpit recording system works right."

"One hour," Rafe said. "You got one hour to fish, then it's a beeline for the *Taladro Grande.*"

"The *what?*"

Tangles came up the steps from the forward berths with a couple of rods under each arm and announced he would thaw out some sardines. He disappeared into the bright sunlight of the cockpit.

"The *Taladro Grande* is the oil rig that my cousin might be working on. A good captain would have remembered that," Holly said.

"It's not a good idea to cross the captain, Missy."

"*Missy*? You just called me, *Missy*?"

"That's right. Captain's call."

"Ughhh. I'll tell you what. If you stop calling yourself 'Captain,' I'll make sandwiches for everybody. Deal?"

"Really? Hmmm. Let me check with the captain."

"Seriously. It's getting old."

"Sorry. I just can't believe this is my new boat. It's so friggin' awesome I guess I'm getting a little carried away."

"Sorry to burst your bubble, Kit, but this boat is the property of Uncle Sam. You just get to use it so long as you don't screw up. That would be a good thing to remember…and thanks Holly, a sandwich would be great," Rafe said.

"Ditto here, babe. Make mine a salami and Swiss with German mustard and I'll have Tangles make your special K4 rig so you can wet a line when you're done."

"Now you're talking!"

I opened the door to the cockpit and motioned to Rafe. "C'mon. Show me how the cameras work, and I'll show you how we catch 'em Shaggy style."

"I can hardly wait."

While Tangles put together Holly's K4 rig, which was nothing more than a four-hook sardine rig instead of the usual three, Rafe pointed out the built-in cameras. They were basically all over the place: on the bridge, underneath the cockpit overhang, on the stern facing the cockpit, and on both sides of the cockpit facing the fighting chair.

"What about microphones?" I asked. Rafe opened one of the drawers next to the bait prep station and pulled out a small clear waterproof bag. Inside were a pair of clip-on mics, and he handed them to me.

"Here you go. Just clip them on, and you're good to go. There's also a multidirectional mic built into the underside of the overhang." He pointed at what I thought was a speaker and added, "That's not a speaker, that's a microphone. When you turn on the cameras, the mics are activated. It's wireless. The clip-ons are lithium battery powered."

Tangles looked up as he finished with Holly's K4 rig. "Technology rocks."

I clipped on a mic and handed the other to Tangles. "Here, put this on." I turned back to Rafe. "So how do we turn on the cameras?"

He showed us a button under the left arm of the fighting chair, another next to the fingerprint scanner by the cabin door, and one more recessed into the transom below the gunwale.

"I'm guessing that's for Tangles?" I wondered aloud.

"How did I know you were going to say that?"

"Very funny," Tangles said.

"No, that wasn't the reasoning. It's so you can activate the cameras with your foot if your busy fighting a fish."

"Man, you guys seem to have thought of everything."

"That's what we do."

"Right. So let's try it out already. Tangles, stand next to me, and we'll do an intro." Rafe stepped under the overhang, and I pressed the button on the fighting chair. "Okay, we're rolling."

"Which, uh, which camera should we be looking at?" asked Tangles.

"Let's try the one in the middle...on the bridge."

"Got it."

I waved at the camera and started my spiel. "Hey there, Shagball and Tangles fans! Long time no see, no pun intended. Although technically this isn't the sea, we're filming in the Gulf of Mexico, in the Dry Tortugas, to be exact. Welcome back to another episode of *Fishing on the Edge with Shagball and Tangles.*"

"Hang on, bro." Tangles held a hand up for me to stop.

"What are you doing?"

"I thought we changed the name of the show."

"Oh, shit. You're right. Look up at the camera again." We both faced the camera again. "Welcome back to the inaugural episode of our newly renamed show, *Fishing for Answers with Shagball and Tangles.*" I spread my arms wide. "As you can see, we have a new and bigger boat, but don't worry, Tangles is still the same little lovable chunk of surliness he's always been." I looked at Tangles, who was frowning. "Well, maybe he's a little bigger too, but trust me, he's not any taller."

"Fuck you."

"You can't say that! This is a family show."

"Really? What family watches TV at four o'clock on Sunday morning?"

Rafe started laughing, which didn't help things.

"That's beside the point."

"Hey, you're the one who just called me surly. I'm just trying to live up to the hype. So what if I drop a few F-bombs? Edit it out."

"What do *I* know about editing? Jamie use to do all that stuff. I'm just the talent."

"That's highly debatable, but you don't have to worry about editing if we don't catch some fish."

"Exactly. So, let's do another intro without any F-bombs, and then we'll start fishing. Okay?"

"Okay, fine."

"You ready?"

"Don't wait on me."

"No F-bombs this time."

"Stop yappin' and get on with it already—it's hot."

"All right, here we go. Welcome back to the inaugural episode of *Fishing for Answers with Shagball and Tangles.* Today we're on our new boat, the *LD3*, about a hundred and ten miles off the west coast of Florida in the Dry Tortugas. For those of you not familiar with the Dry—"

"Hang on a second."

"*Now* what?!"

"What's the question?"

"*What* question? What are you talking about?"

"If we're fishing for answers there must be a question. So what is it?"

"*What?*"

Holly stepped out of the cabin with a platter full of sandwiches.

"You heard me. You can't name the show *Fishing for Answers* without having a question. I thought we were supposed to try to unravel mysteries while we fish our way around the world."

"Shit. I forgot. It's been so long I forgot the premise of the new show."

"I got a question for you," Rafe said.

"What's that?"

"How did you guys ever get a fishing show?"

"Now *there's* a mystery to unravel," said Holly. "You can bet there's a lot of people who would like the answer to that."

"Cute. Do I detect a hint of envy in that flagrant snipe?"

"Not hardly. It's the truth. Putting that aside, I suggest we eat these sandwiches before they melt."

We took Holly's advice, and just as we finished them off, Rafe's phone rang. He looked at the display, said, "I gotta take this," and disappeared into the cabin. Holly picked up the rod with the K4 rig and asked what the depth was as she hooked a sardine on it. I glanced at the depth finder mounted on the underside of the overhang and said, "Ninety-five feet."

She walked over to the port-side corner of the stern and smiled.

"Let me show you how it's done, boys."

As she let out her line, Tangles asked, "So have you come up with a plausible mystery?"

"Nope."

"Then we're not gonna shoot another intro?"

"Negatory."

"So…what then?"

"So fuck it. Let's fish."

Chapter 19

In Pago's dream he was in the Afghanistan desert sinking in a pocket of quicksand. The harder he struggled to keep his head above the soupy sand, the more he sank. But when he cried for help, it wasn't sand that filled his mouth. It was seawater. Instinctively, he spit it out. His eyes shot open as he regained consciousness, and in that moment he realized his dream had turned into a real-life nightmare. His burning orbs picked up the blurry lights of the oil rig above, which seemed to be growing dimmer. No, they *were* growing dimmer. *I'm sinking to the bottom of the ocean!* He kicked toward the surface. His skull throbbed as his hand probed the large knot that had formed on the side of his head. As a trained Navy SEAL, he fought the urge to inhale, even as the oxygen in his lungs grew sparse. Then he realized he was still sinking. Panic began to set in. His hands frantically searched for the cause, and he discovered a pair of weight belts tied around his waist. The panic kept rising as he unsuccessfully struggled to untie them before feeling the emergency air bottle fastened to the inside of one of the belts. *Yes!* He ripped it free from its Velcro enclosure and opened the release valve before biting down on the mouthpiece and inhaling the glorious oxygen. The small bottle contained enough air for only a few minutes, and as he continued to sink, he knew he had to act fast.

In the pitch-black water he struggled for a few more seconds trying to untie the weight belts before remembering the survival knife he always carried. He dug in his cargo shorts pocket and was relieved to find it hadn't fallen out. He quickly snapped open the blade and cut the belts loose. As the belts sunk into the abyss, he tried to slow his breathing rate down to preserve as much oxygen as possible. The lights above were barely visible as he slipped the knife in his pocket and kicked toward the surface. He had no way of knowing how deep he was, but based on the atmospheric pressure crushing his throbbing head, he estimated he was well over a hundred feet deep—maybe 150 feet or more. It was problematic to say the least. With no weight belt or buoyancy compensator, he had no way to regulate his ascent. And he didn't have enough oxygen to stop and decompress along the way. *Details.* A case of the bends was better than a case of the ends.

As he swam toward the surface he pieced together what he remembered. He was locking up the dive locker when he thought he heard something, and then the next thing he knew he was spitting out seawater. His throbbing head told him the rest. Somebody had clubbed him and threw him overboard. *Somebody had tried to kill him!* But who? And why? He hadn't made any enemies on the rig that he knew of, certainly not the kind who would want him dead. Suddenly, he felt a stinging sensation on his right hand and arm, then one on his chest. His breathing quickened as he tried to wipe away the culprit and recognized the slimy substance as a jellyfish. *Great.* He thrashed his arm in the hopes of disengaging the stinging menace but quickly realized it wasn't happening. The only thing that was happening was that he was using up the precious oxygen from his emergency air bottle, which, as if on cue, began sputtering. *He was almost out of air!* He risked opening an eye to try and gauge the distance to the surface but he couldn't see anything. No lights, no nothing. To make matters worse, after thrashing around at the jellyfish, he wasn't positive which way was up. *Shit.* He sucked on the little oxygen bottle until there was nothing left and then spit it out. Then he exhaled a little and used the faintly glowing dial of his dive watch to track a few air bubbles as they rose to the surface. Confident of his bearings, he breaststroked upward as fast as he could.

A minute or so later he burst to the surface and greedily gulped down the sweet salty air. His relief at having made it was quickly doused by the fact that the current had pushed him a good three hundred yards from the rig. His head began to throb even worse, and as he felt the knot, he realized he was bleeding. There was blood in the water. He was in the water. There were sharks in the water. They fed at night. *It just kept getting better.* The one thing going for him was that he was in excellent shape and an exceptional swimmer. He would need to be to have any chance of making it to the rig. As he began swimming he thought about the large hammerhead that snatched the grouper from his line earlier in the day. That did it. The pain from the head wound and jellyfish stings faded as he channeled Michael Phelps and swam for his life.

Chapter 20

We were just finishing dinner when my phone rang. I glanced at the display. The boss. I wasn't sure how he made it happen, but I didn't dwell on it. It was going to take a lot to surprise me after captaining a nuclear-powered, vanish-on-demand fishing boat. I announced who it was.

Rafe said, "Put him on speaker."

I placed the phone in the cradle in the center of the dinette table and answered it. "I was hoping we'd hear from you. There's a problem."

"We all have problems, pal. Let me guess. Tangles did a poor job cleaning the red snapper, and you swallowed a bone. Well boo-hoo to you."

"No, the fillets are fine. What voice are you using? Say something else."

"Something else."

"That's Bill Murray!" Tangles said.

"Congratulations. You just won a pair of platform fishing boots."

"This is weird," Holly said with a shake of the head.

"What are you shaking your head at? I thought you liked weird. Why else would you be with Kit and caboodle there?"

Tangles looked at me. "Did he just call me caboodle? What the hell's a caboodle?"

"Sir, you're doing it again," Rafe said. "You're not just talking in Bill Murray's voice, you're channeling him."

"Sorry, it's a hard habit to break. Like running with the bulls on acid."

"Sir!"

"My bad. I'll try to restrain myself. Not in a Michael Hutchence way, mind you, but I'll try. So, what's the problem, Kit?"

"Aside from the Michael Hutchence reference? Wait a second. How'd you know we were having red snapper? You've been watching us?" I looked toward the TV where Rafe had shown us one of the hidden cameras.

"Like Big Brother. When I was alerted that the boat unexpectedly stopped, I tuned in to watch Holly reel up a sizeable red snapper. I saw Tangles catch a couple of yellowtails, but I didn't see you bring up anything. Did I miss it?"

"No," said Holly. "He got skunked."

"Ouch. I'm guessing that hurts for—"

"I did not get skunked. I caught a grouper."

"You lost him at the boat. He spit the hook." Holly smirked at me.

Bitch. "He was too short. I let him go."

"He didn't look short to me," commented Tangles.

"I guess you would know, you little hobbit."

"Now wait a second! Why do you—"

"Boys, boys, boys," said the boss. "You can squabble later. There's been a slight change of plans. But first, what's this problem you're talking about, Kit?"

"I didn't get skunked."

"And I didn't try to tap Sigourney Weaver during *Ghostbusters.* Oops, I forgot we're in mixed company. Sorry about that, Holly."

"Apology accepted."

"So, what's the problem, Kit?"

"The fishing show name, for one thing. *Fishing for Answers with Shagball and Tangles.* We have to come up with a mystery, right? Something that we're searching for the answer to?"

"You mean like how does Whoopi Goldberg have a career in show business? Good luck solving that one."

Everybody laughed.

"I'm kidding...sort of. You're not going to use *Fishing for Answers.* You're keeping the old name. We reached a settlement with your ex-producer. He's happier than a pig in you know what."

"That's great! I love the old name. What made you change your mind?"

"Since you had a year and a half left on your contract we had to settle with him anyways, so I figured why not buy the rights to the show name as well. The more we kicked it around at headquarters, the more we figured *Fishing for Answers* wasn't such a great name. It seemed like a good idea at the time, but asking questions in far-flung places and trying to solve mysteries would draw too much attention. We want it to be an ordinary fishing show, and you guys do that perfectly."

"Now hang on just a—"

"Relax, my man, that's a compliment. So that's it? You were just worried about the name?"

"Well, that and uh, I hate to admit it, but—"

"But what?"

"He misses the old beanpole," said Tangles.

"The what?"

"Jamie, our old producer."

"I don't miss *him* so much as I miss having somebody to ask me questions, tell me what to do, what not to do, you know...direct me. That sorta thing."

"Doesn't Holly do that?"

"Watch it, mister," she replied.

"Sorry."

Rafe started to talk, but the boss cut him off.

"You don't have to say it, Rafe. I know I'm channeling again. I'm so pleased the boat is running well I can't help myself."

"And I can't talk into a camera with nobody there," I continued. "It's too weird."

"What's with you guys? You think everything's weird. That's weird, this is weird. Look, I don't know what to tell you. You're gonna have to get used to it for now."

"Who's gonna do all the editing?"

"Don't worry about it, I'll hire someone. Remember, the fishing show is just for cover. You guys have a job to do. Speaking of which, as I mentioned before, there's been a slight change of plans."

"How slight?"

"So slight that nobody will care...except maybe Holly."

"I don't like the sound of this. You promised I could go see Alexander Hamilton LeRoux on the *Taladro Grande* so I can see if he's my cousin."

"I also promised Andie McDowell I wouldn't slip her the tongue when we were filming *Groundhog Day*, but—"

"Ewwww!"

"Sorry, that just slipped out, so to speak. Anyhoo, you can still go there. It's just that I'd like you to stop by another rig first. It's a little over ninety miles northeast of the *Taladro Grande*. It's called the *Bluewater*."

"What are we doing there?" Rafe asked.

"Oh, not much, other than taking the forty-third president of the United States out for a little deep-sea fishing."

"Seriously?"

"Seriously."

"The forty-third?" Tangles asked. "What is this, *Jeopardy?* Who's the—"

"George W. Bush," answered Holly. "You want us to take him fishing? Why?"

"Because it's a little hard for me to turn him down since there would be no DICK without him. DICK was his brainchild; the ultimate top-secret terrorist-hunting group formed in direct response to the nine-eleven attacks."

"You said it would be hard for you to turn him down," I repeated. "You're saying he *asked* to go fishing with us? He knows we're part of the DICK team?" There was enough silence to fill a shuttered library, and I thought the connection was lost. "Are you still—"

"Yes. Yes I'm still here. I know this is going to be hard to believe, but he claims to be a fan of your show."

"No way," Rafe said.

"Oh my God," Holly muttered.

I was all smiles as I fist-bumped Tangles and said, "You hear that? Ol' Dubya's a fan!"

"Dude, this is awesome!" he replied. "Maybe we should change the name of the show to *Presidential Fishing with Shagball and Tangles.* Think about it. We travel around the world—"

"Don't let it go to your head, son," the boss interrupted. "My guess is this will be the one and only time you ever fish with a president. Don't make me regret setting it up."

"When is this supposed to happen?" Rafe asked.

"The president started a program with an oil service company that works on the *Bluewater* to hire more veterans. It's been a success, and he's making a surprise visit on Memorial Day to honor them."

"Memorial Day? That's, uh, that's…"

"This Monday, in less than seventy-two hours. You have until the early afternoon to get there. Permission is granted to test out the upper range speed of the *LD3.* The good weather is expected to hold, so you should be able to make it no problem."

"Permission accepted," I replied.

"And *then* we can go to the *Taladro Grande?*" Holly asked.

"Yes. I'll send you the contact information for the OIM, but there's no guarantee—"

"The OIM?"

"Oh, sorry. The offshore installation manager—he runs the show. But like I was saying, there's no guarantee he'll let you aboard. It's up to you to sweet-talk him. From what I gather that shouldn't be a problem."

"Thank you."

"Rafe?"

"Yes."

"I want you on the bridge when Kit puts the pedal to the metal."

"Understood."

"You don't trust me?" I asked. "That hurts. That really hurts."

"You know what else hurts?"

"What?"

"Frying a fast-neutron nuclear reactor and blowing your boat to kingdom come…not to mention the cleanup."

"Now hold on there," Tangles protested. "Rafe said this was like the safest boat ever built. That it couldn't happen."

"In theory it can't, but with you on board and Captain Happy-Go-Lucky at the helm, I'm afraid anything's possible. Please guys, try not to prove me right. Safe travels." *Click.*

Chapter 21

El Primo tossed some pesos onto the front seat of the taxi and exited while pinching his nose. As the taxi drove off, he waved his hand in front of his face and yelled, "You smell worse than you drive you thieving bastard!" He looked around the run-down industrial park and was met with the icy glares of a handful of locals loitering around a dilapidated taco truck. Nervous as always, he unzipped the small duffel bag he was carrying so he would have easy access to his .45. The building directly in front of him had a faded, hand-painted sign above a door that read ROBERTO'S REPARACION AUTOMATICA.

He double-checked the name and address that he had been given and let out a deep breath. He was in the right place. As he knocked on the door, the scary-looking locals started walking his way. *Great.*

"I'm here!" He knocked harder. "It's el Primo! C'mon, let me in already!" He heard the sound of a series of deadbolts being unlocked, and the door swung open. The one called Chaco ushered him in and then relocked the door.

"You make a lot of noise, el Primo."

"Yeah? Well it was gonna get noisier if the taco-truck boys got any closer. My trigger finger's itchier than Madonna's crotch." He took his sunglasses off and glanced around the filthy garage littered with old engines and car parts. "What is this place, anyways? A Shitholes-R-Us franchise?"

Chaco pointed a finger at him. "It may be a shit-hole, but it's a very profitable shithole. Don't piss off Roberto, he's not as nice as me and Jorge."

"That's hard to believe. You guys are such sweet-hearts. So where's the chopper? Don't tell me it's spread out on the floor and I have to put it together."

"It's in the back. Roberto just finished tuning it up. Follow me."

Chaco led him out the back door into the bright sunlight. El Primo put his shades back on and pulled his tattered Cleveland Indians baseball cap down. If possible, the yard was even worse than the shop. It was a junkyard, plain and simple. There were cars and trucks of all makes and sizes scattered all over the place. In the middle of the yard there was a clearing, and in the clearing sat a helicopter. He recognized Jorge standing next to another fat ass. Chaco introduced him as Roberto. He looked like the Frito Bandito, but instead of a sombrero, he wore a sweat-band around his greasy black hair. El Primo walked up to the chopper and rapped his knuckles on the frame next to the passenger door.

"She's a nice helicopter, no?" said Chaco. "You like?"

"I like money. The more the merrier. This is a Helix 29—a Russian job. It can hold a dozen people, no problem. You said I was only transporting a few. If you expect me to be flying around a couple of mariachi bands, the price goes up."

"No, it's just like I said."

"So why such a big bird?"

"It's all we could get. You can fly it, right? You said el Primo can fly anything." Chaco smiled, and Jorge and Roberto laughed.

"What are you two laughing at? If it can fly, I can fly it."

"Of course it can fly. How do you think it got here?"

"How about I ask the questions?" He pointed at Roberto. "You tuned this whirlybird up?"

"No comprendo." Chaco said something to him, and Roberto added,

"Sí, tune up."

"You ever hear of Mr. Goodwrench?"

Roberto held his hands out and shrugged.

"That's what I thought. You got a ladder?"

"Ladder?"

"Is there an echo here? Yeah, a ladder. You know, those things you guys use to scale fences."

Roberto frowned, and Chaco said, "Watch it, amigo." He looked at Roberto. "*Ir a buscar una escalera.*"

Jorge disappeared into the shop and returned with a ladder. El Primo positioned it next to the chopper and pulled a can of T-9 out of his duffel bag. It was a waterproof lubricant developed for aircraft parts that also provided rust and corrosion protection. He climbed up and sprayed the base of the center rotor and then climbed down and did the same to the tail rotor. All the while, Roberto and Chaco conversed in rapid-fire Spanish.

"You don't need to do that," Chaco said. "Roberto says he greased everything up."

"I bet he did. He probably squeezed the burrito juice out of his headband. Tell him gracias, but I prefer my T-9. You want me to fly this thing, I do it my way. I got a preflight routine, and I don't change it for nobody. Tell him to open up the engine compartment."

They conversed in Spanish again, and he could tell Roberto wasn't thrilled, but he did as told. After spraying the engine down, he signaled for Roberto to close it up and turned to Chaco. "All right, amigo, it's time to see how well this thing flies."

"Good, Jorge's going with you."

El Primo pointed at the passenger door and said, "You heard the man. Climb in, big boy." Then he pointed at Roberto and said, "You too, Mr. Jiffy Lube."

Roberto shook his head and fast-talked in Spanish to Chaco.

"He doesn't want to go," said Chaco.

"I'm sure. Did the guy who flew the chopper here say it was having a mechanical problem?"

"No."

"Then why did Mr. Sweatband fuck with the engine? How do I know he knows what he's doing?"

"He's a good mechanic. He fixed the transmission on my Fiero last week. It runs great."

"A *Fiero?* Really?"

"Sí."

"No shit. I didn't peg you for a corn dogger."

"A *what?*"

"Never mind. If he's so good, he shouldn't mind taking a spin, right? Besides, I need to see if the chopper can handle the weight. These two lard asses will be like having an eight-man crew."

Roberto didn't understand a word but continued to shake his head and mutter, "No, no, no."

"Yes, yes, yes, or I don't fly, fly, fly." El Primo dropped his duffel bag and crossed his arms.

A big shouting match ensued between Chaco and Roberto and while they were going at it, he picked up his bag and headed for the shop. He was almost to the door when Chaco yelled, "Wait! He's going. He said he'll go."

El Primo looked at the door and thought seriously about making a run for it. He hadn't flown a helicopter since the end of the cocaine cowboy days in the late eighties, and it hadn't ended well. He was trying to deliver fifty kilos of blow from the Bahamas to Miami but got spotted by a DEA plane. Like smugglers were prone to do at the time, he kept going when he reached Miami and tried to lose the DEA tail in the everglades. He managed to lose the tail, but he also ran out of gas. The only reason he survived the crash was because he was flying low and the swamp cushioned the impact. It took him three days to crawl out of the mosquito- and gator-infested wetlands. It was the last time he flew a helicopter, and he never ate frog legs or turtle soup again. Unfortunately, he now found himself in a fix and didn't have much choice.

"El Primo! I said he's going."

He turned and walked back to the helicopter, eyeing it warily. "All right boys, pile in."

There was a lot of Spanish mumbling and grumbling going on as he settled behind the controls. Fortunately, the Helix was over twenty years old and not so modernized that he couldn't figure out what was what. He flicked a few switches and the engine started. "Fuckin-A, Roberto. Sounds pretty good. Maybe there's hope for you yet."

Chaco ran behind the rusted-out shell of a '57 Chevy and peered out as the rotors spun faster and faster. Sand blew everywhere.

El Primo yelled, "Hang on! This should be fun!" The chopper rose about thirty feet, tilted, and headed off toward the open desert. El Primo cursed at the visibility at the same moment the main rotor clipped off the top of a large cactus. A milky substance splattered across the windshield, and both Jorge and Roberto started praying in Spanish. As the helicopter rose above the dust storm, el Primo felt a warm wetness soak his dirty underwear. He put on his best poker face and yelled, "The blades are sharp! That's good! Muy bueno!" He looked over his shoulder and winked as he gave his terrified passengers a thumbs-up. Roberto had his headband pulled over his eyes, and Jorge's face was whiter than Christmas at Bing Crosby's.

Chapter 22

Franklin Post, a.k.a. Stargazer, hyperdialed the forty-third president of the United States.

As always, he answered, "Stargazer, is that you?"

"Yes, sir. I just wanted to confirm it's a go for Memorial Day. The guys will pick you up at the *Bluewater* and take you out for a little fishing. It'll probably be in the afternoon."

"That's great! Wait a second, what voice are you using? That's a new one. Say something else."

"Goonga...Goonga la doonga."

"*Goonga la doonga?* Goonga la...that's Bill Murray in *Caddyshack*, right!?"

"Bingo."

"Damn, I love that movie. What a great scene. That's pretty much how the Dalai Lama talks, too. I mean, when he's talking Lama. Sure is a shame about that big earthquake out there. Might as well change the name to Khatmandont, 'cause don't nobody wanna go there no more. Even the yaks left."

"You met the Dalai Lama?"

"Hell yeah, I met him. Must be nice not ever having to take off your bathrobe. He's kinda like the Hugh

Hefner of brotherly love...very introprospective. I think he's related to Confucius. Yep, he's a great man, the Dalai. 'Course I met Dolly Parton, too. Between me and you and the fencepost, she's a lot more fun to hug. Heh. I'll let you in on a little secret. She told me I inspired the name of her amusement park."

"How so?"

"How do you think she came up with the name Dollywood? That's what I got when I hugged her—Dollywood. Wooo! I'm on fire today, Stargazer!

"On fire or going down in flames?"

"Cut me a little slack, Jack. I'm just trying to have some fun. Retirement is boring. All I do is kick around the ranch and rassle up some armadillos now and then. A big night for me is going chupacabra hunting with Manny, which ain't been too productive lately. It's why I'm so excited to go fishing with—"

"Hold on there. *What* did you say? A chupa *what?*"

"A chupacabra. You telling me Mr. Smartypants never heard of a chupacabra before?"

"I don't think so, no. What is it?"

"It's like a flying monkey with fangs and beady yellow eyes that glow in the dark. They're mean little buggers. They'll rip your lungs out, Jim, except they're not werewolves, and this ain't London."

"No offense, sir, but I'd know about them if they were real."

"Did I say they're real? Not hardly. They're mythical. Like the Tasmanian devil or Hillary Clinton's ability to tell the truth."

"I hate to break it to you, but the Tasmanian devil *is* real."

"Sure it is—a real cartoon. You ever watch *Finding Bigfoot*? You got about as much chance of finding a Tasmanian devil as they do of finding a Bigfoot. Ol' Bobo and the boys couldn't find wet in the water."

"You said hunting chupacabra hadn't been too productive 'lately.' You're implying you got one before."

"You calling me an impliar?"

"No, of course not...whatever that means."

"It means me and Manny bagged something a couple of months back, but it wasn't a chupacabra. It was a hairy Mexican dwarf with jaundice. I think he had cataracts, too. A truly horrible sight. He jumped out of a tumbleweed and scared the living crap out of us. I still have nightmares about it. I'll never go to the circus again."

"My God, you...you killed him?"

"Nah, my aim's about as good as Cheney's. I only shot him in the foot. We threw him in the four-wheeler and took him to border patrol. Course, being the good sport that I am, I didn't press charges."

"*You* didn't press charges?"

"You know, for trespassing. I got a soft spot for Mexicans, even ones that look like chupacabras. They're good ranchers. I just wished they'd stay on their own."

"That's mighty big of you."

"Yeah, I know. I'm just a big softie—unless you're a terrorist, that is. Heh. Then I bring down the hammer. BOOM goes the dynamite! Man, I miss those days."

"Be careful what you wish for, sir."

"I guess you're right. Last time I went to a Cowboys game, I got to watching them cheerleaders and started having what Jimmy Carter referred to as 'impure thoughts.' When they did the splits I wished I was...well...let's just say it involved an Astroturf mustache. Heh. Thank goodness, I learned from Bill Clinton not to think with my dub-chub. I mean, look at all the trouble it got *him* into. You'd think with all his charm he could manage his one-eyed rattler, but you'd be wrong. Sumbitch does more drillin' than a fleet of West Texas jack-up rigs. Heh. Well, I guess I better get going before the wife starts hollering for me. She's been cooking up armadillo stew all day. You can smell it halfway to Waco. You should try it. She serves it in the shell. I'll send you some."

"Please, sir, you don't need to go to the trouble. I'll take your word for it."

"No trouble at all, Stargazer. I'll freeze some and have Manny FedEx it. The meat can be a little tough and stringy, but I discovered you can use the cartilage strands to floss with. There might be a market for it in Tijuana. On second thought, you'd probly want a better tooth-to-mouth ratio. I'm gonna have to work on that one."

"You, uh...you do that, sir. Don't forget about Memorial Day."

"Are you kidding? You think I would forget about *Fishing on the Edge with Shagball and Tangles* on a super-secret nuclear fishing boat? Sheeit. I'm double-checking the arrangements as soon as I hang up."

"Something tells me you guys are going to hit it off."

"So why do I sense a little treputation in your voice?"

"Trepu—*what?* Come on, sir. I know you know that's not a word. Same with impliar and introperspective."

"That's intro*pro*spective. Everybody knows intro*per*-spective's not a word."

"Neither are words! And you know it. I've read the reports on how well you ran intelligence briefings and your amazing ability to quickly grasp the complex economic issues of the day. The fact is, you're a highly intelligent man, but you project an image to the contrary by your butchery of the English language. You don't have to keep up the charade of being just a good old boy from Texas with me. I know better. It's all an act." After several moments of uncomfortable silence, he added, "Sir? It is just an act, right?"

"Maybe it is, maybe it isn't. I'll never tell. It's called strategery."

"There you go again."

"Now you sound like Reagan."

"I'll take that as a yes."

"Take it however you want, just don't take it for granted."

"What's that supposed to mean?"

"It means if I'm such a smart guy, I'm not gonna do anything stupid. So why are you worried about me going fishing on the new DICK boat?"

"It's not the DICK boat I'm worried about. It's putting you together with Shagball and Tangles. They have a knack for getting into trouble."

"But they also have a knack for getting out of it, right? That's why you made them DICK agents."

"True, it's just...I don't know. I have a funny feeling maybe this isn't such a good idea."

"Let me tell you something, Stargazer, if I didn't do something every time somebody told me it wasn't such a good idea, I'd a never been president. In life you gotta roll the dice and play the cards you're dealt, otherwise, you're not in the game. If things don't work out, you roll 'em again and draw new cards. Live and learn and don't make the same mistake twice. That's all you can do."

"Did you just come up with that? That was great."

"Don't sound so surprised. I minored in psychosis."

"You don't have to tell me."

"Too late. Already did. Quit worrying, Stargazer. I got a funny feeling this is gonna be one memoriable Memorial Day. Heh. Talk to you later." *Click.*

Chapter 23

It took Pago over two hours to swim the three hundred yards back to the rig. Against incredible odds he battled through the current, multiple jellyfish stings, a bleeding head wound, and the onset of the bends. Completely exhausted, he clung to a barnacle-encrusted support strut and pondered his next move. His hands and legs were bleeding, thanks to the barnacles, and he again thought of the large hammerhead he'd encountered earlier in the day. Desperately wanting to climb out of the water but unable to find the strength, he yelled for help. Well, he tried to yell, but it didn't produce much sound. His voice was weak and his throat raspy with dehydration. There was no way someone working on the lower level some forty feet above him would hear his feeble cries over the steady hum of the drilling machinery. To make matters worse, his roommate, Arturo, was working the late shift and wouldn't notice he was gone. It wouldn't be until daybreak, when he was due to dive, that Luis would start looking and eventually report him missing. Somehow, someway, he had to hang on all night and pray that the sharks would stay away. So pray is what he did.

Seven levels above him, his attacker picked up his cell phone and dialed. Chaco was fast asleep on a dirty cot in the safe house when the ring of his phone woke him. He rubbed the sleep from his eyes and saw from the display that it was his cousin.

"Why are you calling so late?"

"Because I just finished my shift and thought you would want to know I took care of the problem."

"What problem?"

"The one we talked about earlier. The diver."

"He's dead?"

"Most certainly."

"Were you able to find out if he was working for somebody?"

"No. I planned to, but there was a fire drill, and I had to improvise."

"Were you able to make it look like an accident?"

"Not really, but chances are he will never be found. It's a deep ocean, and he's on the bottom of it."

"I see. And you're sure no one can connect you to his disappearance?"

"Yes. I slipped away during my shift, and there are no cameras on the lower level."

"Good. Our employers should be pleased."

"*Should* be pleased? They'd *better* be pleased. I have some leave time, and I'm taking it this weekend. I'll be on the first flight out tomorrow morning, and I'm coming to collect my pay. That's fifty thousand dollars, and I want it all."

Chaco crept over to the door and peered out at the darkened hallway before returning to sit on the edge of the bed. He lowered his voice. "That should be no problem. They seem to have an endless supply of money."

"Why are you whispering?"

"Because me and Jorge are trying to figure out where they keep it all. They must have it stashed somewhere. Once we find the mother lode, we will kill them and take it."

"Let me get my money first. Then I will help you look for the rest. I'll be there tomorrow." *Click.*

Down the hall, Noorbi, the security expert, removed his headphones and stopped the recording device.

"What did he say? What were they talking about?" Zahvi asked.

"I don't know. They were talking in Spanish, not Arabic."

"Chaco was whispering. He didn't want us to hear. He must be trying to double-cross us."

"Agreed."

"I am going to cut his head off and piss down his—" He stopped midsentence when footsteps could be heard coming down the hall, followed by a knock on the door.

"It's me, Chaco. I have some news."

"Come in," Zahvi said.

Chaco walked in and commented, "I thought you would be sleeping."

"We could say the same of you."

"I was until my cousin called. He said he took care of the diver who sabotaged the video on the *Dinero Majado.*"

"And how did he take care of him?"

"He didn't say. He only said he is on the bottom of the ocean and will never be found."

"Was he able to interrogate him first?"

"Unfortunately, no."

"Anything else?"

"Yes, he is coming here tomorrow and wants to be paid. You owe him twenty-five thousand for helping set up the room on the *Dinero Majado* and another twenty-five for taking care of the diver."

"You don't have to tell me what I agreed to. He will be paid in full. Has your brother-in-law finished painting the helicopter to match the picture we provided?"

"He said it should be finished tomorrow...Sunday at the latest."

"*Sunday?* It better be done by Sunday. Monday we leave in it."

"Are you taking the woman and child?"

"No. You can do what you want with them once we're gone. Consider it a tip."

"Muchos gracias." Chaco grinned and winked at him. "We will put them to good use."

"I don't care what you put them to. Just make sure the helicopter is painted properly and the fuel tanks are filled."

"There is a truck coming to fill the tanks tomorrow." He looked at the duffel bag on the floor that Zahvi carried the cash in and rubbed his index finger and thumb together. "I need some money to pay them."

"How much?"

"El Primo said it needed about five thousand dollars' worth of fuel. The delivery charge is five hundred dollars so you better give me six to be safe."

Zahvi knelt down and pulled two stacks of hundred-dollar bills out of the duffel. He handed one to Chaco. "Here's five thousand." He peeled off ten more hundreds from the other stack and added, "That makes six."

Chaco stuffed the money in his pockets and announced he was going back to bed. As the sound of his footsteps faded down the hall, Zahvi turned to his security expert.

"What do you think?"

"I think he looks at the money the way he looks at the little girl."

"What about the diver? You think his cousin really killed him?"

"I don't know. You said you heard him whispering, so he's hiding something. I'll anonymously post the audio file to an online chat room and get it translated. We'll know what was said by morning."

"Good. The sooner the better. We can't let anybody get in the way of our mission. It is so close I can taste it…and I taste blood."

Chapter 24

Oskar Medina, the newly honored operations installation manager (OIM), was finishing breakfast when he spotted one of his assistants hustling his way.

The assistant abruptly stopped in front of his table and announced the reason for the concerned look on his face. "Sir, it looks like we have a problem."

Oskar pushed his plate away and gave him his full attention. "What would that be?"

"It seems the diver, Pago, is missing."

"*Missing?* What do you mean *missing?* Luis told me he returned from his fishing trip late yesterday and would be diving this morning."

"I confirmed he returned, but he has not been seen since dinner last night."

"Have you talked to his roommate?"

"Yes, he worked the late shift and said when he got back to the room this morning Pago was gone. He thought he was diving."

"By the look on your face, I assume you have already conducted a preliminary search."

"I have, and he is nowhere to be found."

"Shit!" Oskar stood up and pulled out his radio. "You know the drill. We shut everything down and assemble all hands on the main deck to organize a search. As soon as I'm done talking to the operations center, sound the alarm and spread the word."

"Yes, sir."

Less than five minutes later, the hundred-man crew was gathered on the main deck 140 feet above the water. Only a handful of workers who held critical data-monitoring positions were exempt from the search. With all the drilling machinery and peripheral equipment shut down, the *Taladro Grande* was eerily quiet.

Oskar spoke to the crew through a bullhorn. "As many of you probably know by now, Pago, the diver, has gone missing. He was last seen during dinner last night. If anybody has any information on his whereabouts, please come forward now." As he expected, nobody came forward.

"All right, this is why we practice for such a situation. I want every nook and cranny on every level checked. Assemble into your assigned teams and start searching for Pago. Let's find him. NOW!"

The sound of alarm bells roused Pago from his semiconscious state for the third time since he had reached the relative safety of the support strut he clung to. The first time happened in the middle of the night when he felt something bump his leg. The fear provided a jolt of adrenaline that gave him just enough energy to climb up out of the water despite his hands and feet being sliced by the barnacles. The second time was when he heard the sound of a helicopter, maybe an hour earlier. Now, he was confident the alarm bells signaled that he had been identified as missing. His rescue would hopefully be imminent. It needed to be. What little strength he had was rapidly waning. He simply couldn't hold on much longer. Decompression sickness (the bends), caused by the release of nitrogen bubbles into his bloodstream, resulted in fatigue and severe pain in his elbows and shoulders. On top of that, his head throbbed, and his chest and extremities burned from jellyfish stings. And he itched. He was a bleeding, itchy, aching, dehydrated mess, but he was alive. A few minutes later he heard his name being called and managed to squeak out a feeble, "Help!"

He heard his name called louder and looked up to see a face looking down at him over the railing only thirty feet above.

"Here! I'm here!" He risked a wave of the hand and almost lost his grip on the strut entirely.

"Hang on, Pago! We're coming for you!"

He heard the sound of the lift motor as the skiff was lowered into the water. Within minutes it was positioned under him, and he collapsed after being helped aboard.

After being rushed to the infirmary, he was given some intravenous fluids and a sedative before the doctor tended to his wounds. Two hours later he awoke to find the big boss, Oskar, and one of his assistants at his side. He tried to shake the fog from his brain, but it was too painful, and he winced.

"Take it easy," Oskar said. "You look like you've been through hell and back."

"W-water," was all he could manage. He signaled for something to drink. The assistant quickly handed him a glass of water, and he tried to chug it down, but his chest hurt too much, and he gagged.

"I said take it easy," Oskar said. "There's plenty to drink. Sip slowly. Here, use this straw." He handed him a straw from the bedside table, and Pago steadily drained the glass. The assistant refilled it, and the hoarseness in Pago's voice began to clear.

"Oh that's good…so good, thanks."

"Do you feel well enough to talk?" asked Oskar.

Pago nodded as he sucked more water through the straw.

"Good. Then maybe you should start by telling me what happened."

The doctor came back in the room and took the water away from Pago with an admonishment.

"That's enough. We gave you three liters through the IV."

"I think I need three more. My joints are killing me. I'm pretty sure I have the bends."

"You were diving? Nobody said you were diving."

Pago looked at Oskar. "I'd like to talk to you in private."

"Why? What's this about?"

"Please."

Oskar told his assistant to wait outside, and Pago pointed at the doctor. "Him too."

The doctor protested but Oskar pulled rank, and the doctor left the room, frustrated.

"So what's this about? What happened to you?"

"Somebody tried to kill me."

"WHAT?! What are you talking about? What happened?"

Pago recounted the entire ordeal.

Oskar was stunned. "It's a miracle you survived. I can't believe someone did this to you."

"Believe it. They knocked me out, tied me up with weight belts, and threw me overboard. If I hadn't had an emergency oxygen bottle hidden in the webbing of one of the belts, I wouldn't be here."

"And you didn't get a look at the person responsible?"

"No. It was dark, and they blindsided me."

"But who would do this? Do you have any idea?"

"No."

"Have you had any disagreements with anyone on the rig?"

"Sure, but none that would make someone to want to kill me."

"This is bad, very bad."

"Aghhh!" Pago cried out in pain.

"You want me to call the doctor back?"

"No. I mean, yes, but first I need your help."

"Of course. Anything."

"I have the bends."

"The what?"

"Decompression sickness. By the time I cut the weight belts off, I'm guessing I was at least a hundred and fifty feet deep, maybe even two hundred. When the air in my emergency bottle ran out I had to get to the surface as quickly as possible. I had no choice. I'm not worried about the cuts and bruises and jellyfish stings…but to treat the bends I need to go into the hyperbaric chamber. Probably for the next forty-eight hours."

"You can thank the new regulations that require us to have one on board. I'll instruct the doctor to place you in the chamber for as long as you need and station a member of the security team outside. Is that it?"

"No. Somebody tried to kill me. I want to know why and maybe return the favor. I'd like you to spread word that I've been placed in the hyperbaric chamber with decompression sickness and serious injuries. That I have no recollection of what happened, but the doctor suspects I had a seizure and fell overboard. Maybe the wannabe killer will believe I'm vulnerable and try to finish the job."

"Okay, but I insist on a guard. I don't want anybody getting killed on my rig, be it by an accident or otherwise."

"It has to be someone undercover then. A stationed guard would be a tip-off that something else happened."

"I can do that."

"Thanks."

"It's the least I can do. I don't know what else to say other than I'm sorry for what happened, and we'll try to find who did this and make sure they are punished."

"I'd like the punishing part left up to me."

"Not on the rig, Pago. I don't want to tarnish my perfect safety record." Oskar winked.

Pago started to laugh, but it hurt too much.

"Should I call for the doctor now?"

"Yes, please."

Oskar pulled out his radio and was about to speak when Pago stopped him.

"Wait!"

"What? What is it?"

"It probably doesn't have anything to do with what happened, but my laptop was stolen from my room yesterday."

"*Stolen?* I didn't hear about that. Why didn't you report it?"

"I did."

"To who?"

"I reported it to Luis' assistant Roberto last night after I discovered it was gone."

"It should have been reported to me. I'll look into it."

"Thanks."

Oskar summoned the doctor and his assistant and informed them that Pago had no recollection of how he ended up in the water and suggested he had a seizure and fell overboard. Pago backed up the story by saying he had a seizure some years ago and that it must have been what happened. As the doctor wheeled Pago down the corridor to the hyperbaric chamber, Oskar turned to his assistant and said, "Get me Luis."

"Luis?"

"Yes, Luis. The OTL."

"He's not here, sir."

"What do you mean?"

"He has the weekend off. He took the early flight back to the mainland with some other crew members."

"What's wrong with this picture? I'm working, and he's off. That son of a bitch is never here when I need him."

Chapter 25

Zahvi slammed his fist down next to the computer screen. "I knew it!" He had just read the translation of the conversation between Chaco and his cousin on the *Taladro Grande.*

"I told you," Noorbi said. "He lusts for money the way he does for little girls."

"I suspected from the start they might kill us if they knew where we hid the money and weapons. Now we know it to be true. It was a good idea to stash them under the floorboards of the shed in back. It was also a good idea to monitor their conversations."

"That's why I am in charge of security. At least we know that the diver has been taken care of and the mission hasn't been compromised."

"Yes, that is the most important thing...praise Allah." Zahvi put his hand on his shoulder. "Your skills are second to none, my friend. I was concerned you might have trouble hacking into the helicopter-service computers."

"I told you it would be no problem. The only problem we have at the moment is how to deal with the Mexicans."

Zahvi let out a sinister chuckle. "You have your field of expertise and I have mine. *We* don't have a problem. *They* have a problem...a fatal one."

Suddenly, a high-pitched scream came from down the hall and the two of them dashed toward the source. In the lead, Zahvi flung open the door to the room where the hostages were held. Their colleague, Kahlullah, stood wide-eyed as he zipped up his pants.

"What's going on here?!" Zahvi demanded.

"I was, I was just...I thought—"

"You idiot!" Zahvi backhanded him across the face so hard he fell over a chair.

The little girl was lying on the bed on her stomach. Her skirt was pulled up, and she was sobbing uncontrollably and babbling in Spanish. He mother lay next to her looking horrified, bound and gagged by duct tape.

"I said nobody was to touch the hostages until—"

"I didn't touch her. I swear. She started screaming and—"

"Shut up." Zahvi could see that the girl's panties hadn't been pulled down yet and that the piece of duct tape covering her mouth had come unstuck.

Jorge appeared at the door and asked, "What's going on?"

"There was a misunderstanding. Kahlullah tried to get friendly with the girl. Tell them it won't happen again." As Jorge rattled off some Spanish, Zahvi ordered Kahlullah to get some food and water for the captives. As he headed to the kitchen, Zahvi turned to Jorge.

"Where's Chaco?"

"He went to pick up his cousin and the flight suits you had made."

"Good. Untie the mother so she can tend to the girl. Tell them to keep quiet. Tell them there is some food and water coming and in a couple of days they will be freed," he lied.

Ten miles away at the Matador hotel, el Primo lay sweating and hungover on top of the sheets of his filthy bed. He suddenly felt nauseated and stumbled into the bathroom, dropping to his knees. One look at the excrement- and rust-stained toilet bowl was all it took for him to toss his cookies. He heaved and heaved until there was nothing left, and then he dry heaved until his stomach cramped and tears leaked from his bloodshot eyes. He used the sink for leverage to stand. After splashing some water that smelled like rotten eggs on his face, he fought back another round of dry heaves. He looked at his reflection in the medicine cabinet mirror. The years had not been kind. He was only fifty-nine, but his gaunt, scruffy face and hollow eyes made him look like the geriatric, banjo player from *Deliverance,* with a meth addiction. He was thinking how fucked up it was to end up in such a hellhole looking the way he did when his cell phone rang. He stumbled into the bedroom and snatched his phone off the nightstand as he collapsed on the bed.

"Get me the fuck out of here," he answered.

"Where have you been? Why haven't you called?"

"I had to sort some things out."

"You sound like shit."

"I look like shit, too. It helps me blend into this third world fuck hole."

"You were on a bender…weren't you?"

"You're damn right I was. I almost bought the farm in an old Helix."

"A Helix?"

"It's a Russian chopper…a military job."

"I didn't know you could fly a helicopter."

"El Primo can fly anything."

"Right. How could I forget. So what was the problem?"

"Aside from the Helix being a relic, I hadn't flown a chopper since Christ was a kid. I turned a cactus into porcupine sushi and wet my fucking pants like a kindergartner."

"You said the Helix is a military job. Is it armed?"

"No, it's been stripped out. It's strictly for transport. Three rows of seats and cargo space in back."

"So, who or what are you supposed to move? And where?"

"I got no fucking idea."

"Are you kidding?"

"No, but maybe I'll find out Monday. I'm supposed to meet whoever the Mexicans are working for and take them on a test run."

"This Monday?"

"Yeah."

"That's Memorial Day."

"It is? No shit. Well that settles it, then. I'm bailing."

"What are you talking about?"

"It's a national holiday to honor veterans, and I'm a veteran. I never work on Memorial Day. I'm out."

"First of all, it's not a national holiday in Mexico. Second, it's for honoring deceased veterans, not living ones who were dishonorably discharged. Third, you're working for Homeland Security now, and we don't take holidays."

"Not by choice."

"Sure it is. You're the one who chose a career in drug smuggling and topped it off by getting charged with multiple violations of maritime law, including hijacking, kidnapping, attempted murder—"

"Hey, I don't need a guided trip down memory lane to remember what I allegedly did."

"Maybe not, but you seem to need one to remember what you're *going to do* because if you back out, it's straight to the federal pen for the rest of your sorry life."

"What do you mean *life?* I had it pled down to twenty years before I took this fucked-up deal."

"You don't think twenty years is a life sentence? Have you looked in a mirror lately?"

"Fuck you."

"Look, I don't mean to be a dick, but this is important. We're 99 percent sure ISIS is working with a Mexican cartel—maybe more than one. These guys who hired you work for the Sinaloas, so maybe they're the ones."

"They're definitely working for somebody. They don't seem to know shit about what I'm supposed to do other than fly some fucking death trap they scrounged up from God knows where."

"It makes sense they wouldn't know anything because the chatter we're hearing is ISIS is planning something big. They wouldn't risk a leak. You said it's a transport chopper, so maybe they're planning on flying a team of terrorists over the border for an attack somewhere in Texas. Or maybe they're bringing in a dirty nuke. Maybe both. We just don't know. That's why it's critical you stay in the loop. You're the only one we have on the inside down there."

"Is that right? Well, guess what. I'd say it's time to play Let's Make a Deal again."

"What the hell are you talking about? You already made a deal."

"Not to fly around a bunch of head-chopping, dirty-nuke-carrying goat humpers in a thirty-year-old, piece-of-shit Russian helicopter!" There was an extended silence on the line. "You still there?"

"I'm listening."

"Good. 'Cause I'm telling you if I manage to help stop whatever it is they're planning, I'm never coming back to this godforsaken place...assuming I survive."

"I thought you liked it down there."

"*Like it?* Are you out of your fucking mind? The food is shit, it smells like shit, it's hotter than shit, and the water *gives* you the shits. I've lost at least ten pounds. It's a fucking parasitical paradise is what it is. Even the goddamn tequila has worms. I haven't shaved in two months because I'm worried if I nick myself, I'll get that flesh-eating disease. It itches, man. It itches *so* fucking bad."

"I'll see what I can do."

"That's not good enough. If you'd ever been here you'd know what I'm talking about. This place is like a postapocalyptic Miami, only without as many spics. I gotta get outta here, man. I can't take it anymore. I swear to God, I'm gonna blow my fucking brains out if one of these taco-truck gangsters doesn't do it first."

"All right, already. See this job through, and we'll send you somewhere else."

"You swear? You better not be fucking with me."

"I said it's a deal."

"Thank you, sweet Jesus. Right now I'd crawl a hundred miles over broken beer bottles and hot coals just to suck—"

"Okay. I get it. Call me as soon you find out more."

Click.

Chapter 26

Chaco and his cousin arrived back at the safe house in the late afternoon. After identifying themselves at the door they were let in by Kahlulla, who led them into the living room and pointed at the couch. "Wait here."

They did as told and watched Kahlulla disappear down the hall. He peeked into a doorway and said something. Moments later Zahvi and Noorbi exited the room. Noorbi went into the room where the hostages were held and relieved Jorge, who followed Kahlulla and Zahvi back to the living room. Jorge plopped his considerable bulk down on the couch, and Zahvi placed the duffel bag he was carrying on the dining-room table.

Zahvi addressed Chaco. "While I talk to your cousin I want you to make a couple of calls. First call your brother-in-law and see how the paint job is coming. Tell him we will be arriving in the van at eleven Monday morning. He should be ready to open the overhead door so we can drive inside. Tell him there will be no more communication of any kind until we arrive."

"Why no—"

"Just do it."

"What about the money?"

"He will be paid in full when we arrive, plus a bonus if the paint job looks good."

"Roberto will be pleased. He is an excellent—"

"Then call the pilot. Tell him we will be picking him up in the van at ten thirty. Tell him to be ready and that there will be no more communication until we pick him up."

"He will also want his money."

"And he'll get it…on Monday."

"You'd better not be putting me off until Monday, too," said Chaco's cousin.

"Not at all. I'm taking care of you as soon as you answer a few questions. In fact, I'm going to take care of all three of you."

"Really?" said Jorge.

"You are paying us, too?" asked Chaco.

"After you make the calls, I will take care of you."

"You heard what he said," said the cousin. "Make the calls already. I have plans."

Chaco got up and pulled out his cell as he walked into the kitchen.

"So what do you want to know?" asked the cousin. "You wanted the diver dead, and I killed him."

"How did you kill him?"

"Didn't Chaco tell you?"

"I want to hear it from you."

"I split his head open with a pipe and threw him overboard."

"How do you know he's dead?"

"Because I tied thirty pounds of weights around his waist before I threw him over, and he was unconscious."

"Why didn't you make *sure* he was dead?"

"I planned to slit his throat, but like I told Chaco, a fire alarm went off. If I slit his throat there would have been blood everywhere, and I wouldn't have time to clean up. Trust me, he's dead. He either drowned or the sharks got him. They'll never find a trace of him."

"I was hoping you would have a chance to interrogate him."

"Hey, it's an active oil rig with a lot of people aboard. It's not like there's an interrogation room like the one set up on the *Dinero Majado.*"

"Yes, about that. Don't you find it odd that the diver would fail to report what he saw if he stumbled on it by accident?"

"Not really. Everybody knows it's a restricted area. If you get caught on it, you'd probably get fired."

"What about his computer?"

"That went overboard too."

Chaco walked back in the room and held out his phone for Zahvi to see. "It's done," he announced, before joining Jorge and his cousin on the couch.

"You talked to both of them?"

"Yes, they will be ready on Monday."

"And they understand there will be no more communication until then?"

"Yes."

"Good. I don't want anything or anybody to interfere with our plans."

"So I can get paid now?" the cousin asked.

Zahvi held up his index finger, displaying a long gnarled nail. "One more thing about the computer. You're absolutely sure there was nothing on it regarding what the diver saw on\ the *Dinero Majado?*"

"Yes. His last e-mail was talking about hunting for treasure somewhere in the Caribbean."

"Where in the Caribbean?" Chaco asked.

"I can't remember."

"You like hunting for treasure, don't you, Chaco." Zahvi smiled.

"Sure, I like treasure. Who doesn't?" He laughed.

"How about you, Jorge? You like treasure?"

"Sí." Jorge nodded with a grin.

Zahvi pointed at the cousin. "And I'll bet you do, too. I bet if Chaco told you he was hot on the trail of some treasure, you'd be right there to help him find it."

"I don't know what you are talking about. Right now I only care about getting paid."

"Yes, of course. Fifty thousand, right? No problem." Zahvi reached in the duffel bag. As he started counting out stacks of hundred bills on the table, Chaco and his cousin shared sideways glances. The three Mexicans sat transfixed as they watched him pull out stack after stack.

Chaco licked his lips. "I hope there's enough in there for me and Jorge."

"Don't worry, there's plenty for you. In fact, here it is." He pulled out a small Uzi with a suppressor on the muzzle and pointed it at him. Chaco threw his hands in the air, and his cousin and Jorge scooched to either side of the couch. Zahvi waved the Uzi side to side, and there were quickly six arms in the air.

"I don't know what Chaco did," the cousin said, "but—"

"Shut up."

"But I did everything you—" Zahvi squeezed the trigger, and the Uzi made a soft spitting sound as a single nine-millimeter bullet smashed between his eyes. The cousin slumped into the cushion, and as blood oozed from the bullet hole, he squeezed the trigger again and shot him through the heart.

Panicking now, Chaco said, "Why? Why are you doing this? He did everything you asked."

"Not really. He didn't shut up."

"He didn't—*what?* Are you crazy?"

"No, crazy is what I would call someone trying to double-cross me. That would be you and your friends. You planned on stealing our money and weapons and then killing us."

Jorge mumbled something in Spanish. Zahvi pivoted and squeezed the trigger long enough to riddle the fat man's torso with a dozen rounds. Chaco reached for the weapon tucked under his poncho and was met with a similar barrage of bullets. Zahvi added a couple more head shots to each of the three amigos before turning to Kahlulla, who silently watched the whole thing.

"There's a shovel in the garage. As soon as it gets dark, start digging."

Chapter 27

We ran the *LD3* hard all day Saturday and Sunday to reach the surrounding waters of the *Bluewater* by Memorial Day. By running hard, I mean averaging fifty knots in three- to four-foot seas from sunup to sundown. Rafe and I manned the helm in shifts, relieving each other every couple of hours during the day. At night the boat ran at ten knots on autopilot, utilizing the radar's collision-avoidance system. The alarms went off one time—when we came within a half mile of a passing freighter—but other than that, the gulf crossing was uneventful. When we were within ten miles of the *Bluewater* I throttled down, and we glided to a near stop. The lack of engine noise was astonishing and took some getting used to.

Rafe called up from the interior stairway that led to the bridge. "What's going on?"

"We're only ten miles out," Tangles answered.

Rafe came up the stairs to the bridge and noted the sea conditions. "Looks like it settled down." He was right. Three- to four-foot seas had become one to two feet, and it was an absolutely beautiful morning.

"We're early, aren't we?" I asked.

Tangles sniffed the air and rubbed his hands together. "I think we should do some fishing. It smells fishy."

"It looks fishy too," I added. "Look at that weed line ahead." I pointed at the weed line, and Rafe looked at his watch.

"It's only ten o'clock. Let me call the operations manager on the *Bluewater* and see if the president's there yet—see what he wants to do." He pulled out his cell and called the number he had been given. That was the other great thing about the *LD3*: thanks to the powerful satellite on the top of the bridge, we could make and take calls virtually anywhere. Rafe disappeared down the stairs, and Holly came up.

"What's going on? Who's Rafe talking to?"

"We're only ten miles from the *Bluewater*," I answered. "Rafe's calling to see if Dubya's there yet."

"I can't believe we're actually going to meet him," Tangles said.

"Really?" Holly said. "I can't believe he's a fan of the show."

"Now come on, Holl," I replied. "That's cold."

"I'm just kidding." She gave me a kiss on the cheek. "You do have your niche fans. After all, he *is* retired."

"*Retired?* What does that have to do with anything?"

"What time is the show on?"

"On what day?"

"Any day."

"The last time I saw it was at IHOP on a Friday morning at maybe four thirty or five o'clock. I remember because I took a waitress from the Old Key Lime House to Sunfest to see Sammy Haggar, and that's where we ended up," Tangles said.

"At five in the morning?" Holly asked. "What were you—forget it, I don't want to know."

"Sure you do. Sammy was so awesome my date was like a hot glob of hormonal puddy in my hands. A couple of hours of the horizontal cha-cha works up quite the—"

Holly stuck a finger in each ear. "La-la-la-la, I'm not listening to you."

"I told you we should have gone to see Sammy Haggar," I lamented.

She unplugged her ears. "I'm not listening to you either."

"So what's your point about what time the show airs?"

"Simple. Retirees go to bed early and get up early. That's who probably watches the show—them and night-crawling, alcoholic little perverts."

"Hey, I am *not* an alcoholic," Tangles argued. "I merely enjoy celebrating life with the occasional adult beverage. You know, socially."

"Keep telling your liver that…or whatever's left of it."

"Aren't you being a little bit of a Betty Buzzkill?" I interjected.

"What's the matter? Did that hit a little too close to home?"

"My home, like my liver, is twice as big as his. I can handle a couple of drinks now and then."

"Is that what you're calling it?" She laughed.

"Yes. And as a matter of fact I *could* go for a beer right now."

"I'll take one then," said Tangles. We fist-bumped, and Holly shook her head.

"You guys are getting worse, if that's possible. I think you need a bro intervention."

"I couldn't agree more," Rafe said as he returned to the bridge. "But it'll have to wait. It's time to pick up the prez."

"Now?" said Holly. "Right now?"

"Yes, ma'am."

"Oh my God. I gotta get ready. I can't meet him looking like this."

As Holly darted down the stairs, Tangles yelled, "I think you look great!"

I scowled at him and he held his palms out. "What. It's true. She looks great."

"I know she looks great. She *always* looks great. You don't have to be such a kiss ass."

"I wasn't kissing ass. I only kiss ass when I have a chance of getting some. She's out of my league and frankly, I think she's out of yours, too. I still haven't figured it out."

"That makes two of us," Rafe said.

"Now wait just a goddamn second. I'm the host of a world-class fishing show and a secret agent with a nuclear boat. Did you ever think maybe *I'm* out of *her* league?" Tangles and Rafe erupted with laughter. I knew it was a stretch but wasn't about to admit she had me outclassed. "You guys suck," was all I could muster.

"Oh, man, that was funny. I really hope you don't believe that," Rafe said.

"He might," Tangles said. "He still believes Tiger Woods is gonna make a comeback."

"Don't count him out, especially if he were to hire me as his life coach and Svengali."

"Do me a favor," Rafe said. "Don't be talking crazy when the president's on board. I don't want him to think we have a nut job running the boat."

"I'm serious. With a little hypnosis, acupuncture, and high-grade marijuana—medicinal, of course, I could straighten him right out. He'd win twenty majors no problem. Nicklaus would cry like a baby."

"I told you. He's delusional." Tangles said.

"I'm gonna give you the benefit of the doubt and assume you're kidding," said Rafe. "But if you're not, keep your delusions under wraps while the president's on board."

"All right. So what's the plan?"

"Bring us about a quarter mile away, and we'll deploy the skiff. I'll pick him up, and we'll take him fishing for a couple of hours."

"Just a couple?"

"He needs to be back by one thirty for a ceremony and lunch with the crew."

"Let's get moving, then. Tangles, get the gear out and start rigging some baits."

"You got it, Shag." Tangles hustled down the stairs, and I pushed the throttles forward. With a soft *whoosh* the boat silently accelerated toward the *Bluewater*.

"Before we return on the skiff," Rafe said, "turn on the engine noise."

"Why?"

"The president has to bring a Secret Service agent with him, and I don't want the agent asking questions about why it's so quiet."

"But the president knows, right?"

"Oh, yeah. He knows more than you think he knows."

"Meaning?"

"Meaning the boss said, 'Don't let him fool you.'"

"Why would he wanna fool me? I don't even know him."

"Just don't worry about it, okay? I'm going below to let Tangles and Holly know about the agent."

Left alone on the bridge, I picked up the mic for the intercom system and called the forward berth that Holly and I shared.

"Holly, you there?"

"I'm here, what's up?"

"I just wanted to tell you that Tangles was right. You look great. You *always* look great."

"I'm not bringing you a beer. We're about to meet the president, and it's not even noon yet."

"I don't need you to bring me a beer. There's a fully stocked fridge up here, remember?"

"So what do you want then?"

"Wow, that hurts. I just wanted you to know I appreciate you, and I'm proud of you." After several seconds of radio silence, I said, "Holly?"

"I don't know what to say. Do you...do you really mean that?"

"Of course I do. I'm the luckiest guy on earth to be with you. I just wanted you to know—you know, if I haven't told you lately."

"Lately? You've *never* told me that. But thanks, that really means a lot. I feel lucky to be with you, too. Sometimes you surprise me, Kit Jansen."

"Don't be surprised if we have an epic fishing trip. This should be fun. See you in a few."

"Love you."

"Ditto. Over and out." *Click.*

I thought about what Rafe said. *Don't let him fool you. Puh-leez.* Shagball was nobody's fool.

Chapter 28

El Primo heard a horn beeping and pushed the tattered curtains aside to see a dirty white van parked in front of the hotel. He grabbed his duffel bag and stood in the doorway to survey the decrepit room one final time. As if on cue, a large cockroach scurried out from under the bed into the bathroom. *What a shithole.* He looked both ways to make sure the coast was clear before clearing his nose and letting loose with a giant loogie. It arched across the room and landed with a splat on the control panel of the malfunctioning air conditioner unit. When he reached the lobby he walked up to the front desk. The fat slob who said he was the manager was fast asleep in a chair with his feet propped up and a sombrero pulled over his eyes. There was a bell on the counter, and el Primo slapped it several times.

The manager almost fell out of his chair and pushed the sombrero up to see who was causing such a racket. "Why did you wake me? You already checked out."

"I just wanted to let you know the air conditioner finally started working. I got it cranked down low, but I forgot to turn it off."

"I'll take care of it. No problemo."

"Good."

As he crossed the lobby toward the exit the van's horn blared again, and the manager said, "Adios, amigo. Come back and see us again sometime."

He turned at the door and smiled. "This shithole has a better chance of getting on the cover of *Travel & Leisure.*"

Not exactly sure what he meant, the manager gave him a thumbs-up and winked. *Fucking jerk-off.*

El Primo pushed open the door, and the sweltering heat hit him in the face like a sauna towel. He put his sunglasses on and walked up to the van.

The passenger door swung open and a stranger stepped out. "You are the pilot? The one called el Primo?"

"Yeah, that's right." He could immediately tell the guy wasn't Mexican. He spoke with an odd accent. The stranger slid open the panel door and told him to get in. He saw an unfamiliar face sitting on the bench seat and another behind the wheel, and he hesitated. "Where's Jake and the Fatman?"

"Who?"

"Chaco and Jorge. Where are they?"

"They are meeting us. Get in." The rear bench seats had been removed and the space was filled with crates, so the only place to sit was next to the guy in front of him. He set his duffel on one of the crates and reluctantly slid in next to him. The one doing the talking climbed in next and slid the panel door shut. Instead of taking the passenger seat, however, he pushed his way in next to him on the bench seat, pinning him in.

"This is a little cozy, isn't it?" he complained. "Why don't you sit in the passenger's seat?"

"I am comfortable."

"Yeah? Well I'm a pilot, not a fucking sardine. If you don't want to sit in the passenger's seat, fine, but I do." He tried to get up, but the one doing the talking stuck his arm out, and the guy on his left pulled him back.

"Okay, I get it," he said. He looked at the one calling the shots. "This is ridiculous. You're practically sitting in my lap. How about a little bathhouse etiquette? Before I start cornholing you, we oughta get acquainted." He winked. "You gotta name?"

"You don't need to know. I am nameless to you."

"Anonymous sex—I like it. Hope your friends do too."

"It is a short ride. We will be there soon."

"Not soon enough, No-Name. It's hot in here. Tell the driver to turn the fucking air down already. That shitbox I was staying in is hotter than a Portuguese whorehouse."

No-Name said something, and the driver fiddled with the controls. After a few seconds the driver held his hand in front of a vent. Then he shook his head and shrugged.

"Super," said el Primo. "So, where are we going?"

"We are going to the auto yard," No-Name (Zahvi) replied.

"I figured that. What I meant was, where am I flying to?"

"You will know when we get there."

"No shit, Sherlock. I wanna know now."

"Chaco said you were a smartass. He was right." Zahvi gave him a chilling stare with his beady black eyes, and el Primo squirmed. He looked at the guy sitting on his left and was met with another icy stare.

"Who, uh, who exactly *are* you guys?"

"No more talking until we reach the auto yard."

El Primo didn't push it, and as they drove the rest of the way, he began forming his own conclusions. No-Name had a neatly trimmed goatee and his face was red and chafed like he just shaved. As he looked closer, he noticed several tiny pieces of tissue stuck on his face. He *had* just shaved. The guy on his left had a mustache and also had a couple of pieces of bloody tissue stuck on his neck. The driver was a stocky bastard with a bushy black beard and unibrow. *Hmmm.*

"What are you looking at?" asked Zahvi.

"Huh? What? I was just, you know…looking around. What's in the crates?"

"I said no more talking."

"Right. Got it."

When they reached Roberto's Reparacion Automatica, the driver backed up to the overhead door and sat on the horn. A few moments later the door trundled open, and they pulled in. They piled out of the van and Roberto looked confused. He held out a pair of open hands and asked, "Donde es Chaco?"

Zahvi turned to el Primo. "I heard you speak some Spanish."

"Sí." He nodded, happy that he knew what *donde* meant. "He wants to know where Chaco is."

"Tell him Chaco is on the way."

"Sure, okay." He looked at Roberto and said, "Chaco, uh…Chaco soon come."

"No comprendo."

"Oh, crap. Let's see. Wait, I got it." He held his fists out and moved his arms up and down like he was holding an imaginary steering wheel. "Chaco el drive-o en automobilio…Pronto. Chaco come el pronto."

Roberto pointed a finger at the floor. "Aqui?"

"A key? How would I know? He's got one if you gave him one. I'm not a fuckin' mind reader. El Primo no reado el mindo."

Roberto shook his head and dismissed the gibberish with a wave. Then he turned to Zahvi and rubbed his finger and thumb together, the international sign for show me the money.

"Tell him I want to see the helicopter first," Zahvi said to el Primo.

"Right. Uh, no dinero until we see el helicoptero." He pointed two fingers at his eyes and then spun his index finger around to emulate a helicopter rotor. Amazingly, Roberto understood and signaled for them to follow him out back. Zahvi told the other two to stay with the van and followed el Primo, who trailed Roberto.

As soon as el Primo saw the chopper he couldn't believe his eyes and let out a low whistle. It was freshly painted jet-black with neon green racing stripes and a logo that read RIG HOPPERS.

"Muy hermosa, no?" Roberto smiled.

El Primo wasn't sure what hermosa meant, but judging by the proud smile on Roberto's face, he took a stab.

"Sí. Es muy hermosa. Muy, muy hermosa. Muy bueno."

Zahvi walked around the chopper and nodded in approval. "Ask him if it's all fueled up."

"Oh, boy. Uh…es el helicoptero full of, uh, gasolino?"

"Gasolina? Sí, se alimento hasta."

"What does that mean? See you at the alimento? I don't know what that is but I'm pretty fucking sure I don't wanna go there. No comprendo, amigo."

"Mucho gasolina." Roberto gave them the okay sign and winked.

"That's good," Zahvi said. "Tell him everything looks good. He will be well rewarded."

El Primo shot Roberto a thumbs-up and then rubbed his finger and thumb together. "Mucho dinero por Roberto."

Roberto rubbed his hands together and smiled. "Muchas gracias."

"No problemo. You deservo. El whirlybird es muy hermosa." He winked.

They headed back into the garage. Noorbi and Kahlulla were unloading the crates from the back of the van. Zahvi reached under the bench seat and pulled out a bag. He opened it and presented a pair of flight suits that were matched to the colors of the chopper, complete with a Rig Hoppers logo on the sleeve. He handed one to El Primo, and said,

"Put this on after you shave."

"*Shave?* Nobody said I had to shave."

"You need to look like a pilot someone would employ."

"This may come as a shock, but I don't have a razor on me."

Zahvi reached in the glove box and pulled out a comb, a pair of scissors, a disposable Bic razor, and a can of shaving cream. He handed them over. "Here."

El Primo examined the razor, which had damp dark curly hair stuck between the blades. "You want me to use *this?*"

"It worked for me."

"That's what I was afraid of."

"Get cleaned up and put the suit on while I take care of Roberto."

El Primo knew where the bathroom was from his previous trip, and as soon as he closed the bathroom door behind him, Zahvi signaled to Roberto. He opened the rear doors to the van. There was a large canvas bag sitting behind the crates. He unzipped it so Roberto could see it was crammed full of stacks of one-hundred-dollar bills. Roberto mumbled something, and his eyes bulged out. He had never seen so much money in his life. *Where the hell were Chaco and Jorge?* He looked at the front door and prayed they would come storming through it with guns blazing. There was plenty of money to go around once they killed the three terroristas and the joke of a pilot called el Primo.

Zahvi watched his eyes go to the door and said, "Que pasa?"

"Huh?"

"You expecting company?"

"No comprendo."

"You lie." He nodded at Kahlulla who had slipped behind Roberto with a length of wire in his hands. He deftly slipped it over Roberto's head and cinched it tight around his throat. There was barely a gasp, and he proceeded to strangle him to the point of near decapitation.

As Kahlulla and Noorbi dragged Roberto's body away, Zahvi looked inside el Primo's duffel bag. He found a .45-caliber pistol, some clothes, a few toiletries, a big bottle of water, and a tattered copy of *JUGGS* magazine. There was no cell phone. He silently cursed himself for failing to secure it and immediately headed to the bathroom.

Inside the bathroom, el Primo was sitting on the toilet and whispering into the phone. "One's got a beard like Paul Bunyan that's blacker than midnight in Detroit, and another has a mustache like a Pakistani porn star. The one calling the shots has a goatee and looks like he works in a Syrian Starbucks. He's got the beadiest black eyes of them all and more razor cuts than a suicidal teenager on Prozac…yeah, he just shaved. Probly the first time too—he used a Bic. Now he wants *me* to use it. If the flesh-eating disease don't get me I'll probably get camel AIDS. Of course they're fucking terrorists, they all look like extras in *The Scorpion King*. No, I don't know where we're going, but I'm pretty fuckin' sure this ain't a test run. They got crates in the back of the van…How would I know what's in them? You think they opened them for me? I don't like this one fucking bit. These guys are scary…No, that's another thing, the Mexicans are gone. I thought they were supposed to pick me up, but instead I get some fucking Mesopotamian welcoming committee. Well, fuck that. First chance I get I'm making a break for—Shit! Someone's coming."

Only steps from the bathroom door, Zahvi inadvertently kicked an exhaust pipe that clattered on the floor. In panic mode, el Primo terminated the call and inadvertently dropped the phone into the toilet as he tried to hide it. He watched in horror as it disappeared to the bottom of the bowl beneath a fresh pile of bean-burrito-laden waste. The door handle jiggled, and there were several loud bangs on the door as he grabbed a handful of toilet paper.

"Open the door! Why is it locked?" Zahvi yelled.

"'Cause I'm taking a shit!"

"Open it now!"

"All right, all right." He wiped his ass and dropped it in the bowl before pulling up his pants and opening the door. "What's the matter? You got the squirts too?"

Zahvi brushed past him into the small bathroom and immediately recoiled from the smell. He frantically waved his hand across his face. "Who were you talking to?"

"It's called praying. I was praying to God I don't have to drop another loose deuce when I'm flying."

Zahvi continued to wave his hand, and he glanced into the toilet bowl before using his foot to press the flush lever. El Primo closed his eyes for a moment as he realized his lifeline was headed down the drain.

"Where's your phone?" Zahvi asked.

"My phone?" He feigned not knowing where it was and patted his pockets. "I, uh…it must be in my bag."

"It's not in your bag. Where is it?"

"What do you mean it's not in my bag? You been going through my shit?"

"Answer the question."

"I don't know. If it's not in my bag, I must have left it in the hotel. Shit."

Zahvi grabbed him by the arm and led him out of the bathroom. He quickly frisked him and found nothing. El Primo went on the offensive.

"You notice how there's nothing in my pockets? Well, guess what, if you don't start filling them full of Benjamins, I ain't flying anywhere."

"Once you are cleaned up, you will be paid." He pushed him toward the bathroom and added, "Hand me the flight suit."

El Primo grabbed the flight suit, which was hanging on a towel rack on the bathroom door, and handed it to him.

"I thought you wanted me to change into it."

"Not in there. I don't want the smell on it. Put it on out here." He set the suit on a chair outside the bathroom. El Primo took a whiff. "Smells good to me."

"Quit talking and start shaving...and keep the door open."

Zahvi walked toward the van, and el Primo began cutting the scruff off his face with the scissors. He watched some hair swirl down the drain and realized his life was headed there too...down the drain, down the toilet—just like his fucking phone. He could be playing Ping-Pong in a federal pen somewhere eating three squares a day, but *noooo*...he had to flip and work for Uncle Sam. What seemed like a good idea at the time was now a nightmare. He looked in the mirror and wondered for the umpteenth time where it all went wrong. Whoever said that greed was good had his head up his ass. He had put up a good act, or so he thought, but as he looked in his eyes he could see something he hadn't seen in a long time: fear. He took a deep breath and nearly gagged. It really did smell god-awful in the tiny bathroom. There was no getting around it; el Primo was literally in a world of shit.

Chapter 29

“Here they come!” said Tangles. He set the high-grade military binoculars down, and I aimed the bow at the oncoming skiff before putting the boat in idle. Tangles scampered down the stairs, and I followed him into the salon.

“They’ll be here in a couple of minutes, Holly!” I yelled.

“Coming!”

“C’mon,” I said to Tangles. “Let’s get ready to help them aboard.”

“Aye-aye, Captain.” He saluted and followed me to the cockpit. “So how we gonna do this?”

“Like this.” I stepped to the side of the salon door and pressed the button I saw Rafe use some ten days earlier. There was a soft humming sound, and the swim platform started sliding out from a recessed slot in the transom.

“I forgot,” Tangles commented. “That is so sweet.” No sooner had the platform reached its fully extended position when the skiff pulled up along the port side. The president sat in front with a Secret Service agent behind him and Rafe at the helm.

"I forgot to tell you to put out the swim platform," Rafe said.

"Already did."

"Great." He tossed Tangles a line, and Tangles walked the skiff to the stern. I opened the tuna door and stepped out on the platform to help them aboard.

"How y'all doing?" the president asked. "We gonna catch some fish today?"

"We're sure gonna try."

I helped him onto the platform and as I reached for the Secret Service agent, the president said, "Better use two hands with Blinky. He's not feelin' too good." I did as I was told, and once he was aboard I asked the president to wait in the salon while we put the skiff away.

"Sure thing. Is that where you're hiding your better—" The salon door slid open on cue, and Holly stepped out, looking like a dream. She had on a pair of short fishing shorts that showed off her amazing legs and a white V-neck T-shirt that accentuated her melonious lady humps. Her hair was tied back and tucked under a pink visor that held her sunglasses on top. She extended her hand to the president and smiled.

"Hello, Mr. President. I'm Holly. It's an honor to meet you."

They shook hands, and the president grinned.

"*Your* honor? Please. It's *my* honor. I was just asking Shagball if he was hiding his better half inside. Clearly, I was mistaken. You're way more than his better half; you're like five-sixteenths. That's ninety. You're like 90 percent of him. Heh."

"Um, thank you…I guess."

I looked at Tangles and mouthed the word, "*What?*"

Rafe said, "Holly, will you show the president inside while we put the skiff away? He might like something to drink."

"Sure. Right this way." Holly direct the president and his Secret Service agent inside, and when they passed by her, her eyes went wide and she mouthed "Hurry up!"

It was the first time Tangles and I learned how to hook up the skiff to the davit and operate the controls, so it took a little longer than expected. I was the first to head into the salon and heard Holly laughing before I got there. The president was sitting across the dinette from her, and he laughed, too, as Tangles and Rafe followed me into the room.

"Oh my God, that is sooo funny," Holly said with a big smile.

"That was my sophomore year," Dubya said. "Needless to say, I was still drinking back then. That's when Dubya was a whole lotta trubya. Excuse me." He winked at her and slid out of the booth. Rafe officially introduced me and Tangles by our real names; Kit Jansen and Langostino Dupree.

Once we shook hands, the president laid down the ground rules. "As long as we're on this boat, I don't wanna hear any more Mr. President this or Mr. President that, okay? We call each other by our formal names, we'll spend all day talking." He pointed at Rafe and said, "You're Rafe." Then he pointed at each one of us and added, "You're Shagball, you're Tangles, you're the delightful and lovely Holly, and I'm Dubya. You wanna call me 'George,' no problemo, otherwise I'm just plain ol' Dubya."

"Where's your bodyguard?" I asked.

"Blinky? He's lying down. He's seasick already."

"I gave him some motion-sickness pills," Holly said.

Dubya clapped his hands together and said, "So, what are we waiting for? Let's get fishing!"

"That's what *I'm* talking about." Tangles stuck his little fist out, and Dubya fist-bumped him. Wait. *What?* Rafe shook his head, and Holly rolled her eyes.

"What kind of fishing would you like to do?" I asked. "We're set up to troll, but I can have Tangles put together some bottom-fishing rigs if you want to—"

"Hell no, I don't wanna bottom fish. I want the big stuff."

"Anything in particular you'd like to catch?"

"You know, the usual: marlin, swordfish, sunfish, moonfish, whale, shark, whale-shark. The bigger the better."

"Whale-shark?"

"Sure, why not? SeaWorld's not using them anymore. I'll bet they're thick out here. They're THICK! Heh. Isn't that how you say it on the show?"

"You nailed it, sir," said Tangles. He went in for another fist bump, and Holly covered her eyes in disbelief. Things were getting out of hand, and we had yet to wet a line.

"How about tuna?" I asked. "There's a nice weed line about ten miles back. There might be some tuna around."

"I like it. Tuna's probly good whale-shark bait. Let's do it."

Holly and Dubya joined me on the bridge for the ride out to the weed line while Tangles set up the cockpit and Rafe called the boss from the salon. With Blinky in one of the cabins, Dubya wanted to know everything about the boat, starting with speed.

"So how fast does this baby go?"

"Hang on to your hat, and I'll show you." I pushed the throttles forward, and in seconds we were flying across the water.

"Stop!" said Holly.

"What? Why?"

She pointed down at the cockpit through the glass. Tangles was on his back underneath the transom gunwale. I pulled back the throttles, and Holly slid open the window.

"You all right?" she yelled at him.

He slowly got up and waved his fist at me. "How about a little warning before you put the hammer down?"

"Sorry, dude. My bad."

"Good thing he's so small," Dubya said. "A normal-size person might have gone right over."

"Yeah. He's good like that. Maybe we should just troll our way out to that weed line. Holly, will you ask Rafe to come up here? I'd like him to run the boat so we can fish with our esteemed guest." I nodded at Dubya, and he frowned as Holly went down the stairs.

"What's the matter?" I asked.

"I'm not steamed. I'm fine. I'm having a good time. Believe me. You'll know when I'm steamed."

I started laughing. He was a real ballbuster.

"I'm serious," he said. "You don't wanna get on my bad side, especially with a nuclear reactor on board. Heh. Where is it, anyways? I'd like to give it a hug."

"It's inaccessible, suspended in a lead-lined section of the hull. Works like a charm. We haven't had a single problem since we left Norfolk."

"Norfolk? Man, I used to *love* going there. Being around all those aircraft carriers and nuclear submarines gave me a natural high...like killing mustachioed dictators. Yep. Those were the good old days. Not counting today, of course. I never imagined my little ol' DICK would grow so big it needed its own boat. Heh."

"That's a good one. I'm gonna use that sometime."

"Feel free to reinterpretate me as you like."

"What?"

"Feel free."

"Right. I will. Thanks."

Rafe relieved me at the helm. I asked him to keep the speed between twelve and fifteen knots so we could high-speed troll out to the weed line. Dubya followed me to the cockpit, and I asked Tangles to retrieve the bent butt rods.

He returned a couple of minutes later and stuck each one in a rod holder on either side of the boat. "What do you want to put on these?"

"How about a split-tail mullet on one and San Sal Candy on the other."

"San Sal Candy?"

"It's that long pink Black Bart lure."

"Oooh. I like the looks of that one. I bet she's deadly."

"I like deadly," Dubya agreed.

Holly got us each a bottle of water while Tangles and I put the lines out. Each reel had high-strength braided line attached to it. The line was attached to ten feet of 150-pound monofilament shock cord. The shock cord was attached to a two-pound cigar weight that was attached to thirty feet of hundred-pound fluorocarbon leader, which held the bait. I love using split-tail mullets but wasn't sure how long they would hold together at speed, so I hedged with the artificial lure. Once the lines were deployed, I asked the president if he minded if we filmed.

"You mean, like, for your show?"

"If you don't mind, that would be great."

"Hell no, I don't mind."

"Awesome!" said Tangles.

I activated the cameras and asked Dubya and Holly to stand under the bridge overhang while Tangles and I shot the opening. I stood on one side of the fighting chair, and Tangles stood on the other.

"Okay, here we go."

"Wait a second, where's the camera?" Dubya said.

"They're hidden." I pointed out where the cameras were and added, "I know, it's a little weird."

"Of course they're hidden." He grinned. "I keep forgetting I'm on a secret spy boat. You'd never know it. Okay, do your thing. Never mind me."

"Thanks. Okay. Here we go again." I looked up toward the bridge in the direction of the port-side camera and began my spiel. "Welcome back to another episode of *Fishing on the Edge with Shagball and Tangles.* Today we're—"

"Shouldn't you have your show shirts on?" Holly interrupted.

"What? Oh, crap. You're right. Will you go get—" Suddenly the line on the starboard side started peeling off the reel, and Tangles lunged toward the rod.

He tried to crank the handle, and the line stopped peeling off and went slack.

"Dammit! He's gone." Tangles started reeling up the line, and the other reel on my side started peeling off line. I jumped on it and yelled, "He's back!" I tried to crank the handle, but line kept peeling off at a rapid pace. I waved a hand in the air and yelled, "Stop! Stop the boat!" When the boat didn't stop, I glanced up at the bridge and saw Rafe staring straight ahead. *Shit.* "Holly! Tell Rafe to stop!" Holly opened the salon door and hollered up to Rafe. As the boat slowed, I yelled for Tangles to strap Dubya into the fighting chair and increased the drag on the reel. I finally managed to stop the fish and walked the rod over to the chair, slipping the rod butt into the gimbal. Tangles stood by the president's side and said, "Crank that handle, sir! Keep cranking until I say stop."

He did as he was told, and the fish made another run, peeling off more line. "This baby's got some fight in him!" Dubya said. "What do you think it is?"

"Probably a wahoo," I answered. "Keep cranking."

He managed to turn the fish around, and after ten minutes of fighting, Tangles yelled, "I see the shock cord!"

I stepped to the transom for a better look, and I saw it too. I also saw that I forgot to bring the swim platform in after the president boarded. "Shit!"

"What?"

"I forgot to bring in the swim platform. The line could get caught on it."

"No problem. I'll use it to bring the fish over to the side, and you can stick it." I wasn't sure it was such a good idea, but before I could say anything, Tangles opened the tuna door and stepped onto the swim platform. He grabbed the shock cord just below the braided line and yelled, "Stop reeling!" Tangles pulled up the shock cord hand over hand until he reached the cigar weight.

"You got a good hold?" I asked.

"Yeah, give me some slack and put the weight on the deck so I don't get beaned if he takes off."

I turned to Dubya. "Take the reel out of gear."

"Gear? What gear?"

"Here, let me help," said Holly. She flipped the lever on the reel, putting the line into free spool. I leaned over the transom, took the weight from Tangles, and then laid it in the corner of the deck. "Weight's on the deck! Can you see—"

"Oh my God! It's a slob!" Tangles was braced against the transom and struggled to hold the leader. The fish was fifteen feet from the corner of the boat, and it was definitely a slob—a fat torpedo of a wahoo in the hundred-pound class.

Holly handed me the gaff, and I yelled, "Bring him to the corner!"

"I'm trying!" Tangles wrapped the leader around his hand as he tried to get the monster fish close enough to gaff. It shook a couple of times, but the Black Bart lure wasn't going anywhere. Tangles took another wrap and pulled the fish closer. I leaned over the corner to stick it, and as soon as I did, the fish turned and ran. Tangles slipped, and his foot kicked the gaff out of my hand as he flew off the platform head first. With a loud splash he hit the water and was gone. The cigar weight launched off the floor and nearly nailed me before clanking off the corner of the boat and disappearing with Tangles.

"Tangles!" Holly screamed.

I realized the line was in free spool and put the reel in gear, but it was too late. The line on the spool had bird-nested.

"Where'd he go?" Dubya asked.

"Oh my God! Oh my God!" Holly repeated.

"What happened?" Rafe yelled from the bridge. "Where's Tangles?"

I grabbed the line with both hands and started pulling in a state of panic. I had about twenty feet of line at my feet before I realized something was wrong. It was coming in way too easy. "Shit! Shit! Shit!" Seconds later the shock cord was in my hands, and that was all I had. It was the end of the line. The shock cord had severed just above the cigar weight. Holly had her hand over her mouth and looked horrified. I kicked off my shoes, handed my glasses and visor to her, and then jumped up on the gunwale and into the water. My eyes burned as I searched for him, but he was nowhere to be found. I swam as deep as the oxygen in my lungs would let me before heading up empty handed. I was about thirty yards off the stern when I surfaced.

Rafe yelled as he pointed off the port side. "There he is! He's about fifty yards to your left! I'm bringing the boat around!"

Holly and Dubya were yelling and pointing in the same direction. I swiveled and spotted his arm waving. *Thank God.* I swam over as fast as I could and when I reached him he was struggling to keep his head above the light chop. His sunglasses were hanging on his neck by their safety straps and I wrapped an arm under his chin to help buoy him. The boat completed circling around. As it headed toward us, he spit out some water and said, "Sorry bro. I had to cut that big boy loose. He's gone."

"*He's gone?* Jesus Christ, man, we thought *you* were gone! How did you cut the line?"

He reached down and pulled up a bright-orange J-shaped plastic tool with a blade in the crook of the neck that was on a retractable line. "With this. My mother gave it to me for my birthday."

"Good thing you used mono leader instead of wire."

"No shit. Man, did that happen fast. What a slob that was. You got a good hold of me?"

"Yeah, why?"

"You don't realize how heavy two pounds is until your swimming for your life. I could barely tread water with this thing wrapped around my wrist." He held up his other hand, which was tangled in mono and the cigar weight dangled from it. He used the orange tool to cut the mono above the weight and it sank away. "That's better. You can let me go now."

"Just relax. Here's the boat."

Rafe maneuvered alongside us, and Holly yelled up to him, "Make sure you're out of gear! Put it in idle."

Rafe signaled okay, and I pushed Tangles up onto the swim platform.

The president hoisted him up and then gave me a hand too. "Did I screw up with that reel gear? Was it my fault?"

"No, not at all," I answered. "It was just a freak thing. You didn't do anything wrong."

"You okay, Tangles?" He looked concerned.

"I'm fine, sir. Sorry I couldn't get that monster 'hoo to the boat. He was a lot stronger than I thought."

"Nobody cares about the stupid fish," Holly said. "You almost drowned, for crying out loud!"

"No I didn't. I took a helluva ride, and it was a little dicey there for a few seconds, but—"

"But nothing! That was scary." She handed him a towel. "Are you sure you're all right? You need anything?"

"I could sure use a beer."

Holly shook her head and looked at the president. "Don't worry, he's all right."

The Secret Service agent stepped out from the salon. "What's going on? I heard some yelling. Everything all right, boss?"

"It is now. We had a man go overboard, but we got him back. How are you feeling?"

"Not so good…still queasy."

"Keep lying down then. We'll be back at the rig pretty soon. Looks like our fishing trip just got cut short."

The agent went back in the cabin, and Tangles said, "The hell it did."

"Tangles!" cried Holly.

"Sorry, sir. I didn't mean it that way, but if you still wanna fish, let's fish."

"*Really?* You sure?"

"Sure I'm sure. We're pretty close to that weed line we passed earlier. I'll put the bent butts away, and we can troll some squid and ballyhoo on top. We can't let you off this boat without some fillets to take home. Besides, I need to redeem myself."

"He has a point," I said. "That was a hundred-dollar lure that wahoo swam away with."

"Kit!" Holly had her hands on her hips and scowled at me.

"C'mon, Holl, you know I'm just kidding."

"What do you say, sir?" Tangles asked.

The president lifted his sunglasses and squinted at him.

"I say you're a tough little son of a bitch—that's what I say." He glanced at his watch and dropped his shades back down. "I got an hour and a half before I need to be back. If you're game, I'm game. Let's fish."

"All right!" For the third time, Tangles fist-bumped the president.

I looked up at Rafe who was leaning out the bridge window, watching the whole thing. "You heard the man, Rafe. Give us seven knots out to the weed line. There's fish to be caught."

Rafe saluted. "Aye-aye, Captain."

Tangles tugged on Holly's shirt, and she asked, "What?"

"How about that beer?"

"Me too, babe," I added. "The salt water really got me parched."

She puffed her cheeks out and shook her head. "Some things never change."

"C'mon, it's almost noon."

"I know what time it is."

"I got enough salt in my mouth to start a Morton's factory," Tangles said. "It's pretty much doctor's orders."

"You can stop with the excuses. Nobody got hurt in that little mishap, so I suppose one beer would be okay. Mr. President, can I—"

"It's Dubya, remember? Or George."

"Right. I forgot. Can I get you anything?"

"No beer for me. I been on the wagon since ZZ Top stopped shaving."

"How about a soda?"

"If you happen to have a Dew, that'd be great."

"A Dew?"

"Mountain Dew. I do the Dew. Nothing like a little glucose to pump up your fructose. Or is it the other way around? No matter. It pairs well with armadillo stew, but that's another story. I'll send you guys some when I get home. It's mmm, mmm good!"

Chapter 30

El Primo held the disposable razor over the toilet and urinated on the blade in an effort to disinfect it. He figured having piss face was better than camel AIDS or flesh-eating disease any day. Five minutes later he looked in the mirror and assessed his appearance. He appeared somewhat gaunt due to Montezuma's revenge, but at least with the scraggly facial hair gone he no longer looked like the cover boy for *Trailer Trash Weekly*. With his flight suit on and his hair combed back, he even looked presentable. When he slipped on his aviator sunglasses, the change was remarkable. He actually looked like a real pilot. Feeling marginally better he walked over to the van, where the ringleader was talking on the phone. He heard him mention the name of the shop and the address before ending the call.

"What's going on?" He asked as he looked around. "Where's Roberto?"

"Roberto went to the bank."

"Is that right? Speaking of bank, it's time for my deposit."

"That would be ten thousand now plus ten thousand every time we land?"

"That's right."

Zahvi reached in the van and handed el Primo his duffel. Then he slid over a large canvas bag and handed him ten stacks of hundred-dollar bills.

"I assume you have no problem getting paid the full amount in advance. That's fifty-thousand dollars, five thousand in each stack." As El Primo stuffed the money in his bag, he added, "Your appearance is adequate. I hope your flying is too."

El Primo pulled a bill out of the last stack and slid his sunglasses up on his head so he could take a good look at it. "Don't worry about my flying, and I won't worry if this money is funny."

"There is nothing wrong with the money."

"Good. There's nothing wrong with my flying either. So where are we going? Fifty grand buys you a few stops."

Zahvi pulled a piece of paper out of his pocket and handed it to him. "Here are the coordinates of the first stop."

Noorbi and Kahlulla walked in from the back. Noorbi said, "The cargo is loaded. We are ready to go."

"I don't have a chart on me," said el Primo. "Where is this?"

"It is an oil rig about a hundred and forty miles east of here," Zahvi said.

"*East* of here? But that's—"

"In the Gulf of Mexico. That's why we have a helicopter and not a plane."

There was a sudden banging on the front door to the shop. Zahvi turned to Kahlulla and said, "That should be the others. Let them in."

El Primo was expecting to see Chaco and Jorge come walking through the door, but instead it was three strangers who looked strikingly similar to the rest of *The Scorpion King* crew. "Who the fuck are these guys? Where's Chaco and Jorge?"

"Don't worry about the Mexicans. These are the other passengers."

"Wait a second, pal. The *rest* of the passengers? You're telling me *all* of you guys are coming? *Plus* those crates that were in the back of the van?"

"No. One of us is staying behind."

"So that means five, plus me, plus the cargo."

"That is correct."

"And we got a full load of fuel?"

"Of course."

"Let me ask you something. You ever heard of a weight limit?"

"It's a big helicopter. The weight should be fine."

"It *should* be fine? Right, and I should be on a beach in Bora Bora sipping umbrella drinks with a Polynesian hooker, but I'm not. How much do the crates weigh?"

Zahvi turned to Noorbi and said something in Arabic. Noorbi shrugged and said something to Kahlulla, who also shrugged.

"They're not sure, but they're pretty heavy. What is the weight limit?"

"What am I, a helicopter historian? How the fuck would I know?"

"Then quit worrying. Besides, we are leaving the cargo and most of the men at the first rig."

"The first rig? You mean—?"

"We are flying from one rig to another and then back. No more questions. Let's go. " He said something in Arabic, and the three new guys followed Noorbi and Kahlulla toward the back door. He pointed for El Primo to follow. El Primo reached for his duffel, but Zahvi beat him to it. "Your money and belongings will be placed in the back of the helicopter until we are finished."

"Great," el Primo lied. He had actually been thinking about going postal with his .45 and making a run for it with the money and whatever was in the crates. It was like the beady-eyed bastard was reading his mind.

Zahvi set his duffel to the side and pulled a mini-Uzi out of the big canvas money bag. With a knowing smile, he slung it over his shoulder, picked up both bags, and said, "After you."

It was a typically hot and dusty day in Matamoros. When they reached the helicopter, el Primo said, "I'm thirsty. I need something to drink before we take off. Something cold, preferably without a worm in it."

Zahvi said something to Kahlulla, who headed back into the shop.

He turned to el Primo. "He is getting some water. Let's get moving." Zahvi handed the bags to Noorbi who placed them in the cargo hold on top of the crates. The other three arrivals followed Noorbi into the chopper. El Primo got behind the controls and began entering the rig coordinates into the GPS unit. Kahlulla returned and handed Zahvi several bottles of water. Zahvi handed one to el Primo, and Noorbi grabbed the others. Kahlulla started to climb in, but Zahvi grabbed his arm and pulled him back.

"You're not coming with us."

"I don't understand."

"I know. That is why you are not coming. You don't understand. I tell you to do one thing, and you do the other."

"What are you talking about?"

"I said no one was to touch the hostages, yet you disobeyed me."

"But they are women! Christian women! Sharia law says—"

"I know what Sharia law says! Do not lecture me on Sharia law! I don't care where you stick your filthy cock, but when I give you an order, I expect it to be followed!"

Clearly worried now, Kahlulla instinctively backpedaled. "Yes, of course. I said it wouldn't happen again."

"You are right. It won't." Zahvi leveled the Uzi and squeezed the trigger. A dozen rounds slammed into the stunned terrorist, and he collapsed in the dirt. Zahvi climbed into the copilot's seat and looked el Primo in the eye. "What are you waiting for? Let's go."

El Primo's mouth hung open, and he glanced back at the other passengers who looked unfazed. "What, uh, what did that guy do?"

"He didn't follow orders. I advise you don't make the same mistake."

Chapter 31

It was a good call by Tangles to continue fishing despite nearly getting drowned by a large wahoo. When we reached the weed line, we were rewarded with four nice dolphins in the thirty-pound class and a fifty-pound yellowfin tuna caught off the shotgun line. Holly went inside to iron out a computer issue while Tangles cleaned the fish. On the way back to the *Bluewater* rig, Tangles suggested to the president some different ways to prepare it.

"You can cook these dolphin fillets any number of ways," he said. "You can deep fry them, pan fry them, bake them with lemon and herbs…pretty much however you want."

"I was kinda hoping to surprise the wife and kids back in Corpus Christi tonight with something special. After all, it's Memorial Day."

"Okay. You wanna kick it up a notch? Make Dolphin Oscar."

"Never heard of it."

"Stuff the dolphin fillets with crabmeat, put a couple of asparagus spears on top, drizzle it with hollandaise sauce, and then bake it for twenty minutes or so."

"Wow! That sounds tasty. I'll do the same thing with holiday sauce. We *love* the holiday sauce." He gave a furtive look toward the cockpit door and then lowered his voice. "So, I heard you're going inshore to test out a high-tech eavesdropping system on some possible terrorist activity."

"That's what we've been told," I answered. "That ISIS has enlisted a Mexican cartel to help them get across the border for some type of attack. I hope we pick up some useful information."

"Me too. The border situation is completely out of control. I'm no Trump fan, but he's right about building a wall. I shoulda built one that would make the one in China look like a playpen divider."

"Why didn't you?" Tangles asked.

"Nine eleven. It threw me for a loop. Hell, it threw the whole damn country for a loop. After that, it was game on with the desert rats. My whole focus was on wiping them off the face of the earth. That's why I started DICK. We did a pretty good job, too. Iraq was under control when I left office. I never imagined Obama would pull out all our troops and walk away thinking everything would be hunky dory. Nobody did. Nobody believed he could be that naïve or stupid. Well, until the Iran deal, that is. That sure blows the theory that he's some kinda intellectual all to shreds. The sad truth is, I think he knows what he's doing but doesn't care. How else can you explain him not enforcing our immigration laws? He just doesn't care. He hates America. He hates it worse than a cat hates a bath. He lets illegal aliens get welfare, and when they commit serious crimes, he lets them go. Kidnap someone? You're free to go. Rape someone? Free to go. Murder someone? Free to go. But God forbid a Christian couple won't bake a wedding cake for a pair of bean flickers. No, sirree. Gotta shut their business down and fine them to high heaven. It's flat-out crazy. Anyways, I'm not one for excuses. I shoulda been building a wall at the same time I was hunting terrorists and if Congress didn't go along I shoulda done it anyways—the Great Wall of Bush."

"Shoulda, coulda, woulda—life in a nutshell," I said. "Hopefully the next president secures the border. Obama's like a drunken texter, driving straight down Fuck Street when we need to make a hard right on Wake-the-Fuck-Up Boulevard. Pardon my French."

Tangles fist-bumped me with an "Amen, brother," and Dubya followed with a fist bump of his own and similar words of praise. "Well said, Shagito. I might have to borrow that sometime. Heh."

The boat slowed down, and I leaned out the side to see the *Bluewater* rig looming dead ahead. "Looks like we're about there."

"Guess I better go get Blinky. Sure hope he's feeling better. The last time I checked on him he was greener than Dr. Seuss's eggs."

Chapter 32

El Primo had been in some dicey situations over the course of his checkered smuggling career, but nothing like the one he currently found himself in. As he flew over the open gulf at an altitude of only a hundred feet he thought about the crates in the back of the helicopter. What was in them? *Guns?* Probably. He had smuggled guns before. All kinds of guns. Machine guns, AK-47s, automatics of every type. Guns didn't make him nervous. Bombs made him nervous. Especially terrorists with bombs. Was there a bomb in one of the crates? Maybe. There was no way to know. *Fuck.* Instead of trying to guess what was *in* the crates, he decided to guess what wasn't. *Soap?* No chance. *Mouthwash?* Highly unlikely. *Goat porn?* Check one for the probable list. He let out a nervous chuckle, and the terrorist leader sitting in the copilot's seat adjusted his headset and stared at him.

"Why do you laugh?"

"'Cause I'm nervous, that's why. I don't like this shit. I don't like not knowing where I'm going or what's in the crates."

"I gave you the coordinates."

"And they best be right or its splish, splash, we're taking a bath."

"They are. This isn't our first trip."

"Well, that's comforting. So what happens when we get there?"

"Then I will give you the next set of coordinates."

"To pick somebody up? Chaco said I was picking somebody up. He said it was a simple deal. He didn't say anything about crates or guys with AKs." He glanced back and saw that the other passengers were fast asleep. *Unbelievable.*

"Chaco was a liar and a thief."

"Welcome to Mexico. Wait a second—*was?* What do you mean *was?*"

"Chaco's loss is your gain. There will be more money for you if the mission is successful."

"*Mission?* I didn't sign on for any *mission.* I'm just a pilot. People get killed on missions. What the fuck. I shoulda listened to my mother. I shoulda been a florist. I could be in a greenhouse somewhere banging middle-aged decorators on a bed of tulips instead of—"

"Enough! Just shut up and fly. I will double your fee if everything goes right. That's one hundred thousand dollars."

"Gee thanks, but it doesn't do me any good if I don't get a chance to spend it. Fuck. *Mission.* I shoulda known. The Alamo was a fucking mission. Look how well it ended for them."

"Quit talking. I must meditate."

"Of course you must."

"Approach the rig from the south. When we are five miles away, fly to the south and come in that way."

"Anything else? You sure you don't want me to circle it three times and—"

"Just do it!"

El Primo pondered his fucked-up situation some more as he closed the distance between the chopper and the rig. A hundred thousand big ones was a nice chunk of change but not enough for him to renege on his informant deal with Homeland Security and go AWOL. He hoped to God his handler had someone looking for him after his phone got flushed down the toilet but realized it would do little good. Nobody knew where he was or where he was going. *He* didn't even know where he was going. *Fuck.* His options were few. He had to play it out and look for an opportunity to split the scene when it presented itself. Preferably *before* the smelly gang of goat humpers did whatever it was they planned on doing, like blowing something up. They were always blowing something up. El Primo wanted no part of that shit, he *hated* bombs. Five miles away from the target he swung the chopper in an arc to the south.

"We are five miles away?" Zahvi asked.

"Yep. Smack dab in the middle of fucking nowhere."

"Have you seen any boats or planes?"

"Not lately. I saw a fishing boat about fifty miles back, but that's it. Nothing but waves. Why? You expecting someone?"

"I'm expecting you not to ask any more questions. Just fly the helicopter like you were hired to do." He turned toward the rear of the plane and started speaking loudly in Arabic. El Primo pulled the headset off his ears and complained.

"Hey! Push the mic away from your mouth before you start talking to your buddies." He motioned pushing his own mic away. The men in the rear of the chopper snapped out of their slumber and added to the loud chorus of indecipherable conversation.

"Jesus. Sounds like a fucking Fallujah fire drill." El Primo mumbled.

The *Dinero Majado* gradually appeared in front of them, and El Primo put the chopper in a hover about a hundred yards from the deck. Noting the dilapidated appearance of the old rig, he looked at Zahvi and said, "Are you serious? This is it?"

"Yes. Land on the X."

"I know what a fucking helipad looks like. Thanks a million." As he set the chopper down he spotted what appeared to be a new satellite dish semiconcealed among the rusting metal rooftops. The chopper hit the deck with a thud, and he was surprised it didn't crash straight through the deck into the waters below. He killed the engines, and once the blades stopped spinning, everybody piled out.

Zahvi barked out some orders in Arabic, and one of the guys disappeared through the nearest doorway. El Primo watched as the others unloaded the crates onto a dolly and then carted them away. He casually followed, hoping to see where they were going, but Zahvi stopped him and handed him a slip of paper.

"Here are the coordinates to our next stop. Enter them into the flight computer. We will be leaving shortly."

El Primo waved the paper. "Where is this?"

"It is another oil rig about a hundred miles north of here called the *Bluewater*. Plot a course that takes us ten miles due east before heading there and on the way back do the opposite. Take us ten miles west before flying back here."

"Wait a second. We're flying back *here?* I thought you said we were flying back to Matamoros after going to the second rig."

"You thought wrong."

"I don't think so. I think *you* thought wrong. We've already gone a hundred and forty plus miles. You're talking about another two hundred and twenty miles round trip just to get back here. I'm not sure what the range is in this thing, but four hundred miles is pushing it. We may make it back here, but not back to Matamoros. No way. Not without refueling."

"I am well aware of the fuel constraints, which is why I had a two-hundred-and-fifty gallon drum delivered here," he lied.

"You got *fuel* on this floating shithole? Where?"

Zahvi pointed at one of the small rusted structures. "On the other side of that building." He lied.

"Great. Have your boys wheel it over. Let's fill 'er up."

"We will when we return. There is no time now. We are on a schedule."

"Schedule, my ass. I said we 'may' have enough gas to make it back from the *Bluewater.* I don't know if we do or not."

"I do. It is Allah's will."

"Are you kidding me?" El Primo pointed out at the open water. "That's the Gulf of fucking Mexico. It's a real ocean with sharks that eat you and waves that can crush you and currents that pull you under. It ain't like that putrid pond you call the Dead Sea. There's none of that neutral buoyancy bullshit out *here.* You can't just float around playing circle jerk with your buddies all day while you pray for Allah to swoop down on his magic carpet and—"

Zahvi slammed the butt of his Uzi into el Primo's gut, and he keeled over in pain.

"Never question Allah's will! The only reason I have tolerated your insolence is because I need you to fly. Enter the coordinates into the flight computer… now!"

Zahvi gave orders to one of his men to guard el Primo as he gasped for air.

He slowly caught his breath and stood up. "Why does everybody have to nail me in the gut?" He rubbed his bruised ribs. Zahvi walked into one of the buildings, and the guard pointed his weapon at el Primo as he climbed into the cockpit. While he plotted a course to the *Bluewater* and back, Zahvi was in the interrogation room, peering over Noorbi's shoulder at the computer screen in front of him. Noorbi clicked and sent the e-mail on the screen.

"That's it?" Zahvi asked.

"Yes. The helicopter service has been notified to delay their scheduled pickup by two hours. They won't think twice about it because it was sent through the Secret Service e-mail system."

"You are truly a genius when it comes to hacking computer systems."

"True, but it does not take one to hack the US government. Even a high school kid managed to hack the email account of the head of the CIA."

Zahvi put a hand on his shoulder, and they shared a laugh. Noorbi considered the situation and added, "A follow-up call should be made. Government e-mail is also unreliable, so we can't know for sure that someone at Rig Hoppers has received the message. You speak good English. You should call them."

"No, I speak *excellent* English, thanks to my time at Oxford. Give me the number."

El Primo was just finishing up with the GPS plotting when he noticed the guy posted to guard him had wandered over to the edge of the rig. The guy peered over the side and then slung his AK-47 over his shoulder. El Primo couldn't believe it. It was the break he needed. *The guy had his back to him and was pissing over the side!* Seeing that no one was paying attention, El Primo scrambled to the back of the chopper and located his duffel. He quickly retrieved his .45 and rushed back to the pilot's seat. As if sensing something was happening, the urinator looked back at the chopper while he gave his goat prod a few final shakes. Knowing how severe the punishment could be if Zahvi saw he wasn't on guard, he zipped up and hustled back to the chopper.

El Primo quickly considered his next move. If he didn't do something fast he would be piloting a terrorist mission of some sort. Somehow, he didn't think his handler at Homeland Security would approve. Plus, he would probably be killed. *Not a good plan.* He glanced at the building that the rest of the group had disappeared into and wondered when they would be coming out. The guard stopped only ten feet away and held his AK across his body. *What to do.* Now that he had his .45, he had some options. The one he considered at the moment was to signal the guard over and blast a large hole between the thick black caterpillars on his forehead that some call eyebrows. Then he'd fire up the engines and get the hell out of dodge. Once he got to the mainland he could contact Homeland Security and give them the coordinates of the rig. He would be up fifty thousand bucks and get credit for stopping whatever plot the terrorists had planned. It would also give him a chance at negotiating an early exit from the deal he had agreed to. He needed less than ninety seconds, and he could be airborne. *It was go time.* With the .45 sitting on the seat between his legs, he pushed open the pilot's door and waved the guard over. The guard warily stepped forward a couple of feet and stopped.

"Commere," El Primo urged him. "I gotta ask you something." He had his right hand on his .45, ready to go postal on the smelly bastard. The guard shook his head and kept his finger on the trigger of his assault rifle. "No speak English."

"You don't have to speak. You just have to let me take a leak. I'm about to—" Zahvi and a guy holding an AK walked out of the building. *Shit.* They quickly crossed the deck, and No-Name asked, "What's going on here? Have you plotted the course? Are you ready to leave?"

"Yes and yes and not quite. I was just telling your buddy I need to drain the vein."

"What are you saying? Is there something you need to do to the engine?"

"The engine's fine. I need to make the bladder gladder. You know, put out a fire, bleed the lizard, flush my buffer."

"Flush your *what?*"

"I thought you knew English."

"I do. My English is excellent. I studied at Oxford."

"Apparently not hard enough. Let me translate. I gotta squeeze the scorpion."

"You have to take a leak?"

"Bingo. Give the man a clove-flavored cigar."

"Make it quick. It's time to go."

"You're telling me." The pilot's seat had pouches for maps and personal effects on the left side, the right side, and the middle. He slipped the .45 into the middle pouch and hopped out of the chopper. The guard followed him over to the edge of the rig and watched him piss over the side like he had only minutes before. As they walked back to the chopper, Zahvi finished giving instructions to the others. He turned to el Primo and nodded. "Let's go."

"After you." El Primo held out an open palm and watched as the smallest member of the group climbed in, followed by Zahvi. El Primo got in last. With his headset on and the engines going, he said, "Here goes nothing."

"No." Zahvi smiled. "Here goes history."

Chapter 33

Rafe returned after dropping Dubya off, and it only took a few minutes for us to secure the skiff in the forward hull compartment. Tangles operated the retractable power winch while I directed from the helm. I was a quick study, and he was a quick doer. We were a team. A dream team. Well, we definitely like to sleep. We like to fish, we like to sleep, we like to drink, we like to eat, we like to—

"Kit." Holly came bounding up the steps and caught me inwardly philosophizing as I gazed out at water.

"Huh? What?"

"What are you doing?"

"I was just, uh, thinking about things." I pulled her close and kissed her on the lips. She kissed me back before putting her hand on my chest and gently pushing away. She glanced down the steps toward the voices of Tangles and Rafe in the salon.

"What exactly were you thinking?" She smiled seductively.

"I was just thinking of all the things we like and you're right there at the top."

The smile went neutral. "What do you mean, *we?*"

"You know…me and Tangles."

The smile turned to a distasteful grimace. "You were thinking of Tangles when you kissed me? That's—"

"No! That's not what I meant. I was just thinking how much we're alike in the sense we like to sleep and fish and eat and drink and…you know, I thought about you."

"That's not the top of the list. That's the bottom."

"No. That's not right. I just said it that way. What I meant was; you can have a great day, but it's not perfect unless you have a good woman to love at the end of it."

"So, you don't want me to share in your great day, you just want to bang me at the end of it?"

"*What?* No! I mean yes, of course I do. At the end *and* the beginning. That's what makes it a perfect day. It starts and ends with you."

"You are so full of it." She pushed me in the chest.

"What. I'm serious. The only thing that could be more perfect would be to slip a little afternoon delight in there."

"Three times in one day? At your age? *Puhleez.* You can barely handle two. Three times might throw off your sleep, fish, eat, drink, sequence. You'd probably have a heart attack."

"Now you're playing dirty, bringing my age into it. That hurts. And for your information there is no sequence as long as it begins and ends with you." I smiled and pulled her close again.

"You really expect me to believe that?" She grinned.

"What part?"

"Ugh. You are such an idiot sometimes. Here." She handed me a slip of paper.

"What's this?"

"It's the coordinates of the *Taladro Grande.* It's time to see if Alexander Hamilton LeRoux is my cousin."

"Shouldn't we check with Rafe first?"

"Already did. He said to tell you to set course and leave it on autopilot if you want to come down and grab something to eat."

I talked Holly into making me a sandwich and spent the next few minutes entering the coordinates. A quick check of the radar showed a few scattered showers but nothing threatening—always a good sign. I set the sonar/radar perimeter alert to a one mile, 360-degree radius, and the autopilot at ten knots an hour before heading down to eat. I found Tangles and Rafe happily munching away at the dinette and Holly coming up from the galley with a couple of sandwiches. Noting the half-empty plates in front of the guys I commented, "Feel free to start. Don't wait for me and Holly."

Holly set the plate with the sandwiches on the table, and I slid in next to her. Rafe started to apologize, but Holly held out her hand and cut him off. "Don't listen to him."

"Dude, I was starved," Tangles replied with a mouthful.

"*You're starved?* Please. Lifesaving is hungry work."

"Lifesaving?"

"Yeah, lifesaving. I saved your life again."

"I was fine. I coulda dog-paddled for hours."

"You were struggling. You were about to drown."

"Not hardly. That doesn't count as a save."

"Neither does saving you after you drown, moron."

"Stop it," Holly said. "Just stop it, all right? I thought you were starving. Eat your sandwich."

I took a large bite and washed it down with some water as I studied her closely.

"What are you looking at?"

"Why do you always take his side? You always defend him. What's up with that?"

"I do *not* always defend him."

"Yeah," Tangles said. "Just eat your sandwich and—"

"Enough!" Holly's hand shot up, cutting him off. "When I said stop it, I meant both of you. This stupid game you two play trying to keep score of who saved who is ridiculous. What happened earlier almost ended in tragedy."

"But it didn't because I saved his life."

Holly gave me death laser eyes.

"Not even close," Tangles replied.

"I said stop." Holly looked serious. "Stop or I'm done making sandwiches."

"What?" Tangles said.

"Whoa, wait a second," I said. "Let's not be talking crazy. This is important. It's two to two in saves. This is a tiebreaker. How about we let Rafe make the call, and we'll be done with it. You good with that Tangles?"

"Rafe?"

"Yeah, he's the guy sitting next to you."

"More like the guy who wishes he *wasn't* sitting next to you," Holly said.

Rafe laughed, and I commended her dig. "Nice one, babe."

She turned her head slowly and stared at me. "You either."

"Ouch," Tangles said. "That had to sting a little. All right, I'm good with Rafe making the call. No way that was a save."

I looked at Rafe. "You heard the man. It's your call."

Rafe shook his head and looked at Holly. "Are they always like this?"

"Yes. It really needs to stop."

"Go ahead, Rafe. Give it to him straight. He's a big boy. He can take it. Tell him no save," Tangles said.

Rafe shrugged. "Well, there's no denying Kit frantically searched for you underwater."

"That's right," I added. "It's part of the lifesaving process."

"Oh my God!" Holly cried. "Can you just let him talk?"

"Sorry. I'll save it for the book I'm gonna write: *Lifesaving like a Lifesaver.*"

"As I was saying," continued Rafe. "Because Kit dove in he was first to reach you and helped keep your head out of the water until I brought the boat around."

"I was dog-paddling like a boss. It was my head that was keeping his arm above the water."

"Nevertheless, you did appear to be struggling."

"The shock cord and cigar weight got tangled in my shorts. I was getting a reverse wedgie."

"Like I said, you were struggling."

"Some call it struggling. Most call it drowning," I pointed out.

Holly rolled her eyes, and Rafe looked at me. "However," he said. "To be fair, I was the one who spotted Tangles from the bridge and brought the boat over. At that point, any of us could have jumped in."

"Could have? Yeah, after I *saved* him. What are you saying?"

"Sorry."

"Yes!" Tangles said with a fist pump.

"Are you kidding me?" I was incredulous.

"I didn't finish. I'm sorry, I can't give you credit for a full save."

"What do you, what do you mean, *full save?*" Tangles stuttered.

"Just what I said. I wouldn't call it a full save, but it's definitely worth a half."

"*What?* No. No way. We don't play in fractions."

"We do now," I said. "I'll take a half. A half puts me a half save up. Hah."

"I hate fractions."

"Then look at it this way; it's a half save on a half person. Two halves equal a whole. That's a full save. It's three to two."

"Screw you, you're up a half."

"I'll take it."

"And that better be the end of it, or I'm seriously going to jump ship," Holly said.

"The sandwich was great." I winked at her.

She looked at my empty plate and shook her head.

"How can you clear a plate without stopping talking?"

"It's a gift. Like lifesaving."

"Really?"

There's a look she gives me that's a cousin of the death laser stare. I think all women have it. It's a cross between the "I'm about to throw my drink in your face" look and the "I'm about to kick you in the balls" look. I watched her lips contort and her teeth grind together and realized I was wrong. I was witnessing the birth of a new look. She sneered at me like Billy Idol with Bell's palsy. It was the "I'm about to throw my drink in your face *and then* kick you in the balls" look. *Whoa.* Time to change subjects.

"Sooo," I said. "Bet you're excited to meet your cousin."

"What?" I saw her eyes snap back into focus. The look was gone. She was back. "Yes, of course. I hope it's him."

"Speaking of your cousin, the *Taladro Grande* is in international waters and is owned by a Mexican conglomerate," Rafe said.

"So?"

"So, it's not owned by an American company like the *Bluewater.* We can't just make a few calls and get cleared to see somebody. And because this excursion is a personal matter, the boss said we're not to try to bluff our way onboard using US government credentials. Not that it would do us any good. We have no jurisdiction there."

"So what are you saying?"

"I have the number for the head guy, but it's up to you to talk your way on board."

"So give me the number already." She smiled optimistically. "How could he say no?"

***

Approximately ninety-five miles to the south, in his office on the *Taladro Grande,* Oskar Medina popped a couple of aspirin. Things had been going nice and smooth, just the way he liked it. The perfect safety record, the recognition ceremony from company executives for his many years of service, the outstanding production numbers—everything had been going great and then BOOM! He's got a diver with the bends claiming somebody tried to kill him. Even worse, he believed him.

His cell phone rang. Incoming call. *No kidding.* Half the calls he got on the rig failed to show who the caller was. "Hola."

"Oh nuts, uh, I no habla español muy bueno. Do you habla English?"

"Do I speak English? Yes. Who is this?"

"My name is Holly Lutes. Is this Oskar Medina?"

"Yes. Who are you and why did you call?"

"Are you on the *Taladro Grande*?"

"Of course I am. I run this rig."

"That's why I called. There's a man who works on the rig I believe may be my cousin."

"Lady, everybody has a cousin who works on this rig. It's one of the biggest offshore rigs in the world. So what? How did you get my number?"

"Please, you don't understand. He may be a long-lost cousin of mine that I've been searching for for years. I'm in the neighborhood, and I was hoping I could stop by and meet him."

"What neighborhood is that? We're in the middle of the gulf."

"So are we. Less than a hundred miles north of you. We just left the *Bluewater.*"

"The *Bluewater*? Talk about big. What were you doing on the *Bluewater*?"

"We weren't exactly *on* it; we just picked somebody up and took him fishing."

"Good for you. Lady, I'm sorry, but I got a rig to run. And if your cousin works for me, he has a job to do too. This isn't a resort. There's no stopping by to say hi. You want to see him, make arrangements to see him onshore, like everybody else. I have to go now. Please don't call this—"

"Wait! Please! I just need to—"

"What you need to do is take your charter back to Houston or Corpus Christi or wherever you—"

"This isn't a charter boat. We came from Palm Beach."

"*Palm Beach?* Palm Beach as in Florida?"

"Yes."

"You came from Palm Beach by boat?"

"Sure beats swimming."

"Funny lady. What are you trying to pull here? You say you came all the way across the gulf just to take somebody fishing? That's crazy. How did you get my number?"

"Please, I'm not crazy. We also came to try to meet my cousin. And it wasn't just to take somebody fishing. We've been filming a fishing show."

"Show? What show?"

"You probably haven't heard of it."

"We have satellite TV. Is it *Chix with Stix*? I love that show."

"What? No. That sounds gross. We were filming for a show called *Fishing on the Edge with Shagball and Tangles.*"

"*Fishing on the Edge*? I think I've seen it. I thought it was cancelled."

"No, their boat just blew up. Now that they have a new boat, they're filming again."

"Wait...is that the show with the midget?"

"Yes, that's Tangles. But technically he's not a midget."

"I *have* seen it. It's funny. Midgets are funny. They are with you right now?"

"Yes, sir."

"I have a lot of guys on this rig who like to fish. It might be good for morale if they got to meet Shagball and Tangles. Especially Tangles. Midgets are very big in Mexico. Very popular."

"If you can arrange for me to see my cousin, you can consider it done."

"What's his name?"

"Alexander Hamilton LeRoux."

"Are you sure? I don't recognize that name."

"That's the name I have."

"Let me look for his file. Hang on." Oskar spun around in his chair and rolled over to the file cabinet. "How do you spell his last name?"

"L-E-R-O-U-X."

Oskar leafed through the files and pulled out the one marked A. H. LeRoux. "Here it is." He opened it, and when he saw the photo inside, he said, "Merda."

"What?"

"It's Pago. No wonder I didn't recognize the name. He goes by Pago. He's a diver."

"So what's the matter? He's not there?"

"No, he had, uh...he had an accident the other day."

"What kind of accident? Is he okay?"

"I think he'll be fine. It was a diving accident. He's been in a hyperbaric chamber for the last couple of days recovering from the bends." Oskar glanced at his watch. "He might be out by now. The doctor said he was getting out today. He wants him to go ashore for some tests."

"When?"

"If he's cleared by the doctor he'll be on the first flight out tomorrow."

"We can be there in less than an hour and a half."

"From a hundred miles away? What kind of boat you got, lady?"

"A fast one."

"I guess. What's your name again? I better write it down for Pago."

"It's Holly Lutes. L-U-T-E-S...but he won't recognize my name. If he is who I think he is, my late aunt is his grandmother."

"You mean you don't know?"

"No, that's why I need to see him and talk to him—to find out for sure."

"The accident shook Pago up. He might not want to see you."

"Tell him my aunt left me instructions to find her grandson so he can get what she left him in her will."

"Her *will?*"

"Yes, I'm the executor of her estate."

"That should interest him. Call me when you're near."

"Thank you sooo much, Oskar. We'll see you soon."

"No problemo. Don't forget the midget." *Click.*

Chapter 34

El Primo said nothing as he guided the helicopter deeper into the gulf. He spent the time trying to envision a scenario that gave him the best chance of survival. He didn't need much. He didn't need much at all. You don't get to be an AARP-card-carrying intercontinental smuggler without having some serious survival skills—skills that include killing people as needed. He had no qualms in that regard. The fact that he had his .45 concealed and ready made him feel immensely better. At the ten-mile mark he swung the chopper north on a beeline toward the *Bluewater.*

El Primo was old school when it came to the ammo in his .45. That meant full metal jacket. That meant he ran the risk of having a bullet pass through his target and then through the shell of the helicopter. Depending on what it hit along the way, that could determine whether he lived or died. He had no desire to go down in the gulf. He had been stranded at sea before. *No thanks.* The choices were few, though. No-Name let it slip that Jorge and Chaco had eaten their last taco. Given the way he offed one of his own men just prior to takeoff, el Primo suspected the garage owner had also rotated his last tire. He had little doubt that once his own services were no longer required, he was a dead man. A dead man flying…or not. It was kill or be killed. *Fuck it.* He glanced at No-Name and decided to put one through his left temple. The trajectory and angle of the shot had to be just right so that the back of No-Name's head wouldn't explode through the side window. Once he turned No-Name into No-Head he would pivot and fire a couple of rounds into the chest of the guy sitting in back—a little messy, but game over. Cha-ching. He glanced back to get a read on him, but he wasn't there. *What?*

El Primo spoke into his headset. "Where did your buddy go?"

No-Name glanced back. "He's probably sleeping. Don't worry about him."

"Where? On the floor behind the rear seat?"

"Why do you care?"

"Regulations. I'm supposed to know where my passengers are."

"Maybe you should focus on what's ahead of you instead of what's behind you."

"Tell that to Little Red Riding Hood."

"Who?"

"Forget it."

El Primo silently cursed his downward-spiraling luck. Without knowing where the other passenger was, his plan went *kapoof.* Blindly pumping full metal rounds through the backseat hoping to hit his target wasn't feasible. Not when his target was armed and would fire back. Getting shot was no fun. Getting shot and crashing into the gulf was even worse. *Shit.* He had to wait. He had to wait, and waiting wasn't easy.

Not when you're flying 125 miles an hour at an altitude of only two hundred feet. No-Name had his eyes closed and was softly chanting some Arabic mumbo jumbo as mile after mile of open water passed by. El Primo was more than ready to blow the bastard's brains out, but the guy in back remained out of sight. When they were ten miles away from the *Bluewater,* el Primo spoke.

"Hey, No-Name, we'll be there in a few minutes."

Zahvi's eyes popped open. "How faraway are we?"

"Ten miles. So what's the plan?"

"The plan is for you to do exactly what I tell you to do."

"Which is what?"

"Land on the rig and keep the helicopter running until we get our guests aboard. Then fly us back to the *Dinero Majado* on the flight path I requested. It is important we are seen leaving the *Bluewater* heading west toward land."

El Primo had been thinking about the odd flight plan request since mapping it out on the GPS plotter. Coupled with the slick paint job and the matching Rig Hopper flight suits they wore, el Primo came to the obvious conclusion.

"You're kidnapping someone. That's what this is all about, right?"

"Yes. It is Allah's will."

"Will schmill. What's in it for me?"

"What are you talking about?"

"I charge extra for kidnapping—a lot extra, particularly when it's oil executives. That's the gig, right?"

"You could say that. Yes, the president and at least two others."

"Nice. Who else, the CEO, maybe the CFO? Oil companies have all the money. They gotta be worth at least five million each, right?"

"I would think so. The president alone is priceless."

"That's great, but el Primo's not. My price for kidnapping oil executives is a million a head—firm."

"One million dollars each?"

"Firm, and don't try to pass off the guys with the president as middle management. El Primo no buy-o."

"If you play the role of a professional charter pilot and get us back to the *Dinero Majado*, you can have it."

"That's three million clams, pal, maybe more." El Primo licked his lips. He had heard terrorists were well funded, but this was ridiculous. With three million bucks in hand, Homeland Security would never hear from him again. Assuming, of course, that he wasn't killed. It was a big assumption.

"I attended Oxford. I can add. Money is just a means to an end."

"You're damn right it is; it's an end to el Primo's cash-flow problems." He fought to convince himself he had a chance of collecting and the money told him he did. "I gotta tell you, you had me a little worried there. I was thinking you were planning on blowing something up, including us. I know you think you get brownie points for that, but el Primo no diggy. I was two seconds away from turning your head into shepherd's pie."

"What does that mean?"

"It means you're lucky. Why didn't you *tell* me this was a kidnapping? That and hijacking are my specialties. Hell, last time I was in the Bahamas I did both.

Kidnapping can be very profitable. Risky, but profitable. I got no problem with it. It's bombs I got a problem with. Stepped on a dud in Kuwait back in ninety-one. Every time I stub my toe I shit my pants. Had to stop wearing flip-flops. How fucked up is that."

"Is that a question?"

"No. I know it's fucked up. The important thing is, this isn't some kind of bombing suicide mission, right?"

"That is correct."

"You plan on making a video of the hostages getting their heads chopped off, or set on fire, or some other sick trick?"

"No," he lied.

"I'm serious. I can't be part of that. El Primo's got scruples."

"I assure you that is not the plan." He lied again.

"As long as it's a straight snatch for cash, I'm good with it."

"We are not snatching them. They are expecting us to pick them up."

"You mean Rig Hoppers?"

"Yes."

"So I take it you have them handled? We're pulling the old switcheroo?"

"They were notified of a delay and will not be coming for two hours. By the time they figure out what happened, we will be back at the *Dinero Majado.*"

"Pretty slick if it works. There it is, dead ahead." El Primo pointed at the hulking structure and flew the chopper in a slow circle around it. "Holy shit! Is this fucking thing big!"

"It is one of the largest in the world."

"I bet they got cameras everywhere. Fuck. I don't know, man."

"Don't worry about cameras. You're staying in the helicopter. Think of the money."

"I am. I'm thinking about the gas, too. We got less than a half a tank."

"It is enough. I prayed to Allah."

"From your lips to his hairy balls. Hang on, No-Name, I'm putting this baby down!"

Chapter 35

The helicopter hit the deck with a thud, and el Primo looked around. There was a large group of men about fifty yards away standing outside a small building. "What now?"

"Now we pick up our guests. As soon as we get them in the helicopter, we leave. Don't say a word."

"Got it."

"When I get out, don't do anything stupid, either." He pulled a small device out of his pocket that looked like an automobile remote lock opener.

"What's that?"

"It's insurance in case you were thinking of flying off. One press of the button, and the helicopter will be blown to pieces."

"You just had to have a fuckin' bomb. I knew it. Where's the trust, man?"

"It's in my hand." Zahvi slipped it in his pocket before taking off his headset and exiting the chopper.

El Primo cursed under his breath and watched the group of men finish shaking hands. Zahvi stood outside the chopper door and motioned for the passengers to come. Three men approached. As they neared the spinning overhead blades, they ducked and jogged to the open door. The man in the middle carried what appeared to be a small cooler. He had on boat shoes, jeans, a short-sleeve fishing shirt, a Texas Rangers baseball cap, and aviator sunglasses. He was flanked by two guys in khakis and windbreakers. *Who wore windbreakers when it was eighty-five degrees and sunny?* Zahvi shook hands with the first guy and directed him into the seat behind el Primo. The guy in the ball cap followed. El Primo avoided eye contact by pretending to write on a chart. The second guy with a windbreaker climbed in and sat on the other side of ball-cap guy. As the three new passengers adjusted their headsets, Zahvi climbed in and shut the door. He quickly slipped on his headset and nodded before pointing at the windshield. El Primo took the cue and a deep breath before piloting the helicopter up and away on a due west heading.

With the sun beating down on the water, the glare had el Primo squinting behind his Ray-Bans. His nerves were holding up, but he was definitely on edge. At the end of the day, kidnapping was still kidnapping. Things could go wrong and often did. At least that was his experience. He tried to think about the money but then started thinking about the bomb and it caused him to fart so hard it felt like his scrotum got tickled by a centipede playing patty-cakes. Then came the smell. *Yikes.*

"Sorry," he said, to no one in particular.

Zahvi shot him a stern look and then caught a whiff and started waving his hand in front of his nose.

"I smell something funny," said one of the other passengers. El Primo glanced back to see who said it.

It was the guy in the middle. He had his sunglasses perched on his Texas Rangers baseball cap, and he looked strangely familiar.

"That was me. Sorry about that," el Primo confessed.

"I'm not talking about the fart. I know what a fart smells like. I eat armadillo stew. Heh. I'm talking about that other smell. What is that?" He turned to the guy on his right. "You smell that Blinky?"

Blinky had his nose buried in his shoulder, trying to escape the fart smell, and shook his head no.

"I'm telling you, I smelled that smell before." He turned to the guy on the left. "How about you?"

"Sorry, sir, just smells like shit to me."

Sir? El Primo glanced back at the three passengers and started reevaluating things. *What kind of oil executive calls the other, sir?* He looked at the guy in the middle again with the graying temples and the southern twang. He looked familiar. *Why was that?*

"You got a name there, flyboy?" the man asked.

El Primo was caught off guard. "What's that?"

"Your name. What's your name?"

"Oh, uh, it's, uh..." El Primo looked at the controls and saw a name. He went with it. "Helix."

"What's that? Helix?"

"Helix? No...no, I said Felix. My name's Felix."

"That's pretty funny. Felix flying a Helix. Heh. Haven't seen a chopper this big since Iraq. Didn't realize Rig Hoppers had one of these babies in their fleet. I'll have to remember that next time we throw a hoedown at the ranch. I could fit the Gatlin Brothers in this thing. Seems like a little overkill for the three of us but what do I know about cargonomics? I'm from

Texas, the bigger the better. Just look at my wife. Heh. That was, uh…that was a joke there. You know, for the record."

El Primo let out a nervous laugh and thought about what the guy with the southern twang said and the way he said it. Iraq, the Gatlin Brothers, the Ranch…cargonomics. Cargonomics? It wasn't even a word, was it? The guy reminded him of—*No, no, it can't be.* He looked over his shoulder. The guy pointed a finger and winked at him with a smile. El Primo's mouth hung open and his blood ran cold as he recognized who he was looking at: the forty-third president of the United States of God Bless America. George W. Bush. *Holy fucking shit.*

"Watch where you're going," Zahvi said.

El Primo turned and stared out the windshield, stunned to the core.

"Ohhh, shit. Oh, shit, shit, shit."

"What's the matter, Felix? Another fart go rogue?" He sniffed the air. "Smells okay to me except for that underlying odor I just can't put my finger on…no pun intended. Heh."

El Primo looked at Zahvi in near panic. "You didn't tell me it was the…it's President Bush!"

"Pay attention to what you're doing. Fly the helicopter."

"Yup, it's me," said the president. "What is this, your first day? Is that why the copilot's telling you what to do?"

"Yes, he's in training," Zahvi answered.

"Well, I say he's doing fine. Just keep us in the air, son, it's not too complicated. Hey!" He sniffed the air again. "I figured it out. I figured out that smell. I haven't been on a chopper like this since Iraq, and that's what it smells like in here. Like Iraq. Why is that?"

"I don't smell anything," Zahvi said.

"What about you, Felix?"

"I just came from Matamoros. Everything smells like shit to me."

"Yeah? Well, I got a nose like a hungry beagle. I can sniff out a chupacabra in a hollered-out cactus from a quarter mile, and I'm telling you it smells like Iraq in here—like a tiny clingin' turd gettin' a ball-sweat bath from two camels humpin' in the hot desert sun. Heh." The Secret Service agents on either side of the president shared knowing looks and shook their heads.

El Primo, on the other hand, let out a big snorting laugh. "That's why I can't smell it. It smells just like Matamoros."

Zahvi was not amused. "It smells fine. Pay attention to the course." He pointed to the south. "You know the way."

El Primo looked to the south and then back at Zahvi. Kidnapping was one thing, but helping a terrorist kidnap a former president of the United States was another. It was off-the-charts insane and traitorous to boot. He had spent a lifetime on the wrong side of the law and had been dishonorably discharged by the navy, but he was no traitor. And he knew he was kidding himself to think No-Name would give him three million bucks and let him fly off into the sunset. More likely he would let him fly off and then press the little red button—turning him into bite-size fish food. He took a deep breath and assessed the situation: The men on either side of the president were undoubtedly

Secret Service agents and armed. He had a gun, too. It was three to two. Pretty good odds…except for the bomb. The bomb was the wildcard. He had to make sure No-Name didn't press the button. He took a deep breath and leaned forward, preparing to go for his gun.

"Did you not hear me?" said Zahvi. "I said, 'You know the way.'" He took his hand out of his pocket and discreetly pointed south. El Primo could see both hands were empty. *It was go time.*

"Yeah, I heard you, dick breath. I heard you blow camels." He grabbed the controls with his left hand, and with his right, he snatched the .45 out of the seat pouch and stuck it in Zahvi's face. "Put your hands in the air, motherfucker!" The agents reacted with surprising speed and each pulled out a pistol. One was pointed at el Primo and the other at No-Name, who had his hands raised.

"He's a terrorist!" el Primo cried. "I got him covered! There's another behind you!"

Both agents turned around, and Zahvi calmly reached into his pocket and pulled out a pistol. El Primo pulled the trigger and expected to see No-Name's brains get splattered, but nothing happened. The gun clicked empty. He yelled, "Look out!" and pulled the trigger again, but it was too late.

"Allah akbar!" Zahvi yelled and shot both agents in the back of the head.

The president cried, "You son of a bitch!" and lunged at Zahvi, only to be yanked back by the other terrorist, who jumped up from behind his seat. An ether-soaked rag was clamped over his mouth and nose, and it was lights out for Dubya.

Zahvi pointed his gun at el Primo and smiled. "Did you really think I would leave a loaded gun in your bag? Drop your useless weapon and take us directly to the *Dinero Majado*! Now!"

Stunned, el Primo let the gun slip to the floor and retook the controls with his right hand. "You didn't tell me you were kidnapping the fucking president! You just killed two Secret Service agents!"

"And you didn't tell me you planned on shooting me in the head."

"I *didn't* plan it. It just happened…seriously. You gotta—"

"Trust me?" He reached in his pocket and held out the remote with the red button. "Seriously?"

"Actually, I was going to say believe me, but sure, a little trust would be good. I trust you, you trust me… together, we're trusty. So don't break the bond and put that thing away. You know how much el Primo hates bombs."

"Then el Primo should trust me when I say that if he doesn't turn south in the next three seconds, I will blow this helicopter out of the sky. It may be plan B, but it works for me. I *love* bombs."

"Christ, you really *are* sick bastards. All right, we're heading south."

El Primo steered the chopper south out of the direct glare of the sun and considered his fate. It was like he was on death row at two hundred feet. He was a dead man—totally and undeniably fucked. He suddenly remembered the fuel situation and looked at the gauge. It showed less than a quarter tank. Over a hundred miles of open water to go and less than a quarter tank. *Super.* It seemed inevitable that one way or the other, he was going in the drink. The question was whether he would be dead before he hit it. Only one thing seemed certain: it was not going to end well for el Primo.

Chapter 36

Time flies when you have a nuclear fishing boat. Actually, the boat flies, but you get the idea. We were going fast. Very fast. I had the *LD3* zipping along at seventy-five knots at one point before Rafe's voice came over the bridge intercom. "SLOW DOWN!"

I did as instructed and throttled back to a more comfortable sixty knots. Tangles poked me in the side and pointed out the port window. "Look at that."

"Look at what?" I glanced but didn't see anything.

"That helicopter. It just passed us to the east. It's heading in the same direction. There it is, at ten o'clock." He pointed out the front window toward the bow, and I saw it growing smaller and smaller as it got farther away.

"I wonder what they're doing way out here?"

"That's what I was thinking. It's kinda weird, right? Especially heading south. Land is that way." He pointed to the west.

"Maybe it's the coast guard."

"The coast guard's colors are orange and white. I got a good look at it. It was black with a neon-green stripe across it. It's definitely not coast guard."

"Then it must be one of those oil service choppers. Maybe they're going to the same rig we are, the *Taladro Grande*."

"Wouldn't they be coming from the west?" He pointed toward land again.

"Maybe they came from New Orleans."

"New Orleans has to be close to a thousand miles from here."

"So maybe it's a nuclear helicopter. How the hell would I know?" I laughed.

"Yeah, right. Well, whoever they are, I hope they got plenty of gas. This is like the middle of Bumfuck, Egypt, out here."

"Egypt is the desert. This is the gulf."

"Yeah, the Gulf of Bumfuck, Egypt. You know what I mean."

"Unfortunately, I do."

"What the hell does that mean?"

"It means I hear you. I can read your little mind. It's like reading the CliffsNotes to a normal mind. Boom—done. It's scary."

"What's scary?" Rafe came up the steps.

"Huh? Oh, nothing much. Tangles saw a helicopter."

"So what."

"That's pretty much what I was thinking."

"That's not what you said before," Tangles said. "You wondered what they were doing out here in Bumfuck, Egypt, just like I was."

"Egypt's in the desert," Rafe replied. "This is the gulf."

I started laughing again.

"What the hell. Have you been listening in on us?"

"You really think anybody would choose to listen to a conversation between you two?"

"He has a point," I agreed. "So what's going on?"

"I got a call from the boss. Headquarters detected a minor problem with one of the heat-exchanger sensors. It's going to require some specialized diagnostic testing. Once we get a handle on the issue we'll need to upload some software to fix it."

"*Software?*" I said. "That's right up Holly's alley. If it has to do with software she can fix it."

"I've already discussed it with her. Like you said, she can handle the software side, but she hasn't had any training on the diagnostic testing. Neither have I. That's why Judy Larson is flying into Corpus Christi. She knows how to do it. We're picking her up after our stopover at the *Taladro Grande.*"

"We're picking up Judy?" said Tangles. "*My* Judy?"

I shook my head. "Dude, you got a long way to go before referring to her as 'my Judy.'"

Rafe nodded. "Don't be creeping her out. There's a saying when it comes to nuclear-related issues. 'There's minor problems, and there's mushroom problems.' Trust me when I tell you we don't want a mushroom problem. Okay? Don't be pestering Miss Larson when she's got work to do."

"*Me* pester *her?* Puh-leez. Try the other way around. We had some serious sparks going on before she got called away, the kind that gave me a mushroom problem in my pants. I bet she volunteered to come back just to see me."

"Actually, she's one of only a few people in the world who are trained in this particular type of work and the others aren't available. When she was told she needed to come back, her exact words were 'Do I have to?'"

"Doesn't sound like sparks to me. Sounds like a wet blanket." I laughed.

"That's bullshit. No way she said that. If she did, she's in denial."

"Somebody sure is."

"Nevertheless," continued Rafe. "The orders are straight from the top. No bothering Miss Larson unless you want to end up back in the bayou working on a shrimp boat."

"Back on a...*what?* Wait a second, how'd you know?"

"I know everything."

"*Everything?*"

"Pretty much. Like you also used to be an Elvis impersonator on a cruise ship until you jumped overboard after catching your girlfriend in the act with another woman. I believe that's how you and Shagball met, right?"

"That's right," I chipped in. "Her name was Darlene. Last I heard she traded her Mustang for a Subaru." Rafe started laughing.

"You are so full of shit." Tangles said.

"No, seriously. Heard she got a pimped-out Forester. You know, four-wheel drive, tent strapped to the top, bikes on a rack."

"You lie."

"Camping bag in the back."

"*Camping bag?* You mean sleeping bag?"

"Yeah. Heard it's just big enough for two." I winked.

"You dick."

Tangles huffed his way down the stairs, and Rafe followed, leaving me alone at the helm. It was nice. The weather was good, and the seas were calm. It was near perfect conditions for running fast, so I took it upon myself to do exactly that. I pushed the throttles forward again and watched the speedometer climb back to seventy-five knots per hour. The lack of engine noise was astonishing as the *LD3* flew across the water. It was like the Tesla of boats—silent but blisteringly fast. I almost felt sorry for the flying fish that tried to flee from the bow's wake. It was a certainty that more than a few of the silvery winged creatures got splattered on the bow and became seafood. Oh well. *Ashes to ashes, fish to fish.* It was the circle of life or something like that. I was just passing through it on a badass boat. Surprisingly, the intercom didn't crackle to life with Rafe ordering me to slow down again, and two beers later we were nearly there. I slowed down to trolling speed and set the autopilot before heading below.

Tangles was lying on the couch, and Rafe and Holly came up the hallway that led to the forward berths.

Rafe said, "I take it we're there."

"Yeah we are. I gotta tell you, I really like this nuclear program. It's the only way to fly. We covered almost a hundred miles in less than an hour and a half. That's frickin' crazy."

"We were going that fast?" said Holly. "I can't believe it. I was working on the computer the whole time. It didn't seem bumpy at all."

"That's the motion stabilizer at work," Rafe said.

"And my expert navigating," I added.

"Expert my ass," Tangles said as he rolled over on the couch to face us. "It's practically dead calm. That's why it wasn't bouncy."

"Yeah, that's right, that and my expert navigating. Some captains are made, and some are born. I was born already made."

"Say *what?*"

"I wouldn't expect you to get it because you're not a captain. To be a great one takes vast knowledge, expert seamanship, and profound humility." I smiled at Holly but she was having none of it.

"Kit, knock it off. You sound like Donald Trump."

"You mean presidential?"

"No, I mean like a pompous ass."

"Hey, I was just kidding."

"Well I'm not."

"All right, all right, all right."

"And quit doing that stupid Matthew McConaughey impression. It's terrible."

"Really?"

"Yes, really."

"She's right," Tangles said. "Your McConaughey sucks, just like your navigating."

Sometimes I know when to stop, but not usually. Usually I just keep going until things start flying at my head. This was one of those times. Maybe it was the beers and the hot sun or maybe it was just me being me. I gave my McConaughey one more shot and drawled, "That's cool…I'm cool with that."

I expected to see Holly reach for something handy like a lamp or coffee mug, but she just closed her eyes and gritted her teeth. When she let out a deep breath

I knew she was on the verge of exploding and wisely decided to throw in the towel.

"I'm done. Sorry. No more McConaughey."

"Well, now that that's settled, we need to get this show on the road," said Rafe. "Since we have to pick up Judy we don't have a lot of time. Holly, I'll take you over to the rig on the skiff for your meeting. You guys can stay here and get more familiarized with—"

"Sorry to interrupt," Holly cut in. "But I, uh…sorta made a deal with the gentleman in charge of the *Taladro Grande*."

"*Deal?* What kind of deal?"

"I told him I would bring Kit and Tangles with me."

"Why would you do that?"

"As unlikely as it seems, he's seen their fishing show and thinks it would be good for morale to have them meet some of the guys on the rig. Apparently, quite a few of them like to fish and may have also seen the show. I told him if he arranged for me to meet Alexander Hamilton LeRoux, then I would bring the guys along."

"You hear that Tangles?" I beamed. "Even in Bumfuck we got fans."

"Egypt's in the desert, we're in the gulf."

"Hah. Right. Well, well, well. Look who needs our help…Little Miss Holly. I don't recall her asking if she could utilize our star power. Did she ask you?"

"No sir."

"Hmmm. Seems like we have once again been taken for granted."

"I hate being taken for granted."

"Me too."

Holly pointed at me.

"Don't push it, Kit. I'm warning you, don't push it."

As I considered pushing it, Tangles saved me from myself and got off the couch. "I'll get the skiff ready," he said.

"Thank you. Thank you very much," acknowledged Holly.

As he walked past, I whispered, "Brown nose."

"What was that?" Holly asked.

"Huh? Oh, I, uh, just said I'm gonna…change my clothes. Maybe clean up a little, too."

"Hmm." She wasn't buying it.

"What? I need to look proper for a meet and greet with my fans."

As I headed off, Holly said, "*Really?* It's just some oil rig workers."

I turned at the top of the hall and shook my head. "Maybe to you, but to me they're fans, and I never let down my fans. *Ever.* You know what they say, once a star, always a star. I'll be ready in five."

I walked down the hall with a big grin on my face and heard Holly say, "Oh my God."

Stardom—it has its moments.

Chapter 37

Three days in the hyperbaric chamber worked wonders for Pago. The effects of the bends were all but gone, and his head wound was healing nicely. The doctor finished cleaning the wound and then covered it by wrapping gauze around his entire head.

"Do you really have to do that?" asked Pago.

"Yes. It's healing well, but the cut is pretty deep. The risk of infection is greater now that you're out of the chamber. No sense taking chances. How do you feel?"

"Tired. Pretty good, but tired."

"You should be, you've been sedated for a couple of days."

"Did I miss anything?"

"Your bunkmate, Arturo, and a few others stopped by to see how you were doing. Oh, and the big boss called about an hour ago."

"Oskar?"

"Yes. He said he needed to talk to you. I told him to wait until after I got you out of the chamber and redressed your wounds." The doctor glanced at his watch. "He should be here any minute."

"Thanks for patching me up, doc. I appreciate it."

"That's my job. Unfortunately, we don't have any CT scanning equipment."

"For what?"

"For your head. It doesn't appear you have a skull fracture, but there's no way to know for sure until you get a scan. I told Oskar, and he has you scheduled to fly to a clinic in Corpus Christi first thing tomorrow. Here's a card with the clinic's information. They're expecting you." He handed it to Pago.

"Really? My head feels pretty good. I think I'd know if my skull was busted."

"You've still got painkillers and sedatives in your system. You could have a hairline fracture and not know it."

"So what if I do? What do you do for that?"

"Wear a helmet."

"Seriously?"

There was a knock on the door, and the doctor opened it. It was Oskar. He looked at Pago with his big head bandage. "How is he?"

"Ask him yourself."

"I'm much better, thanks."

"Good. Great. That's great." Oskar turned to the doctor. "Could I have a few minutes alone with him?"

"Sure. I'm done for now." The doctor stepped past him and addressed Pago at the door. "My advice to you is rest. Don't do anything strenuous and watch your head. Please bring back a copy of the CT scan and lab results when you return, and if you need me, you know where to find me."

"Thanks, doc."

As soon as the door shut, Pago asked, "So, did you find anything on the security footage?"

"Nothing useful. One of the exterior cameras caught the moment you went over the rail but it was just a blur. The only thing it did was establish the time. I put in a requisition for more cameras to be placed throughout the lower levels...including the area where your incident occurred."

"*Incident?* Somebody tried to kill me."

"About that. I reported what you told me to my superiors. Due to the lack of evidence to support your claim, they believe this to be a medical incident."

"*Medical incident? Lack of evidence?* I was tied up with weight belts!"

"It's not that I don't believe you, but you had no weight belts on when you were found."

"No shit. I cut them off. If you found me with weight belts, I'd be dead."

"I understand. It's just the way big company's work. Unless it's proved otherwise, they're saying you had a seizure and fell overboard, hitting your head in the process."

"What bullshit. I've never had a seizure in my life."

"That's not what you told the doctor."

"I made that up to try and lure out the guy who tried to kill me! We discussed it."

"I know, but you are now deemed to be an insurance risk."

"What are you saying?"

"Pemex has agreed to a settlement with the company you work for. They are paying for your medical expenses related to the incident plus two month's pay. They are bringing in a new diver."

"What?!"

"I'm sorry, Pago. You can no longer work on any Pemex-owned rigs."

"Fuck Pemex! If word gets out I had a seizure and went overboard, I won't be able to get a job on *any* rig!"

"I don't know how that works."

"I do. If the word 'seizure' gets on my medical records, I'm fucked."

"You are a US citizen, right?"

"So what."

"Look at the bright side. You can probably collect disability. I have a cousin in Brownsville who fell off a ladder and gets a thousand a month."

"He broke his back?"

"No, just the ladder. His back is fine."

"Figures."

"Oh, I almost forgot." Oskar looked at his watch. "I think I have some good news for you."

"You found out who swiped my computer tablet?"

"No, not that. You have a visitor coming."

"What are you talking about?"

Oskar pulled out a piece of paper and read it. "Her name is Holly Lutes. She thinks her aunt is your grandmother or something like that."

"Is this a joke?"

"I don't think so. She says if you're the person she's been looking for, your grandmother left you something in her will."

"*Will?* What will?"

"Don't ask me, she just called a little while ago. I would normally never allow such a visit, but taking into account your situation, I figured it was the least I could do."

"I never even met my grandmother."

"Grandmothers are great. They're like mothers, only nicer and fatter." Oskar's phone rang. "Hola? Yes, yes, hang on a second." Oskar pressed the phone against his shirt. "It's her."

"Who?"

"The lady that wants to see you. She's here. You want to see her, right?"

"Sure, I guess."

Oskar put the phone back to his mouth. "Pago said he'll see you—uh-huh, uh-huh, sure. We'll meet you down below...yes, you'll see it. Are you bringing the midget? Great...that's great, see you soon."

Click.

"Are you bringing the *midget?*" Pago asked.

"Yes, she's bringing him with her. She came by boat."

Pago's ears perked up. "What kind of boat?"

"She said it was a fishing boat, but I don't know, it must be very fast."

"I like to fish."

"I like to watch people fish...especially midgets. It's fun and relaxing at the same time."

"What's with the midget?"

"He's short. It's very funny."

"That's not what I meant."

"I know, it's a special surprise for the crew. The midget is on a fishing show. Maybe you're related to him, too."

"What fishing show?"

"I forget the name, but they have a new boat. C'mon, I've got some binoculars in my office. Let's go take a look."

Chapter 38

Pago looked through the binoculars at the boat holding steady about a half mile from the *Taladro Grande.* It had a classic sport-fisher design but with a sleeker, low-slung look. The blue hull blended seamlessly into the gently lapping waters of the gulf. Nice. *Very nice.* He estimated the length at fifty to sixty feet and watched as a small skiff pulled away from it and headed toward the rig.

"Here they come," he said.

"Can you see the midget?" asked Oskar.

Pago tried to focus on the skiff but couldn't keep it in his sights.

"I can't tell, the skiff is moving too fast." He lowered the binoculars and handed them back to Oskar.

"Well, let's go down and meet them. This might be your ticket, Pago. Maybe you inherited enough money, you don't need to worry about working anymore."

"I wish I shared your optimism. This whole thing seems farfetched to me."

"Well, you're about to find out. C'mon."

By the time they reached the lower level, the skiff and its occupants were pulling into the lift area. Oskar nudged him in the side and whispered, "Look. Look at the midget. Wow, he's a short one."

"Most of them are."

"This is gonna be great. The guys are gonna love this."

Pago waved and the beautiful blonde standing next to the guy driving the skiff smiled and waved back at him.

Oskar gave directions to the driver.

"That's good where you are. Just keep it there, and I'll bring the lift up."

The driver gave a thumbs-up, and Oskar activated the lift. As the skiff slowly ascended, Pago studied the occupants. The midget and the guy at the helm wore matching shirts, and both wore visors and sunglasses. The guy at the helm was good sized, about six two and maybe 225 pounds. The name on his shirt read: Shagball. He appeared to be in decent shape. The midget was short and semistocky, and the name on his shirt read: Tangles. Shagball and Tangles? Interesting. Interesting, but not nearly as interesting as the leggy blonde who wore cutoffs and a tank top and had her hair pulled up under a Miami Dolphins cap. Pago lowered the walkway to the skiff and held his hand out to help her disembark. She said thanks and stepped past him onto the platform. "Welcome to the *Taladro Grande*," said Oskar, as he shook Holly's hand. "You are the one who called me earlier?"

"Yes. You're Oskar, the manager?"

"Yes, ma'am."

"Thank you so much for meeting us. As you can probably tell from their shirts, this is Shagball and Tangles."

As Oskar shook our hands, he gushed over the unexpected chance to meet us. "Thank you for coming. It is an honor to have you here. You have many fans on the *Taladro Grande.* Myself included."

"Don't mention it," I said. "We have fans all over the world. Any chance we get to pay back the love, we do it in spades, right, Tangles?"

"That's right. Spades, hearts, diamonds, clubs… every card in the deck of love."

"That's good. We like cards. We play a lot of cards. Maybe you can play some cards with the crew?"

"Or maybe you can introduce me," said Pago.

"Oh, right. Of course. Sorry about that. Miss Holly, this is Pago, the man you think is your cousin."

"*Pago?*" Holly extended her hand.

As they shook, he explained, "It's a nickname. I'm from Pago Pago, in American Samoa. My given name is Alexander Hamilton LeRoux. I go by Pago for obvious reasons."

"What happened to your head?"

"Somebody tried to—"

"Pago?" Oskar cut him off. "You have yet to collect your severance pay and have your medical bills paid."

"Right. I, uh…just hit my head. It was an accident. It's nothing."

"Yes, it was an unfortunate accident," Oskar confirmed. "Okay, then, why don't we go up to my office? You two can discuss your family tree there and I will take Shagball and Tangles to meet some of the crew."

"Sounds like a plan," I said. "We don't want to keep our fans waiting."

As we followed Oskar and Pago, we got several looks from some of the rig workers. Tangles was undoubtedly the subject of their interest. There was lots of pointing and laughing that was drowned out by the hum of machinery. To his credit, he played the part by smiling and waving back like he was on a Rose Bowl parade float. It seemed my steady stream of ribbing over the years had finally started to thicken up his skin.

On the other hand, Pago's skin, in the literal sense, didn't seem so thick. I noticed some fresh scratches and cuts on his legs and arms that were starting to scab up, not to mention the big bandage wrapped around his head. The way Oskar cut him off when he started to tell Holly what happened made it pretty clear that his wounds were the result of something more than a simple accident. Pago had the physique of a swimmer with narrow hips and wide shoulders. He was a few inches shorter than me. A weathered face made it hard to pinpoint his age, and the color of his skin was light brown. Whether or not he was related to Holly was about to be determined.

The *Taladro Grande* wasn't as big as the *Bluewater*, but it was still pretty damn big. We made our way across the top deck and stopped outside a door to a small structure.

"This is my office," said Oskar. "Miss Holly, you and Pago can talk in private inside. Pago, when you are finished, use the radio on my desk to call me. I am taking our guests down to the cafeteria to meet some of the crew. Okay?"

"Sure. I just have one question."

"What's that?"

Pago turned to me and asked, "Is this some kind of joke?"

"What?"

"You heard me. Is this some kind of prank? You wearing a hidden camera for some stupid reality show or something?"

"I hate reality shows. They're too fake."

"That's not an answer. Are you in on this, Oskar? Please tell me I didn't really get fired."

"No. I mean, yes. You're still fired. But no, this isn't a prank. At least I don't think it is." He turned to Holly and scowled. "It better not be."

"I assure you this is no joke," Holly said. She looked Pago square in the eye. "I just need a few minutes with you to try and determine if you are who I think you are. I am the executor of an estate which you may be entitled to a portion of."

"Don't be pulling my leg. I'm really not in the mood."

"I'm not."

"She pulls my leg all the time," Tangles quipped. "Unfortunately, not my third leg."

"Tangles!"

"Sorry. You better listen to her, dude. If you're her cousin, you're one lucky bastard, and you look like you could use some right now."

"I can't argue with that." Pago swung open the door to the office and waved Holly in. "Okay, let's hear what you have to say."

Chapter 39

Less than ten miles away, el Primo held the Helix in a hover above the *Dinero Majado* and eyed the landing spot. There was a crudely drawn X on top of a platform covering the old landing area. The platform had two wheels on each side that looked like they came off a forklift. It looked like a makeshift trailer without the sides.

"What are you waiting for?" Zahvi asked. "Set us down."

"On *that* fucking thing? Are you serious?"

"What's the matter, is it too difficult for you?" Zahvi smiled.

"Of course not. I could land a hang glider on a pontoon boat in a hurricane."

"Then do it."

"All right, but your little Tonka Toy trailer's probably gonna get crushed. This chopper ain't exactly light. What's it there for, anyways?"

Zahvi pointed his gun at el Primo's head. "No more questions."

"I don't know what you're doing here, pal, but here we go."

El Primo lowered the chopper onto the platform, which surprisingly didn't collapse. Zahvi instructed el Primo to shut down the engine and when the rotors stopped spinning, two of Zahvi's armed associates opened the passenger door. El Primo unbuckled his seatbelt, and Zahvi again pointed his gun at him.

"You're not going anywhere."

"I gotta take a leak."

"Too bad."

El Primo watched the men remove the president's unconscious body and drag him across the deck into a building. The men returned, and Zahvi barked some orders in Arabic. The men ran to the side, where a third man helped them lug a heavy chain over to the front of the trailer-like platform that the chopper sat on.

"What the…what are they doing?"

"You'll know soon enough." Zahvi exited the chopper but kept the door open. He picked up one of the AK-47s one of the men left on the ground and trained it on el Primo. With the chain fastened to a giant eyebolt screwed into the front of the platform, the men hauled the rest of the chain over to the edge about forty feet away. El Primo hadn't noticed it before, but a section of railing along the edge was missing, and what appeared to be a large diesel generator sat on the precipice. The men attached the chain to the generator, and then one of the men ran back to the chopper and told Zahvi, "It is ready."

"Excellent."

El Primo was no math whiz, but he could put two and two together. He looked at Zahvi. "You lousy fucking bastard. After all I did for you, you're gonna send me to Davy Jones's locker with fresh shark meat in the back?" He glanced back at the two dead Secret Service agents.

"You tried to shoot me in the head about an hour ago."

"Fuck you if you can't take a joke. I hope you get camel AIDS."

"You have no idea how much I'd love to blow you to pieces but I can't risk anybody seeing the explosion. Consider yourself lucky. Don't worry though, you'll be dead before you hit the water." He whispered something to the man standing next to him who then pointed his AK at el Primo. Then he shouted instructions in Arabic to the two men standing by the generator at the edge of the platform. The instructions were to push the generator over the side when he gave the signal, which would come after el Primo was shot dead. One of the men had trouble hearing him and asked him to repeat it. Zahvi slung his AK over his shoulder and motioned to push the generator over the side while repeating the instructions. The men saw him signal to push the generator over, and that's what they did.

"NO!" Zahvi yelled. "Not yet!" But it was too late. The generator disappeared over the side.

El Primo braced himself and yelled, "Bin Laden was gay!" The chain snapped taut, and the chopper lurched forward, gaining speed as it rolled to the edge. Zahvi and the other man started firing into the chopper as they chased after it. With glass exploding all around him, el Primo dove behind the rear seat. He looped the strap of his duffel bag through his arm and wedged himself between the seat frame and the rear of the chopper.

A second later he felt the chopper go over the side. The windshield exploded as the two dead agents crashed through it. The weight of the chopper caused the generator to swing under the rig and get snagged on a support beam. The chopper somersaulted and hit the water tail first. His gun, which had been lying on the floor by the pilot's seat, landed next to him, and he stuck it inside his flight suit. He looked up through the busted out windshield and felt lucky to be alive. It didn't last long. He felt the chopper jerk and a split second later he realized the dark object rapidly blotting out the sunlight was the generator. He screamed as it hit the chopper with a horrifying crunch and tore off the entire passenger side. The generator kept descending toward the ocean floor while the chopper rolled over, and water gushed in.

El Primo found himself with his head in a rapidly diminishing air pocket, and panic set in. Just when he thought it couldn't get any worse, bullets started tearing through shell of the chopper. He didn't have long to worry about getting hit because the generator pulled the chopper down and next thing he knew the air pocket was gone. He took a deep breath and swam out the gaping hole in the side, still clinging to his precious carry-on bag. His eyes burned when he tried to get his bearings, and he figured he was about thirty feet below the surface. He swam for the shade of the rig and was surprised at how fast he closed the gap before realizing the current was helping him. With his chest pounding, he reached the cover of the rig and grabbed one of the support legs. He swung himself to the inside corner of the leg where he felt he couldn't be seen from above and shot to the surface. *YES!* He made it.

As he sucked down the sweet salty air, he realized his hand was bleeding, but he didn't really care. *El Primo was still kicking.* After he caught his breath, he opened the carry-on and pulled out the bottle of water inside. He took a few gulps and put it back inside along with his gun. He looked up at the underbelly of the old rusty rig and saw a ladder in the center that was about ten feet above the water's surface. He knew he had to get to the ladder. The ladder led to payback time. He had terrorists to kill and a president to save. Maybe he'd even get a reward. It would take some tricky climbing to make his way over to it but he knew it had to be done. He was tired, though. *Fuck, was he tired.* He figured he would just hang on to the support leg of the rig for a little while until he got some strength back and then start climbing. Then something bumped his foot.

"Shit!" he cried, and in a lower voice, said, "What the fuck." He hoisted himself up the barnacle-laden structure and something splashed in front of him. A triangular fin came out of the water, and he looked down on the unmistakable head of large hammerhead shark. "You have got to be fucking kidding me," he muttered. He looked up at the ladder and shook his head. With adrenaline pumping through his veins, he started climbing.

Chapter 40

Zahvi and the other men peered over the side at the small debris field that remained floating on the surface. The makeshift helicopter platform had disintegrated, and the planks floated about, mixed with seat cushions and other effects from inside the chopper. That was it. Everything else was presumably on its way to the bottom.

"What do you think?" Zahvi wondered aloud. "Does anybody see the pilot?"

"Only the fish see him now," one of the men said. "Unless he has gills, he is a dead man."

"Even if he has gills, he is dead," another said. "If the generator didn't crush him, one of the bullets must have hit him."

"El Primo is el Deado," another said, and everybody laughed but Zahvi, who continued to scan the surface. As he did so he noticed the debris was floating under the rig, with the current. He quickly walked over to the corner of the rig and looked down, but there was no sign of el Primo. The men followed, and he quickly instructed two of them to go back to where they were and keep looking.

"Look for what?"

"For el Primo, you idiot! I want to be positive he is dead." He looked at his watch. "Give it five minutes. If there is still no sign of him then I will believe it."

***

Roughly 110 miles to the north, the real Rig Hoppers helicopter set down on the deck of the *Bluewater.* The pilot kept the engine running and waited for his charter, the former president of the United States and his Secret Service agents. When they didn't appear after a couple of minutes, he shut the engine down and went to see what was going on. As he made his way across the deck, the deck foreman came walking up and inquired as to the reason he was there.

"What do you mean? I'm here to pick up President Bush. I figured he'd be waiting 'cause I'm running a few minutes late. Is he tied up or something?"

"*Tied up?* What are you talking about? He left a couple of hours ago."

"*What?*"

The deck foreman pointed at the helicopter. "You're Rig Hoppers, right?"

"Of course."

"Well, you should know, you guys picked him up."

"We did? What the hell. Let me call the office and see what's going on. There must have been a mix-up." The pilot walked back to the chopper, got in, and picked up the radio mic.

"You there, Alison? It's Steve."

"Yeah, I'm here, Stevie. What's up? Everything all right?"

"No, not exactly. I just got to the *Bluewater*, and they said the president got picked up a couple of hours ago."

"*What?* By who?"

"By us."

"What do you mean, *us?* You *are* us. You're the one that's supposed to pick him up."

"I know, but the deck foreman said he left on one of our birds a couple of hours ago."

"A couple of hours ago? That was the originally scheduled pickup time but we got an e-mail from the service, and they pushed it back until now. They even confirmed it. Hang on a second. Let me pull up the tracking screen. Okay, I can see where every one of our helicopters is and where they've been and...yeah, it didn't happen. If he got picked up, it wasn't by us. This is weird. Maybe he had an emergency or something? I don't know what's going on, but the deck foreman has to be mistaken."

"Huh. That's what I figured. I don't know how he could mistake one of our birds for somebody else's, but I'll ask him again."

"Okay, call me back and let me know what he says. I'm gonna put a call into the Secret Service."

"Will do." *Click.*

The pilot opened the door to get out, and the deck foreman was standing right there.

"Did you figure it out?"

"Sort of. It definitely wasn't one of our choppers that picked him up."

"Buddy, I saw him leave myself. It was a helicopter just like this, same paint job, same name, same everything, only…" The foreman took a few steps back and looked from the tail to the front and back.

"Only what?"

"It was bigger than this one. Yeah, it was definitely bigger."

"Bigger how?"

"You know, a little longer, maybe a little wider, too."

"Couldn't be. Every transport chopper in our fleet is the same model, same size."

"Hey, I'm just telling you what I saw. It was bigger than this."

The pilot shook his head, confused by what the foreman was telling him.

"This is fucked up. Let me call the office again." He picked up the mic and said, "Alison, it's Steve." After five seconds of silence he called again. "Alison, it's Steve, come back."

"Stevie, hang on, don't go anywhere. Oh shit!"

"What? What's going on?" The alarm in Alison's voice had him concerned.

"What is it?" asked the foreman.

"I don't know, but it doesn't sound good." The radio crackled and Alison's panicked voice came over the speaker.

"Stevie! Stevie, you there?"

"What the hell's going on, Al?"

"Oh my God, I can't believe this. This is bad. This is really bad."

"What happened?"

"Are you by yourself? Can anybody else hear me?"

"Yeah, the deck foreman's standing right here."

"Put your headset on and head home."

"Why? What happ—?"

"Just do it!" *Click.*

Stevie looked at the foreman and said, "You heard her, I gotta go!"

"But what—?" He shut the door on the perplexed foreman, put his headset on, and fired up the engine. As soon as he lifted off, he radioed back in.

"Alison, pick up!"

"Stevie! Oh my God. Oh my fricking God!"

"Will you tell me what happened already!?"

"The Secret Service computers got hacked! They never e-mailed us this morning, and they didn't call either. There *was* no change to the president's schedule."

"Are you serious?"

"I wish I wasn't. They're in a panic, just like me. They don't know who picked him up or where he is."

"WHAT?!"

"Yeah, that's what I said. We're not supposed to leave the premises and if we tell anybody they threatened to throw us in jail for the rest of our lives. Our computers and phone lines have been disconnected, the satellite is down, and nobody's cell phone is getting a signal."

"Holy shit! What do they think happened?"

"They don't know and probably wouldn't tell us anyways, but it looks like he's been kidnapped. Oh shit, the FBI just pulled into the parking lot. If I were you, I'd stay away from here. You can always claim you had a mechanical issue and had to land somewhere else. Be safe, Stevie. I gotta go!"

Click.

Chapter 41

The story of Holly's aunt Millie and her taboo-breaking interracial love affair back in 1948 was a complicated one...especially the aftermath that resulted in her husband, Joseph, being murdered and her babies being stolen at birth. If Joseph was indeed Pago's grandfather, then he certainly had a right to know what happened, but it was a big if. Holly didn't know how much time she had to spend with him and wanted to get the bottom of it quickly.

"What is your father's name?" she asked.

"His name was Patrick, he died in Vietnam."

"That's what I was told. I'm sorry. Did he ever speak about his childhood?"

"Not much. The only thing he said was that his mother sent him away when he was a young man because she feared his brother would kill him."

"What about you? Do you have any brothers or sisters?"

"No. As far as I know, I'm an only child."

"Me too. What about your mother? Is she—"

"She passed away two years ago—breast cancer."

"I'm so sorry."

"Look, lady—"

"Please, it's Holly."

"Right. Holly. So it's like this. I got a lot on my mind right now. Can we just cut to the chase?"

"Of course. Your answers lead me to believe you're the person I've been looking for. There's just one more question I have for right now."

"What's that?"

"Your father, did he have a birthmark?"

"You mean like this?" Pago gingerly peeled back a large bandage on his forearm and rotated it over for Holly to see. There on the underside next to a nasty scrape was the image of a four leaf clover.

"Oh my God! You have the same birthmark?"

"Not exactly. Dad's was more of a dark purple. Mine's green. It's a tattoo. I got it in his honor after he was killed."

Holly's eyes started to well up with tears, and her lips trembled.

"What's the matter? Why are you crying?"

"I can't...I just can't believe it." She sniffled. "After all these years, it *is* you. Your grandmother and my aunt were one and the same. Boy, do I have a story to tell *you.* We're...we're *family.*"

Holly stepped forward and when she gave Pago a big hug, he winced.

She pulled away and apologized. "I'm sorry. I forgot about your accident."

"It was no accident. Somebody tried to kill me."

"*What?!* But Oskar said—"

"Oskar's full of shit. Actually, it's the oil company that's full of shit. Oskar's not a bad guy; he's just not willing to stick his neck out for me. He's toeing the company line, even though he knows I'm telling the truth."

"So what *is* the truth?"

"You said you had a story to tell. You first."

***

We walked into the cafeteria, and there were about twenty men sitting at tables and a few more going through a buffet line. Oskar brought a bullhorn with him, and he used it to address the men. "Hello, everybody. We have some special guests today! Maybe you recognize them. This is señor Shagball and señor Tangles. They have a fishing show that I know some of you have seen." He lowered the bullhorn and whispered to me, "What is the name of the show again?"

"*Fishing on the Edge with Shagball and Tangles.*"

"Yes, of course." He raised the bullhorn and said, "The name of the show is *Fishing on the Ledge with Shagball and Tangles.* It is very funny."

I gave him a friendly nudge. "That's not quite right. May I?" I held my hand out for the bullhorn, and he lowered it.

"Sure. No problem. Let me just say one more thing." He raised the bullhorn and said, "Señor Shagball is going to speak to you now. If you have any fishing questions, I am sure he can answer them. If you prefer short answers then maybe you should ask señor Tangles." The men erupted in laughter, and Oskar winked at Tangles as he handed me the bullhorn.

"Yeah that was, uh, not funny," Tangles said.

"I was only joking, my friend." He pulled out a chair from the table we were standing in front of and added, "Please stand on the chair so the men can see you."

"Seriously?"

"Oh yes, midgets are very popular in Mexico."

"That's great, but I'm not a midget."

"Maybe, but you're not exactly NBA material either. Have you looked in a mirror lately?"

Tangles looked at me with disbelief written all over his face. "What the fuck? I didn't sign up for this shit."

"Please, I did not mean to disrespect you, señor Tangles. It was a bad joke. I am sorry. Believe me when I say midg—I mean, people of your stature, are revered in our country."

"People of my stature?"

"We call them *gente diminuta,* or tiny people."

"*Tiny?* I'm not tiny. Lapdogs are tiny. Do I look like a fucking lapdog to you?"

I could tell we were losing the crowd's attention and had heard enough. "Just get on the goddamn chair already."

"Trust me," Oskar said. "When the men get a good look at you, they will love you more than the Frito Bandito."

"I hate Fritos. They're like corn-flavored pretzels without the twist."

"On the chair! Now!"

He shook his head and stepped up on the chair. "This is fucked up."

Immediately, the men started clapping and laughing. One of them said, "Look! It's a meeegit. Hey, hey!"

I raised the bullhorn to my mouth and tried to take control of the situation before Tangles blew a fuse. "Please, may I have your attention. A couple of things I'd like to clear up before we get into the question-and-answer period. Number one, Señor Tangles is not a midget. He is what you call a *gente diminuta.*"

"Sí," said one of the men. "Muy diminuta!" This caused another round of laughter and some high-fiving between the men.

Tangles's face went red, and a vein on his neck started to pulse. I gave him a hand gesture to calm down and counterattacked. "That may be true, but looking around the cafeteria, I can see he's not the only one who's never been allowed on a roller coaster."

Oskar laughed, but the men seemed to not get it until Oskar spoke some Spanish. A few started laughing and pointing at the short guys in the audience, who didn't think it so funny.

"Okay then, number two. The name of the show is *Fishing on the Edge with Shagball and Tangles*, not *Fishing on the Ledge.*"

"What's the difference?" one guy asked.

"Simple. One's the name of our show, and one's not."

"No, I mean an edge is a ledge, and a ledge is an edge, right?'

"Not always. You could be fishing a current edge, which has no ledge, or you could be fishing on the edge of a color change, which again, has no ledge. Comprendo? It's different. Muy differento." I was met with mostly blank stares. "All right, let's just move along then. How about another question?"

"I have a question," said a guy at the table in front of me.

"Great. Shoot."

"I like to fish at Lake Baccarac but haven't landed any big ones yet. What bait would you recommend to catch trophy-size bass?"

"Whoa. *Bass?* We're strictly saltwater guys, pal. The big leagues. We don't play in the kiddie pool."

"But fishing is fishing, no?"

"No, not even close. Tangles, would you like to handle this one?"

"Yeah, I got this." I handed him the bullhorn. He raised it to his mouth. "Lemme see if I can make this a little easier to understand." He pointed at the plate of food in front of the guy. "What are you eating there?"

"A burrito."

"Okay, very simple. The difference between freshwater fishing and saltwater fishing is like the difference between a burrito and a chimichanga."

"But a chimichanga is just a fried burrito. They are pretty much the same."

"Is that right? Huh, didn't know that. Okay, it's like the difference between a taco and a tostada."

"No difference there either," another guy pointed out. "A tostada is just a flat taco."

"No kidding. You must be sick of eating that shit if it's all the same. So how about this. It's like the difference between a plate of hot nachos and a cold beer—two completely different things. Got it?"

"They may be different, but you can't have one without the other. They go perfectly together."

"Oh, for Christ's sake. You know what I mean."

"I think I do. It's like the difference between you and a piñata. You are the same, but different," a guy sitting at a table in back said. Most everyone started laughing, including me.

"*What?* No. No it's not like that at all."

"You are wrong," the man in front said. "You are the same. I want to hit you both with a stick and see what comes out. Hey, hey. Ha-ha. Woooo!"

The whole cafeteria erupted in laughter. Well, everyone but Tangles. He glared at the guy and stepped from the chair onto the man's table. I knew it was about to get ugly and tried to grab him, but he swatted my arm away and kicked the guy's burrito plate into his chest. What was left of the burrito and a heaping pile of rice, beans, and salsa went flying. Half the crowd was eating Mexican whether they liked it or not. Tangles dropped the bullhorn and held his fists up like a boxer. "C'mon, Pedro! You wanna take a shot at me, take a shot!" I'm guessing his name wasn't Pedro, but he stood up, visibly stunned. His mouth hung open, and his face looked like it got hit with a Mexican potpie.

"Stop! Please!" Oskar yelled.

But Tangles wasn't hearing it. He danced on the table like Muhammad Ali and continued his taunting. "C'mon, motherfucker! You wanna dance with the king? Let's dance!"

I had to admit it was pretty awesome. The guy took a swing at Tangles, and he jumped to the left, successfully dodging it. Tangles was in front of me and was winding up to kick him in the head when I grabbed him in a bear hug and wrestled him off the table. The cafeteria was in near pandemonium, and Oskar smartly opened the door behind us. "This way!"

As soon as the door shut behind us we heard the sound of various food items splatting against it. I set Tangles down, and Oskar quickly ushered us down the hall. He looked at me and said, "You should have warned me the little one has such a temper."

"I don't have a fucking temper! That bozo said he wanted to hit me so I gave him the chance. I thought you said Mexicans *love* midgets."

"They do, but as you pointed out, you're not a midget. You are a very angry little person. Now I know why you spend most of your time on a boat in the middle of the ocean."

I couldn't help it and laughed again. "I think he's got you pegged,"

"Shut the fuck up."

"I hope Miss Holly is done speaking with Pago, because for the safety of my men, I must ask you to leave."

"Gladly," Tangles said. "Fucking bass fishermen."

When we reached Oskar's office, Pago was sitting in a chair, and Holly was on the phone.

She said, "Thanks, Rafe," and hung up.

"Thank you for what?" I asked.

"For checking to see if it was okay to give Pago a ride to Corpus Christi for some medical tests. He checked, and it's okay. Pago's coming with us."

"He is? Does that mean—"

"Yes, Pago is my cousin. There's no doubt about it."

"I can't believe it," Pago said. "The story she told is incredible, but it all adds up. I can't believe my father had a twin sister he never knew about. I have to find out what happened to her. This is crazy."

"So what about the inheritance?" Oskar asked.

"What about it?"

"You know, what did you get?"

"It's none of your business."

"None of my business? I didn't have to arrange for you to meet Miss Holly. I could have said no."

"And you could have said no when management told you to cover up the fact that somebody tried to kill me by blaming it on some bullshit seizure I never had."

"There is no proof that—"

"Somebody tried to kill you?" I blurted out.

"I bet his name was Pedro," Tangles said.

"His name is not Pedro!" Oskar fumed.

"Hold on. So you know who tried to kill me then?"

"*What?* No. I don't know. Damn it, Pago, you said you wouldn't go around making this accusation."

"I forgot. The seizure must have affected my memory."

"Nice one," Tangles commented.

Oskar pointed at Tangles. "If I hear one more word out of you, I am going to drag you back to the cafeteria for a game of pin the tail on the midget."

"Now wait just a god—"

"Maybe we should be going," Holly suggested.

"That is an excellent idea," Oskar said. "Señor Tangles has a very bad temper."

Holly looked at Tangles and shook her head. "I swear I can't take you anywhere. What did you do this time?"

"I'll tell you later," I said.

"Some burrito-eating bastard picked a fight with me."

"Oh, Tangles, you didn't."

"Yeah, he did," I said. "Actually, it was more like vice versa."

"Tangles!" Holly had her hands on her hips. It was nice to see her pissed at somebody other than me.

"I'll go grab my gear," Pago said. "I just need a few minutes. I'll meet you at the skiff."

"You're not a bass fisherman, are you?" Tangles asked.

"Not unless you count Chilean sea bass. I grew up on an island in the South Pacific."

"Good. Great. I like you already."

Pago scratched his head, and we followed him out the door. As Pago headed off, Oskar offered up a curt good-bye and good luck and headed the other way.

"What was that about being a bass fisherman?" Holly asked.

"You don't wanna know," I answered with a chuckle. "Believe me, you don't wanna know."

Chapter 42

No sooner had Franklin Post reluctantly given permission to Rafe to give Holly's injured cousin a lift to Corpus Christi than the alarm lights on his command center recliner started flashing. First it was the FBI, then Homeland Security, then the CIA…right down the line. When he got to the bottom of what all the fuss was about, he sat stunned. Former president George W. Bush, the man who'd created DICK and hired him to run it, was missing and presumed kidnapped. A few hours earlier he had been fishing on the newly commissioned *LD3* with Shagball and company, and now he was kidnapped? It seemed inconceivable.

He studied the images of the black-and-white security video from the deck of the *Bluewater* and shook his head. It showed the president and two of his Secret Service agents climbing into a helicopter and taking off. The helicopter had a stripe on it and Rig Hoppers was written inside a logo. Unfortunately, the helicopter wasn't part of the Rig Hoppers fleet, and the Secret Service had confirmed their computers were hacked and the president's schedule had been altered.

The FBI was reviewing flight and radar data from every airport along the Texas and Louisiana coast. It was a daunting task. He zoomed in on the man in the flight suit standing outside the chopper. He was wearing sunglasses, and it was difficult to make out any distinguishing features. Suddenly, the large computer screen on the wall in front of him lit up. The NSA had fed a still image of the man's face into their advanced facial-recognition program and got a hit. The news was bad. They were saying there was a 99 percent chance that the man in the flight suit was none other than Mohammed Zahvi. Zahvi was a former GITMO detainee and member of the notorious Taliban Five who was traded for Bowe Bergdahl, the US Army deserter.

Homeland Security had been investigating rumors that a terrorist organization had hired one of the Mexican drug cartels to help them across the border and that there was a major strike against the United States planned. Now it looked like they knew what it was, and the shit was hitting the fan big-time.

The White House had been notified, and a decision had been made to keep the incident under wraps for as long as possible. The Obama administration was already under critical fire on a number of fronts and the last thing they needed was to be blamed for the kidnapping of a former president of the United States. Especially one that they time and again blamed for their numerous domestic and foreign policy blunders. There was little to go on, but they hoped to somehow locate and rescue him before the kidnappers made their demands or the media got wind of it. *Incredible.*

Given the location of the *Bluewater*, it seemed likely that the kidnappers were either headed for Mexico or perhaps to a ship in the gulf. Franklin Post had a ship in the gulf, too, a nuclear-powered one with enough state-of-the-art gadgetry to give James Bond a hard-on. He scrolled through the Oralator to the voice of James Earl Jones and hyperdialed Rafe on the *LD3*.

***

Rafe was in the forward berth getting briefed by Holly on some software updates to the navigational system when his phone alerted him that the boss was calling. "Hey, boss," he answered. "What's up?"

"There's a problem. A very big problem."

Rafe identified the rich baritone voice as that of the famous African American actor, James Earl Jones. It was a voice the boss had never used before, and he was immediately concerned.

"Is there a problem with the boat? It seems to be—"

"No. Not with the boat, thank God. We need to talk. Where's Holly's cousin?"

"He's lying down in one of the rooms, resting. He's got a pretty nasty head wound by the looks of the bandaging."

"Good. Don't disturb him. Assemble the crew in the salon."

"Why? What's—"

"*Now*, Rafe. Do it now."

"Okay. Sure. Hang on." Rafe put the phone against his chest and whispered to Holly, "Tell Kit to put us on autopilot and come down to the salon with Tangles ASAP."

"What's going on?" she whispered back.

"I don't know. The boss says just do it." Rafe followed Holly down the hall and into the salon. When she headed up to the bridge, Rafe spoke into the phone again. "Okay, boss. I'm in the salon, and Holly's getting the guys down from the bridge."

"Put the phone in the cradle and turn off all the speakers except for the ones on the wall behind the dinette. Turn on the video monitor, too. I'll be sending some images."

"Got it."

***

The sun was low in the western sky when Holly came up to the bridge and loudly told me to put the boat on autopilot. She had to holler because the below deck generator was running, and the engine was rumbling. Rafe had put the boat into fake-diesel mode prior to our return from the *Taladro Grande* because Pago was to be kept in the dark regarding the boat's many unique features. Holly's instruction struck me as odd because my last orders were to bust ass all the way to Corpus Christi.

"Say what?"

"Slow it down!" She gave me a hand signal, and I complied.

"What's going on?" Tangles asked.

"I don't know. The boss called, and he said to put the boat on autopilot and come down to the salon." Tangles followed Holly down the steps, and a minute or so later I entered the salon to find everybody sitting at the dinette.

I plopped down next to Holly. "So what happened, somebody buy the farm?"

Holly gave me a look, and Rafe said, "Okay, boss, we're all here."

"Good," said the deep voice over the speaker. "To answer your question, Kit, nobody bought the farm, at least not yet. Hopefully we can help keep it that way."

"He sounds like Darth Vader," Tangles said. "Wow. That's cool."

"Please, I need your complete attention. There has been a startling development since your fishing trip with the president earlier today," the voice of James Earl Jones responded.

"Lemme guess," I said. "He wants his own fishing show."

"This is no time for jokes, Mr. Jansen. It appears that President Bush has been kidnapped."

We all said it at the same time. "*What?*"

"I'm afraid you heard me right."

"Oh, c'mon!" I said. "I thought you said this was no time for jokes."

"I wish I were joking. Believe me."

"Oh my God," Holly said.

"How?" Rafe asked. "How did it happen?"

"The Secret Service e-mail system got hacked, and somebody sent a message to the helicopter charter service notifying them that the president's pickup time had been moved back two hours. The helicopter service is called Rig Hoppers. They even received a confirmation call, which was recorded and is currently being analyzed by the FBI. The e-mail and call were ruses. The president and his Secret Service agents were picked up at their scheduled time. Look at the monitor." The video monitor above the bar lit up, and there was a black-and-white shot of a helicopter landing on the deck. "A security camera shows a helicopter that appears to be from Rig Hopper's landing on the deck. A man in a flight suit gets out and stands by the door. Less than two minutes later you will see the president and the agents cross the deck and get in the chopper. I sped up the tape to where the president appears. You should be seeing him now."

"We see him," Rafe acknowledged.

"That's my man, Dubya," Tangles commented. "He's carrying the fish he caught in that cooler." We watched as the helicopter rose off the deck, pivoted, and disappeared from view. "Wait a second," Tangles added. "What color is the helicopter and the stripe on the side of it?"

"I'm not sure. Why?"

"'Cause a helicopter passed by us on the way to Pago's rig. I couldn't make out the logo from where we were, but it looked like the helicopter was dark blue or black with a neon-green accent stripe on the side."

"But the *Taladro Grande* is almost a hundred miles south of the *Bluewater.*"

"So?"

"There are eyewitness reports saying the helicopter flew due west toward the coast when it left the *Bluewater.*"

"Tangles isn't mistaken," I confirmed. "I saw it too. Can you rewind the video and freeze the picture when the helicopter pivots?"

"Sure, hang on." A few moments later the video went in slow-motion reverse, and the picture froze, exposing the side of the helicopter as it hovered over the deck of the *Bluewater.*

"What do you think?" I asked Tangles.

"I don't know, except I know what I saw, and what I saw was a dark helicopter with a neon-green stripe. There's no way to tell from a black-and-white picture."

"Hang on a second," the boss said. "I'm pulling up the Rig Hoppers website right now and…son of a bitch! Good eyes, guys. Their helicopters are black with a neon-green stripe, just like you said. I'll be damned."

"I told you so," Tangles boasted.

"Of course, the helicopter you guys spotted may actually be from the Rig Hoppers fleet. I'll have to check it out. Can you give me an estimate of where and when you saw it?"

"Let's see," I wondered aloud. "We had lunch after we dropped Dubya off, so we didn't head south for about forty-five minutes. I didn't start putting the hammer down until we were out of sight of the *Bluewater,* which took a while. I'm thinking we saw that chopper about an hour later, so I don't know. Maybe we were thirty or forty miles north of the *Taladro Grande.* Does that sound about right?"

"Don't look at me," said Holly. "I was working on the computer. I didn't see any helicopters."

"Me neither," Rafe agreed.

"I'd say thirty miles north of the *Taladro Grande,*" Tangles said. "That seems about right. I can't believe

Dubya got kidnapped. That's crazy. Who would do that?"

"Unfortunately, we think we know, and it's not good."

"Who?" asked Rafe.

"Let me roll the video back to the guy standing outside the chopper." The video reversed, and the picture froze with Dubya in front of the guy in the flight suit. "The NSA entered the image of the guy in the flight suit into the facial recognition program that they've perfected over the last fifteen years. They're 99 percent sure the person on the screen is a terrorist by the name of Mohammed Zahvi."

"How can they be so sure?" I asked. "The image isn't that good."

"It's good enough when you have something to compare it to like a prison mug shot. Mohammed Zahvi spent nine years in Guantanamo Bay."

"You have to be kidding," Rafe said. "They let this guy out?"

"Yes. And it gets worse. They let him out along with four others a couple of years ago in a trade for Bowe Bergdahl. He was one of the so called Taliban Five."

"Holy moly," Holly said.

"Holy moly is right," I said. "You're telling me Bush got kidnapped by a terrorist Obama released? People must be going nuts."

"Not yet they aren't, but they will once they find out. The White House is keeping a lid on it for as long as possible. They're pulling out all the stops to try to find him and mount a rescue effort before the terrorists start making demands or the media get a whiff of it. They're frantic. Zahvi is rumored to be with ISIS—everybody's seen the horrific acts they're capable of."

"This is terrible. We have to find him," Holly said. "I can't believe President Bush got kidnapped!"

Pago appeared from the hallway. "President Bush has been kidnapped?"

"Oh, shit," Rafe said.

"What is it?" the boss asked. "Who said that?"

"It's Holly's cousin, Pago," I answered.

"Who are you guys talking to? Darth Vader?" Pago asked. He looked at the video monitor. "Is that Bush? That *is* Bush. He got kidnapped?"

"Damn it! I was afraid this might happen. Tell him to sit down at the table."

"You heard the man. Sit down," Rafe said.

"The man sounds like James Earl Jones. You guys pranking me? What's going on here?"

"Please, sit down." Holly scooched over to make room.

Pago sat down, and the boss said, "Thank you."

"Wait a second, you can see me? I mean us?"

"I can now. I just turned on the video. That's quite a bandage on your head. I bet it hurts." Pago looked around the table, confused. "It does...a little."

"Well it's gonna hurt a lot more if you ever tell anybody anything about what you see, hear, or become privy to while on board this vessel."

"Look, I just wanted a ride to Corpus Christi. I didn't ask to—"

"I don't care *what* you asked for, Mr. Alexander Hamilton LeRoux. Things have changed. We have a national emergency of epic proportions on our hands. You were a Navy SEAL, were you not?"

"Yes, how did—"

"I've seen your file…it's impressive. Were it not crystal clear that you are a patriot, you would have never been allowed to board, Holly's cousin or not. Do you understand?"

"Not really. Where are you? *Who* are you?"

"Rafe, I need to check with Rig Hoppers to see if any of their choppers were in the vicinity where Kit and Tangles saw one. While I do that, swear Mr. LeRoux in and brief him on what's happened. Maybe he'll be useful."

"Are you sure?"

"Of course not, but what choice do I have?" *Click.*

"Swear me in? I thought you were filming a fishing show." He looked around the table. "What do you mean, swear me in? Who *are* you guys?"

"I hate to break it to you, Pago," I said. "But you're about to get dicked."

Chapter 43

El Primo climbed and shimmied his way along the underbelly of the rusty rig and finally reached the ladder that led up to the lower deck of the *Dinero Majado.* The surge of adrenaline he felt earlier was all but gone, and he rested for a few minutes, trying to gather his strength. His flight suit was shredded from the climb, and his hands, arms, and legs were nicked and cut. He reached in the wet duffel bag that hung from his neck and fished around for the bottle of water inside. Despite his wretched condition, he was glad to be alive, and he smiled as his fingers felt the stacks of cash before settling on the bottle. He took a few swigs and looked up the ladder, estimating he had about forty rungs to climb before reaching the top. He put the bottle back in the duffel.

There was a loud splash in the water. He looked down and saw a large triangular fin glisten in the setting sun as it circled below. It was the big hammerhead he'd seen earlier. The tiny drops of blood dripping from his numerous cuts had the primeval predator licking its chops. He murmured, "Well, fuck me," and started up the ladder.

A couple of times on the tedious climb he thought the rungs might give way due to rust and corrosion, but miraculously, they held. Halfway up, his energy was gone, and it was the fear of ending up in the water with a hungry hammerhead that propelled him. Four rungs from the top he stopped and eyeballed the situation. There was a trapdoor with a combination padlock on it. *Fuck.* He thought about chambering a round in his trusty .45 and blasting the lock, but both the ammo and pistol were wet and the risk of a misfire was very real. And if didn't misfire or blow up in his face, the blast might be heard, alerting the terrorists he was still alive. That would not be good. He was badly outnumbered and needed to keep the element of surprise on his side if he was to have any chance of turning the tables. He looked around and noticed a small platform off to the side. It looked like a sheet of marine plywood fastened to some support beams. It wasn't very big but neither was he. He slipped the duffel bag over his head and slung it onto the platform before testing the sturdiness of the wood and climbing onto it.

There was just enough headroom to allow him to almost fully sit up, and that's what he did. In short order he pulled out the .45 and several clips of ammo from the duffel bag and laid them on the plywood. He took his shredded flight suit off and hung it on a cross beam along with his undershirt and another wet T-shirt from the bag. In the shade of the rig and with the sun going down he knew it would get chilly, but he had little choice if he wanted dry clothes. He carefully removed the bullets from the clips and lined them up inside the lip of an overhanging metal strut. Satisfied he had everything drying as best he could; he drank some water and stretched out. He had been trying to quit but he never wanted a cigarette so bad in his miserable life. With his head resting on a damp duffel bag containing fifty thousand dollars cash, exhaustion washed over him like a gentle wave of lullabies. In seconds, el Primo was out like a light.

***

Three levels above the snoozing el Primo, the former president was semiconscious and strapped to a chair in the middle of the windowless maintenance room. Zahvi ordered one of his associates to revive him, and an ammonia tube was placed under his nose. With a shake of the head, he woke up and tried to get his bearings. There was a guy with an AK-47 by the door and a guy sitting in front of a bunch of electronic devices. Standing in front of him was the man in the flight suit who shot his Secret Service agents.

"You lousy bastard!" he cried. He tried lunging at the man but the chair was bolted to the floor and the flex-tie bindings were secure.

"Relax. You're not going anywhere," Zahvi replied.

"You killed two good men!"

"So what. You killed thousands when you invaded Iraq."

"I said *good* men. Not animals like you."

"We are all Allah's creatures."

"Maybe, but you're the kind that's best squished. And that's exactly what's gonna happen to your sorry ass when the Special Forces drop in and give you and your buddies the bin Laden treatment."

Zahvi laughed. "That's funny. If you think you'll be rescued, you're even dumber than I was led to believe."

"You think *I'm* dumb? Look in a mirror. You'll never get away with this."

"But I already have. The greatest kidnapping of all time has been pulled off, and nobody knows where you are...including you."

The president looked around the room. "So what. That's nothing new. I'm retired. I have people to tell me where I am."

"Not anymore you don't."

"So where are we, then? If you're so sure of yourself, what's the big secret? Chicken say chicken."

"Chicken say what? What does that mean?"

"Heh. And you're calling *me* dumb? It means you're chicken—chicken. You're too scared to tell me 'cause you know the Special Forces are probably on their way right now...wherever we are."

"We are in the middle of the ocean where no one will think to look for you."

"Seems pretty dry to me."

"Not *in* the ocean, you idiot. We're on an abandoned oil rig a hundred miles from the Texas-Mexico border."

"Heh. See how easy that was for me to find out where I am? That's called being played. I learned that technique watching *Columbo.* Now all I have to do is let the good guys know where I am, and bing-bang-boom, I'm outta here. So who's the idiot now?"

"And just how do you propose to contact them?"

He laughed. "That's for me to know and for you not to find out until you got a severe case of high-velocity-lead poisoning."

"You are a fool. No one is coming for you except the grim reaper, but only after you have served your purpose."

"Which is what? What do you want from me?"

"I think you mean, what do I want *for* you. What I want *from* you is excruciating pain and suffering."

"Don't tell me you're gonna make me watch *The View*. Heh. Anything but that. Seriously, feel free to waterboard me first."

"Your apparent lack of concern for the situation you find yourself in is astonishing. I shall remedy that shortly."

"Huh. I didn't have you pegged for a doctor. Glad to hear you got remedies. I'll take a couple of Advil and—"

Whack! Zahvi backhanded him across the face. "I'm not a doctor! Soon our demands and the image of you being held captive will be broadcast worldwide. Then *we* will be the ones laughing while your fellow countrymen will be in shock."

The president's face reddened from the blow, and he shook his head a few times before glaring at Zahvi. "You fell for it again. Now I know you're not a doctor. Heh. Thank you, Columbo. The student has become the pupil."

"The *what?*"

"Forget it, Slappy. It's over your head. Who the hell are you and what are your demands?"

Zahvi crouched down in front of him so that his face was only inches away. "You mean you don't recognize me? Take a good look."

The president squinted and examined his face closely. There were several fresh nicks throughout his five o'clock shadow, and the face looked chafed. "What's the matter?" he teased. "Grandpappy Slappy never taught you how to shave? Wait a minute. I *have* seen your face before." The president's eyes went wide. "I can't believe it's you!"

"I thought you might recognize me if you looked close enough."

"I never forget a face, especially one that I see all the time."

Zahvi stood up, looking confused.

"What do you mean? Who do you think I am?"

"*Think?* I never think. I know. You're the guy that works the counter at the 7-Eleven on I-35 in Waco. Small world."

Zahvi backhanded him again. "I am not a 7-Eleven clerk! My name is Mohammed Zahvi. You incarcerated me in Guantanamo Bay for nine long years."

The president shook off the second blow and smiled. "You married?"

"*What?* No."

"Then you don't know what long is. So you're a terrorist. Big deal, Neal. Who are you with? Don't make me guess 'cause I can't pronounce the names."

"I was a member of the Taliban Five."

"*Was?*"

"Now I am with ISIS. We are going to take over the world."

"After what Obama's done to it, you can have it. Just stay the hell out of Texas. So what are your demands?"

"We are asking for the immediate release of all the prisoners in Guantanamo Bay."

"I hate to break it to you, but it's already in the works. How do you think you got out? Obama can't do it fast enough."

"We are also asking for Israel to release all their prisoners of war."

"Whoa now. My buddy Bibi's not gonna be liking that one bit."

"That is what we are anticipating. He will need encouragement, which Obama will provide."

"Are you kidding me? Bibi hates Obama. He wouldn't piss on his face if it was on fire."

"We are anticipating that, too."

"Well, if you've got everything all anticipated out, what's the end game?"

"The end game?"

"Yeah, you know, what's the point? What are you *really* trying to accomplish here?"

"I would think that would be obvious."

"So obviate me."

"*What?*"

"Just tell me already. I'm gettin' too old for this shit."

"Fine. Aside from avenging the lives of our brothers by torturing and killing you in the most heinous of manners and broadcasting it live on the Internet, we expect to start World War Three. What do you think about that?"

"To be honest, I could do without the torturing and killing, but on the bright side, at least I won't have to listen to Obama blame me for everything anymore, so there's that. Heh."

Chapter 44

Pago's jaw dropped when he heard Rafe say the name of the ubersecret organization we all worked for, and he repeated it in disbelief. "The Department of International Criminal Knowledge?"

"Yup," Tangles said. "Otherwise known as DICK. Has it sunk in yet?"

"That's what she said." I laughed.

"Kit, C'mon!" Holly punched me in the shoulder. "This is serious."

"Sorry, I couldn't resist."

"This is for real?" Pago asked.

"Very real," Rafe said.

"It's true, but of all the names they could have chosen, they had to pick DICK." Holly rolled her eyes.

"Which can be painful," Tangles said, and we both laughed.

"Tangles!" Holly glared at him.

"All right, that's enough of the DICK jokes…for now," I said.

"I'm sorry, but I'm having a real hard time believing this," Pago said.

"I had the same reaction when I was recruited," said Rafe. "But if you think about it, it's the perfect cover for a secret organization because nobody believes it."

"I believe in DICK," Tangles said. Holly gave him a death-laser stare, and he sheepishly added, "Sorry. I'll stop now."

"Good idea," she answered through clenched teeth.

"So what exactly does DICK do?" Pago asked. I knew if I looked at Tangles he'd make some kind of face that would crack me up, so I looked away and tried not to think about it.

"We're intelligence gatherers and assemblers of information in the hunt for terrorists and international criminals," Rafe answered. He went on to explain how DICK was formed by George W. Bush after the terrorist attacks on September 11, 2001, and the decision to keep its existence a secret.

"You're telling me that Congress doesn't even know of its existence?"

"Not only that, Obama doesn't know either."

"Holy shit. That's crazy."

"Not really, considering Obama's right-hand man, or woman, Valerie Jarrett, is an Iranian-born Muslim, and there are several other members of the Muslim Brotherhood in his administration."

"But still."

"But still *what?*" I said. "I'd say it was a prudent decision to keep them out of the loop. Just look at the Iranian nuke deal that Obama pushed for and eventually passed."

"Yeah, I didn't get that. How can you give the leading sponsor of terrorism in the world a hundred and fifty billion dollars and a legitimate path to nuclear weapons? The Iranians say they need enriched uranium so they can build nuclear power plants. That's its just for peaceful purposes. Sure it is. Why do they need nuclear power plants when they're sitting on all that oil and gas? Did Obama think to have Kerry ask them that? Everybody knows they're gonna use the money to help finance more terrorism and build nuclear weapons to use against us. It makes no sense. A lot of what he does makes no sense to me."

"It does once you realize what side he's on," Tangles said.

"You really believe that?"

"I believe in actions, not words. Don't listen to what he says. Look at what he does. End of story."

Rafe's phone rang. He glanced at it in the cradle and clicked on the speakerphone.

"You there, Rafe?" the voice of James Earl Jones bellowed.

"We all are. Pago's been sworn in. What did you find out?"

"Rig Hoppers didn't have any flights anywhere near the *Taladro Grande.* If Shagball and Tangles weren't mistaken in what they saw, then it had to be the kidnappers."

"I know what I saw," Tangles said.

"We weren't mistaken," I assured him.

"But why would they be heading south? We know they didn't land on the *Taladro Grande,* and it's nothing but open water south of there."

"Maybe they were heading for a ship?" I wondered aloud.

"The NSA checked the satellite images in the central southern gulf and identified three possible targets.

Two of them are cargo ships operated by American interests. They've been contacted and neither reported seeing any aircraft in the area whatsoever. The third is a Mexican-registered freighter on its way to the Yucatan Peninsula but it's a good hundred and fifty miles southeast of the *Taladro Grande.* We don't know where the flight originated from, but if it was from northern Mexico or southern Texas that would likely be beyond its fuel range. Nevertheless, a coast guard cutter on patrol north of Cozumel has been sent to intercept it and check it out. It doesn't feel right, though. We have to be missing something here."

"Maybe the helicopter that Kit and Tangles saw was a decoy," Holly said.

"A decoy?"

"I don't know. I'm just thinking. Maybe they want everybody to believe they were heading for a ship when they were really headed to the coast."

"But it was a fluke I spotted them," Tangles said. "They had no idea we would be where we were. It's the middle of nowhere."

"And the decoy had to land *somewhere,*" Rafe said.

"Unless it was a suicide mission, and they ditched in the gulf," the boss responded. "Never to be seen again—the ultimate red herring."

"Hold on a second," Pago said. "It's not *all* open water to the south of the *Taladro Grande.*"

"What do you mean?" the boss asked.

"I forgot about it until now. Jesus, I wonder if…no, I doubt—"

"Doubt *what?*" Rafe asked.

"If you know something, *anything,* that might be related to what happened, spit it out *now*!"

"Right. Sorry. About ten miles south of the *Taladro Grande* is a decommissioned rig called the *Dinero Majado*."

"Spell that for me."

Pago spelled it out.

"Go on."

"I worked on it for a little while until the *Taladro Grande* was completed. It's a thirty-year-old rust bucket of a rig. When the weather permitted, I liked to take the skiff from the *Taladro Grande* and go there to fish."

"Good call," I commented. "I bet there's some nice snapper and—"

"Let the man finish!"

"Sorry."

"Anyways, it's been too rough lately, but the weather finally turned late last week and the water lay down. On my day off I decided to make the trip over."

"What day?"

Pago rubbed his bandaged head. "Let me think. *Wednesday?* Maybe Wednesday or Thursday."

"Okay. So?"

"So I pulled up a grouper and—"

"A gag or a red?" Tangles asked.

"A gag. A big gag."

"Please. Can you just get to the point?"

"Right. So I have this nice gag next to the skiff, and a big shark comes out of nowhere and chomps it, almost capsizing me."

"What kind of shark?" I asked. "A tiger? A—"

"Enough questions! Let him finish!"

"Sorry, chief."

"It was a fifteen-foot hammerhead. At least. He took everything. I had a couple of cutoffs before that, and I was out of leader. I didn't want to go back because it was still early, so I thought I'd go on the rig and look around for something to use. It was a little dicey climbing up the ladder, but I managed my way to the access door. There was a lock on it, but I knew the combination and got through. I knew some of the maintenance guys liked to fish, so I headed to the maintenance room to see if anything got left behind. It was dark on the interior, but I had a penlight with me. When I got to the maintenance room, I found a bunch of brand-new electronic equipment, floor lights, and cases of water and canned foods."

"I thought you said it was an abandoned rig."

"It was. I mean, it's supposed to be. It was decommissioned over six months ago, but it looked like somebody set up a friggin' television studio. There was a brand-new generator, too. It was weird. I figured maybe the company was shooting a commercial or something. I don't know. I didn't give it much thought. I cut myself a section of cable to make a leader and left."

"So what did your boss say when you told him about it?"

"I didn't."

"Why?"

"It was strictly off limits—you know, because of liability or whatever. If I told my boss I was on the *Dinero Majado,* I probably would have been fired."

"Lot of good that did," Tangles said. "You got fired anyways."

Pago gave him a look. "Thanks. I know. Somebody tried to kill me, too. It's been a great week."

"Tell me," the boss said. "This attempt on your life. It happened after you went on the *Dinero Majado*?"

"Well... yeah. It was early the next morning."

"Why would somebody try to kill you?"

"I have no idea, but I'd like to ask them myself right before I give them the same treatment."

"And you're sure you didn't tell anybody about what you saw?"

"Positive."

"Tell me more about the room. What else did you see?"

"Like what?"

"You were there, not me. Think."

"Like I said, just a bunch of fancy electronics, lights, food, water, a generator...oh, and there was a satellite dish hidden on the top deck."

"*A satellite dish?*"

"Yeah, I forgot. I saw a cable leading up through the ceiling, and I traced it to the top deck. It was hooked to a dish. Oh, shit. I forgot."

"Forgot what?"

"There was a single chair in the middle of the room. All the floor lamps were pointed toward it. Do you think—"

"That's where they took Dubya!" Tangles said. "It has to be!"

The urgency in the boss's voice came across loud and clear. "Tangles is right. You've described what could be an interrogation room, and I don't believe in coincidences. Somebody tried to kill you because of what you saw, and what you saw is where the terrorists have taken the president. It's the only thing that makes sense."

"But I didn't tell anybody."

"If somebody went to the effort of setting up an interrogation room on an abandoned oil rig in the middle of the gulf, you can bet they set up security cameras too. You said it yourself. It was dark. Even if it wasn't, you probably wouldn't have seen them. They'd be hidden."

"Son of a bitch!"

"I'm looking at the tracking screen right now. You're only thirty-two miles northwest of the *Dinero Majado.* Kit, you've been wanting to test the top speed of the *LD3.* Now's your chance to do it. Switch to stealth mode and when you get five miles away, slow down and activate the cloaking system. Rafe, get the heat-imaging sensors and parabolic microphone ready."

"I'm on it." Rafe got up from the dinette and headed down the hall.

"Holly, you're responsible for the onboard security system. You know where to go."

"Yes, sir." Holly disappeared toward the forward berth.

"Pago?"

"Yes. What can I do?"

"Try not to bump your head." *Click.*

"What the hell." Pago looked at me and Tangles. "My head's fine. I'm taking this ridiculous bandage off." Pago followed me and Tangles up to the bridge. By the time we got there, his bandage was gone. I spun the boat around and turned off the generator and the audio making the motor sound. It was eerily silent with flat seas sparkling in the setting sun.

"Why did you kill the engines?" Pago asked.

"He didn't," Tangles answered, "the engine noise is just for show."

"Say what?"

"Have you ever seen a boat fly?" I asked.

"What do you mean?"

"What I mean is we're going nuclear. Hang on!"

Chapter 45

As we accelerated toward the *Dinero Majado*, I pushed a button on the dash. The front windshield slid closed, followed by the stern-facing windows.

"That's pretty cool," Pago said. "I've never seen that on a boat before."

"Trust me. There's a lot on this boat you've never seen," I answered. "Tangles, be my spotter."

"You got it, Shag." Tangles stood up on the bench seat in front of the helm and grabbed one of the hard-top supports for balance. It was getting dark fast, and I didn't want to run over a floating log or any other nasty object. That would be bad. Having a second set of eyes is always a good idea, especially at high speed. Within seconds we were skimming along at fifty knots.

"How is it so quiet?" Pago asked.

"I told you, we're going nuclear."

"Seriously. What do you have, some kind of electric hybrid engines?"

"This ain't a floating Prius, my friend. I think Rafe said it has a forty-megawatt fast-neutron nuclear reactor under the hood. Check it out." I pushed the throttles forward, and Pago fell back against the stand-up passenger seat.

"Hammer it, Shag! Let 'er rip!" Tangles yelled.

"Jesus Christ!" Pago said. "Are you serious? You're not serious, are you? How fast are we going?"

"Seventy knots. You can hardly tell right? It's smooth. Like Black Velvet. Let's see what else she's got." I pushed the throttles forward and within seconds we were doing eighty-five knots.

Tangles jumped up and down and yelled, "Go, cat, go!"

I glanced at Pago, and the g-force had him pinned against the seat. He was biracial but his face was definitely appearing more white than black.

After several minutes, Tangles pointed and yelled, "Watch out! One o'clock!"

I swerved to the left, and Tangles flew across the bench seat and tumbled to the deck. Pago slammed into my shoulder and caused me to jerk the wheel farther left, but I managed to pull back on the throttle and straighten us out.

Immediately, Rafe's voice came over the intercom, "What the hell are you doing up there!?"

"Sorry, I had to dodge something in the water," I answered.

"Well, watch where you're going!"

"Will do." I clicked off the intercom.

Tangles got up from the deck. "Dude, I said to watch out, not swerve like Merv!"

"You said watch out and pointed, and I went the other way. What was I supposed to do?"

"Not swerve like a maniac—that's what."

"What was it, anyways?"

"Looked like an oil drum. It's getting too dark to see; you better slow down more."

I slowed down to trolling speed, and Pago said, "Thank God. Boats this big aren't meant to go that fast. That was *nuts.*"

I looked at the radar, which showed the *Dinero Majado* to be six miles dead ahead. I picked up the intercom mic and said, "Rafe, you there?"

"Yeah."

"I'm gonna activate the cloaking device."

"We five miles away?"

"Close enough."

"Okay, do it and get down here after you put us on autopilot. The boss is calling." *Click.*

"Cloaking device?" Pago asked.

"You better put that bandage back on," Tangles warned, "'cause your head might explode."

"My head feels fine."

"Tell me that in about three seconds," I said and flicked the cloaking switch.

The boat vibrated briefly and made a humming sound before going silent.

"What was that?"

I pointed toward the bow and answered, "Check it out. Now you see it, now you don't."

Pago leaned forward and shook his head. "I can't see anything. What the hell?"

"Look down at the cockpit," Tangles said.

Pago spun around and peered through the enclosed glass. "It's just…there's nothing. Just water. Where did it go? What in God's name is going on here?" He put his hands over his ears like that *Home Alone* kid and shook his head.

"Haven't you ever heard of cloaking technology?" I said. "It's the latest greatest thing."

"But how—?"

"Who am I, Stephen Hawking? It uses holograms and physics and, you know, scientific stuff. What difference does it make? It works."

"Nuclear power," Tangles crowed. "It's the bomb."

"I need to sit down."

I turned on the autopilot and pointed at the steps. "After you. To the salon."

We joined Rafe and Holly at the dinette. Rafe's phone was in the cradle with the speaker on.

"Say *what?*" Rafe said.

"You heard me," the boss said. "The pilot might be an undercover agent for Homeland Security."

"That's crazy. Did he switch sides?" I asked.

"His handler doesn't know what happened. He lost contact with him this morning. The phone he was using has been traced and appears to be moving through the sewers of Matamoros. It's possible his cover was blown."

"So what do they think?" Rafe asked. "They didn't kill him because they needed him to fly the chopper?"

"Nobody knows, but somebody flew it. The video from the *Bluewater* was inconclusive because the pilot never left the helicopter. So did you have any luck with the parabolic mic?"

"Yes. I picked up a voice, maybe two. It was definitely Arabic."

"What do you mean, maybe *two?*" queried the boss.

"It's hard to tell. They all sound alike to me. It was probably two…Unless he was talking to himself."

"I think it's safe to say there are more than two of them. All right, here's the deal. I can call it in that we're pretty sure we know where the president's being held, but there's a couple of problems with that. Number one, time. No matter which agency gets tasked with making a rescue effort, it will take time to organize and time to get out here. Time the president may not have. Number two, they'll either have to come by boat or by air, and they'll be seen or heard. We, on the other hand—"

"Say no more," Tangles said. "I'm in. Dubya's like family now."

"Ditto here," I agreed. "No way are we sitting by while Mohammed what's his name has his dirty hands on our fishing buddy. Plus, he's a fan."

"Kit, I don't know," Holly said. "These guys are terrorists!"

"Holly, I understand your concern," the boss said. "This is the last thing I want to do, but we're the best chance the president has of getting rescued. We can get next to the rig without being spotted, and Pago knows the way from there. He can map it out for the guys and stay on the boat with you while you monitor—"

"Hold the phone," said Pago. "*Map it out?* Bullshit. I don't even know if I could. I'll lead the way. Once a SEAL, always a SEAL."

"Are you sure? How are you feeling?"

"Considering a few minutes ago I was going ninety miles an hour in a fifty-some-odd-foot, nuclear-powered fishing boat that is now invisible, pretty good, I guess."

"I meant, how is your head? I see you took the bandage off."

"Oh. My head's feeling okay. I'm pretty sure I don't have a skull fracture. The rest of me is a little dinged up but nothing serious. I'll manage."

"Holly, can you handle the boat by yourself?"

"I ran the *C-Love* back in Boynton a few times for private charters. It's seventy-seven feet long. With a few pointers, I'll be fine. It's the guys I'm worried about. This is scary."

"Rafe?"

"Yeah?"

"Make sure everybody wears a vest."

"Will do."

"And use a transmitting device so you can keep in contact with Holly."

"Got it."

"What about weapons?" Pago asked.

"Not to worry," Rafe said. "We got that covered."

"Okay, then," the boss said. "You're only a few miles from the target. Better get geared up."

"You heard him, guys," Rafe said. "Follow me."

Chapter 46

El Primo woke up with a shiver. For a moment he forgot where he was and when he sat up, he hit his head on a metal strut. "Shit!"

The sun had set and darkness descended like an ominous fog. He felt along the ledge where he'd lined up the bullets and retrieved them. Working by feel he reloaded the clips and stuck one into his .45. His T-shirts were almost dry, and he slipped one on before squirming into his damp and shredded flight suit. The only sound was a gentle rippling of waves as the current swished around the support legs of the rig. He thought about blasting the lock again, but it was far too quiet. He pulled the bottle of water out of his duffel and took a swig. There was maybe half of it left. His perch was protected from the elements, and he figured he could survive at least four or five days after the water ran out, which would be soon. *Not to worry*, he thought. Uncle Sam had to have every agency of the government searching for Bush, and they would find him before he died of thirst. *Wouldn't they?*

He wondered what the terrorists were doing to the president and thought about how to get through the trapdoor. Maybe if he could break off one of the rusty metal struts he could use it to pry open the lock. *Doubtful.* If it was rusty enough to break off, it would be too weak to pop the lock. He laid his head down on the duffel and rubbed his arms for warmth. In the morning he would reassess the situation and see if there was any way he could climb his way to the side and work his way up to the deck that way. His whole body ached, but at least most of the cuts and scrapes seemed to have stopped bleeding. He felt like fifty-nine going on a hundred. His stomach growled from hunger, and he wished he had stashed some snacks in his duffel before leaving the hotel in Matamoros. *What a day.*

He closed his eyes and was trying not to think about how hungry he was when he heard a weird sound. Thinking it was his stomach, he ignored it. Then he thought he heard a voice and bolted upright, hitting his head on the metal strut again. He bit his tongue to keep from cursing and rolled over on his stomach. After rubbing the rising lump on his head, he peered over the edge of the platform. The moon had started to rise and cast a little light along the edge of the rig, but he didn't see or hear anything. He reached out his hand to grab the ladder and scooched forward to get a better look. There was nothing to be heard, but he felt it in his hand. The ladder vibrated. *Someone was coming up the ladder.*

***

Rafe used a heat-imaging device to identify two lookouts stationed on the rig. One patrolled along the northwest corner and the other on the southwest corner.

We deployed the electric skiff from a mile away and made a rapid approach from the east. The four of us wore bulletproof vests concealed by dark-camo jumpsuits and were reasonably well armed. All of us had semiautomatic .45-caliber pistols, and Rafe also carried an Uzi and some other goodies in a backpack. Although the *LD3* was to be used primarily for snooping and information-gathering purposes the boss made sure we were well equipped to handle unforeseen situations like the one we found ourselves in. Since Pago was familiar with the *Dinero Majado* it was decided he should drive. He deftly avoided the shafts of moonlight that peeked out from behind the clouds, and in less than three minutes we slipped under the rig undetected.

According to Pago, the trapdoor at the top of the ladder led to an electrical room that was accessible only through an adjacent office. It was unlikely the terrorists would be guarding it or even knew it was there, for that matter. At least that was the hope. He was skeptical of how much weight the rusty ladder could bear, and it was decided no more than two people at a time should be on it. Pago went first. When he was halfway up, I started climbing.

It was pitch black until Pago reached the top and activated the variable-wattage light he had strapped to his head. He removed his protective gloves. By the time he spun the dial on the combination lock, I was maybe fifteen rungs below him. I heard him snap open the lock and then a loud whisper made me freeze in my tracks.

"Don't make a move, Spider-Man, or I'll blow your fucking head off. Who are you and what are you doing?"

I couldn't see where the oddly familiar voice came from but figured it out when Pago slowly turned his head to the left. His headlight shone toward a little cubbyhole platform that somebody was hiding in. I pulled the Glock out of my shoulder holster and crept up the rungs.

"*McGirt?*" whispered Pago. "Is that *you?*"

I stopped climbing and shook my head. Did he say McGirt? Not McGirt. Not possible.

"Holy crap. *Pago?* Pago! Fuckin-A. What are *you* doing here? Is that an Uzi?"

I heard enough of his squirrelly voice to realize that against all odds, it was definitely the dirtbag of the century, McGirt. I quickly climbed the last few rungs and pointed my gun at him.

"Drop it you lousy shitheel," I hissed. "On second thought, don't. I should have shot you a long time ago."

He was on his stomach and laid his gun down on the platform.

"Easy there, big guy. What do you mean, you should have shot me? What did I ever do to you? I don't even know you."

"You know him?" whispered Pago.

"Unfortunately, yes. He tried to kill me. Twice. How do *you* know him?"

"We served in the navy together."

"Lemme guess, on a submarine."

"Yeah, how did you—"

"Oh, shit," said McGirt.

"*Now* you remember me?" I asked. Suddenly, I felt the ladder shake. Tangles was on his way up. "We gotta move, Pago. Grab McGirt's gun, and we'll follow you in."

"You can't take—"

"Shut up, McGirt. No more talking."

Pago switched off his headlight, and the three of us climbed into the electrical room. A smidgen of ambient light filtered up through the trapdoor opening but that was it. Pago flicked his light back on and pressed his ear against the door on the other side of the room.

"I don't hear anything," he whispered. "That's good."

I pointed my Glock at the shadowy McGirt, who had a duffel bag slung over his shoulder. He was wearing a tattered jumpsuit and looked even worse than I remembered.

"Start talking McGirt," I whispered. "How did you end up in that little cubbyhole? How are you even here? You're supposed to be in jail."

"How am I here? How are *you* here? You said you were just some fishing-show schmuck. What a fuckin' liar. What's your name again? Snotball?"

I reached in my pocket and pulled out a disposable silencer which I quickly pushed on to the barrel of my Glock. "Mind if I shoot him?" I asked Pago. "I don't know how well you know this guy, but he's a piece of shit."

"I know. He owes me fifteen hundred bucks."

"You know, I was hoping I'd bump into you, ol' buddy. It just so happens—"

"We're not buddies. Fire away, Shagball."

"Now hold on there." His voice rose a little. "First of all, I can pay you in cash, with interest. How does two grand sound? Second, if you shoot me, you won't know what you're getting into here." He pointed at the door and added, "I *know.* I know exactly how many camel rammers are holding Bush hostage and what they're packing."

"*What?*" I lowered the Glock. "How do you—"

"What's going on here?" Tangles popped his head through the trapdoor. "Who the hell is—"

"Oh no," McGirt said. "Not that rabid little munchkin. What's his name? *Jingles?* Keep that little fucker away from me. My ribs are *still* sore from the Tom Dempsey treatment he gave me."

"*McGirt?*" Tangles said as he stood up next to me. "What the fuck. I thought you were in jail."

"I was, thanks to you guys. Every time I turn around, you fuck my world."

"*We* fuck *your* world?" I said. "You hijacked and blew up my boat!"

"Keep it down," Rafe whispered as he climbed through the trapdoor. He pointed at McGirt. "Who the hell is this?"

"His name is Mac McGirt," Pago said. "I served with him in the Straits of Hormuz where he stiffed me for fifteen hundred bucks. Haven't seen him in nearly twenty years. Last I heard he got dishonorably discharged."

"For what?"

"Smuggling drugs, weapons—anything and everything—by any means."

"He hasn't changed his ways," I said. "A few years back we had a run-in with him while we were fishing in the Caribbean. He was piloting a sub filled with seven tons of coke."

"Hey, it was gonna be my swan song. I was set to retire after that job until you fucked it all up."

"Too bad, you asshat. You stole my boat and tried to kill me and my crew."

"Wait a second, you know him, too?" Rafe asked.

"Yeah, we know him," Tangles said. "Every time we run into him he tries to steal our boat and kill us. Last time was off the Bahamas. He was trying to go from one stolen boat to another."

"You forgot to mention you shot me with a fucking flare gun and your buddy here broke my nose before you kicked the shit out of me."

"That was after you tried to hijack us, dickhead."

"Well, you know what I say. Let bygones be bygones. Especially since we're all on the same team now."

"*What?* How do you figure?" I asked.

"Simple. You guys are here to rescue Bush, right? Me too. I'm with Homeland Security. Who you with? I thought it was the DEA, after the Cordero brothers fiasco, but it looks like I was wrong."

"Never mind who we're with," Rafe said. "You're telling me *Homeland* sent you?"

I looked closer at his tattered jumpsuit. There was a torn logo on the sleeve. I asked Pago to shine his headlight on it.

"Well, they didn't exactly *send* me. I just sorta, you know, ended up here."

"How? In what capacity?"

"What else? I cut a deal. I'm an informant."

Pago shone his headlamp on McGirt's sleeve and the part of the logo I could see read Rig Hop—wait. *What?*

"Holy shit. You're wearing a flight suit. *You're* the pilot? *You?*"

"Yeah, me. Choppers don't fly themselves."

"You kidnapped Bush!"

"Quiet!" Rafe said.

I pointed my Glock at McGirt again. "Now can I kill him?"

Rafe reached out and pushed the gun down. "Let him talk. We need to know what he knows."

"I didn't kidnap him, the camel rammers did. I just flew the chopper. If I'da known they planned on kidnapping somebody I woulda charged more. Once I realized it was Bush I tried to stop 'em, but the sneaky bastards unloaded my clip. The guy in charge shot both Secret Service agents in the head, and the other one knocked out Bush."

"The guy in charge," said Rafe. "You're talking about the guy that got out of the chopper on the *Bluewater?* Zahvi?"

"Yeah. Is that his name? I thought it was Camelcock Breath. After he shot the agents he threatened to blow up the chopper if I didn't fly here. They tried to kill me when we landed, but as you can see"—He held out his arms wide for emphasis—"El Primo don't go easy."

"*El Primo?*" said Pago.

"That's what they call me—it's my undercover name. El Primo. They think I'm dead."

"What a pleasant thought," Tangles said.

"Up yours, Jingles."

"It's Tangles."

"Whatever."

"Enough," Rafe said. "How many of them are there?"

"Five."

"You sure?"

"That's how many rode in the chopper. Five plus me. I suppose there could be a few more that were already here, but I don't think so. They would have helped move the crates."

"What crates?" Rafe asked.

"They had crates. Don't ask me what was in them 'cause I don't know. They looked pretty heavy, though, so it was probably weapons, bombs, whatever. They carry AKs and Uzis."

"There's five of them and five of us," said Pago. "This is doable."

"So let's do it," said McGirt. "Can I have my gun back?"

"Yeah, right," I said. "I say we tie him up. We can't trust him."

"Okay, I'll admit I made a few bad decisions here and there but c'mon, man, we're talking about saving the president. I told you I already tried once. You gotta give me another shot, especially at Camelcock Breath. He's mine."

"What do you think, Pago?" Rafe asked. "You've known him the longest. Can we trust him?"

"Definitely not with your money."

"I told you I can—here," He unzipped his duffel and handed Pago a stack of bills. "That's five grand, Pago. I only owed you fifteen hundred. Call it even?"

As Pago leafed through the stack I pointed at the open duffel. "Where did you get all that money?"

"They paid me. El Primo don't fly for free. You want the best, you gotta—"

"Shut up already."

"All right," Rafe said. "I don't see where we have a choice. We need all the help we can get. Give him his gun. I'm warning you, though, you point it near any of us, and I will personally take you out. Got it?"

Pago handed McGirt his .45.

"Yeah, I got it. No need to worry unless you pray to Allah and like to swalla."

"This is a mistake," Tangles said. "A big mistake."

"That's what your momma said on the delivery table."

"I'm gonna punch you square in the nuts, you—"

"That's enough," Rafe said. "We need to act as a team. These guys are trained killers. The first step is to take out the lookouts. Quietly." He slung his knapsack forward, flicked his headlamp on, and pulled out two big military style knives. He handed one to Pago and said, "Okay, here's the plan."

Chapter 47

Zahvi anxiously paced back and forth as the video camera was set up. “Soon the world will be stunned and amazed by the greatest kidnapping in history!” he said. “And that’s before our demands are made.”

“Better hurry up,” replied the president. “’Cause there’s probly Special Forces guys parachuting in right now.”

“You are even more delusional than I thought. Nobody knows where you are.”

“If I figured it out, so can they.”

“You didn’t figure it out. I *told* you. And the reason I told you is because I am going to kill you. The only question is how.”

“Keep breathing on me. That should do it.”

Zahvi smiled and smashed the butt of his Uzi into the president’s gut. The president hunched over in pain, and Zahvi turned to his electronics and security expert, Noorbi, who was fiddling with some cables. “What is taking so long?”

“One of the cables is kinked. I need to replace it.”

“Hurry up then. I can’t wait to show the world how pathetic the great infidel has become.”

"Speaking of becoming," the president wheezed. He tilted his head so an ear was pointed at the ceiling. "What's that I hear? Why, I think it's the sound of a parachute fluttering on the roof. Better hang on to your hookahs, boys, here be coming the Special Forces. Gonna turn you into Giza goulash."

"Shut up," Zahvi said, clearly annoyed. "There is no chance they figured out where we are yet. But if they do, I have lookouts posted. If a rescue mission is attempted it will be like shooting fish in a barrel."

"What the hell do you know about fish in a barrel? You live in the desert. The only fishing you do is in your pants trying to find your dirty little—"

Zahvi backhanded him across the face.

"One more word, and you will be gagged." He turned to Noorbi. "Get that damned thing fixed. I want to give our guest the full attention he deserves."

"Hey, I'm retired now. I don't want any attention. I'm fine flying under the radar…just like a drone. Speaking of drones, there's probably—"

"That's it! I warned you!" he yelled.

The guard posted outside the door came bursting in with his AK-47. "Is everything okay?"

"No, everything is not okay. It is all I can do to keep from killing him before we make our demands. Gag him. He talks more than—" Suddenly, there was a sound from above like a folding chair falling on the floor. "What was that?" He nodded at the guard and said, "Go see what that was."

"We are ready to tape," Noorbi said. "The cable is replaced. Everything seems to be working."

"Good. I'm going to have a look around, and then we will get down to business."

As he turned to leave, the president said, "Better hit the prayer rug, pal. Sounds like SEAL Team Seven's here. They're like SEAL Team Six with a bad attitude. They got your buddy bin Laden, they can sure get—"

Zahvi turned and smashed the butt of his Uzi into the side of his head, knocking him out.

"Thank you," Noorbi said.

"My pleasure. If I'm not back in five minutes, go to plan B."

"Plan B? What's plan B?"

"Barricade the door, broadcast live, and chop his fucking head off."

***

The plan was for Rafe and Pago to take out the lookouts quickly and silently. Rafe explained that it was better to use a knife, if possible, because you could stop a body from falling that way. The problem with using a silenced weapon was the sound a body might make as it fell on the deck. While it made perfect sense, I was glad it wasn't me doing the knifing. I have a fear of needles, and the thought of sticking someone with a knife gave me the willies.

Like Rafe, I had a device in my ear about the size of a small hearing aid that allowed Holly to speak to me and a tiny mic clipped to my collar that allowed me to talk back. Armed with guns, knives, and stun grenades, Rafe and Pago slipped out of the electrical room. The device in my ear vibrated to let me know Holly was calling, and I pressed it to answer.

"What's up?" I whispered.

"You tell me."

"Rafe and Pago went to neutralize the lookouts."

"*Neutralize?*"

"Sorry, I guess I've watched too many spy movies. They went to kill them."

"I can't believe we're doing this. Please be careful."

"I'm trying, but it's not easy. We got more to worry about than just the terrorists. McGirt's here."

"*McGirt?* No. No way. You're kidding, right?"

McGirt nudged me in the side and whispered, "Is that your girlfriend? Tell her I said hi."

"Shut up."

"What?" Holly said.

"Sorry. I was talking to McGirt."

"You're serious? Oh my God. What is *he* doing there?"

"He piloted the chopper for the terrorists. Supposedly he's an informant for Homeland Security."

"That's crazy. He tried to kill you twice. He blew up your boat. He's supposed to be in jail."

"I know. I wanted to shoot him but got overruled. Rafe thinks we need all the help we can get."

Tangles had his head stuck out the open door and suddenly ducked back in. "Did you hear that?"

"I heard it," said McGirt. "We better check it out."

"I gotta go, babe. Something's going on."

"Be careful. I love you."

"Back at you." *Click.* I put my hand on Tangles shoulder and said, "What was that?"

"I'm not sure. But if we could hear it, so could somebody else."

"That's right," McGirt said. "And that somebody wears robes and rams camels. We gotta move."

"Which way do we go? We don't know our way around like Pago."

"We go up. I got a pretty good view of things when we landed. You guys follow me. Lock and load."

All three of us chambered a round, and we followed McGirt. We crept through the adjacent room toward the faint light sifting through an open door. McGirt gently pushed it open and peered around before proceeding into the night. The gentle sound of waves rippling below us and the salty humid air filling our lungs did little to calm the nerves. We went up a set of stairs.

McGirt stopped at the top. "We should split up," he whispered.

"Why?" Tangles asked.

"They got AKs and Uzis. One guy could take us out with a single trigger pull."

"Good point," I acknowledged.

"So who goes where?" Tangles said.

"Pago said the maintenance room where they're probably holding Dubya is somewhere in the middle of rig."

"All right," McGirt said. "I'll work my way toward the middle, and you guys go around the sides. Shoot anybody who looks like an extra in *Laurence of Arabia.*"

"But you don't have a silencer. As soon as you—"

The sound of automatic gunfire erupted, and we instinctively ducked.

"That was an AK!" McGirt said. "Let's roll!"

McGirt took off straight ahead, Tangles went left, and I went right. I was on the outer edge of a grated walkway and went up a short flight of stairs. I peeked around a corner, and it looked like the coast was clear.

I went into a running crouch and stopped when I heard more gunfire. My back was against the wall and I heard voices when the gunfire stopped. Actually, it wasn't voices I heard but the sound of a struggle taking place above me. I was about thirty feet from a set of stairs that would take me up to the next level and was about to make a run for it when two bodies fell onto the walkway in front of me. There was a sheet of plywood covering the grates where they landed, and the plywood made a loud *crack.* One person was on top of the other, and I saw an arm rise up. I stepped closer with my gun pointed at whoever it was, and a glint of moonlight reflected off the blade of a knife. Thinking it might be Rafe, I called his name. The person with the raised knife looked up at me, and I instantly knew I had been mistaken. The darkness did nothing to conceal the whites of a pair of crazy eyes staring at me. *Holy shit.* The knife started down, and I squeezed the trigger twice. The silencer muted the sound of the .45 but not the devastating effect of the bullets that smashed into his chest and knocked him off whoever it was. I knelt down next to the other person who whispered, "Thanks. That was too close for comfort."

"Pago?"

"Yeah."

"Are you hurt?"

"I was already hurt."

"Sorry. Anything new?"

"Let me check." He sat up. "Aghh."

"What is it?"

"My back. I wrenched it."

"How's your head?"

"I'm seeing stars. The fall didn't help."

More gunfire erupted, and there was an explosion—possibly from one of Rafe's stun grenades.

"Go," he said. "Go do what you can. I'll wait here."

"Where's your gun?"

"I lost it in the struggle. Ahkmed lost his, too."

I helped prop him up against the wall and handed him my gun.

"Are you sure?" he asked. "What about you?"

"Don't worry, I'll find one."

I quickly searched the dead terrorist but came up empty and rolled him under the rail. A couple of seconds later there was a loud splash. I looked back at Pago and said, "I'll be back."

"Good luck. Give 'em hell."

I took off running and bounded up the stairs. At the top I doubled back and found Ahkmed's AK lying on the deck. No sooner had I picked it up when I heard, "Shaggy!" It was Tangles.

"Where are you?"

"Over here." I followed the sound of his voice and found him crouched down next to the base of the drilling tower. I knelt next to him and said, "Pago's hurt."

"Bad?"

"I don't think so, but he took a good tumble. He's seeing stars, and he hurt his back. He's not going anywhere."

"I found a terrorist with his throat slit. Rafe must have got him."

"I killed one, too."

"No shit. That's how you got the rifle?"

"Sort of. He was about to kill Pago. You seen McGirt?"

"No. You hear the explosion?"

"Yeah, this is bad. So much for the element of surprise."

My ear bud vibrated again. I pressed it and answered, "This is a really bad time, babe."

"Kit, what's going on? I can't get through to Rafe. I heard gunfire. Are you all right?"

"Yeah, everybody's okay…I think. There's two terrorists down and three to go. I can't talk now. I gotta go." *Click.*

"So, what's the plan?" Tangles asked.

"Where'd that explosion come from?"

He leaned around the corner and pointed. "From inside that flat-roofed building over there."

"That's where we're going then."

"Okay, cover me, I guess."

"Cover you?"

"Yeah, you're the one with rifle. If somebody starts shooting at me, shoot back. A lot."

"Right. Got it." I hoisted the AK-47 up to my shoulder and pointed it over his head. "Anytime you're ready."

"That's what she said. Hah."

"You're not ready, are you?"

"Nope."

"I can't blame you. This terrorist-hunting shit is dicey. You should have seen the crazy eyes of the one I shot. He was stone-cold nuts."

"You really suck at pep talks."

"Sorry. This rifle's heavy. You gonna go or not?"

"Wow. Okay. I see where this is going."

"Then go already. We're Dubya's best chance."

"Shit. You're right. I hate it when you're right. You got the safety off?"

"Are you gonna go, or do you want me to go?"

"All right, all right, I'm going." He took a deep breath and scampered across forty feet of open deck to the door of the building. Fortunately, nobody shot at him, and I quickly followed. We were crouched down next to the door and plotting our next move when there was a loud blast behind us. We both flinched and spun around in time to see a robed body hit the deck. An AK-47 clattered on the grates next to the body and a voice from above said, "You're welcome." It was McGirt. He stuck his head over the edge of the roof and asked, "Where's the other guys?"

"Pago's on the north side of the deck below," I answered. "He took a bad fall. He's okay, but he's not going anywhere. I killed one terrorist, and Tangles found another with his throat slit. Rafe must have done it, but we don't know where he is, and Holly can't reach him."

"That makes three down and two to—"

A second explosion came from inside the building.

"I think we know where he is now," McGirt said. "There's another entrance on the other side of this building. I'll go in there, and you go in here. Try not to shoot me. You guys owe me one now." He took off before we had a chance to respond.

"I can't believe that piece of shit just saved our ass," Tangles said.

"I owe him fuck all. He blew up my boat."

"True, but you can't deny—"

"I can deny whatever I want. I still hate him."

"Haters gonna hate, hate, hate, hate, hate."

"*What?*"

"Taylor Swift. She's no Debby Gibson, but she's still hot."

"You are so gay." I opened the door to the building and added, "C'mon, we got a president to save."

Chapter 48

McGirt carefully jogged across the roof and climbed down the ladder affixed to the side of the building. As soon as his feet hit the deck the barrel of a gun was stuck in his back and a familiar voice whispered, "Drop your weapon." He dropped his .45 and the voice said, "Turn around." He turned around and was face to face with the terrorist leader, Zahvi, who had his mini-Uzi pointed at him.

"*You?*" said Zahvi in disbelief. "How did—?"

"El Primo's got nine lives. I'm like a cat with flippers. I gotta say that wasn't very nice what you did to me. You know, after all I did for you."

"You tried to shoot me in the head."

"I thought we put that behind us."

"I'm going to kill you. I'm going to kill you right now."

El Primo raised his hands. "Now hold on there. You might want to rethink things. You fire that Uzi, and the Special Forces are gonna be on you before you can say 'Allah akbar.' I'm pretty sure they took out all your buddies."

"*Special Forces?* How is that possible? How did they find us?"

"How do you think? They're special."

Zahvi cursed and jabbed the barrel of his Uzi in his rib cage. "I swear if I had a knife I would cut your tongue out and shove it down your throat."

"I'm sure that turns you on, but then you wouldn't know how to get off this rig in one piece. I do."

"What do you mean?"

"There's a skiff tied up under the rig. First come, first serve."

"How do we get there without climbing down the side or jumping?"

"El Primo's no dummy. If I told you that, you might be tempted to pick up some cutlery and give me the old Fallujah french kiss."

"So? I thought you had nine lives."

"I do, but I only got one tongue, and there's an island full of Polynesian hookers waiting for it."

"That's disgusting."

"Thank you."

"Lead the way."

***

Tangles and I slipped inside the building, and it went from dark to darker.

"I can't see shit in here," Tangles complained.

"That's good. That means we're hard to see, too."

"Unless they got night-vision goggles. Then we're sitting ducks."

"If they had night-vision goggles, we'd already be dead. Start waddling your way forward. I'll cover you again."

"How you gonna cover me if you can't see me?"

"I'll aim high. Quit talking and start moving…and hurry."

"All right, Peter Pushy. Here goes nothing."

Tangles took off, and within steps he knocked over something. I heard him say, "Shit."

"What was that?"

"A fucking chair, I think. I wish I had one of those headlights." I heard him move forward. "There's another one…and a table."

"Go around it."

"No shit."

"Quiet!"

"You be quiet!"

I figured with all the noise he was making there was nobody hiding in the dark ready to mow us down, so I followed him. I ran into a couple of chairs like he did, and he whispered back at me, "What are you doing?"

"Same thing as you. Come on, we gotta hurry." I passed him, pushing chairs and tables out of my way as I went. It must have been a lunchroom or something. At the other end of the room we reached a hallway, and I called out, "Rafe!" When no reply came, we continued down the hall until it intersected with another corridor. I peered around it and could see light spilling out from a room ahead. I called for Rafe again.

"In here!"

When we reached the open door, I warned of our arrival. "It's me and Tangles. Don't shoot."

"Okay!"

Rafe had just finished cutting Dubya loose from a chair in the middle of the room. He looked dead, and

Tangles asked what I was thinking. "Is he dead? Jesus, he looks dead."

"No, he's breathing, but he's got a bad head wound."

I stepped closer to look at the large welt on the side of his head. It was split open, and blood was oozing down his face and neck. There was lingering smoke from the stun grenade that Rafe must have used. A bullet-riddled terrorist was sprawled over some electronic equipment.

"That dead guy there makes four down, Rafe. There still one more unaccounted for."

"Better cover the hall. Tangles, get me a couple of those waters over there."

As I stood in the doorway with the barrel of the AK sticking out, I surveyed the room. It did look like a friggin' television studio. There were floor lights, a big video camera on a tripod, and a slew of electronic equipment. There were cases of water piled against the wall along with some canned foods. I heard a faint hum coming from above and noticed a thick electrical cord next to some cables running up through a hole in the ceiling. I figured there had to be a generator on the roof providing power to the room. *The roof.*

"Hey, where's McGirt?" I wondered aloud.

"I haven't seen him," Rafe said as he poured a bottle of water over the president's head. Dubya slowly shook his head, and his eyes fluttered open.

"What, uh, what's going on?" he said. He put his hand up to the side of his head and touched it. "Damn, that hurts."

"Tangles, hold him steady while I take my backpack off," Rafe said. He slipped off the backpack and pulled out a small first aid kit. In short order he deftly cleaned the wound and wrapped the president's head in gauze.

"Where's Pago?" he asked.

"He had a bad fall," I answered. "He wrenched his back and rehurt his head. I left him propped up against a wall and gave him my pistol. Is your ear transmitter working? Holly said she couldn't reach you."

"No, it went dead after I tossed the first stun grenade."

Rafe peeled off his shirt, and Tangles asked, "What are you doing?"

"Giving the president my vest. Like Kit said, there's still one more unaccounted for." He took his vest off and plucked a pair of deformed bullets out of it.

"You got shot?"

"No, the vest did. There's a big difference." He leaned the president forward and helped him into the vest.

"How'd you guys find me?" Dubya asked. "I thought I was a goner."

"It's a long story, but we're not out of this yet, Mr. President." Rafe tore open a small pack of Advil and handed them to him with a bottle of water. "Here, take these. We gotta get moving."

"Wouldn't we be safer staying in here until reinforcements arrive?" I asked.

"Not necessarily. There's a bunch of crates on the back side of this building. One of them might contain a bomb set to go off. We need to get off this rig pronto."

The president downed the Advil and chugged the entire bottle of water. He smacked his lips. "All right. I'm good to go."

My ear bud vibrated again, and I answered, "We got him, babe. We got the president."

"Thank God."

"Rafe's okay, too, but his transmitter's shot."

"Great. So everybody's good?"

"Pretty much, unless you carpool by camel and your girlfriend's a goat. We got four of 'em. There's one more unaccounted for plus McGirt. We're headed for the skiff."

"Be careful."

"Always. Tell the boss the good news. Gotta go." *Click.* Rafe had the president standing and held him by the arm. They took a step toward me, and the president swooned.

"I got you." Rafe steadied him.

"Whoa. That first step was a doozy. Sorta felt like the seventies. Wait a second. Where's my fish?"

"What?"

"My little cooler full of fish. You know, the mahimahimahi."

"It's just mahimahi, sir," Tangles said.

"I'm pretty sure there was three fillets, son."

"Don't worry about the fish," I said. "We'll get you some more."

"That'd be great. I promised the girls some fish."

"We have to go." Rafe guided him to the door.

"Let's go out the back," I said. "McGirt was supposed to be coming that way. I wonder where the hell he is."

Chapter 49

McGirt, a.k.a. el Primo, figured his nine lives were about up. He quickly guided Zahvi down to the lowest level while avoiding the injured Pago and desperately trying to come up with a plan that didn't involve him being dead. It wasn't easy. He knew that as soon as they got to the electrical room, Zahvi would have little use for him. He slowed his pace to buy some time, but as soon as he did, Zahvi stuck the Uzi in his back and whispered, "Hurry up."

"I am. It's dark, in case you didn't notice."

"Be quiet and keep moving."

When he reached the open door to the small building that held the electrical room, he stopped.

"This is it?" Zahvi asked.

"Yeah. You go through an office, and there's another door that goes to the electrical room. There's a trapdoor in the floor."

"Show me." Zahvi pushed the barrel into his back and prodded him into the darkened room, closing the door behind them. He briefly thought about trying a spin move and grabbing for the Uzi, but Zahvi was younger and stronger. It would be suicidal. *Ix-nay on the ab-gray.* He shuffled his way across the floor and into the electrical room with Zahvi breathing down his neck. The trapdoor was open, and the sea air filled the room.

Zahvi pressed the barrel into his side and directed him into the corner with an ominous instruction.

"Get on your knees, el Primo."

"Now wait a sec—"

"Do it!"

El Primo dropped to his knees in near panic. The only thing he could think of was to keep Zahvi talking.

"You shoot me, and they're gonna hear it."

"It will only take one shot to your demented head. It's worth the risk. You are a liar, a thief, and a double-crossing murderer."

"On a good day, yeah, but at least I'm not a Christian. Can't you cut me some slack? I'm just a free-lancer. I could convert to Buddhism, or Muslimism, or whatever it is you guys are, and join up with you. We'd have a ball. Whadda you say?"

"I say no, and our religion is Islam."

"Islam. Right. That's what I meant to say. I love that law you guys have where you're allowed to rape, pil-lage, and plunder anybody and everybody. What's it called? *Sharif law?* I love Omar Sharif. I didn't know he had such a dark side, but whatever. I'm down with it."

"It's Sharia law, you idiot."

"Potato, potahto. Bottom line is you guys got it right when it comes to women. They have no rights. You can do whatever you want with them. But who needs women when you have camels and goats at your disposal? I mean, they're all pink on the inside. Am I right or am I right? You ride 'em hard, give 'em a little water once in a while, and when they get tired you get a fresh one. It's lather, rinse, and repeat, minus the nagging. Sounds like heaven to me."

"Would you prefer the bullet between your eyes or in your ear?"

"Hold on. I'm serious now. Don't be getting twitchy on me. You *need* me."

"I need you? I don't think so. What I *need* is to kill you." Zahvi flicked the switch on the Uzi to single shot.

"No! Wait! Think about it. There's a skiff tied off below. That means there's a bigger boat close by. Now I know a couple of these guys from before. They say they have a fishing show. Maybe they do, maybe they don't. I've never seen it. Only thing I know for sure is they work undercover for the feds. Don't ask me which agency 'cause I don't know. But I know they use a fishing boat and that's probably what's waiting for them. And my guess is there's not many people on it 'cause they got everybody trying to rescue the president. You and I could go down the ladder, take the skiff to the boat, and hijack it. That's sorta my specialty."

"I could do that myself after I kill you."

"No chance. Special Forces will be coming through the door any minute. They might even have the president with them. You gonna pass up your last chance to take him out?"

"I instructed one of my brothers to kill him if I didn't return in five minutes. He is already dead."

"Don't be so sure. Special Forces can fuck up even the best laid plans."

"Hmmm. Then we shall wait until they arrive, and I will ambush them."

"They're not stupid. No way are they coming in here without clearing the room first…especially if they have Bush. They know you're unaccounted for. They'll toss another stun grenade in here just to be safe, unless."

"Unless what?"

"Unless I tell them it's all clear. They think I'm on their side, and I was, but like I said, I'm a freelancer. So what's it worth to you? What do you got in those crates up top? You got any more cash?"

"You want me to *pay you!?*"

"Shhh. Keep it down. A successful ambush requires stealth, and el Primo *always* requires compensation. That being said, we're in uncharted territory here. I haven't established my rates for presidential kidnappings and assassinations just yet, but I'm thinking—"

"There is thirty million in one of the crates."

El Primo let out a low whistle.

"Quiet. I think I heard something," whispered Zahvi.

"That's gotta be them," he whispered back. "So what do you say, partner? I'll lure them in, you mow them down, we push the cash crate over the side, grab a few weapons, hijack a boat, pick up the cash, and start living the Sharia life."

"If you double-cross me again, I swear I will make you the star of the most heinous snuff video ever produced."

"Great. I'll take that as a yes."

Chapter 50

We carefully worked our way through the rig. The going was slow because at every turn we had to consider the possibility that the fifth terrorist was waiting to ambush us. It was eerily quiet, and fortunately it stayed that way. Exactly where McGirt was and where number five was remained a mystery.

When we got to the walkway where I left Pago, I stuck my head around the corner and called out in a loud whisper, "Pago! It's us. Don't shoot."

"Okay. C'mon."

We came down the walkway single file, with me in front, then Tangles, then the president, with Rafe covering the rear. When I got close, Pago whispered, "It sounded like all hell broke loose. Did you get to the president in time?"

"Yeah, they did," answered the president. "Just like I knew they would."

"Mr. *President?* Is that you?"

"Actually, I'm not president anymore. I'm retired. I just screw around all day...like Obama. Heh."

I helped Pago to his feet, and Rafe said, "Pago, there's still one more terrorist we haven't located. Have you seen or heard anything?"

"McGirt's missing, too," I added.

"That's not surprising, but yes, I did hear something about five minutes ago from the lower level. It might have been nothing, but I did hear something creak."

"Well, we're headed that way, so stay alert," said Rafe. I led the way down to the lower level. When we reached the door that opened to the office outside the electrical room, Rafe whispered, "Hold up. Let me open it. Mr. President, stay behind the guys."

Rafe slowly opened the door, and it made a creaking sound from all the rust on the hinges.

"That's what I heard," Pago whispered.

Suddenly, McGirt's voice sliced through the pitch-black room.

"It's all clear guys. C'mon in. I just offed the last camel rammer." Rafe flicked on his headlight, and I followed him in. McGirt was standing in the doorway to the electrical room, about fifteen feet away.

"What are you doing in here?" I asked.

"I wanted the bottle of water from my bag. Killing rag heads is thirsty work. Hey, how's Bush? Did he make it?"

"Where is he?" Rafe asked.

"Where's who?"

"The one you just killed."

"Did somebody call my name?" the president said as he stepped in the room behind Tangles. "Hey, it's Felix."

"Who's Felix?" Tangles asked.

"Him," he pointed at McGirt. "The helicopter pilot. I didn't expect to see *you* here."

"I was thinking the same about—"

"Where's your gun?" Rafe asked as he stepped toward McGirt.

"My gun?"

Rafe was leery and my spidey senses started tingling. Where *was* McGirt's gun?

"Yeah, your gun. Where is it, and where's the dead guy?"

McGirt was suddenly shoved aside and another guy in a flight suit stepped into the doorway and opened fire with an automatic weapon. Rafe spun and went down, and his gun clattered to the floor. I felt a couple of bullets slam into my midsection and fell backward on top of Tangles. Pago darted out the doorway to the exterior walkway, and the president was left standing in the middle of the room, apparently unscathed. The gunman retrained his weapon on the president, and Rafe sprang up from the floor and charged him as he pulled the trigger. Despite taking several rounds at point blank range, Rafe tackled the gunman, and they tumbled backward into the electrical room. A moment later somebody screamed, and it sounded like they were falling. They were. Then it went silent.

Tangles scrambled out from under me and rushed into the electrical room "Rafe!" he cried. "No! Oh my God!"

I got to my feet, thankful the bulletproof vest had done its job, and staggered into the electrical room. Tangles was hunched over Rafe, who was lying on his back. His headlamp was shining on the ceiling and cast enough light that I could see blood pooling on the floor around him. I knelt down and tore open Rafe's jumpsuit. It was bad. There were three holes in his chest and one in his shoulder. Blood was pumping out at an astonishing rate. Tangles tore off his T-shirt and tried to stem the flow.

Pago came in the room with his weapon drawn. "What happened?"

"Rafe tackled the gunman, and he fell through the trapdoor. Pago, shine your headlamp on him. He's hurt bad." Pago directed the light onto Rafe. It was worse than bad. Blood was coming out his mouth, and his eyes started rolling back in his head. He managed to lift a hand up and gently grab Tangles by the wrist as he tried to plug the bullet holes with his shirt.

"Too late," he murmured and spit out a mouthful of blood. "Get...president...to boat."

"No!" Tangles yelled. "It's not too late! You can't die on us. Don't die on us, Rafe!"

Rafe's hand slipped off Tangles's wrist, and his head rolled to the side. It was too late. Tangles started pumping Rafe's chest in an effort to restart his heart but only succeeded in causing more blood to gush from the devastating bullet wounds.

I put my hand on his shoulder and said, "He's gone, buddy. Let him go." Tangles slowly stopped pumping on Rafe's chest and started crying softly. I had tears welling up too. I stood up to see the president standing next to Pago. I asked him if he was all right.

"Thanks to that heroic young man, yes."

McGirt stepped out from the corner of the room and said, "Sorry about your buddy. That was crazy. Man, I thought—"

I don't know *what* McGirt thought because I turned and drilled him in the chops. He went down like a bag of bones.

"Good call," said Pago.

I had Tangles hand me Rafe's headlight and after I narrowed the beam I knelt down over the trapdoor and shone it on the water below.

The gunman was flailing his arms and yelling, "Help! Help! I can't swim!"

"Anybody think we should try and rescue the guy who just killed Rafe?" I asked.

"*Rescue him?*" said Tangles. "Fuck no! I'm gonna—"

A blood-curdling scream pierced the air like a cruise missile. I focused the beam directly on the gunman who was being thrashed around like a rag doll. A large triangular fin appeared in the light, and the scream cut off as the gunman was pulled under.

"What the hell was that?" the president asked, and everybody knelt around the trapdoor to have a look.

Pago said, "My guess is a shark—a big hammerhead."

Another scream erupted as the gunman's torso was lifted out of the water at an unnatural angle. The shark had him around the waist and when it rolled over I could clearly see the hammer-shape head. It was big. Very big. *Yikes.* The gunman went under, and the screaming abruptly stopped. The shark submerged with a final tail slap on the surface, and all was quiet. This time for good.

"How'd you know it was a hammerhead?" the president asked.

"It ate a big grouper off my line last week and almost flipped my boat."

"Fucker got what he deserved," said Tangles. "What are we gonna do about Rafe?"

"I don't know." I replied.

"He gave me his vest," a choked-up Dubya said. "He gave me his vest, and he *still* charged him. Those bullets were meant for me."

My ear bud vibrated, and I turned it on as I stood up.

"Kit, what's happening?" Holly asked. "I saw a light shining on the water."

I thought about telling her what happened to Rafe but was worried how she would react. I knew she would be upset and we needed her to run the boat. I decided to wait.

"I was looking for a terrorist who ended up in the water. It looks like we got 'em all."

"That's it? Is everything okay?"

"The president's fine. We're gonna climb down to the skiff right now. In five minutes take the boat out of stealth mode and turn on some lights. We'll be there soon."

"Okay, but you didn't answer my question. Are you all right? You don't sound right."

"I'm fine. We'll see you shortly." *Click.*

"You didn't tell her," Pago said.

"No. It can wait. We can't. Rafe said we need to get the president to the boat, so that's what we're gonna do. Tangles, you go down first, then Pago, then the president."

"What about Rafe?"

"There's no way we can get him down the ladder into the skiff. We need to talk to the boss. He'll know how to handle it."

"What about McGirt?" Pago asked. I shone the headlight on him, and he looked to be sleeping peacefully on the floor.

"He's got some serious explaining to do, but right now I don't feel like hearing it. I say he stays for now. Let him get his beauty rest. God knows he needs it." I handed the headlight to the president. "Here, you should wear this. Tangles, lead the way."

"Wait," said the president. "I'd like to say a few words first."

Chapter 51

About three weeks later I found myself at the Sky Bar at the Old Key Lime House in Lantana. It was a beautiful Thursday afternoon, and the bartender, Mike, was just setting up for happy hour. I was the only one there. It was a good place to find myself.

"Mr. Jansen," Mike said. "The usual?"

"Sure, why not."

"Tito's and soda with a splash of cran, no fruit?"

"You got it."

As I took in the incredible view looking south down the Intracoastal, I thought about what Mike said: the usual. I like the usual. I like things predictable. I like my beer cold, my women hot, my steak rare, and my showers warm. I don't see that ever changing. Whoever came up with the line "The more things change, the more they stay the same" was full of crap. The more things change, the more things change. That's why they call it change. Some times it's good change, sometimes it's bad change. Losing a few pounds when you're dieting is good change. Having a friend die in front of you and losing them forever is bad change—very bad change. The worst. Especially when it's a friend who valiantly sacrificed his life to save yours.

It makes you stop and think. Could I do the same? *Would* I do the same? I'd like to think so, but I guess it's one of those things you don't know until it happens. McGirt knows. When Zahvi opened fire on us, *he* could have tackled him and not left it up to a defenseless Rafe to be the hero that he was. It was clear to me that the only reason McGirt saved me and Tangles earlier that night was because he had the drop on the terrorist about to shoot us, and his life wasn't at risk. If it had been, we'd be dead, and you wouldn't be reading this.

About that night: A half hour after we got back to the boat, two unmarked choppers arrived. One landed on the *Dinero Majado* to pick up McGirt and Rafe, and the other hovered over us and airlifted out the president and Pago. Holly was understandably upset, as we all were, about what happened to Rafe, and she got Pago to agree to visit her after he got a good looking-over by the doctors.

The next day a DICK team was sent to the rig to do a thorough sweep and to inspect and remove the crates and electronic equipment that luckily never got used the way it was intended. It turned out to be Dubya's ranch foreman who tipped ISIS off to his travel schedule after they kidnapped his wife and daughter. Thankfully, they were found relatively unharmed. Much to the chagrin of the Secret Service, but to no surprise to us, Dubya forgave the foreman, and refused to fire him.

It was a somber boat ride home for the three of us, and we never once stopped to fish. When we pulled up to the dock at Holly's house in Ocean Ridge, we were met by DICK agent Judy Larson and three others. After getting all our stuff off the boat they took it back to the naval shipyards in Norfolk to have it examined and serviced as necessary. Tangles was still subdued and made no effort to hit on Judy Larson. A first. The fact was, we were all in a funk, and we stayed that way until just recently when a FedEx package arrived.

The package was actually a small cooler, and it came from Crawford, Texas. It was from President Bush. Inside the cooler was a container of armadillo stew and a small ziplock bag with some of Rafe's remains. There was a handwritten note, thanking us for the fishing trip and rescuing him. It explained that he requested some of Rafe's remains from his family when he discovered he was being cremated. He thought we might like to have them. He was right.

The three of us decided to scatter Rafe's ashes at sea, like we had done with Holly's aunt Millie some years before. Today was the day, and I was waiting for Holly and Tangles to pick me up in the Robalo. I was just finishing my second drink when I saw them coming up the Intracoastal. As I closed out my tab I felt a hand on my shoulder and a friendly familiar voice in my ear. "Well, well, well, look what the cat dragged in." It was the owner of the bar, Layne. Layne is one of those guys that are hardly ever in a bad mood. I guess owning one of the largest, most popular, and most successful waterfront restaurants in the state of Florida will do that for you. He had become a good friend, and I like being around him because his jovial nature helps diffuse my naturally cynical and surly disposition. It's true and it's what I tell Holly whenever she suggests that I'm spending too much time at the Key Lime. *I'm not drinking at the bar, honey; I'm working on my personality deficiencies.*

We shook hands, and I greeted him with my usual, "Layne-O!"

"Where you been buddy? Let me buy you a drink."

"I'd love one, but I'm gonna have to take a rain check. My ride just got here." I pointed at the Robalo pulling up to the dock.

"You like to play hard to get, don't you?" He winked at me, and we both laughed. It was classic Layne. "Come on, I'll walk down with you. I want to say hi to that gorgeous girlfriend of yours."

As we walked down to the dock I explained that we just got back from a trip to the gulf and that we were going to spread some ashes at sea. After saying hi to Holly and Tangles, he made us promise to come back that night to see the local band favorite, Acoustic Mayhem. They were great, and it was a promise we all vowed to keep. Less than ten minutes later we were heading out the Boynton inlet. We passed my buddy Hambone who was on his way in following an afternoon charter. He gave us a horn blast and signaled for me to give him a call. I texted him to meet us at the Key Lime later.

The sky was blue, the seas were calm, and it was just about as perfect as a June day could get. I put my arm around Holly as Tangles drove the boat out to a hundred feet of water off the old Ritz Carlton in Manalapan, now known as the Eau de Palm Beach. Whatever the name, it was still a nice place and a well-known boater's landmark. Tangles pointed the bow into the current and put the motors in idle.

"This looks like as good a spot as any," he said. "Holly, you do the honors."

Holly had the baggie with Rafe's remains in her hands and looked at me. "We need to say something. Kit, do you have anything?"

"There's nothing I could say that would even come close to what the president said back on the rig."

"Tangles? Do you want to say something?"

"Yeah. I'm sure that if Rafe tasted it, he would agree that armadillo stew sucks."

While some people might consider such words inappropriate for a eulogy, the three of us laughed until we cried. I'm sure Rafe would have laughed, too. Holly proceeded to dump the ashes, Tangles threw a dozen roses on top, and I followed by pouring an ice-cold can of Budweiser, Rafe's favorite, over the side.

"We'll miss you, Rafe," Holly choked out with a wave.

"God bless," Tangles croaked.

"This Bud's for you, pal," I managed to spit out. "Thanks for saving our skin." I gave a salute and pulled three Budweisers out of the cooler so we could have a toast in his honor.

"Here's to Rafe," I said.

"Hear, hear," echoed Holly and Tangles. We had just finished taking our swigs when Holly's phone rang. She looked at it and said, "Three, four, zero. Isn't that the area code for Saint Croix?"

"Hell if I know," I said. "Go ahead and answer it."

"I'm going to put it on speaker, I'm all sweaty." She left the phone on the console and answered.

"Is this Holly Lutes?" It sounded like an elderly woman.

"Yes, who is this?"

"Oh, my goodness. I can't believe I'm speaking to you. My name is Althea Trace."

"Althea Trace? Okay. I see you're calling from area code three, four, zero. Are you in Saint Croix?"

"No, Saint John."

"Oh. What can I do for you?"

"Do you know who Genevieve VanderGrift is?"

"Genevieve? Sure. How's she doing?"

"I'm afraid she just passed away."

"Oh, no. I'm so sorry to hear that."

"I am too, but that's not the main reason I called."

"Sooo, what's this about then?"

"I was contacted by a private investigator she hired and was told that my mother and your aunt are one and the same. Her name was Milfred Lutes. Is that possible?"

Holly had a Bud in one hand and grabbed one of the T-top supports with the other to steady herself.

"Oh my God!"

"Holy shit," said Tangles.

"Quiet!" said Holly.

"Hello? Are you still there?"

"Yes, yes, I'm sorry about that. Please, if you don't mind me asking, what day is your birthday?"

"That's the same thing the investigator asked. It's on February 22, 1948."

"Oh my God! President's day!"

"Well, now it is. Are you all right?"

"I'm not sure. Tell me one more thing. Is one of your eyes a different color than the other?"

"Why yes, one is blue, and the other is green. How did you know?"

"I don't believe it! It has to be you! Did you know you had a twin brother?"

"That's what I was told. I'm in a state of shock. Do you have any information about him?"

"Yes, I do, but I can't go into it right now. I'm just finishing up a memorial service for a dear friend. Can I call you back at this number in like a half hour or so?"

"Of course, please do."

"You can count on it, Althea. Talk to you soon." *Click.*

"This is incredible," Holly continued. "Tangles, back to the house! This is great. I can't wait to talk to her. Heck, I can't wait to meet her. Genevieve said she was making me an executor of her estate. I'll probably be hearing from her lawyer soon. You know what this means, Kit. We're going to Saint John! We're going to Saint Martin *and* Saint John. This is so exciting. Oh my gosh. I can't *wait* to tell Pago. Althea's his aunt! He should probably go with us. We need to go to Saint Croix, too. Millie and Joseph's gold is still buried there, and it belongs to Pago and Althea. Kit, how come you're not saying anything?"

I shook my head in disbelief and smiled as Tangles pushed the throttles down. Lucky's twin had been found. It was all coming full circle. I was wrong. The more things change, the more they *do* stay the same. Here we go again.

THE END

Note to readers: If you are wondering about some of the spelling please read the disclaimer at the front of the book.

Coming in 2016: The next Shagball and Tangles DICK Files adventure.

For more information go to: www.acbrooks.net

Made in the USA
Charleston, SC
17 May 2016